THE SISTER

VALERIE KEOGH

Boldwood

First published in 2018 as *Secrets Between Us*. This edition published in Great Britain in 2025 by Boldwood Books Ltd.

Cover Design by Head Design Ltd.

Cover Images: iStock

Every effort has been made to obtain the necessary permissions with reference to copyright material, both illustrative and quoted. We apologise for any omissions in this respect and will be pleased to make the appropriate acknowledgements in any future edition.

A CIP catalogue record for this book is available from the British Library.

Paperback ISBN 978-1-80656-109-4

Large Print ISBN 978-1-80656-119-3

Hardback ISBN 978-1-80656-108-7

Trade Paperback ISBN 978-1-80656-112-4

Ebook ISBN 978-1-80656-111-7

Kindle ISBN 978-1-80656-107-0

Audio CD ISBN 978-1-80656-101-8

MP3 CD ISBN 978-1-80656-106-3

Digital audio download ISBN 978-1-80656-110-0

This book is printed on certified sustainable paper. Boldwood Books is dedicated to putting sustainability at the heart of our business. For more information please visit https://www.boldwoodbooks.com/about-us/sustainability/

Boldwood Books Ltd, 23 Bowerdean Street, London, SW6 3TN

www.boldwoodbooks.com

In loving memory of my mother
Kathleen Foley
13th November 1920–11th November 2015

1

The letter came every Monday. It was delivered to the reception desk of St Germaine's school for the Differently Abled sometime during the morning, the postman cycling from the nearby Scottish border town of Peebles, come rain, shine or winter snow. He never complained, delivering the bag of post with a customary smile and wave.

In the basement kitchen, which served not only the school but the attached sheltered accommodation, Tia Bradshaw spent the morning as she always did, baking bread from a recipe she had memorised many years before. Occasionally, a new chef – and there had been several over the years – suggested changing the recipe. It always ended in disaster; Tia would start with one recipe but in the middle of mixing the ingredients, she'd forget and revert back to the ingredients from her old memorised recipe. The outcome was usually inedible.

The current chef left her to her own devices, making the same bread, morning after morning, never taking a day off, the concept of such a thing beyond her. A previous manager, appalled, had insisted she have at least one morning a week off. 'You can't work every morning, Tia,' she'd said kindly. 'You need to rest, go for a walk, maybe go into town with one of the staff and do some shopping.'

Tia had looked blankly at her and then, to the manager's dismay, she'd started to cry. She was one of those rare people who could cry beautifully; fat tears appearing in the corner of her brown eyes, getting fatter and fatter until suddenly they'd overflow and run slowly down her cheeks. She never brushed them away, letting them fall until she was persuaded to stop.

'I don't want to have a day off,' she had said, her voice thick. 'I don't like going outside.'

The manager could have insisted but, like everyone, faced with those rolling tears, she had conceded defeat. 'Well, if you are quite sure?'

The change had been immediate and startling. The tears stopped, and Tia's usual bland look returned. She was never asked to take a day off again, left alone to live her days as she chose.

She always finished her bread-making at two, leaving the last loaves cooling on wire racks for the kitchen staff to put away when they were ready. She usually took her time – she never had anything to rush away for – and sometimes she'd sit and have a cup of tea with the kitchen staff who'd finished their busy lunchtime slot.

But on a Monday, as soon as the minute hand reached twelve, she would rush to tear off her apron and run from the kitchen, flour on her face, dough on her hands, leaving a trail of both as she ran along the corridors and up the stairs to the floor where she lived. The house-keeping staff would later mutter, '*Tia!*' under their breath as they wiped floury handprints from the walls and banister and swept up specks of dried dough from the floor.

Sometimes she'd see the letter before she got to her door, a corner of the envelope sticking out. If she wasn't careful the letter caught when she opened the door, becoming pleated and torn. When this happened, she cried, her tears plopping onto the damaged envelope, rendering it soft and difficult to open.

It was best when the administrator sent the envelope sliding across the polished floor to land in the middle of her bedroom, sometimes as far as the opposite wall. She'd open the door, bright eyes full of expectation, and look around the room until she spotted it. She never doubted it would be there, some-where. In all the years, her sister had never failed her.

Taking the precious letter out, she would sit in her chair in front of the window, curling her legs under her, and read every word. Her sister wrote of the everyday things she did, the people she met, boyfriends, lovers, enemies, friends. She shared secrets with her, intimate details of her life, a life as different from Tia's as it was possible to be. In simple, easy-to-read language, she shared everything. At the end of each letter, after signing *Your loving sister, Ellie*, there would be one final sentence. *Don't forget to burn this after you've read it.*

Tia finished each letter quickly, and would immediately read it again. Sometimes there would be a word she didn't understand and she'd carefully write it down on a blank piece of paper and head to reception. 'Can you tell me what this means?' she'd ask the duty receptionist, handing her the piece of paper. It wasn't always easy because a word out of context can have many different meanings, but the staff did their best.

'Thanks,' Tia would say before heading back to finish the letter, slowly this time, taking in every word. Sometimes, when the letter was long she'd reread it several more times before she was satisfied. And then, almost reluctantly, she'd fold it and head to the administration office.

In the beginning, she'd tried to do exactly as Ellie wanted, to burn the letters when she'd finished, becoming inconsolable when she was told she wasn't allowed. 'I have to,' she'd said.

It had taken a lot of time and patient words to convince her that using a shredder was just as effective. 'Your sister just wants to make sure her letters are destroyed. She wouldn't mind if you shredded them instead. See,' the manager had said, sliding a page into the shredder, pressing the button, and then opening the case to show her the resultant mass of shredded paper. 'Just as good as burning.'

Only after several weeks had Tia become reconciled to it.

Now, she didn't think twice. 'Is it okay if I use the shredder,' she'd ask, politely. Each time, the staff would smile, nod and point to where the machine sat under the desk. When she was younger, they'd switch it on for her but now they left her to it. Sometimes, if it were someone new on the desk, they'd say she didn't have to ask. But she always did.

And then Tia would wait, patiently, eagerly, for the next letter to come.

Every Monday, for fifteen years, the letters came.

If Tia had known the word, she would have said that for her sister the letters were cathartic; that in writing them, Ellie released the pent-up frustrations of a woman determined to make it in a tough world. And if for Ellie they were cathartic, for Tia they were fantasy stories about a different reality that she read and enjoyed like a multi-part novel, unfolding a chapter at a time.

Sometimes, a new resident or member of staff would ask Tia where she rushed off to every Monday. She would explain about her letter, and they would ask the inevitable question.

'*Who's it from?*' For a moment, Tia's brow would crease, and she would blink rapidly. Then her face would clear, her usual smile return, and she'd say, 'It's from Ellie.'

Rarely was she questioned further, but if anyone ever asked, '*Who's Ellie?*' a look of puzzlement would skim across her face, her eyelids would flutter faster, and she'd walk away without answering and then, she'd turn and say, 'She's my twin.'

2

Ellie Armstrong was beyond tired. She waited until everyone had left the boardroom before stretching, feeling muscles creak and a piercing pain in her right shoulder that told of too many hours hunched over her computer. The meeting had gone on for an hour longer than she'd expected. God Almighty, if she had to listen to Jeff Harper wittering on one more time, she might just have to do what she'd been promising her husband she'd do for the last two years and quit.

Standing slowly and looking around the boardroom table, she knew that wasn't ever going to happen, no matter what Will wanted. She'd told him before they got married that she was a career woman, that if he wanted a stay-at-home wife he'd better say so. He swore then that he liked things just the way they were.

'But we will have children,' he added; not a question, a statement. He was willing to accept some compromise, just not with this.

'Eventually,' Ellie had said.

'When?' Will had pushed her, wanting to know, needing a time frame.

Ellie felt cornered and stayed silent.

'It's not because of your mother, is it?' Will had asked. 'You're not afraid?'

Was she? She'd be lying if she said it had never crossed her mind. Her mother had, after all, died during childbirth. But it wasn't as simple as that. There were other things that worried her, things she tried not to think about. She looked at the open, honest face of this man she loved, and knew she couldn't lie to him. Not about this.

'No, it's not,' she said softly, patting him on the cheek. 'My mother was just unlucky, that's all.' She slid her hands around his neck and moulded her body to his. 'There's a lot of change in the company, Will. If I play my cards right, I could get that promotion I want. Just give me another year or two,' she promised.

* * *

Before the two years were up, Ellie spent a considerable amount of time planning the best time to conceive, poring over the calendar, discounting months that were certain to be too busy. Finally, she settled on a month.

'How about April,' she said to Will, over dinner one evening. He frowned. 'How about April for what?'

She smiled. 'For making babies?'

His fork clattered to his plate and he looked at her for a moment before getting up and pulling her into his arms. 'You sure?' he said.

She buried her face in his neck. Yes, she was sure. She loved him and wanted his child, but that niggling worry in the back of her head still wouldn't go away. She kissed him to block out her thoughts, watched as his eyes softened and wondered if it was possible to love anyone more.

That night she stopped taking the contraceptive pill she'd been taking since her university days, and entered into the conception with the same drive and focus she did everything else.

She'd left some wriggle room on the dates, so it didn't matter if it didn't happen immediately, but she expected to be pregnant within a month or two. She planned to work up to a week before her due date, take a couple of weeks off for the birth and recovery, find a good nanny and slot back into work before she was missed, and, more importantly, before any of her colleagues began to question her commitment.

But months passed, and nothing happened. She tried to convince herself she didn't really want children, that it didn't matter because she had her career. If she repeated this to herself often enough, perhaps she'd start to believe it, but she knew she'd never be able to convince Will. She noticed him at friends' homes, silently watching Joe and Steve and even that pain-in-the-ass, Carlos, playing with their children, and her heart ached for him.

It was at his urging that they had the tests, scans, invasive examinations and meetings with insufferably condescending doctors. And, yesterday, a final meeting.

'Final,' Ellie said as they left the clinic, her voice thick with unshed tears. 'That's it, no more.'

They'd waited in the expensively furnished offices, Will reading a magazine, trying to look relaxed, Ellie refraining from tapping her fingers on the wooden arm of the chair as she watched the minute hand of her watch drag.

Finally, the office door had opened and the consultant

gynaecologist waved them in, apologising perfunctorily, smiling, and offering coffee. Ellie, feeling Will's warm hand in the small of her back as a gentle warning not to complain about being kept waiting, shook her head. 'No,' she managed to say, 'we'd just like to hear the results of the tests.'

The consultant, Jeremiah Gardiner, sat behind his large, polished desk, and opened a file on his laptop. His eyes lingered on it for a moment before he looked up.

'We've done exhaustive tests, as you both know,' he said, his eyes meeting theirs with an almost apologetic look.

With a flash of insight, Ellie knew she wasn't going to like what he said.

'Mrs Armstrong,' he said, 'you say your doctors put your primary amenorrhoea down to stress following the loss of your father, and then to a subsequent eating disorder.'

She nodded.

'The eating disorder, bulimia, I gather. That went on for how long?'

Biting the inside of her lip, Ellie weighed the question. Surely, they weren't going to blame her inability to conceive on bulimia that lasted only a few months, were they? 'Six months, at the most,' she said, shrugging dismissively. 'It wasn't serious; all the girls were doing it. I'd never have described myself as having had an eating disorder, as such.'

Dr Gardiner, who'd heard denial in all its many and varied forms, nodded as if he agreed, and continued as if he didn't. 'And you were how old at the time?'

Ellie sighed. Loudly. 'Seventeen.'

'But you didn't begin to menstruate then.' It wasn't a question. 'Why didn't your GP advise further investigations?'

Ellie shrugged again. She probably should have gone to the school nurse, but after the bulimia she'd had enough of the concerned faces and lectures, so hadn't wanted to bother. 'I never told anyone,' she said, without elaborating.

The consultant's eyes flicked to the computer screen and when they returned to Ellie's face, his gaze was a little softer.

Her hands trembled in her lap. She wanted to tell him to get on with it, whatever it was. She guessed bad news. But she'd known, hadn't she? Wasn't it always in the back of her mind, the notion that something wasn't quite right, that she wasn't normal? She'd refused to address it, went on the pill her first week in university like everyone else and had been on it ever since.

In their early years, before they'd started to properly think of a future together, she could have mentioned her doubts to Will, but the opportunity had passed and then it was too late. Because, by then, she knew how desperately he wanted to have a child and how desperate she was not to lose him.

She'd clung to the hope that when she stopped taking the pill everything would be as it should be. Her period would come. She'd get pregnant. It would be happy ever after. But that worry never went away. And when it didn't happen, she hoped for a while that he would accept it. That they'd drift into being one of those couples who'd just not been lucky enough to have children. They loved each other, they were happy, wasn't that enough?

But no, he had insisted on the damn tests, and she had no choice but to go along with it. For a brief moment, she resented him. Denial wasn't a bad place to live.

'I've consulted with a few of my colleagues,' Dr Gardiner said, his voice dropping in pitch, becoming softer, deeper. 'I'm afraid our conclusions are incontrovertible, Mrs Armstrong. At first, we thought you had a version of Mayer-Rokitansky-Kuster-Hauser syndrome.' He held up a hand at the sudden look of panic on Will's face. 'It's okay, Mrs Armstrong doesn't have it. It's called MRKH, for short, and, as I said, it was something we considered but,' he looked at Ellie, 'you don't have any of the other symptoms of that syndrome, and your blood tests have come back negative.'

'So why did you think I might have it?' Ellie asked, relieved to be talking about anything rather than her non-existent period. She looked across the desk, meeting Dr Gardiner's cool gaze before dropping her eyes to where his long-fingered hands rested on the desk in front of him, his fingertips pushing together with such force that the top of each nail shone white. Mesmerised by them, Ellie wondered how much force was necessary and if it equated to how bad the news was. Her eyes flicked back to his face. Because it *was* bad, she could see the pity in his eyes. Dr Gardiner took a deep breath and answered her question. 'Because you don't have a uterus, Mrs Armstrong.'

3

They left the clinic and got back into the car in silence, driving home in a vacuum of unsaid words and unshed tears. There was, as usual, no parking space outside their house on Gibson Square. It had been Will's family home before they married and often Ellie would wait a moment in the car before she got out, taking in the Edwardian terraced house she'd come to love. The symmetry of it pleased her, the arched ground-floor window echoing the fan light over the front door, the two twelve-paned windows on the first floor, the square nine-paned windows on the second. When she'd moved in, she'd planned to put red geraniums in the small ironwork balconies that hung in front of both first-floor windows, but it had never happened.

A decorative iron railing ran in front of the house and divided it from the houses on each side. Two narrow, stone steps led up to a wide step in front of the glossy, black front door. To the right of the door, a small gateway opened onto a stairway down to a converted basement. Will's father had moved into it after she and Will got engaged, insisting they take the house. 'It's a family house,' he'd said, more than once. Ellie always looked away quickly so she'd miss the accompanying wink in her direction.

When he died suddenly, a year later, Will was grief-stricken and the basement apartment sat empty for several months. It was let now and the income from it allowed them a very comfortable lifestyle.

'You'll be able to give up work if you want to when we have children,' Will had once said to her.

'*If* we have children, it will allow us to pay for a good child-minder,' she had replied, a twinkle in her brown eyes, as she reached forward to plant a warm kiss on his cheek.

She remembered the conversation as if it had taken place yesterday, remembered putting extra emphasis on the *if*. Had she hoped it would put a doubt in his mind? It would have been the perfect opportunity to have mentioned her concerns. How deep was the pit of denial she had trapped herself in?

Very deep, she guessed.

Will stopped on a double yellow line to let her out. She closed the car door behind her and left him to drive around until he could find a parking space. Unlocking their front door, she stepped into the hallway and leaned back against the door to close it behind her, feeling weak. She bit down painfully on her lower lip and told herself not to cry. If she started, she wasn't sure she could stop.

She pushed away and felt a moment's panic. Will would be back soon, and she didn't want to talk to him. Not now. She needed to get herself under control first. To process what she'd learned. There was a pile of post on the floor at her feet; she bent down and picked it up, sorting it automatically into his and hers. Leaving Will's pile neatly on the hall table, she took hers upstairs. The normality of the act gave her a sense of calm.

Upstairs, she stood undecided for a moment and then

made her way into the main bathroom. She'd have a bath. It was an unwritten rule in their relationship; in the bath, she was incommunicado. He'd leave her in peace for a while. She dropped her post on the small table beside the bath and turned both taps on full.

Locking the door, she stripped, dropped her clothes on the floor, added a generous amount of her most expensive bath oil to the running water and stood naked waiting for the bath to be deep enough. A few minutes later, she climbed into the hot water, lay back with her eyes closed, and tried to relax.

It was impossible. The gynaecologist's words rang inside her head: *Because you don't have a uterus, Mrs Armstrong.* All these years railing against being a twin, trying to prove she was unique, one of a kind, never realising until now that she already was.

'You have ovaries, so hormonally you are completely normal. You even produce eggs,' he'd added, as if that were cause for celebration. 'They're just harmlessly reabsorbed.'

'Harmlessly,' Ellie had said, feeling a heavy weight in her chest as she imagined each egg on its monthly fool's errand.

'They could be harvested,' he said. 'It's something—'

She'd held up her hand to stop him, stood, and left the room, waiting outside for Will to join her.

What had he been about to say? That it was something she should think about? To have her eggs harvested and inserted into a surrogate? 'Oh God,' she said, feeling her eyes burn. For some other woman to carry their child? She didn't think she could bear it. She already felt so unbearably inadequate.

She forced it all into a dark corner of her mind, dried her hands on a towel and reached for the first of her letters. It was the usual glut of rubbish, and she dropped them one after the other to the floor. She opened the last, her eyes narrowing as she saw the logo on the envelope. It was unusual to hear from the school. The bill was paid by direct debit every quarter and any additions were invoiced at the end of the year.

Skimming it, she sat up abruptly in the water, her eyes racing across and re-reading every word. Her brow creased, and her mouth tightened. 'I don't believe it,' she muttered, turning over the letter to see if more was written on the back. But there wasn't; the letter was as short as it was shocking.

Dear Mrs Armstrong,

We are sorry to inform you that St Germaine's School for the Differently Abled is to close in three months. We also plan to close the attached sheltered accommodation where your sister, Tia, presently resides. We are informing you at this early juncture to enable you to make alternative arrangements for her accommodation.

'Alternative arrangements? What on earth do they expect me to do?' It was just too much. Everything. All of it. She leaned her head back against the bath and, finally, sobbed.

Will passed the door, his feet loud on the wooden floor of the hallway. Through her sobs she heard him pause. He was a good man, but she never truly believed she deserved him. It was, she knew, a relic of her childhood. No matter what she did then, it wasn't good enough. And now, here she was again. Not good enough. Not *woman* enough. 'Damn it,' she whispered on a sob, 'hardly a woman at all.' The one thing Will really wanted and she couldn't give it to him.

He would sit, she knew, in the privacy of their bedroom and cry tears of his own. Then he'd start thinking about the future, thinking up ways around what he would no doubt call *their* problem. Not for one moment would he blame her. It didn't matter, she carried blame enough for both of them.

She looked at the letter in her hand again before dropping it on the floor. As if she didn't have enough to worry about. What was she going to do about Tia?

4

She'd been fifteen when their father died in a freak accident; a car mounting a kerb and killing him instantly, a seismic event that had changed their lives irrevocably. But the death of his young wife had made John Bradshaw a careful man and he had organised an old and trusted friend to act as guardian for his girls if anything ever happened to him.

Adam Dawson, shocked at the death of his friend, had taken his responsibilities seriously, but he wasn't a family man and the care of two teenage girls was definitely a challenge.

He'd quickly found a suitable boarding school for Ellie in London, and finally one appropriate for Tia's additional needs in Peebles on the Scottish borders. He'd never asked Ellie how she felt at being separated from her twin, and she was glad. It was hard to describe the relief she felt; her father had loved them both equally, but differently. To look at, they were identical, but the minutes separating their arrival had been all it took to make Tia different. A little slow, innocent, vulnerable and needy. She was the soft twin, easily brought to tears that had people rushing to do whatever she wanted them to do; to pick her up, cuddle her, give her whatever she wanted. The world was a dangerous and scary place for a girl like Tia, Ellie was told; she needed to be watched and protected at all times.

So, no matter what Ellie did, the prizes she won, the honours she received, she couldn't compete for that same level of attention and affection. The assumption was always that she would be fine because she was *normal*.

If she was ever upset and sought solace from her father, tears in her eyes, her lower lip trembling, he'd take her face in his hands and simply say, 'You have to be strong, Ellie. You have to look out for your sister.'

And that was the way it continued. She had to look out for her, had to be strong and sensible. Forever. At twelve, it was a heavy burden. By fifteen, she'd grown to resent her sister. So, when Adam explained they'd be going to separate boarding schools, that he wasn't able to look after them both in his upmarket Kensington apartment, she had to bite her lip to stop her smile of relief.

Boarding school was a revelation. Ellie was no longer one of two, the mirror image of a girl so different to her. At last, she was unique. Just *Ellie*. If she were sick, she was looked after; if she were upset, she got extra attention. She missed her father desperately but, if she were honest, she never really missed her sister.

At school, she'd quickly made friends who were happy to invite her to spend part or all of the summer with them. Her friends' parents, discovering she was an orphan, frequently included her in holidays abroad, Adam giving permission with alacrity. The one holiday she spent in his Knightsbridge apartment terrified her, worried the whole time she was there that she would break something, or dirty the pristine carpets.

But like many of the other students, she spent most weekends at the school. Sometimes, Adam would visit and take her out for lunch or an ice cream. She enjoyed his company and would laugh at his risqué stories, feeling very grown up in the elegant places he'd take her, enjoying the glamour.

She learned news of her sister through his regular, if infrequent, visits to St Germaine's and so she knew Tia had settled in and was doing well. Adam never asked if she missed her, so she never needed to lie.

She didn't miss her, but it was impossible not to think about her. She wondered how much of it was guilt that she was happier without her and how much was because, no matter how much she might dislike it, she was her twin and there was that indefinable, indelible connection between them.

'I write to her every week,' she told Adam over a milkshake one Saturday. 'I tell her all about my school, the places I go and the people I meet.'

Adam smiled at her. 'Does she answer?' he asked.

Ellie shook her head. 'But I don't mind,' she said. 'I just want her to know that I think about her. Perhaps I might visit her sometime? I could go up on the train on my own. You wouldn't need to come.'

'Maybe next year,' he said, waving a hand towards the future. But she guessed his determination to do his duty as their guardian made him baulk at allowing a young girl to travel so far unaccompanied. Maybe he considered going with her, she didn't know, but the visit never happened.

She didn't really mind; although she'd have liked to have visited, the offer had been made from a sense of duty rather than genuine desire. The resentment she'd felt when she was younger had faded with their separation, but the memory of it hadn't. She'd learned to like being *just Ellie;* seeing Tia would remind her that she wasn't, she was a twin.

When she finished school five years later, she did an internet search for Peebles, determined at last to visit. She looked up train timetables, flight times, even car hire.

She decided on the train, imagining a long journey through the heart of England as an adventure. But it was not to be. The day before she was due to travel, she tripped on the stairs and sprained her ankle. In pain, and limping badly, she reluctantly cancelled the trip thinking she might go later but, by the time it had healed, she was due to start university.

University, four glorious years in Oxford, put all ideas of visiting out of her head. The business and economics degree course she'd chosen was tough and challenging. And, when she wasn't studying, she was mixing with the right people; networking, because that was what it was all about, knowing the right people, making the right contacts. Days of freedom, when they came, were spent somewhere sunny, with like-minded friends or lovers, not in the wilds of the Scottish borders.

She dealt with the occasional pang of guilt by writing a longer weekly letter to Tia, sitting in the quiet of the library and writing of people she'd met, parties she'd been to, detailed and colourful letters, written longhand at first and then typed on her laptop, but always sent every Friday.

The Oxford years were a dream compared to the tough internship with one of London's top finance companies. It wasn't said straight-out, but she and the three other interns that started at the same time quickly learned this was a kill or be killed industry. And Ellie, determined to make it, and brought up to be strong, quickly learned how to kill.

It was during a particularly busy time that Adam had rung and invited her out to dinner, refusing to accept her plea of exhaustion. 'You need to eat,' he argued reasonably. 'I'll pick you up at your office, we can eat nearby and you'll still be home to get eight hours' sleep.'

Eight hours' sleep? She couldn't remember the last time she had more than six. Running one hand over her sleek chignon, she gripped the phone tightly with her other hand and said, 'Okay, but don't pick me up till eight. I have a stack of things to finish. I'll see you in the lobby.' And then, because she was genuinely fond of him, she added, 'It will be lovely to see you.'

It was eight fifteen before she rushed out of the lift, one hand coming up in an apologetic wave. 'I'm so sorry,' she said, putting her other hand on his arm and leaning in to give him a dry peck on the cheek. They ate in a small French restaurant a few metres from the office. It was the type of restaurant she knew Adam would enjoy; heavy white linen tablecloths and napkins, lots of candles and excellent food and wine. Ellie ate there regularly and was greeted by name and taken to their table.

They chatted about nothing until they'd finished their meals, Adam's eyes widening when he saw just how little she'd eaten. 'You're not having problems again, are you?'

'Oh, for goodness' sake, Adam, of course not,' she said shortly, immediately relenting when she saw his worried face, reaching a hand out to rest it on his arm. 'I promise. I'm not hungry because we had a lunchtime meeting.' She smiled. 'They had crab patties that were to die for. I think I ate most of them.'

He smiled back, relieved.

She watched him. There was something he wanted to say, she could tell by the slight furrow on his otherwise smooth brow. 'What did you want to speak to me about?'

He didn't insult her intelligence by saying he'd just wanted to see her. She knew him better than that. 'We've sold the Knightsbridge apartment,' he said.

She was stunned. 'But you love that place.'

'We'll love this even more,' he said, taking a photograph from his pocket and placing it on the table in front of her.

'Wow,' she said, picking it up and staring at the low building on white sand, a crystal-blue sky as a backdrop. Her eyes met his. 'Where?'

'Barbados.'

She handed the photograph back with a smile. 'It will suit you both very well. You *and* Tyler, I assume?'

He nodded. 'I waited until everything was definite before telling you. We're set to leave in two weeks, Ellie.'

Reaching across the table, she laid a hand on his arm again. 'I'm happy for you, Adam,' she said, the pleasure in her voice sincere.

'There's just one thing,' he added, patting her hand. 'I stopped being your legal guardian, as you know, when you turned twenty-one, but because of Tia's status I'm still registered as hers.' He stopped and looked at her. 'It makes sense for me to relinquish that now, Ellie, Barbados is too far away to react in case of problems.'

Ellie blinked. This wasn't something she'd expected. 'You want me to take over?'

He nodded. 'It makes sense, doesn't it?'

Of course, it did. It didn't mean, however, that she wanted to take on the responsibility. 'Couldn't our solicitor become her guardian?'

Adam's eyes became hard, and his voice was cold when he said, 'Well, of course, if you feel you can't take the responsibility on yourself, then that's my next option.'

Ellie bit her lip. Memories came flooding back. Her father

and his constant plea: *Take care of your sister, Ellie, remember she needs you to look out for her.*

She should have said no, should have explained to him then about her resentment, the relief she'd felt when she was separated from her twin, the feeling of never being good enough when she was with her. But guilt washed over her, and she found herself shaking her head. 'No, that's okay, I'll do it.'

Two days later, she signed the papers. She checked them over, made sure everything was satisfactory and then tried to put it out of her head.

And now, with her heart breaking, that decision was back to haunt her.

5

Will sat on their bed and thought of the child he'd never see born; the best of him, the best of Ellie, wrapped up in one precious little package. He cried silently for a few minutes before snuffling and wiping his eyes with his hand.

When he'd composed himself, he came out to listen at the bathroom door, taking a deep breath when he heard nothing. He rested a hand on the door wishing he could enter but knowing the door would be locked, and, even if it weren't, he wouldn't go in. He'd done so once, in their early days together, and she'd accused him of intruding into her *unassailably personal space*. He'd been amused at her phrase, surprised at her anger and relieved at her eventual forgiveness. And he'd never tried it again.

She tried to explain to him later how early years of being forced to share everything with her sister had left its mark and how, now and then, she really needed time and space to herself. He didn't really understand, but he was an only child so what did he know? 'In future,' he'd said, putting an arm around her to draw her close, 'if you're in the bathroom, you're out of bounds. We'll make it a house rule.' He laughed and kissed her, watching as her face softened and her lips curved into a smile.

He guessed she'd be tense now and, for a second, he rested his forehead on his hand as he felt tears sting. Then, with a shake of his head, he headed downstairs.

The kitchen was a big L-shaped room with a kitchen-dining room spreading across the length, a cosy living room in the smaller section. A big island separated the kitchen and dining areas. Around it, on high stools, they ate casual meals, drank coffee, read the paper. When Will cooked, she'd sit at it with a glass of wine and watch him, sometimes criticising his technique, laughing when things went wrong, full of praise for his successes. She rarely cooked. 'Why would I when I can buy better food from M&S?' she argued, opening packets and arranging the food on plates before popping them into the microwave.

He was a good cook, but he needed to be in the right mood and tonight definitely wasn't one of those times, so he crossed the kitchen and opened a drawer that was full of takeaway menus. Flicking through them, he took out the one for a local Indian he knew they both liked.

It didn't take long to decide; they invariably ate the same dishes. He picked up the phone and rang the order through. It would be thirty minutes, he was told.

He hoped she'd have come down by the time it arrived; preferably hungry. She rarely ate breakfast, and they'd skipped lunch in their anxiety about the meeting with the consultant. She needed to eat.

But not for two.

The thought popped into his mind, unbidden, unwanted and painful. He opened the large American-style fridge and took out a bottle of wine. Twisting the cap, he tossed it on the counter where it rolled too far and landed on the floor. He didn't bother picking it up, he wasn't planning to use it again.

Pouring a large glass, he took a mouthful. He'd like a whiskey really, but he guessed getting drunk wouldn't help. Glass in hand, he leaned against the cold granite of the island and thought of the future he'd planned.

He loved Ellie and had looked forward to seeing her swelling with his child, waddling slightly the way he'd seen very pregnant women do. In his imagination he'd pictured himself in the wee hours, driving around London trying to find an open shop because she had a craving for something weird to eat. He'd pictured them laughing together, planning their future. Maybe even talking about schools. He gave a sad smile. He'd wanted it all.

It wasn't his way to wallow, but he allowed himself a few more minutes. Soon enough, she would be downstairs, and he could concentrate on her but, just for now, he wanted to recognise his own grief and mourn that dream.

He also wanted to deal with the faint feeling that he'd been cheated somehow. Had she known? She was such a private person, it had never entered his head to talk about things like her period. If she'd never had one, how did she expect to get pregnant? He didn't want to think she'd deliberately misled him but, the truth was it didn't matter, he loved her with a passion that would forgive anything.

He topped up his glass and sat on a stool, elbows resting on the counter-top, staring out the window into the fading light, blinking only occasionally, his eyes still gritty from the tears he'd shed earlier. He was on his third glass of wine by the time he gave up waiting for her and headed into the sitting room to light the fire.

Growing up, the beginning of wintertime was marked by the start of real fires burning in the grate. An only child, he would sit around the fire with his parents in the evening to watch television. When he was older, and had schoolwork to do, his mother would light it earlier in the day so he could do his homework on the floor in front of it.

He and Ellie rarely lit it during the week but, at the weekend, if they weren't going out, he liked to have a blazing fire. It made the room cosy. And now a fire would help to counteract the chill of disappointment that curled around them.

The grate was empty. They hadn't lit a fire in a while, the weather being unseasonably warm for February. He wasn't particularly good at lighting them, but he made up for lack of skill with a generous amount of firelighters. He screwed up newspaper, added four firelighters and then another for good measure, piled some kindling on top and lit a match. Sitting back on his heels, he smiled in satisfaction when flames shot up. He added lumps of coal, using his fingers rather than the tongs to drop them on the flames, waiting a moment before adding more. It was tempting to use the poker, his face softening when he remembered his father constantly telling him to *leave it alone, you'll put it out.* With those words ringing in his ears he resisted the temptation, sat back and watched it take hold.

A few minutes later, he stood, red-faced from the heat, pins and needles shooting down his legs. He shook them out and went back to the kitchen to fetch a bottle of red wine. Opening it, he left it near the fire and sank back into the couch with his glass of white, eyes fixed on the flames.

He was still sitting when Ellie appeared, wrapped in a cashmere robe tied tightly around her waist. It was one he'd bought for her last birthday. He'd planned to buy blue, one of her favourite colours, but he'd seen the baby pink and immediately imagined her wearing it, swelling with their child. He'd taken the chance and bought it and, luckily, she'd loved it. When he told her why, she'd laughed but her eyes had gone soft and he knew she was imagining the same thing.

Watching her stand in the doorway, her face pale and drawn, eyes red, he thought he'd never loved her more. 'I ordered a takeaway,' he said, knowing that asking her if she was okay was the last thing he should do. 'Indian,' he added, 'with extra coriander.' He was pleased to see this quip drew the usual smile, even if she shook her head at his predictability. She hated coriander.

Instead of joining him on the couch, she moved to the fire and lifted the poker. She spent a couple of minutes moving pieces of coal about. It didn't make the slightest difference to the fire, but with a satisfied look on her face, she put the poker down, kicked off her slippers and sat cross-legged on the rug in front of it. Her hair was damp and lay in inky curls around her shoulders. It would dry naturally and the curls would be riotous, just the way Will liked them.

'Have a glass of wine,' he said, turning to reach for one of the wine glasses he'd put on the side table.

She shook her head. 'I'll wait till the food comes,' she said, giving him a quick smile before turning her face back to the glow of the fire.

They sat in a silence that was neither comfortable nor uncomfortable, but loaded with questions he wanted to ask, discussions he wanted to have. But not tonight, he guessed, looking at her profile, chin slightly raised as if she was struggling to keep herself together. There'd be time enough for discussions about what to do. Time enough to talk about a future that looked... different, he decided, refusing to use the word *lonely* that had first popped into his head.

The front doorbell, loud and insistent, made them both jump and give a little laugh of embarrassment. Will went to answer it, grabbing the money he'd left on the hall table.

When he came back, the takeaway bags in one hand, plates and cutlery in the other, she was still staring into the fire. Without asking, he opened the containers and spooned food onto the plate for her, nudging her shoulder with his knee before bending and putting the plate on her lap.

He watched as she picked up the fork and then put it down again. She turned her big brown eyes to him and said, simply, 'I'm sorry, Will.' Waiting a beat, she picked the fork up and started to eat, as if those three words were the end of the story.

For what? He wondered, gripping his fork tightly. For misleading him, or for being unwilling to listen to the alternatives that were available to them? Forgiving her for misleading him was easy.

He remembered the look of shock on her face; she might have had her suspicions, but he was sure she didn't know.

He could even forgive her for not listening to the alternatives. Not in that office, with the look of pity on the consultant's face. Those options would still be available in a few days, or maybe weeks. He swallowed the lump in his throat and felt the sadness that curdled inside. He knew she was hurting, but so was he.

He looked at his stunningly beautiful wife, in the bubblegum-pink robe he now hated with a vengeance, and wondered what their offspring would have looked like. Beautiful, he guessed, closing his eyes on the sharp pain of loss for the child he had wanted all his adult life.

6

They finished the wine and most of the food. 'Another glass?' Will asked her, getting up to fetch another bottle when she nodded. Ellie waited until he was back and the wine was poured before she took the letter from St Germaine's out of her pocket. 'I've had some bad news,' she said, unfolding it.

Seeing Will's face, she shook her head and managed a half-smile. 'I should have said, *more* bad news, I suppose.' She held out the letter to him and watched as he read it, a look of bewilderment crossing his face.

'Tia is in sheltered accommodation? I thought she was profoundly disabled,' he said, sounding puzzled.

Ellie had told him very little about her sister. She'd mentioned when they first met that she had a sister in care but when he suggested they go and meet her, she'd said the home didn't encourage visits; that, afterwards, Tia became too upset and unmanageable. So he hadn't suggested it again.

She put birthday and Christmas cards in front of him to sign but if he asked about her, she'd shrug and say there was no news. 'It's just hard,' she'd said with a shake of her head and without going into detail, letting him know that Tia was a subject she wasn't comfortable discussing. The sympathetic look on his face implied he thought Tia to be more disabled than she was, and if he did, she let him continue. It was simpler than the truth.

When they married, she dismissed a quiver of guilt and explained to Will her decision not to invite her sister. 'She'd never cope. It would distress her to be out of her normal environment and routine.'

Adam, who had flown in from Barbados for the occasion, was surprised not to see Tia, and slightly taken aback when Ellie told him she hadn't been invited. 'She's all right, isn't she?' he'd asked, concerned.

'Yes, she's fine. It's just the logistics of it, Adam, it would have been a nightmare,' she'd explained, relaxing when he accepted this statement with slightly narrowed eyes but without further comment.

And since then, she'd continued with her weekly letters, the Christmas and birthday cards that both she and Will signed, and the occasional brief mention of Tia when the quarterly account came from St Germaine's. But she had always managed to skirt around any proper discussion about her.

Now, however, it was easier to talk about Tia than have the conversation she knew Will wanted to have. She wasn't ready to talk about what they'd do next. Not just yet. She loved him, she had wanted to have a child with him, but now, everything was different, and she needed time to think. It was better to talk about Tia. And anyway, she might need some help in finding alternative accommodation for her.

'No, not disabled,' she said, taking the letter back, 'she's differently abled.' She laughed softly and put the letter back into her pocket. 'That's how my father used to describe her; he hated words like handicapped or disabled. It was one of the reasons Adam chose the school for her after he died, it's the word they use.' She shrugged. 'Not that there were many suitable schools to choose from.'

With a sigh and smile for Will, she continued. 'It's a word that suits Tia perfectly. Intellectual disability,' she explained, 'can range between profound at the worst end, to mild at the other. Tia falls into the mild category; her IQ is around sixty.' She brushed a lock of hair back behind her ear and frowned. Despite writing to her every week, she realised it had been a while since she'd actually thought about her sister. 'She can read, as long as it isn't complicated, and can count but couldn't do complex maths. It takes her a while to pick up things and she forgets easily. She's naive, very impressionable.'

'But she can look after herself, to some extent?' Will asked, when Ellie hadn't spoken for a while.

Shaking her head, she said, 'Sorry, I was thinking about her. Yes, she's fairly independent, just needs some guidance. She's classified as a *vulnerable adult*. Ten years ago, when she finished school, she took a job in the kitchen doing something relatively simple. Baking, I think,' she frowned, trying to remember exactly what it was that Tia did, and gave up. 'Something like that, anyway.'

Will frowned. 'So, what's the problem? Can't she get an apartment? Didn't your father leave her well taken care of?' He remembered Ellie telling him something about her father's will, but he couldn't remember the details. 'Was there something about your father's will? You told me...'

Ellie finished her wine and held her glass out for a refill. 'I told you. He left almost everything to her. It paid for her tuition and boarding in St Germaine's. When she finished school, she moved from dormitory accommodation into what they term sheltered housing but I gather it's just a room in a different wing of the same complex. Adam went to visit her there a few times before he went away. He said, if I remember correctly, that it wasn't the Savoy but that she was safe and comfortable and that was all that mattered.'

'Safe and comfortable,' Will repeated, twisting his lips, 'it sounds pretty grim.'

Ellie shrugged. 'Adam was horrified at how naive and easily persuadable Tia was. Honestly, Will, if you offered her an ice cream or sweets, she'd do anything you asked. It left her open to being abused in all manner of ways. Adam became almost fixated on keeping her safe. He looked at places nearer to London but found an issue with many of them. Some were designed for more profoundly disabled people and totally unsuitable for her. So, when he found St Germaine's, although it was a long way away, he discovered it to be the best of what was available. Anyway, she seems happy there so there was never a serious consideration to moving her. When I took over her guardianship, I just followed what he'd done.'

Will's eyes opened wide. 'You're her guardian? You never told me. What about Adam?'

She shrugged. 'He stopped being my legal guardian when I turned twenty-one, but because of Tia's status he was still hers. When he moved to Barbados it made sense for me to take over. It isn't a huge responsibility. At least,' she smiled, 'it wasn't up until now.' She swilled wine around her glass, watched as he did the same and waited for the next question he would ask, preparing herself for his reaction.

'How old is she?'

She took a gulp of her wine and then looked down at her hands, both of them clasping the stem of the glass with such force she wondered it hadn't snapped. She hadn't kept it a secret, well, not precisely, she'd just never mentioned it.

Sins of omission.

Was that a quotation? She didn't know, but she did know she was just trying to put off giving him an answer. She looked up then and met his steady gaze, keeping her eyes locked on his, unconsciously begging him to understand.

'She's my twin, Will. My identical twin.'

7

Ellie watched his face change, the half-smile that appeared tentatively on his lips. He thought she was joking she realised and was waiting for the punchline of a joke she hadn't made.

'We're identical twins,' she repeated, reaching a hand up and laying it on his knee.

Brushing it away, he stood abruptly, still holding the glass, wine sloshing unnoticed onto his hand, one drop falling to the sofa where it shimmered for a moment before soaking in. Ellie watched the round red circle and wondered absent-mindedly how she could remove the stain. It helped to focus on something so mundane rather than watching the hurt disbelief on her husband's face.

Will walked across the room, kicking a floor cushion out of the way.

'You're serious,' he said finally.

She turned her face away, unable to look at his eyes begging her to tell him it was just a bad joke, that of course Tia wasn't her twin. Her identical twin. Because surely, she'd have told him something this important in the ten years they'd known each other.

'I'm sorry—'

'Don't,' he said, running a hand through his hair and giving a distinctly unamused laugh. 'Wow,' he said, 'just how many other secrets have you been keeping from me, Ellie?'

She cringed at the anger in his voice. 'I didn't—'

'Please,' he interrupted her again, his voice louder, 'don't tell me you haven't kept secrets from me. There's never having had a period for one. And now I find out that Tia is your twin.' He raised a finger and pointed at her, stabbing the air with each word as he shouted, 'Your identical twin.'

As she looked at him, wondering how or if she could explain, she saw his face change from angry to sad puzzlement before he returned to his seat and sat with his head in his hands.

Ellie turned away from him and sat looking into the fire, hearing his heavy breathing behind her. She had to try to make him understand. 'It was hard being a twin,' she said quietly, 'especially an identical twin of a girl with a such a mild learning disability. Yes, she needed a little more help than most, but everyone wrapped her up in cotton wool like she was this special, fragile thing and I just got left out in the cold. They'd be nicer to her, gentler with her, more understanding and forgiving when she did something wrong. And, all the time, more loving.' She heard Will move behind her.

'It almost sounds like you were jealous of her,' he said, his voice quiet.

She gave a bitter laugh. 'Jealous? I've never thought of it like that but, yes, I suppose I was.' She stared into the flames for a moment before sighing. 'I resented her, Will. As a child, I didn't understand the restricted life that was in store for her, I just saw how everyone loved her more than me.'

There was silence for a few minutes, broken only by the sputtering of the fire. Ellie reached out and dropped another log on the embers and then sat back. 'When I went to boarding school after Daddy died, it was a revelation. I was just me. A whole person, not half of a couple.' She turned to meet his eyes. 'I never told the friends I made there that I had a sister, let alone a twin, and it helped.'

'An identical twin,' Will said.

Ellie bit her lip. 'Can you hear,' she said, and her voice was sad, 'the way you said that? You're fascinated. People are fascinated by the idea of identical twins, they stare as if they can't believe their eyes.' She waited for him to contradict her but the silence stretched on. Picking up the poker, she pushed the log causing flames to shoot up again and then just held it in her hand bouncing it up and down.

'What am I going to do with her now?' she muttered.

'Could she live in an apartment with someone dropping in to make sure she was okay?' Will suggested. 'Maybe the apartment downstairs? We could give Mr Dempsey a month's notice. Would that suit?'

Taking a sip of the wine, Ellie thought a moment before shaking her head. 'No, she wouldn't be able to live on her own. It wouldn't be safe, she's too vulnerable, Will, too easily taken advantage of. It might even be frightening for her to live alone.' She sighed heavily. 'I'll have to start looking. Maybe there are more sheltered housing places available since Adam had a look. It's been fifteen years after all.'

The conversation might have stopped there but alcohol had softened their minds offering solutions they wouldn't have considered had they both been stone-cold sober.

'Why don't we let her live here with us?' Will said, when neither of them had spoken for several minutes.

Ellie turned to look at him over the rim of her glass. *Let her live here.* Had he not heard what she'd said? Had he not understood how difficult she had found it to be a twin?

She met her husband's eyes. He was such a good and generous man and he was looking at her with that gentle look on his face that she loved. *Let her live here?* If she said no, his face would change, the same way Adam's had when she hesitated about taking on the guardianship, the same way her father's used to when Tia was upset, and he blamed Ellie for not watching out for her properly. If she said no, if she said she wouldn't even consider the idea, he'd be disappointed in her. Once again, and for the second time that day, she wouldn't be good enough.

'She might find it difficult being here,' she said vaguely, hoping he'd say *yes, it was a crazy idea, ignore me.*

But he didn't, he looked at her with that same expression on his face and said, 'Isn't it worth a try?'

Her mouth was suddenly dry. Taking a sip of her wine, she nodded slowly and said, 'I suppose we could have her here for a few days and see how it goes?'

He slipped to the floor beside her and took her in his arms. 'I think we're doing the right thing, darling. You'll see, I bet she fits right in, and you'll wonder why we didn't have her here years ago.' Ellie felt his arms around her, holding her tightly. But despite his arms, despite the fire that still blazed behind her, she suddenly felt very cold.

8

In the sober light of the following morning, Ellie hoped Will would say that maybe inviting Tia to stay wasn't such a good idea. She'd lain awake most of the night worrying about it and felt tired and irritable.

'Are you sure you don't mind Tia coming to live here?' she asked over her breakfast of liquidised spinach, cucumber and lemon, the resulting green drink making her stomach churn. It had better be good for her because it tasted bloody awful. She waited for an answer to her carefully neutral question. She didn't want him to see her doubts. If, on the other hand, he had a rethink, she'd jump right in.

He drained a pint glass of water, leaned against the sink and considered her question. 'It was easier last night,' he admitted. 'Maybe too much wine.' He shrugged and then winced. Reaching into a cupboard, he took out a packet of paracetamol, pushed two from their foil and popped them into his mouth. 'Why don't we give it a go?' he said, filling the pint glass again and draining half before he continued. 'If it doesn't work out, we can look for sheltered accommodation. Perhaps somewhere nearby so you can see her more often.'

Ellie looked for criticism in the words, on his face, knowing he'd been surprised, even a little shocked, when she'd admitted she'd never once visited Tia. She sipped more of the foul drink, wishing she could tip it out but aware of his eyes on her. He'd told her she was crazy for drinking these smoothies on more than one occasion and she'd defended them. Maybe next time she'd halve the amount of spinach and see what it was like. It couldn't be worse. She was aware she was putting off answering his question. Putting the glass down slowly, she nodded. 'Okay,' she said. 'I suppose there'd be no harm trying for a couple of weeks. Meanwhile, I can have a look at what alternatives are available.' If she got a moment, she'd start looking that day. Maybe if she found somewhere exceptional, she could argue for Tia going straight there.

'I suppose you'll have to go and collect her,' Will said. 'Where did you say the place was?'

'Peebles,' Ellie said, picking up her drink again and taking a sip, allowing Will to see her suddenly closed eyes as a reaction to that, rather than the enormity of what they were taking on, of the stupidity of her agreeing. She'd told him how she'd felt as a child, but she hadn't told him she was afraid it wouldn't have changed, that she'd once again be a twin; a half, not a whole. He'd think she was being silly. It was fifteen years ago, she'd been a child. Now she was an adult, a corporate high-flyer. Things would be different.

But a bit of the child remains in us always. She heard it now, saying quietly, *what if things are exactly the same*, and she felt a quiver of fear.

It was too late to back down now, anyway. Focusing on the details would help put things into perspective. 'And yes, of course, I'll have to go and fetch her. She wouldn't be safe to travel alone. I can fly to Edinburgh,' she said. 'She'll need some form of photographic identification, I'll check with them that she has something when I ring. It's only about an hour's drive from the airport. I'll hire a car at the airport and pick her up.'

It could be done in a day; she wouldn't need to take precious time off work. She'd pick Tia up on a Saturday and would have the Sunday then to help her settle in.

Later, sitting at her desk, coffee in hand, she rang the number written in small print on the bottom of the letter she'd received and waited, tapping a carefully manicured nail on the desk until it was answered. When it was, and she started to explain why she was ringing, she was stopped mid-sentence and asked to wait. For five minutes she listened to irritating music that had her gritting her teeth. 'This is a bad idea,' she muttered and was just about to hang up when a cheerful voice shouted, '*Hello?*' down the line.

If Ellie had hoped for the plans to be cast aside for any of a hundred reasons, she was destined to be let down. The owner of the cheerful voice turned out to be the manager. 'Thank you so much for getting back to us so quickly, Mrs Armstrong,' he all but gushed down the line. 'We're keen to make the transition as smooth and painless as possible and the sooner families become involved, the easier that will be.'

Ellie explained that they'd decided to have Tia stay with them for a while. 'Just until we can find something suitable nearer to London,' she added hurriedly. 'I am slightly concerned, however, that we may be expecting too much from her. She's been with you for fifteen years, there's bound to be an element of institutionalisation. Will she cope with being at home alone all day while we're at work? I suppose what I'm asking is,' she gave a nervous laugh, 'can I be sure she'll be safe?'

The manager's voice was cooler when he replied, perhaps she shouldn't have used the word *institutionalisation*. 'I would imagine she would be as safe in your home as she is here, Mrs Armstrong,' he said. 'Tia is used to spending afternoons on her own. We've never had any worries, nor has she shown any desire to leave the campus. In fact,' he added, his voice thawing slightly, 'the only slight concern I would have, is that, despite continued encouragement to do so, she has always refused to leave the school and has no knowledge of life in the real world.'

'She has never left the school?' Ellie was appalled.

'Her previous guardian, Mr Dawson, was aware of the situation. We had a number of discussions about it, all of which,' he added, 'have been documented. I assume when you took over guardianship of your sister, our concerns were discussed.'

Were they? Ellie didn't remember Adam raising any problems. He always said Tia appeared content. But never to have left the school. In fifteen years? Unable to imagine such a restricted life, she didn't try, and brushed away a twinge of guilt.

'I'll pick her up in a week,' she said firmly. 'We'll be flying so will you arrange to have the bulk of her belongings sent to my address? I'll settle her account with you when I arrive. And she'll need some form of ID, can you make sure she has that?'

He assured her he'd have everything organised. They decided on a date, discussed essential paperwork, and that was that. Ellie hung up and sat back in her chair. 'Dear God,' she murmured. 'What have I done?'

She sat for a long time before shaking her head and getting back to work, but she couldn't get the numbers on her screen to make sense. With a hiss, she turned off the programme she was using and went on the internet. No harm in looking for her get-out-of-jail card, was there?

Forty minutes later, despite an extensive search for suitable accommodation for Tia, moving further and further from London in desperation, she had two numbers to ring. Two. Taking a deep breath, she rang the first. The conversation was brief. There were no vacancies and their waiting list for places was long. Finding the same situation at the second sheltered accommodation, she hung up in disbelief. Nothing!

Nothing, and next week Tia was coming to live with them.

She rested her forehead on her hand, there had to be something she could do, but right at that moment, apart from screaming in frustration, she couldn't think what.

9

On the appointed day, earlier than she'd been out of her bed in years, Ellie dressed in her standard weekend wardrobe of jeans, white cotton shirt and navy jacket. She wouldn't bother with a coat; she'd be inside, one way or another, the entire day.

'Are you excited?' Will asked, watching as she buttoned her shirt.

She looked at him, surprised, and then looked back at her reflection in the mirror. She had a fleeting memory of looking at her sister and seeing her own face looking back. They'd been so alike. Surely that would have changed.

'Of course, I am,' she lied. Apprehensive was the word she'd have used. Actually, if she were being honest, she'd have used the word *terrified*. But he wouldn't understand, and she wasn't sure she could explain.

He'd wanted to go with her, but she'd insisted it would be better if she went alone. Better for her, she meant, but she could see by the sudden softness in Will's eyes that he thought she was being protective of her twin and she hadn't the heart to enlighten him, hadn't the heart to tell him that this first encounter was likely to be difficult for her, traumatic even. What if nothing had changed?

She enjoyed flying and the flight from London Stansted was no exception. She'd paid extra and got a window seat, lying her jacket across the middle seat when it was obvious nobody was going to sit in it before sitting back to look out the window and watch airport personnel doing whatever it was they were supposed to be doing.

Normally, she'd have had a glass of wine, but not this time, she was driving. Maybe she should have organised a taxi to take her to Peebles, as Adam always did, but when she'd thought about the hour's drive, the two of them sitting in the back making small talk, she'd immediately booked a rental car.

On the return journey, she would have some wine. Probably more than one glass.

The car hire had been arranged through the airline when she'd booked her flights. The airport was busy but she was in luck and there was no queue at the car hire desk.

She handed her confirmation paperwork to the smartly dressed man behind the desk and, a few minutes later, having signed her name in numerous places, she was handed the car keys. 'You've driven a Suzuki before?' he asked.

She took the keys and nodded. 'It has a satnav?' she asked, nodding at his quick *yes* before following the directions he'd given her to the rental car section. 'Row five, bay thirty-six,' she muttered to herself walking up and down until she found the correct bay. She gave the small Suzuki a quick once-over and pressed the fob to open it.

St Germaine's School for the Differently Abled was a mile outside the town of Peebles. She followed the satnav directions and found it with little problem, just once having to reverse on the road to make a turn she'd missed. There was a tight turn-around time to catch the flight back to London, she didn't have time to waste, and so she heaved a sigh of relief as she saw a large, ornate sign hanging above an imposing gateway.

She turned in and slowly drove down a long winding drive, the school building looming into view as she turned a corner. It was a strikingly large and grim building. Victorian, she guessed, pulling into a parking space in front of it. She'd have taken a bet it was built as an asylum, it had that sorrowful air that lingered on some old buildings with a less-than-happy history.

Shivering, she went up the five stone steps that led to the large front door. Looking around for a bell, or maybe even a knocker, she frowned to see neither. Frustrated, she risked a gentle push on the door, and was surprised when it immediately opened. Thankfully, it didn't squeak; she might have run away if it had.

Inside, in stark contrast to the forbidding exterior, the entrance hall was bright and decidedly cheerful. 'Overcompensating,' she muttered, seeing the garishly bright colours, the childish decals, the whimsical furniture.

Wooden double doors with clear glass panes led from the entrance hall and here, on the wall beside the door, Ellie found the doorbells she had sought outside. She stooped slightly to read the small print beside each bell, choosing the one that said *Reception*, and pressed it firmly.

If it rang somewhere within, it wasn't audible outside. Ellie, feeling a bubble of anxiety that had nothing to do with worrying about missing the flight, pressed her nose to the glass just as the door was opened. She stepped back, a slight flush to her cheeks, a distinctly guilty look on her face.

The man who opened the door grinned. 'You'd never believe how often that happens,' he said, standing back and waving her inside. His grin faded and he stared at her, a strange look crossing his rather pleasant features.

She recognised the look of disbelief. Biting her lip, she ignored him and looked around. Whoever had decorated the entrance hall hadn't been given the same leeway here. It was stuck fast in the Victorian era but, unlike the exterior, this was Victorian at its best. The tiled floor was stunning, the hues muted, the design intricate. A huge, cantilevered oak stairway curved upward, its steps carpeted in deep red, brass stair rods on each step gleaming. Under it sat a huge mahogany desk. It wasn't Victorian, but it looked the part.

'This is very nice,' she said.

'Unlike the entrance hall,' he said, smiling. He led her to the desk, waving a hand toward a chair while he took the one behind the desk.

The manager had apologised and said he'd be unavailable on the day, which Ellie rightly read as meaning he didn't work weekends. 'I was told to ask for the deputy, Felix Porter,' she said.

'That's me,' he said. 'I don't have to ask who you are. Tia's sister. Forgive me if you've heard it a million times, but you look so alike.' Ellie kept the slight smile fixed on her face as she felt her heart plummet. She wanted to quiz him, wanted to ask *how alike* but she was afraid to. Surely fifteen years of different experiences would have left some mark, wouldn't they?

He stood abruptly. 'Jim said you wouldn't have time to spare, so I won't bother offering you refreshments and take you straight to Tia's room. She's been told, several times, about your arrival. She was understandably a little upset, at first, when she was told she'd be leaving. Refused to go, actually. Jim had to be quite firm with her, said she didn't have a choice, not this time.' He shrugged. 'I don't know if she understood, or not, but anyway, she has packed her things. I think she's just finishing with the last few bits and pieces.' He indicated a door behind. 'I'll take you over,' he said, and led the way from the reception across a courtyard into another building, opening a door onto a long corridor. Ellie's heels click-clacked on the cheaper modern floor tiles as she followed him, her nose crinkling in defence as unidentifiable smells assaulted from every direction.

'The main kitchen is one floor down,' Porter explained.

But it wasn't just food – although there was an overpowering smell of cabbage – it was the distinct odour of decay. Looking up, she noted damp patches on the ceiling, mould on the walls, wallpaper peeling off, and here and there fungal growths hinting at an underlying problem. No wonder it was closing.

Porter stopped at a door and, with a reassuring smile in her direction, he knocked, waiting only a second before turning the handle to push the door open. 'Tia,' he said, 'your sister is here.' He moved back into the corridor to allow Ellie to enter the small room where Tia sat on the narrow bed, her hair unbound, falling forward over her face. She was folding a jumper, her whole concentration fixed on the task.

'Tia,' Ellie called gently as she moved into the room, suddenly and frighteningly aware of how little she knew about her sister. Fifteen years. She'd changed so much in that time, it was likely her sister had too.

Tia finished folding the jumper, put it into the suitcase that lay open on the bed, and only then did she stand, brush her hair back and smile at Ellie.

Stunned, Ellie took a step backward. She hadn't expected dramatic change; they were identical twins, for goodness' sake, but if she'd expected their different life experiences to have had some impact, different choices to have made a superficial difference, she was disappointed. Unbelievably, they even wore their hair the same length: loose and slightly curling. Tia wasn't wearing make-up, she guessed, but at the weekends Ellie favoured natural make-up that was so subtle as to be almost unnoticeable. To all intents and purposes, looking at her sister was like looking in a mirror. And, for the first time, as she felt her gut curl, she didn't feel doubt, she knew with certainty that she'd made a terrible mistake.

10

Ellie gritted her teeth when Tia came towards her with a raised hand and gently touched her cheek. She would have stepped back, but she was conscious of the deputy behind her. Conscious too, that Tia didn't mean any harm, not even when she moved the hand on her cheek to pat it lightly and say, 'You're me.'

Lost for words, Ellie looked back to where Felix Porter hovered in the doorway. She could change her mind, couldn't she? Then the noxious smell hit her once more, and she knew she couldn't. Not now. Taking a deep breath, she said, 'Hello, Tia.' There was so much to say, and nothing to say; so much had changed and, terrifyingly, nothing had changed. She forced a smile. 'We need to get going,' she said to her, 'we can chat later.'

She turned back to the deputy. 'Has she much more stuff?'

'No,' he said, and nodded toward the suitcase, 'that's it. The heavier stuff was sent yesterday, they promised it would arrive in a day or two. It was books and folders mostly. Tia likes to collect things.'

'More clothes, too, I hope,' Ellie said, staring at the small suitcase open on the bed. She caught his eye, saw the negative in them before he needed to say a word. 'Surely she must have more clothes than this?' Ellie said, horrified that everything Tia owned fit into this one little suitcase.

He shook his head and shrugged. 'She had everything she needed, Mrs Armstrong.'

Ellie felt a stab of remorse. She should have come to see her, or at least she could have phoned and asked if she needed anything.

But if she had, would she have heard the, '*She has everything she needed,*' and hung up, satisfied? Probably, she admitted.

'We'd better get going,' she said again, with a gentle smile for her sister.

Tia nodded. Turning, she closed her suitcase, picked it up and stood with it in her hand waiting to be told what to do next.

'Don't forget your coat,' Porter said from the doorway.

Immediately, Tia dropped the suitcase and took her coat from where she'd left it on the back of the only chair in the room. She put it on, buttoned it, and picked up her suitcase again.

Ellie expected her to show sadness when, in the reception, they were met by some of the staff and other residents who had come to say goodbye. They hugged her and wished her well; some, Ellie noticed as she stood waiting, had tears in their eyes. But Tia showed little emotion, merely accepting their wishes and hugs with a slight smile.

Ellie glanced her way as they drove down the long winding drive away from the school. 'Are you sad to leave?'

Tia turned to stare at her. 'Why would I be?' Ellie swallowed. Why indeed?

The journey back to the airport was made almost in silence. Now and then, Ellie asked her if she were all right and Tia nodded, her eyes glued to the scenes they passed. As they approached the airport, Ellie became worried. Tia had never been in an aeroplane; she might be terrified.

But, to her relief, when she explained to Tia about flying, she accepted the concept in the same passive way she seemed to accept everything else. Ellie had been afraid the world outside St Germaine's would be overwhelming. If it were, if Tia were nervous or afraid, she didn't show the slightest sign. Inside the airport her almost blank expression was replaced by a wide-eyed fascination as she took in the sounds and smells of the busy airport. She constantly stopped to stare at things, reaching out a hand to run her fingers along each new surface they passed.

Ellie quickly became conscious of people staring and pointing fingers and frowned. It was starting already. Opening her bag, she took out a pair of sunglasses and put them on. They helped, a little. Putting a hand on Tia's elbow, she increased her pace. 'We have to walk quickly,' she explained to her, 'we don't want to miss our flight.'

To Ellie's relief, the flight was on time. Apart from a brief moment at check-in, where eyebrows were raised as she handed over her passport and Tia's identification, she kept her glasses on, hiding behind their ridiculously oversized frames, glad for the first time she hadn't listened to Will and gone for something much more discreet.

At Stansted, they waited for Tia's suitcase. Fascinated by the luggage carousel, she shouted out in delight when she saw her suitcase appear out of the tunnel and, before Ellie could stop her, she rushed to grab it, elbowing people out of the way in her haste. 'It's all right,' Ellie reassured her when she missed it and it disappeared around the bend of the carousel. 'Watch, it will come around again in a minute.' She kept a hold of her arm, murmuring *wait* into her ear when the case did appear, releasing her when the case trundled in front of them. Tia grabbed it and pulled it from the belt, her face beaming with such pleasure it brought a smile to Ellie's face.

Outside, rain had started to fall as Ellie guided her sister toward the taxi rank. There was a queue, but it wasn't endless. As the taxi negotiated the streets of London, Tia sat forward and stared, her mouth slightly open. She said nothing and Ellie, watching her, wondering what was going through her mind. It was such a contrast to the quiet of St Germaine's. For the first time, she wondered if they were being fair to her by bringing her to the city. As if she'd read her mind, Tia turned to look at her, a serious expression on her face. 'I like London,' she said.

Ellie met her gaze. She wished she could say she was welcome to stay with them as long as she wanted, but she wasn't going to start their reacquaintance with a lie. 'It will be like a holiday for you until we can find somewhere else like St Germaine's,' she said with what she hoped was a reassuring smile.

Tia's expression didn't change. 'I like London,' she said again and with a nod turned back to watch the passing scenery of the city streets and the people who milled about as the taxi stopped in traffic.

Ellie bit her lip. She turned to look out the window as they passed a darkened office block. All she could see was her reflection. With a gulp she shut her eyes, keeping them shut until the taxi slowed to a stop over an hour later.

'This is where we live,' she said, paying the driver. It had stopped raining, so she stood on the path for a moment after the taxi had gone, giving Tia time to take in her surroundings. If she'd expected her to be impressed by this evidence of her success, she was disappointed; she smiled in the same way she'd done at the luggage carousel.

'There's an apartment down on the lower-ground floor,' Ellie explained as they passed the well-camouflaged gate in the fence that gave entrance to the steps leading downstairs. 'There's a very nice gentleman living there, Mr Dempsey, you might see him now and then.'

It wasn't like her to babble. She stopped, fished in her bag for the door key and opened the front door. 'Come in,' she said, standing back to let her in. 'It's nice to be home.'

Tia stood looking at her, her expression inscrutable. Ellie pinned on a smile. Was that the way *she* looked, did people think the same of her? 'Would you like to go straight to your room,' she asked her, 'or have a cup of tea? Or there's coffee, if you'd prefer?'

She knew what she wanted: a large, no make that a very large, glass of wine. On the flight home, when she'd really wanted a drink, she'd been struck by the sudden realisation of the responsibility she'd taken on and had an espresso instead.

'My room, please,' Tia said.

'Great, follow me.' Ellie could hear the forced jollity in her voice. She took a deep breath and let it out slowly as she led the way, stopping and smiling at Tia before pushing open the door to the spare bedroom. She'd cleared the room during the week, removing the clutter that had drifted in over the years, dressing the bed in pale-pink bed linen, adding a small desk and chair. She'd also added a television, in case she liked to watch TV late at night or early in the morning.

Tia looked around the room but said nothing. Ellie, who had really made an effort to make the room as homely and comfortable as possible, was a little taken aback at her lack of response, then she remembered her bedroom in St Germaine's, and the miserable few clothes. Really, what did Tia have to thank her for?

'You can put your stuff in there,' she said, pointing to the wardrobe and chest of drawers. She hadn't meant right away, of course, but she'd no sooner made this remark than Tia lifted her suitcase onto the small table, opened it and started unpacking.

Ellie was about to explain that there was no urgency but stopped when she saw the contents of Tia's suitcase. She'd been horrified when she saw that all her clothes fit in one miserable case, now she was appalled at the clothes themselves; basic white, now faded-to-grey underwear; two pairs of cheap, unbranded jeans; a few long-sleeved T-shirts that had seen better days; a couple of out-of-shape jumpers and a few other unidentifiable garments with one common denominator: grey. What colour they had started out as Ellie had no idea but guilt, her companion for the day, once again twisted her gut painfully.

'Hang on,' she said and went to her bedroom. When she'd moved in with Will she'd been surprised at the small amount of space available for her clothes. She'd said nothing, squeezing her suits and shirts alongside his, leaving some of her clothes in suitcases until she needed them. A few weeks later, she arrived home after a hard day at work to discover he'd organised a surprise for her. He'd brought her upstairs, his hands over her eyes, and shown her what he'd had done. A door had been knocked through from their bedroom into what had previously been a small spare bedroom. Builders had closed off the door from it to the hallway and fitters had lined it with shelves and hanging racks. It was a perfect dressing room, and she'd squealed with pleasure. Of course, it didn't take long to fill it. And there was so much she didn't wear. Frowning in concentration now, she took down blouses, trousers and skirts, grabbing the hangers together, taking them and dropping them on her bed. She returned for T-shirts and jumpers, dropping them on top of the rest. 'That should do it,' she murmured and, grabbing the lot, brought the bundle to Tia's bedroom and placed them on her bed.

'Here,' she said with a smile. 'I don't wear half the clothes I have, have a look through these, see if there's anything you like. Tomorrow,' she continued, seeing her twin's eyes light with excitement at last, 'I'll take you shopping for underwear and other stuff you'll need.'

Tia moved to the mound of clothes and picked up a jumper. Her hands caressed the fabric, holding it to her face. 'So soft,' she said, 'is it really all for me?'

Ellie felt a catch in her throat. Why hadn't she sent her things over the years? 'Yes, it is. Would you like to change into something while I go and make dinner?'

Tia nodded. With a sigh of relief, Ellie left her and headed to the kitchen. She'd planned a simple dinner: fillet steak and salad. Will had gone to a football match. Normally, he would have gone to the pub afterwards, drowning sorrows or cele-brating success; whichever the case he was usually pretty drunk on his return. But not today, today he'd promised to have only a couple of pints, come home for dinner and meet his sister-in-law for the first time. Ellie resisted the temptation to open a bottle of wine. The day had been long, tiring and emotionally draining, and she hadn't eaten. It would be safer to wait. Slipping an apron on, she started dinner, feeling herself relax as she prepared the marinade for the steak. She poured it over the meat and put it to one side before starting on the salad, slicing tomatoes, peeling and chopping cucumber and beetroot.

The steak was grilling and she was just putting the salad bowl onto the dining room table when Tia opened the door slowly and made her entrance in Ellie's cast-offs. She stood a moment in the doorway before moving into the room and then suddenly, like a child, she did a twirl.

'This is my favourite,' she said, spinning again.

Ellie could see why. The gossamer-thin white voile blouse made her look angelic and the white silk skirt, brushing the floor, added to the effect.

Just as Ellie was about to say it wasn't really suitable, that she must have added the outfit by accident, she heard the front door open and then Will's voice shouting a cheery, slightly inebriated *hello*.

Tia, startled, moved backward towards Ellie so when he walked in they were standing almost side by side.

Ellie had told him that she and Tia were identical twins, but she hadn't warned him how alike they were, maybe because she'd hoped it was no longer true. But all the evidence she needed was right there on his face: disbelief coupled with confusion. For a moment, Ellie was certain he wasn't sure which of the two women in front of him was his wife.

Before Ellie could move, before she could stop him making a mistake she'd find impossible to forget, he moved toward her.

She smiled in relief. Of course, he'd recognise her. She was just being silly, oversensitive.

'Tia,' he said, reaching forward to peck her on the cheek, 'how nice to finally meet you.'

11

Will, hearing Ellie's quick intake of breath, realised his mistake immediately and tried to laugh it off. 'Just joking,' he said to his clearly horrified wife, his laugh sounding forced even to his ears.

He turned to face his sister-in-law. 'Tia,' he said. 'How lovely to meet you. Did you have a good journey?'

Ellie, still reeling from the shock of his mistake, answered for her sister, her voice tight. 'It was fine, the flight was on time. No problems.' Turning to Tia, she pointed to one of the chairs, 'You can sit there, Tia. Dinner is ready.'

'Can I help you?' Will asked. She ignored him. With an embarrassed laugh, he turned to Tia again and gave her a friendly smile, 'I hope your room is all right.'

Tia looked at him and blinked rapidly. 'It's pink,' Will tried again, helplessly. She smiled. 'Yes. I like pink.'

Will gulped. It was just like looking at Ellie. And then he frowned. No, it wasn't, not really. He couldn't remember the last time he'd seen his wife's face as relaxed as Tia's. 'Sit, please make yourself comfortable,' he said. 'I just need to go and wash up, I'll be back in a minute.'

By the time he returned, dinner was on the table, the sisters sitting opposite each other, his plate at the end. 'This looks nice,' he said appreciatively, sitting down and giving both women an awkward smile. 'Ellie is a good cook,' he said to Tia. 'I hear you worked in a bakery?'

As a conversation starter it didn't work. Tia looked blankly at him, her mouth slightly open. Will picked up his knife and fork and cut into his steak, trying to ignore the heat of Ellie's stare.

'Didn't you bake bread? At St Germaine's,' he tried again between mouthfuls.

Tia nodded. 'Every day. Brown bread.'

'Very good,' Will said and then, glancing up to see both women looking at him, he qualified, 'the steak. It's very good.'

Tia hadn't started hers. Ellie, a hint of panic in her voice, said, 'Don't you like steak?'

Her laugh rang out, an earthy belly laugh that made Will grin and Ellie frown. 'Is that what it is?' she said, her laugh reducing quickly to a giggle that continued as she explained, 'I didn't know what it was. I've never had steak like this before.'

Ellie's frown, like Tia's giggle, continued. 'It's fillet steak, Tia. Very expensive and very good. Eat it up, you must be hungry.'

Still smiling, Tia picked up her knife and fork and proceeded to cut the steak and eat. She ate quickly, barely slowing to nod or shake her head in reply to the questions Will threw her way. *Did she enjoy the flight? Was she sad leaving St Germaine's?*

Eventually, he gave up trying to make conversation and

concentrated on his dinner, ignoring the occasional baleful glance from Ellie.

Tia's plate was empty well before either Will or Ellie had finished and he watched as she put her knife and fork down carefully, side by side.

'Did you enjoy that?' he asked, expecting another nod.

Tia smiled at him, a dazzling smile that lit up her face, animating it and making her even more like her sister. 'It was very nice, thank you.'

'Good,' he said, avoiding looking Ellie's way.

'There's some apple tart and ice cream,' Ellie said, standing and collecting the plates.

Will watched her go without a glance in his direction and sighed before turning to look at his sister-in-law. He wondered if they'd made the right decision. How would he feel if he had to live with his double? In a flash of understanding, he thought this was why Ellie hadn't spoken much of her sister in the past. She was a very strong-willed, independent woman – and she was one of a pair. But not quite. It gave him a headache just thinking about it. It hadn't helped that he'd mixed them up. What an idiot he'd been. He glanced over to where Ellie was scooping ice cream, her face a picture of concentration and he shook his head. He'd always known she wasn't as tough as she liked to make herself out to be, but now, suddenly, he saw a vulnerability he hadn't known existed. He looked across the table at his sister-in-law. What had Ellie said? *Everyone loved her more than me.* He frowned. That was fifteen years ago. They were children then, but was Ellie worried that not enough had changed since? They certainly still looked identical. Maybe she was afraid everything else would be the same too? He needed to be more careful.

He could already see that Tia's arrival was bringing out

something in his wife that he'd never seen before, complex emotions she'd kept buried for a very long time. Had it been a crazy idea to bring Tia here?

A slight movement brought his attention back to Tia. Feeling a little guilty for ignoring her, he said, 'You must miss St Germaine's.'

'Why?' she said, her face guileless.

He was taken aback. 'Didn't you have friends there?'

Tia thought a moment. 'I did. Her name was Mandy. She died.'

'Who died?' Ellie asked, returning with the promised apple tart and ice cream. Handing plates out, she sat and looked around, a polite expression of interest on her face.

'Her friend, Mandy,' Will explained. 'I was asking her if she missed the school and her friends.'

Ellie looked at her sister. 'I'm so sorry,' she said, 'when did she die?'

Tia looked at her blankly.

Will nudged his wife under the table with his foot; it was obvious that Tia couldn't remember and also obvious, because he knew her so well, that Ellie wasn't going to let it lie. He ignored her cross look and sought desperately for something else to say. 'So, you baked bread,' he tried, 'what else did you do all day?'

Tia mirrored his smile. 'I had breakfast and then I baked bread. Then I had lunch. After that I went to my room and read magazines or watched television. At five, I went for my supper and, afterwards, watched television and went to bed.'

The dull routine of the institution. Will's tart suddenly tasted dry and bland. 'What did you do on your days off?' he asked.

Tia looked blankly at him and it dawned on him that it was

her default expression when she didn't know the answer or didn't understand the question. Or both.

'The days you didn't bake bread, I mean,' Will explained.

Tia laughed. 'I always baked bread. How would they have bread, if I didn't bake it?' Like a light switched off, her smile vanished. 'Where will they get their bread now?' she whispered as tears silently and unexpectedly appeared and slowly made their way down her cheeks.

Ellie and Will looked at each other, panicked and helpless. But even as Will wondered what to say, he saw a change appear in Ellie's eyes as she saw the tears.

'They'll have to buy it like everyone else does,' she said gently.

'They will,' he quickly agreed, reaching out to grasp Tia's hand and adding, 'I bet it won't taste nearly as good as yours though, and they'll be sorry that you're gone.'

This idea seemed to appeal. Tia looked up and gave him a beaming smile.

Ellie's face, he noticed, looked tense and strained again. Deciding it might be a good idea to give her some space, he stood. 'Why don't we go for a walk,' he said to Tia. 'I know it's late, but we can do a quick tour of the neighbourhood. Plus,' he smiled at her conspiratorially, 'we get out of doing the cleaning up.'

He'd no idea if she made any sense of what he'd said, but when he reached out a hand toward her, she took it automatically. He remembered what Ellie had said. She'd be vulnerable to anyone who wanted to take advantage. Now he saw how true that was.

Ellie looked up at him with a look of gratitude. 'She'll need to change.'

Will grimaced, suddenly taking in what Tia was wearing for

the first time. He was sure that was the outfit Ellie had worn at that wedding in Mexico. Why on earth was Tia wearing it? He'd ask Ellie later, maybe she'd understand then why he'd made that terrible mix-up.

'Ellie's right, you can't go walking in that. Can you change into something warmer?'

A mulish look crossed her face.

'It would be a shame to spoil such a pretty skirt by getting it muddy,' he said, coaxingly, hoping there wouldn't be more tears. 'Okay,' she said and headed out of the room. Moments later he heard her footsteps on the stairs.

'I'm sorry,' he said, moving to stand beside Ellie, putting a gentle hand on her shoulder. She didn't immediately brush it away which he took as a good sign, bending to place a kiss on her cheek.

'It will work,' he said, desperately hoping he was right.

'Go for your walk,' she said without looking at him. 'Don't rush.'

He stood looking down at her for a moment, wanting to offer reassurance but then the door opened, and Tia was there, in a coat and boots, smiling.

Ellie must have given Tia some of her clothes; he definitely recognised the coat she was wearing, he'd been with her when she'd bought it.

He looked from one sister to the other. He couldn't remember now whose idea it was to invite her to come live with them. It didn't matter; it had been a bad one.

He'd lied to Ellie, he didn't think it was going to work at all.

12

Ellie closed her eyes briefly when she heard the front door opening and closing. She hoped they'd be gone a long time, that he'd show her the entire neighbourhood and the surrounding ones. Dammit, she thought with the first sting of tears, she hoped he'd show her the whole of the blasted city of London. She needed time. Time to put Will's mistake into perspective. After all, Tia was wearing her clothes, and they were identical. But it scared her how identical they were, much more than she remembered. How could that be when their lives had been so different?

She pushed away her empty plate, rested her elbows on the table and dropped her head into her hands. It was already proving worse than she'd expected. It was never going to work. Rubbing her eyes, she decided that on Monday she would start looking again for residential accommodation for Tia. There had to be something somewhere, she didn't care how far away it was. In fact, she admitted quietly to herself, the farther away the better. Taking her glass, she moved to the sitting room and sank into the sofa with a sigh. She'd like nothing better than to sit here, peacefully drinking and pretending the last few weeks had never happened. She gave a soft laugh. At least worrying about Tia had put any talk of their childless future to one side. She knew Will wanted to explore their options, wanted to talk about what the consultant had said. He wanted to talk. Most women complained that their husbands never wanted to talk; just now, she'd swap in a heartbeat.

She'd finished another glass of wine before she heard the front door opening and the sound of voices in the hallway. They sounded cheerful. She wondered, vaguely, what they'd found to talk about.

She was stretched out on the sofa when they came through the door and she saw Will's eyebrows rising. Raising her glass to him, she grinned. She was a happy drunk, becoming mellow after a few, and generally more amusing after a few more. He knew it, and with a shake of his head he returned her grin.

Taking Tia's coat, he ushered her into the room. When it looked like she was heading to the seat beside Ellie, Will gently pointed her towards an armchair that sat on the other side of the television. 'This can be your seat,' he said, patting the arm of the chair. 'You'll be able to see the television better from here.' To demonstrate, he switched it on, flicking channels until he hit on a cookery programme.

Having settled her into the chair, he turned and cocked an eyebrow at Ellie who gave an elegant shrug in return but said nothing. With a shake of his head, he left the room, returning minutes later with a bottle of beer. He drank it straight from the bottle, a habit Ellie hated and something he rarely did. It was a subtle protest, Ellie knew; his gentle way of indicating that he didn't approve of her getting drunk on the first night her sister was there. God, she did love him. And it wasn't his fault after all, was it? She'd overreacted. It was an easy mistake to have made, since Tia was wearing her clothes. An easy mistake because they were so damn alike. She kept the smile on her face with difficulty and tapped the sofa beside her. The smile was lopsided, but it was enough. Will sat beside her and reached a free hand over to take hers, pulling her closer to him. Ellie relaxed against him, feeling the warmth of his body, basking in it. Resting her head against his shoulder, she closed her eyes. She was just beginning to relax when she was overcome with the strangest feeling she was being watched. She opened her eyes and looked over to where Tia sat staring at her, a cold, hard expression on her face. Ellie's quick intake of breath caused Will to look down at her with concern. 'You okay?'

She gave him a reassuring smile before looking back to where her sister sat, her eyes glued to the television screen like she had been watching it all along.

Maybe she'd imagined it? She closed her eyes for a few seconds. It had been a nightmare of a week. Opening her eyes again, she watched her sister for a few minutes.

She'd imagined it. Of course, she had.

13

The next morning, Ellie woke and lay with her eyes shut for a few minutes thinking of the previous day. She shivered when she thought of Will's mistake. That couldn't happen again. Throwing back the duvet, she headed to the bathroom. Will, as usual, had already left to pick up the Sunday newspapers. He'd be back soon and would cook a big breakfast. Sunday morning bliss, he always called it. The thought brought a smile to her face.

A short while later, dressed, she looked at her reflection in the bathroom mirror, seeing her clear sallow skin, long dark curling eyelashes and dark wavy hair without any pleasure. Usually, she left her hair loose at the weekend, but today she caught it and twisted it into a tight, neat bun, using several clips to keep every strand in place. She was reaching for the heavy, dark eyeshadow she usually wore on nights out when she stopped herself with a firm shake of her head. She was being silly.

The bun stayed though, and when she joined Will in the kitchen, she saw his eyes linger on it for a moment too long and knew from the regretful look on his face that he understood. He'd not make the same mistake again.

After breakfast, she looked across the table at her sister. 'Let's go shopping,' she said. 'We'll get you some new clothes. Would you like that?'

Tia, a slice of toast in one hand and a mug of tea in the other, took a few seconds to answer. 'Yes,' she said finally and then looked across the table to where Will was reading the Sunday paper. 'Are you coming?'

He laughed, shooting Ellie an amused look. 'I'll leave that to you two.'

Ellie took Tia to the John Lewis shop on Oxford Street, taking a taxi for convenience rather than the underground.

Tia wanted to stop and look at everything, but Ellie guided her through the beauty department and up the stairs to women's fashion, Tia smiling when her hand reached out to touch the garments, her eyes widening in amazement at the fabrics and choices available. Ellie steered her towards bright colours and prints that she herself would never wear. She was relieved to see Tia appeared to prefer them, happily choosing a number of shirts and jumpers in bright colours and pretty patterns.

Two hours later, they left, each of them carrying several bags. Ellie knew she was overcompensating for years of not buying her presents, but she also knew that, with plenty of new clothes of her own, Tia had no need of hers.

Back at home, she made room in Tia's wardrobe for the new clothes, removing the ones she had given her without explanation. 'Why don't you change into something new now,' she suggested, and Tia immediately agreed, stripping off the jeans and white shirt she'd given her the day before. Ellie, expecting her to stop at that, was taken aback when she stripped off her bra and knickers without hesitation, standing naked as she chose which of her new clothes to wear.

Ellie was not one of those people who felt comfortable in front of other naked women. At her health club, she'd have a towel tightly tied around her while other women showered and dried their hair without bothering to cover up. She always wore a swimming costume in the women-only sauna too. It was just the way she was; she didn't feel the need to apologise for it.

It was instinctive then to look away from the nakedness of her sister, from a body so like her own. But she also found herself glancing back as Tia bent forward to open the lower drawer of the dresser, taking a sharp breath as her breasts swung softly. *To see ourselves as others see us,* the line of the Robbie Burns' poem popped into her head. She turned away, scooped up the discarded clothes and left Tia alone.

Downstairs, she dumped the clothes in the washing machine. She'd wash them and donate them to charity. She held up the white voile blouse and the silk skirt that had caused such trouble. The skirt had been very expensive, but she knew she could never wear it again. The label inside stated dry clean only. She hesitated a few seconds, a frown creasing her brow before, swearing under her breath, she scrunched it up and threw it into the rubbish bin.

When Tia came down, dressed in bright pink jeans and a cream jumper patterned with tiny pink flowers, Ellie nodded. 'You look very nice,' she said, biting her lip. She was suddenly aware that she'd made another mistake. Yes, they looked different now, but this wasn't the kind of difference she wanted. She had wanted Tia to have better clothes and her own identity. What she hadn't expected was that she'd look like a full-colour version of her. She didn't look *nice*, she looked stunning.

Gritting her teeth, she watched as Tia went into the living

room where Will was lounging on the sofa with a beer, watching the rugby. She held her breath, waiting for his reaction, and with a twinge of pain noticed his double take when he saw Tia.

Tia stood between him and the television. 'What do you think?' she asked him.

'You look very nice,' he said, echoing Ellie's words.

Ellie, hearing the constraint in his voice, knew he'd chosen his words carefully. She also knew, without a doubt, he was thinking exactly what she had. She waited for her to leave but Tia stood as if waiting for further compliments. 'Why don't you come and help me with dinner?' she asked her, slightly surprised when she was ignored. 'Tia,' she said again, raising her voice to be heard over the commentary.

Tia slowly turned to look at her then, unsmiling. With obvious reluctance, she moved back to the kitchen. 'What shall I do?'

'Perhaps you could set the table,' Ellie said, pasting on a smile that wasn't returned. She pulled open a drawer. 'The cutlery is here,' she said, and then opened a cupboard, 'and the glasses are here.' She turned away to check the pasta and left her to it.

* * *

The following day, Will and Ellie returned to work, leaving Tia alone.

'You sure you'll be all right?' Ellie had asked her several times. She had showed her how to use the phone. 'That button,' she said pointing it out, 'will get you through to me automatically. If you have any problems or are worried about anything, anything at all, just ring me.'

Ellie worried all day, checking her phone several times, and rushed from the office on the dot of five. But she needn't have worried, when she returned home Tia was curled up on the sofa watching television.

The days settled quickly into a routine. Will suggested that Tia might be able to go to the local shops unaccompanied once she had done the journey a few times. There were, after all, no roads to cross on the way; she simply had to follow the path until she got there.

Ellie had reservations about allowing her walk alone. 'Don't forget, she's been more or less institutionalised her whole life. It might frighten her to go on her own.'

'It's five minutes, tops, Ellie,' he argued, raising an eyebrow. 'Aren't you being too protective? She's not a child—'

'She might as well be,' she interrupted, a worried look on her face. She stood and walked across the kitchen to the French doors, crossed her arms and stood staring out over the small, neat garden.

Will waited for a moment before trying again. 'She held down a job.' His hands shot up defensively when she turned. 'Yes, I know, a simple job baking bread. But it was a job, none-theless, one where she had responsibilities, even if they were very limited ones. If we don't allow her some freedom, our home will become more of an institution than St Germaine's ever was. We should be encouraging her to lead as normal a life as possible. Maybe, someday, she'll be able to move into her own place.'

Ellie said nothing. He didn't understand, and she couldn't explain to him how responsible she felt for Tia. It was her childhood all over again. The enormity of the mistake she'd made in bringing her to their home hammered inside her head. She brought her hands up and wiped her face, rubbing the corners of her eyes where tears always appeared to be waiting.

The answer was simple. Tia had to go. She should turn around and say as much, but she couldn't because, so far, she hadn't been able to find anywhere that could offer her a place.

It worried her that after only a few days Will had become more reconciled to her being there. In the first day or two, she thought he'd felt as she did, that they'd made a mistake. Now, he seemed to have accepted her presence. She'd even go so far as to say they were getting on.

Tia certainly seemed to like him, always beaming when he came into a room. Ellie blinked, trying to remember if Tia smiled at her in the same way.

Despite her reservations, every evening before dinner, Will did the five minutes' walk with Tia to the shops and back while she got dinner ready. She said nothing but was conscious of waiting anxiously until they returned.

'I think you'll be able to go alone tomorrow,' Will suggested to Tia that night over dinner, watching Ellie's reaction from the corner of his eye as they ate.

'If you think she'll be safe.' It was all she could muster. There was, after all, no point in arguing. And perhaps if Tia was more independent, there would be more care options open to her.

The next evening, she watched as Will handed Tia a key, showed her how to use it and sent her off in the right direction. 'It's five minutes there, the same back and a few minutes perhaps to look in the shop window,' he said to Ellie, nodding towards the kitchen clock.

When Tia arrived back exactly eleven minutes after she'd left, Will looked at his wife and grinned. 'I told you, no problem. It will be good for her, and for us. She'll be able to go down and pick up stuff if we run out.'

The local shop was small and well stocked but they rarely bought anything in it. Ellie ordered all their groceries online and they were delivered once a fortnight on the same day their cleaner came so it was all tidily put away before she returned from work. Occasionally, they might run out of something, but one of them would pick up whatever it was on the way home or make the short journey to the shop.

Ellie reluctantly accepted that Tia could take on this job when necessary. 'It might be best if you open an account with the shop so that she can buy stuff without having to worry about money,' Ellie said to Will the following day. 'Explain to them that she's a little...' She searched for the right word but couldn't find it. Having decided that *differently abled* was such a mouthful and, in any case, people tended to look confused when she used it, as if they expected her sister to have three legs rather than two, she settled on *simple*. 'Simple,' she said. 'Tell them she's a little simple.' Seeing a disapproving look in his eyes, she guessed he might not use that term. He didn't tell her what he did say, and she never asked, but the account was set up and if they needed something Tia went and got it. She was always delighted to be asked, taking the request with a seriousness that had Will looking at Ellie with a delighted *see what I mean* look in his eye.

* * *

It was nearing the end of their first week together when Ellie arrived home to find the house empty. Suddenly and unexpectedly panicked, she ran from room to room calling Tia's name. Running back down the stairs, she launched herself at her bag, grabbing her phone to ring Will and wondering if she should ring the police. She was just dialling his number when the front door opened behind her and Tia entered, a plastic shopping bag hanging from her hand. 'Hi,' she said, taking off her coat.

'I was worried about you,' Ellie said.

Tia looked at her curiously. 'Why?'

Why? The question threw Ellie.

Before she could think of an answer Tia reached into the bag and pulled out a box of tampons. 'I have my period,' she said simply before turning and heading upstairs.

Ellie watched her go upstairs, stunned into silence. The unfairness of it hit her like a blow, sending her reeling and clutching the bannisters for support. They weren't so identical after all, were they? Tia had a uterus. She could have a baby. Resting her head against the wood, she bit her lip painfully. She would not cry; Will would be home soon. She didn't want him to see her crying, didn't want to have to explain until she had herself under control. She tried to look at the funny side of it. All the years disliking the idea of being a twin and, for the first time ever, she wished they were even more alike. What had Will said? That it sounded like she had been jealous of Tia. She may have been.

And now? She wrapped her arms around herself and acknowledged with the bitter taste of reality that Tia could do the one thing she could never do. How could she possibly face this monthly reminder of her own failure? Her lower lip quivered. For everything Tia lacked, she was more of a woman than Ellie could – and would – ever be.

She told Will that night as she lay in his arms, trying to pretend she found it amusing, ironic even. But she knew he wasn't fooled as he pulled her tighter and, after a few seconds, she did what she'd wanted to do for hours: she sobbed.

14

Ellie and Will rarely went out during the week but, at the weekend, they enjoyed going to the cinema or theatre or out for dinner on their own, or with friends. Will, horrified that Tia had never been to either the theatre or cinema, suggested they go together the following Saturday.

Ellie wasn't surprised when he said he'd booked tickets to see the latest *Star Wars* movie, merely raising her eyes to heaven and grinning. She wasn't a fan, but she went to them for his sake.

'It's got really good reviews,' he said persuasively.

'I'm sure it will be fantastic,' she said with a smile before turning to Tia. 'You'll enjoy it, I think, it's very...' She sought for an appropriate word, settling in the end for, 'colourful'.

Will laughed. 'Colourful? This is *Star Wars*, woman!'

'He's a fan,' Ellie said, looking at a bemused Tia.

Saturday was chilly, so Ellie felt justified in wearing a beanie pulled down to cover her hair and the collar of her coat turned up. She felt Will's eyes assessing her and ignored him.

In the cinema, Will told Tia she had to buy popcorn. 'It's

part of the experience,' he said. At the kiosk Tia, faced with the choices available, looked from one option to the other, unable to decide. 'Have the toffee popcorn,' Ellie said finally, pointing. 'It's really good.'

Tia hesitated.

'Or the salted?' Will said, checking the time. Tia smiled at him. 'Salted.'

'I swear, if you said poisoned, she'd say yes,' Ellie said to him under her breath, trying to sound amused.

The row they were in was almost full, but the house lights were still on. 'We need to move down to our seats,' Ellie explained to Tia, pointing them out. 'Excuse us,' she said to the first couple who stood to allow them to pass.

'Let me go first,' Will said, taking Tia's hand and sliding into the row, tugging her after him, apologising and offering thanks as they moved along.

Ellie followed, frowning when they passed a group of young men who gave Tia admiring glances that she returned with a wide, almost flirtatious, smile, slowing down as she did so.

'Move on,' Ellie said to her, causing the men's eyes to switch to her, their eyes widening as they saw a second beautiful woman. She tried to ignore the whisper of *'twins'* as she moved past as quickly as she could.

Finally, they were seated. Ellie looked at her sister, now munching happily on the popcorn and frowned. Had she been deliberately flirtatious or did she just smile broadly at everyone? Maybe every man. Certainly, she smiled at Will. Maybe she should have a word with her, go through the whole birds and bees thing. *Especially since...*

The thought flashed across her mind and, as she had done every time since she'd discovered that Tia was probably fertile, she brushed it away and refused to think about it. She also refused to acknowledge the twisting knot of envy that was dragging her down, putting her low mood down to being overworked in the office. Sighing, she tried to concentrate on the movie.

To her surprise, Tia loved it. She and Will chatted about it all the way home. Ellie was even more surprised that Tia managed to follow the story. Better, in fact, than she had.

'Her memory seems to be a lot better than I remembered,' she said to Will later when they were lying in bed.

He yawned. 'Maybe she's better with visual things,' he suggested. 'It might be worth remembering.'

'Maybe,' Ellie agreed. She waited a moment and then pushed herself onto her elbow and looked down at him. 'Sometimes, I catch her looking at me, Will, as if she's weighing me up. It makes me feel... a little uneasy.'

He reached for her face to bring it nearer and kissed her. 'You're imagining things, Ellie. You need to relax more.' He hugged her close and kissed her again before rolling over and falling asleep in seconds.

Ellie lay awake for a long time. She didn't think she was imagining it at all. Will hadn't noticed but women were better at reading facial expressions than men. Tia's memory was definitely better than she remembered; she wondered what other things had changed in the fifteen years since they'd lived together.

* * *

The next morning, they were having breakfast when the phone rang. Ellie answered, listened for a while and then took the phone out into the hallway.

When she returned a few minutes later, Will could tell it hadn't been good news.

'What's wrong?'

Ellie picked up her coffee and took a sip before replying. 'That was Barbara,' she said. 'She couldn't come on Friday because she fell and hurt her hip. She's not badly hurt, but she's decided she's not able for the job any more. She's not coming back.'

'Who's Barbara?' Tia asked, reaching for some toast.

'Our cleaning lady,' Ellie said, taking another sip of her coffee.

Will shrugged. 'She must be seventy, Ellie. It's not a job for an older woman.'

'I'll have to advertise and interview,' she said, rubbing her forehead, 'as if I haven't enough to be doing. It would happen now, of course, when we're so busy at work.'

'I can do it,' Tia said to both Will and Ellie's surprise.

They'd become used to her silence at the table. At first, they'd tried to involve her in their conversation, but it was increasingly obvious that she preferred to sit and listen rather than join in. Sometimes, Ellie caught her smiling, as if she found something they'd said funny, but it was hard to tell what. She was quickly realising that her sister puzzled her.

'That's sweet, Tia, but you can't,' Ellie said, then, her frustration making her tetchy, she added, 'don't be silly.'

'Yes, I can,' she said simply and continued to eat her toast before explaining, 'I used to do it when Nicky went on holiday.' Will and Ellie looked at each other for enlightenment. Will, shrugging, put his cup down and asked, 'Who is Nicky?'

'The cleaner at St Germaine's,' Tia said. 'She taught me what to do. She said I was very good.' She looked at Ellie, her eyes sharp. 'She never called me silly.'

Will laughed, drawing both women's eyes to him. 'Ah, so when you said you could do it, you meant the housekeeping, not the advertising and interviewing?'

Tia looked at him blankly.

Ellie pushed her plate away. 'Oh, for goodness' sake,' she said. 'You can't possibly do it. Imagine what people would say if they knew I had my sister working as a cleaner!'

There was a moment's silence. 'Why not let her?' Will said, keeping his voice calm. 'It would be good for her to have some responsibility. Plus, it will give her something to do. She must be bored sitting here all day on her own. And,' he added, 'maybe she *is* good at it.'

'I am,' Tia said before Ellie could reply.

It broke the ice and all three laughed, but Ellie's laughter was short-lived. Tia wouldn't be doing their cleaning. If things worked out, she wouldn't be living with them for much longer. She needed to get the timing right to tell Will.

She had almost despaired of finding sheltered accommodation, or assisted living as she'd been informed it was called now. Very quickly, she'd discovered that there was a dearth of places available for people like Tia. So, when one of her contacts had rung on Friday to tell her of a new sheltered housing development that was being built close to Brighton, she didn't wait to discuss it with Will and rang the number she'd been given immediately. After a long conversation with the coordinator, she realised it was perfect and made a provisional reservation.

Now all she needed to do was to persuade Will that it was for the best.

15

Ellie was normally good at dealing with the harsher realities and, in her office, she was the go-to girl when someone wanted somebody to break bad news. But a week had passed, and she still hadn't told Will about finding somewhere for Tia to live. Her reluctance was less to do with what he'd say, than with her own mixed feelings about Tia. Mixed? Not mixed at all, she was increasingly uneasy around her twin.

The rational side of her knew that her sister's fertility had a big part to play, but there were also the strange looks she caught Tia giving her from time to time; the sudden flash of ice on her soft, pretty face. And, of course, there was also the slightly hungry way she looked at Will when she thought Ellie wasn't looking.

'You need to be careful,' she warned him when they had a moment alone together, 'maybe be a little less friendly with her.' Will had laughed. 'I treat her like a big brother would, Ellie, you're worrying about nothing.'

To her surprise, Tia hadn't lied about her abilities as a

housekeeper; the place had never been so clean. She'd taken to adding her own touch too; fresh flowers from the local shop now adorned the living room and the hall table.

At first it pleased Ellie that Tia had a purpose, that she had something to fill her days with other than television. But her initial surprise changed to unease as she came home to find new additions and changes each day; framed photographs that used to sit barely noticed on the living room bookshelf joined the flowers on the hall table. Opening kitchen cupboards, she'd find things had been rearranged and her peppermint teabags were now in a drawer by the kettle. She had to admit that each change was for the better, but that only made her gut twist tighter.

She knew she was overreacting, being oversensitive and unreasonable, but Tia's natural homemaking ability pinched at a nerve inside her head. *Was it because she was more of a woman?*

'Isn't it supposed to be her home too?' Will asked quietly when she mentioned it. She really should have told him about the Brighton development then; it was the perfect opportunity to address the idea of her having a place of her own, but she let it slide, feeling guilty about her own pettiness, shaking her head and heading upstairs.

That night, when both Tia and Will had gone to bed, she couldn't sleep. Creeping downstairs, she returned all the photographs to their original places and although tempted to throw the flowers out altogether, she resisted and settled for moving them to a window sill in the kitchen.

The next morning, it was doubtful if Will noticed and if Tia did, she made no comment. But when Ellie arrived home that night, after a trying day at work where nothing had gone her way, she wanted to scream when the flowers and photographs were back in the hallway. This time, she didn't hesitate.

'Tia,' she called, dropping her briefcase on the floor and folding her coat over the banisters. When her twin's face appeared around the kitchen door, she pointed at the photographs and flowers. 'I want these left where *I* put them.'

'But they look nice there,' Tia said, coming forward and adjusting one of the frames slightly.

Ellie took a deep breath. 'They looked nice where they were too,' she said, biting her lip as she said it because, damn the woman, she was right, they did look better in the hallway. But being right wasn't the point; it was her house, and she wanted things left where she'd put them, regardless of what they looked like. 'Put them back, please,' she said. Without waiting for a response, she picked up her briefcase, grabbed her coat and headed upstairs.

When she came down, thirty minutes later, she was pleased to see Tia had done as she asked, even as she felt a slight twinge of guilt at her overreaction. But she'd made her point. And obviously Tia hadn't minded too much as she could hear her in the living room singing along to her favourite country music on the radio. Things would be better now, she thought. She was still wearing a slight smile of satisfaction when the front door opened and Will came in, raising an eyebrow when he saw her standing there.

'Everything all right,' he asked, taking off his coat. He threw it over the banisters before reaching for her and planting a kiss on her still-curved lips. 'You're looking very pleased with yourself,' he said. 'Had a good day at work?'

'Just success in a minor skirmish,' she said, without elaborating.

'Not Jeff Harper again?' Will asked, picking up his post. She watched as he flicked through it and then threw it back onto the hall table. 'What happened to the flowers? They looked nice there.'

Ellie gave a forced laugh. 'Jeff Harper isn't the only person who gets on my nerves, you know,' she said, avoiding his second question. She linked her arm through his and walked with him toward the kitchen. 'Let's have a glass of wine before dinner.' She went straight to the fridge and took out a bottle. 'White?' Will nodded and yawned. 'God, I'm exhausted,' he said, running a hand over his face.

Ellie took two glasses to the central island, opened the bottle and half-filled each glass. 'Sit and have a drink. It's lasagne for dinner; it'll be ready in about forty minutes.' She took the shop-bought lasagne from the fridge, removed the wrapping and put it into the oven.

'I'm sure Tia would manage to put stuff into the oven and it would be ready when we got home, why don't you ask her?' Will asked before looking around. 'Speaking of which, where is she?' Ellie was about to say she was listening to music when she realised it had stopped. She paused and in the sudden silence they both heard it. The sound of someone sobbing. Their eyes met and they rushed together to the corner of the living room. 'Tia?' Will said, seeing her in a chair at the far end of the room. 'What's the matter?'

Tia didn't look up. If anything, her sobs grew louder.

Ellie stood rooted to the spot as Will hurried to her side, crouching down beside her, his face creased with worry. 'What's happened? Are you all right?'

Tia's head was buried in the crook of her arm, her shoulders heaving.

Will stood up. 'What the hell is going on?' He felt Ellie come up beside him and turned to her. 'What's the matter with her?' he said in a barely audible whisper.

Before she could answer, Tia lifted her tear-stained face and wailed, 'I was just trying to make it look nicer.' And then she buried her head in her arm again.

Will turned to Ellie with a shrug. 'What is she...?'

Ellie avoided his eyes and bit her lower lip while trying to think of a reasonable explanation. But Tia's sobs filled the room. How could anything compete with it? She didn't need to explain anyway; she saw his eyes widen as he realised what had happened. 'Success in a minor skirmish? Really?' Will said, looking at her, disappointment in his eyes. He shook his head, then ignored her while he crouched down beside Tia again and spoke soothingly to her.

Helplessly, feeling like a child again, Ellie looked on. Tia had been fine until Will came home, hadn't she? She'd been singing along to the music in the kitchen? *She's manipulating us*, she wanted to shout at him, *and she's bloody good at it. She always was.* But she knew there was no point.

A few minutes later, Will stood and took Tia's hand. 'It's fine, honestly,' he said to her. 'We'll put them back. You were right, the frames looked much better on the hall table.'

Ellie didn't move as they collected the frames and flowers and returned them to the place Tia had chosen. 'They look much better there,' he said before moving her gently toward the stairs. 'Why don't you go wash your face,' he said, 'dinner will be ready soon.'

Ellie leaned against the kitchen doorway and looked at him. 'So, if I start crying now,' she said, trying to disguise the hurt in her voice, 'are you going to move them back?'

'*Are* you going to start crying?' he asked, keeping his tone measured. He waited until she shook her head before continuing, 'Well then, that's that sorted, isn't it?'

He passed her without another word, sat down and picked up his wine.

Ellie stared at the photograph frames and wanted to smash them all, one by one; she just wasn't sure over whose head she wanted to smash them. As she stood with her eyes filling and her lower lip trembling, the only thing she could cling to was the fact that Tia wasn't going to be with them for much longer.

16

They barely spoke over dinner. Will ate, rinsed his plate in the sink before putting it into the dishwasher and left the kitchen saying he had work to do. Ellie, her lasagne only half-eaten, toyed with a few more mouthfuls before dropping her fork and reaching for the wine bottle. She filled her glass and lifted it to her mouth, holding it there as she looked at Tia over the rim. She seemed completely oblivious to the trouble she'd caused. Ellie sipped, swilled the wine around her mouth and swallowed. She supposed she could have handled it better. Sighing, she took another, bigger mouthful of wine and wished alcohol helped.

Putting her plate in the dishwasher, Ellie took her glass through to the sitting room, closing the door after her. She was tempted to turn the key in the lock, wanting to wallow in self-pity for a while but she didn't. Not, she admitted, because she was afraid of offending Tia who seemed to prefer the living room television anyway, but she hoped Will would come down and sit with her once he had cooled off.

The hope dwindled as her glass emptied. It crossed her

mind to go and refill it but, instead, she left the glass on the table and went to look for Will. He rarely worked from home; it was, she guessed, a pretext for avoiding her. Sighing, she headed to their bedroom. He wasn't there so she opened the door into the small spare bedroom and found him sitting on a rickety old chair among boxes of seldom-worn clothes and stuff they'd brought from her previous home but had no need for here.

'We really should go through these boxes sometime and take a lot of this stuff to charity shops,' she said, leaning against the door frame.

'The recycling centre is probably more appropriate,' he said, his eyes on the laptop open on the box in front of him.

'It's not rubbish,' she said, mock offended. 'There's priceless and valuable stuff in them.' She waited for him to say something, but he kept tapping away on the keyboard. 'Does it taste sweet?' she asked. Curiosity made him turn to look at her, their eyes meeting.

Nothing was said for a moment, until with a shake of his head, he said, 'I give in, does what taste sweet?'

'The frosty icing you've covered yourself in,' she said.

He groaned and then laughed. 'Jesus, Ellie, that's awful.' She smiled. 'It was the best I could come up with.'

Shaking his head, he tapped a few keys and then closed the laptop and looked at her. 'She was only trying to be nice, Ellie. You could just have left things as she wanted. And,' he added, rubbing salt into her wounds, 'you must admit, she has a good eye.' There was no better time to break her news. Ellie pushed away from the door frame and moved to stand in front of him. 'We agreed we'd give it a go, Will, and that if it didn't work out, we'd find her somewhere better to live. Well, it's not working.' She paused and tried to read his face. Whatever he was thinking, it wasn't written there. His face was set, eyes cool. Was he listening, or judging?

She wrapped her arms around herself, suddenly cold. 'I can't do it, Will. I've found a place, in Brighton. Sheltered housing where she can live as she did in St Germaine's. There's even the possibility of a job in a cafe in the grounds.' She was babbling. She stopped abruptly and waited for him to say something. When he didn't, she asked, 'Well, what do you think?'

He stood up suddenly, startling her. 'I need a drink,' he said, 'let's go downstairs.'

Ellie bit her lip. That he didn't immediately agree worried her. Couldn't he see it wasn't working? Luckily, Tia had gone to her room, so they sat where they had sat earlier, around the island, the cold granite under their hands only slightly warmer than the atmosphere that hung over them both. Ellie was tempted to try another joke, but looking at his face, she guessed the moment had gone. She took the bottle of wine from the fridge and poured him a glass before turning to put the kettle on. He sat silently until she'd made a mug of tea and perched on the stool opposite.

'So, what do you think?' she asked.

'I think you're being unfair,' he said. 'She's only been here a short time, she's hardly had time to settle in and now you want to move her again.' His brow furrowed. 'I don't understand why you want her to go, she seems happy here. I was a little worried initially but she's no problem and, you have to admit, she keeps the place very clean.'

Ellie smiled sadly. 'I told you how I felt when we were children—'

'Yes, but you're not children any more,' he interrupted her.

She knew how childish she was going to sound, but she

couldn't stop herself. 'You took her side, Will. You comforted her and made a fuss over her. You let her win.'

'Oh, for goodness' sake,' he said, running a hand over his hair, 'she was in tears, what was I supposed to do?'

'She was manipulating you.' Ellie half-laughed, half-pleaded, standing up and moving to the window. 'And, when I look back, I can see now it was what she always did. Always.' She turned back to stare at him. 'She was singing along to that blasted country music just minutes before you came in, Will. There was no indication she was upset until you came home with a shoulder for her to cry on.'

She came back to her stool and sat. 'Sometimes I see her looking at me with such a—'

'Please don't say evil look, Ellie,' he said with a shake of his head, 'this is getting ridiculous.'

'I wasn't going to say evil,' she said quietly. 'I was going to say calculating. I told you before, I feel as if she's constantly weighing me up.' She picked up her tea and cradled the mug between her two hands. 'I thought you understood, Will. I did try to explain before she came.'

'You said you resented her because she got more attention than you did and you felt people loved her more than you. But you were a child, Ellie, you're not a child any more,' he said.

She sipped her tea pensively and then put the mug down, keeping her hands around it. 'She got so much more of everything but when I looked at her, I saw myself and I didn't understand.' Her eyes lost focus for a moment, she gave a quick shake of her head and continued. 'There wasn't a huge difference between us then, she was slower, more forgetful but that was all, really. I remember thinking that people must see something special in her to love her so much more than me. When we were separated, people thought I'd be upset.' She met his gaze without faltering. 'I wasn't. Not in the slightest. For once, I was just me, Ellie.' She played with the mug in front of her, looking into it as if the answer to her dilemma was written there. She gave a short laugh. 'When we agreed to have her here, it never entered my head that we would still look so alike. And then you came home,' she looked at him accusingly, 'and you couldn't tell us apart.'

Will reached a hand out, but she moved away.

'And now,' Ellie went on, 'I see myself in her every day, but softer—' She held her hand up when Will tried to interrupt. 'No, let me finish, she *is* a softer version of me, why wouldn't she be, for pity's sake? She's never had to worry about exam results, interviews, guys like Jeff Harper just waiting in the wings to kick you when you're down.' She gulped, the sound loud in the silence.

'Harper isn't going to steal your job,' Will said, grasping the only part of her explanation she assumed he really understood. There was silence for a few minutes. 'I think you're just over-wrought,' he said. 'A lot has happened in the last few weeks. I know you don't want to discuss it, but what the consultant said must have hit you hard.'

Her fingers tightened on the handle of the mug. If it broke and cut her, she doubted if she'd feel it. 'Overwrought,' she said, 'how very Victorian. Next, you'll be asking me if I need smelling salts.'

'Sarcasm isn't helping, Ellie.'

She gulped again before putting what she felt into words she knew he would understand. 'What the consultant said? Yes, don't you realise, Will? Tia is literally everything I'm not; she can have children. And I can't bear it any longer.'

Will shook his head. 'It's not her fault, Ellie,' he said softly.

No, it wasn't. And nor was Tia's vulnerability Ellie's fault. Two different accidents of birth. They'd both missed out.

Ellie lifted her chin. 'You don't agree, but it doesn't matter. I've organised the sheltered housing, and Tia will be moving out as soon as it is ready.'

Will made a sound of disgust and stood. 'So, I've no say in the matter. Is that what you're telling me?'

She pushed her mug away so hard that it slid across the surface and fell to the floor, the loud crash barely registering on either of their faces. She stood so she could look him in the eye. 'If that's the way you want to take it, Will, well then fine, yes, you've no say in the matter. I'm her guardian, not you. I'll make the decisions as to what's best for her.'

Without another word, she turned and left the room.

17

Will slept downstairs that night. Ellie heard him moving around as she lay in their bed, twisting from side to side, trying all the tricks she had to put everything out of her mind. She'd done a few courses on mindfulness and tried some of their techniques now, counting slowly with each breath in and out, but nothing worked. It was too hot, so she climbed out of bed to open the window only to think, moments later, that it was too cold. She closed it again and then stood naked at the window, looking out at the street below.

Perhaps only a twin could understand her predicament? For a second, she wondered what Tia thought about their situation. Did she like seeing herself in Ellie? She rested her forehead against the cold glass and gave a weary sigh. She could go down, snuggle up beside Will and let the wound heal, couldn't she? But, like a splinter, it would always niggle.

No, perhaps going down to Will wasn't a good idea. She tried to dismiss the trickle of fear that he might rebuff her. Better to let sleeping husbands lie. He wasn't one to bear a grudge, tomorrow they'd sort things out. Now that he knew how she really felt, he'd have to agree to Tia leaving. And with that convincing argument in her head, Ellie climbed back into bed to twist and turn until morning. She woke an hour past her usual time, stretching out an arm automatically for Will's body beside her, feeling only the cold emptiness of his space. Her bedside clock told her the bad news, and she leapt out of bed swearing loudly. 'Damn it,' she cursed as she swung open the bedroom door and hollered down the stairs. 'Will, it's eight forty-five!'

Her face in the bathroom mirror told her worse news; red eyes hung with dark circles looked back at her critically. 'Don't you start,' she told her reflection and then put her hand on the glass. 'How many of us are there?' She shook her head. Sleepless nights and philosophical questions didn't mix.

She had a quick shower and dressed in her standard work clothes of dark trouser suit and shirt, choosing a brighter coloured shirt than usual, hoping it would deflect eyes from her weary-looking face. Make-up, also little heavier than usual, and she was ready to face the day.

Will usually used the main bathroom and kept his clothes in a wardrobe in the spare bedroom. The bathroom door hung open. It was empty. Ellie paused outside the spare bedroom before knocking gently. A moment later, she knocked again, the sound this time ringing around the landing. 'Will?' As she called, she turned the knob and pushed open the door. He wasn't there.

He must be still asleep. Ellie checked the clock on the wall. It was nine fifteen. She squeezed her eyes shut for a moment; she was going to be so late. What was the betting the first person she'd meet would be Jeff? Shaking her head at the thought, she ran down the stairs and pushed the door into the sitting room open. 'Will,' she said, 'it's so late. Get up.'

The room was empty. Ellie blinked and took in the crumpled cushions on the chair, the last of her hope fizzling as she made her way to the kitchen and found nothing but an empty coffee cup on the island. No matter what, Will would never leave the house without at least one dose of caffeine. She picked it up, it was cold. He'd been gone for a while.

Her heart twisted. It was worse than she'd thought. In all their years together, the years before they married and the years since, he'd never done something like this. It was irrational, unfair and probably downright stupid, but she blamed Tia.

Yes, it was all Tia's fault and she'd probably still be asleep, peacefully oblivious to all the trouble and heartache she'd caused. Slamming the door hard enough to have the sound reverberate throughout the house gave her a slight feeling of satisfaction that was quickly lost in acknowledgement of how unreasonable she was being. They'd invited Tia into their home; she'd never asked to come.

A tiny voice whispered in her ear, '*And now you're throwing her out.*' A fresh wave of guilt, which seemed never too far from the surface these days, broke over her. She tried to brush it away, but she couldn't stop thinking how awful it must be to have everything – where you lived, what you did, what you ate – decided on by someone else. She couldn't even begin to imagine what it would be like.

Perhaps she could ask her? She dismissed the thought as soon as it arrived. Did she really want to know the answer? Anyway, she reasoned, it wasn't as though she was placing her in some unsuitable place. The Brighton development was brand new, top of the range, and incredibly expensive. Tia would be happier in sheltered accommodation. She'd have a certain amount of independence, there would be other people to mix with, there was even the promise of a job. It was what she was used to. And Brighton wasn't far away; they could visit. She could visit.

* * *

She had never once been late to work and the raised eyebrows as she arrived made her bristle with annoyance; none of the many times she had arrived early, and stayed long after everyone else had left, would count in the face of this one damn time she was late. It was the way it went. Throwing herself into work, she put Will and Tia into the part of her brain clearly labelled *Don't go there*.

She managed it, but only by working twice as hard as usual and deciding not to stop for lunch, waiting for someone to ask her if she was going out, waiting for the opportunity to say she was making up for being late. But nobody asked, and her martyrdom only served to make her tired and crotchety as the afternoon ticked by.

Only when everyone else had left, did she shut down her computer with a sigh of relief. She was aware that most of the afternoon had been spent worrying why she hadn't heard from Will. Not a call, not a text. It was so out of character for him. She wasn't sure what to make of it, worse, she wasn't sure what to do. Backing down wasn't an option. She rubbed the corner of her eyes, careful not to disturb the make-up she'd put on what felt like so many hours before. She was truly exhausted, going home to face Will wasn't something she relished. This tired, she might say something to make the rift between them even deeper.

The Tube was packed with quiet, weary Friday evening commuters. Another hour and it would be raucous with weekend revellers. Looking around, she wondered how many of her fellow travellers would transform themselves and hit the town later. She was thinking about anything rather than what she'd have to face when she got home. The crush around her ebbed and flowed as doors opened and closed. And then it was her stop and, minutes later, she opened her front door.

Usually, she enjoyed the peace of their house when she got home. She dropped her briefcase on the floor at the bottom of the stairs and took off her coat as the maudlin lyrics of some country song drifted past her from the kitchen.

She gave a sigh, picked up her briefcase and trudged upstairs. For possibly the millionth time that day, she checked her mobile and then threw it on the bed. Still no message from Will. Maybe the house phone? She picked it up, pressed the four-digit code to access messages and waited, holding her breath. *You have no new messages.* She sighed and then smiled. God, she was pathetic. He'd be home soon; she was making a fuss about nothing.

She slipped on silk pyjamas and headed downstairs. The plan had been to do a stir fry for dinner, but she wasn't in the mood for all the chopping the dish required. It would have to be a takeaway night. In the kitchen, she ignored the music that was blaring away from the other end of the room, opened the drawer holding the menus and took out the one she wanted.

Her eyes flicked over the choices. She fancied pizza and always ordered the same: mushroom and artichoke for her, pepperoni and olives for Will. She'd get Tia a chicken pizza. Years of living in an institution had taught her to eat anything she was given and, as she'd shown no particular preference or dislike of anything, it was easier just to order for her. It was nearly seven. Will was late, but she was certain he'd be home soon. She might as well place the order now.

'That's fine,' she said as she finished the call and hung up. She took the exact change plus a tip from a bowl in the same drawer and went to leave it handy on the hall table. Her post was there, she'd not bothered looking at it when she came in and picked it up now with little real interest.

Her breath caught when she saw, tucked among the letters, a scribbled note from Will. He'd been home, changed and gone out again.

Going out with the boys. I'll be late back. Don't wait up.

No endearments, no apologies for not sending her a message, or for leaving her alone for the evening. Nothing. She crumpled the piece of paper and threw it across the wooden floor. Then she picked it up, smoothed out the creases and read it again. The words hadn't changed, nor had the way they made her feel.

Her throat clogged with tears she refused to cry as she headed back into the kitchen. Unfortunately, Tia had chosen that moment to come over for a drink and she stood in front of Ellie with the slightest hint of a smile on her face.

'What are you smiling about?' Ellie asked, moving to the fridge to take out a bottle of wine. Pouring a glassful, she took a sip and looked at Tia over the rim. Did her smile mean she was happy? Will seemed to think so, but maybe her smiles were just a meaningless imitation of the smiles she saw around her, or on the TV.

'I've ordered pizza,' she said.

Tia turned to her, the smile still in place. 'Good, I like pizza. When is Will going to be home?'

'Soon,' Ellie said, hoping she was right. She sipped her wine as she looked at her sister. The smile never went to her eyes, she thought. And as she looked at her, she realised Tia was staring back in a calculating, assessing way that made her shiver. She looked away.

The doorbell interrupted her thoughts. 'The money is on the table,' she said as Tia immediately rushed off to answer the door. They took their pizzas, still in their boxes, through to the sitting room and Ellie switched on the television. She flicked through channels before landing on a movie channel where *Gone with the Wind* had just started. It fit the bill, and for a few hours she munched pizza, drank wine and lost herself in the problems of the South and of women who struck her as being just a little bit more pathetic than she was.

Will's pepperoni pizza sat on the table between them. Tia had offered to put it in the oven to keep warm for him but sat back when Ellie just shook her head. They ate in silence, the film playing out on the screen, the occasional rustle as one or the other of them fumbled for the next slice of pizza or when Ellie reached for the wine bottle she'd left within reach.

Will would be drunk when he arrived home. A boys' night out had been a regular occurrence when they had first met, years before, but as his friends had settled down, married and had kids, they were less and less frequent and, now, almost non-existent.

'Pathetic,' she said drawing a wary glance from Tia who reached for her last slice of pizza without a word. 'Oh,' Ellie said, quickly, 'don't worry, I didn't mean you.'

When the movie ended, Tia took the pizza boxes out and didn't return. Ellie flicked through the channels for something to watch, one eye on the mantel clock, the other on the screen. Midnight came and went. Ellie stood, swaying slightly before getting her balance.

Heading to bed, she left the empty wine bottle and the glass where they were.

18

Will struggled to get his wallet out to pay the taxi driver. When he did finally manage, he found it hard to focus on the contents. 'How about I do that?' the driver said, taking the wallet from his hands, opening it and extracting two ten-pound notes. He waved them in front of Will's face. 'Two tens, okay? The fare is sixteen. How much of a tip do you want to give?'

'Keep the change,' Will said, moving to walk away before being called back by the driver who was shaking his head and rolling his eyes as he waved Will's wallet.

'Oops,' Will said, taking it and shoving it into his jacket pocket. He gave a wave and headed up the short path and steps to his front door, pulling his keys out as he moved. Alcohol numbed his brain and unfocused his eyes. He jabbed at the keyhole, missing it several times. He looked at the doorbell, tempted to press it, but he hadn't forgiven her yet. A final determined effort to focus and he got the key in, giving a muttered cheer as he turned it in the lock. He pushed the front door open as quietly as he could, taking a step forward into the darkness. One step more, and he tripped over the doormat he had forgotten was there, stumbled and landed face-first on the floor, the clatter echoing in the stillness of the dark hall.

He lay where he was for several minutes, wondering sleepily if the best course of action was inaction. He had almost drifted off to sleep when he heard the soft shuffle of feet on the stairs and, looking up, he saw Ellie.

She looked like a ghost, a light from behind backlighting her, making the fine nightdress she was wearing almost totally transparent. His heavy eyes stared at her body curving in all the right places, a dark shadow between her legs and, despite the alcohol, lust shot through him, making him instantly so hard he had to adjust his position on the floor.

'Come here,' he said, lifting a hand to reach for her.

He expected hands on hips and a shake of her head, but she took the last few steps towards him tantalisingly slowly.

God, he thought, *I love her so much*. As soon as she was near enough, he reached for her ankle and slid his hand upward. Then it was both hands, reaching, seeking, finding. There was a time and a place for the slow foreplay that they both loved, but this wasn't one of them. He pulled her down onto the floor beside him, pushing the nightdress up and out of the way and, with a speed he didn't think he'd manage, he unzipped his trousers to release his erection.

'Oh God, my darling,' he said, 'I can't wait.' Lifting her hips, he slipped inside her with a groan of pleasure and then with a few swift movements and a louder grunt, he came, almost immediately, his orgasm short but intense. Seconds later, he felt his limp penis slip out of her. 'I'm sorry,' he muttered, his head swirling as he levered himself onto his elbows to look down at her. 'I'll make it up to you.'

She whispered something he didn't catch as he rolled off

her, pulled her to him, and fell into a deep, boozy, post-orgasmic sleep.

* * *

When he woke, it was still dark. Had it been a dream? He reached a hand out to sit up, pulling it back with a sound of disgust. Not a dream. Wiping his hand on his shirt, he stood up shakily and went into the kitchen. He switched on the light, pulled several pieces from the kitchen roll and returned to the hallway to wipe up the sticky mess.

The wall clock told him the bad news. It was almost five. His head banged as if his brain was trying to escape. Heading back to the kitchen to dispose of the paper towels, he reached into the kitchen cupboard, pulled out a packet of paracetamol and popped two, swallowing them with a pint of tepid water from the tap. There was no point in disturbing Ellie at this time of the morning. He pushed open the door into the sitting room, kicked off his shoes and lay on the sofa. Within minutes, despite the thumping in his head, he was asleep.

* * *

By the time he woke, two hours later, the medication had done its business. He sat up slowly, nonetheless. The distinct sound of the electric shower overhead told him that Ellie was already awake. He smiled and stretched. It was going to be all right.

Swinging his feet to the floor, he made his way up to the spare bedroom – a room Ellie laughingly referred to as his dressing room – stripped and dropped all his clothes into the laundry basket.

Thirty minutes later, he was showered, shaved and dressed

and feeling much better until he looked in the mirror, where his reflection told him plainly that he'd had too much to drink last night. His skin was pasty, the whites of his eyes red.

'Never again,' he muttered, turning away and reaching for the door, which he opened at the exact moment Ellie opened hers. For a long moment, neither said a word.

Then Ellie smiled, her eyes flicking up and down his body. 'You look pretty okay after your late night. You had a good time?'

He gave her a crooked smile. The storm had passed. 'The best bit was when I got home,' he said, moving closer to kiss her gently on her lips. 'I'm sorry,' he said.

'Me too,' Ellie said. 'But now,' she added, checking her watch, 'I have to run. I've got a presentation first thing that I need to get in and prepare for.'

He reached out a hand to stop her. 'How about we go out for dinner tonight?' he said, and then saw the hesitation in her eyes. She was so easy to read. 'Just us,' he reassured her. 'Me and you. A date, if you like.'

Ellie smiled and put her hand over his. 'A date. Perfect.'

He stood listening for the light tap of her feet as she reached the wooden floor of the hallway and then the opening and closing of the front door. Taking a deep breath, he let it out slowly. It *would* all be okay.

As that thought crossed his mind, he heard laughter drift up from downstairs; even their laugh sounded the same. If he hadn't already heard Ellie leaving the house, he would have assumed it was her. He shook his head, checked his watch, swore and ran down the stairs. Coffee would have to wait until he was in the office. He grabbed his keys from the hall table drawer and left.

19

Typically, Ellie was late home that night. She rushed in the front door, shouting, 'I'm home,' before taking the stairs two steps at a time. She had a quick shower before slipping on a red dress she knew he liked. Dressed, hair loose, she looked at herself in the mirror and smiled. She wasn't particularly vain, but she knew she looked good. She could hear him humming a happy tune from somewhere in the house and smiled, feeling happier than she had in days.

He was at the bottom of the stairs waiting when she went down, taking the steps slowly, deliberately swaying her hips, watching that certain look appear in his eyes.

'We don't have to go for dinner,' he said, putting a hand around her waist and drawing her close.

Her laugh tickled against his ear. 'I'm the kind of starving that only calories will fix,' she said, pushing away from him and reaching for her coat. They left together, Will stopping in the doorway to call a quick goodbye to Tia before the door clicked shut.

He had booked dinner at a French restaurant he knew she

liked, asking for a table by the window overlooking a neat garden filled with solar-powered fairy lights. Even in the weak winter sun they lit up the trees beautifully at night. It was the closest to magic he could organise and she appreciated it. The service and the food were as good as ever and they sat looking out at the lights and talked of nothing of great importance, hands entwined.

Finally, over coffee, Will brought up the subject they'd carefully avoided all evening. 'I'm never going to understand about Tia,' he said, his fingers tightening on hers. 'She seems so content with us, I really didn't think there was an issue with her staying.'

Ellie returned the pressure on his fingers. 'I don't know if it's because of what happened as children, but I see her differently from you, Will. There's something about her that makes me uneasy. Some of it is the way she can manipulate you so easily.'

He shook his head. 'You're on about those picture frames again?' Ellie squeezed his fingers tighter. 'I know you find it hard to believe, but she was singing just minutes before and then suddenly she was sobbing! She used to do the same when we were children. She'd cry those big tears until she got whatever it was she wanted.'

She watched him give that idea some thought. It might make it easier for him to understand if he thought of her behaviour as being manipulative.

Cunning and manipulative, she wanted to say, but decided she'd said enough to give him some thought.

She wanted to bring up the other matter, Tia's fertility and the pain it would cause her to see evidence of it every month. But it was still too raw, too gut-wrenchingly difficult to accept and, anyway, she wasn't sure, despite his protestations, that Will really understood.

Thankfully, she didn't need to use it to close her argument. She saw the decision on Will's face break before he spoke and felt the knot of tension somewhere inside her ease.

'Maybe it's just impossible to understand what it's like to be a twin,' Will conceded. 'To see someone so like you every day.' He sighed. 'I'm not 100 per cent happy about it but, if it is that important to you, we'll do as you want.'

Ellie took in a deep breath and let it out slowly. 'Thank you,' she said. She didn't say anything else, instead she ran her free hand over her face and let relief sweep over her. A few months and Tia would be gone. There was no way to explain the inexplicable, so she didn't try, merely raising his hand to her mouth and pressing her lips to it. She held his gaze. 'Let's go home.'

'Better?' Will whispered in her ear much later.

Multiple orgasms had left her slick with sweat. 'Much,' she said, wiping her face with the sheet. She sat up. 'I need a shower,' she said, and then, with a sideways glance at him, 'you want to come and wash my back?'

She knew it wasn't an offer he was likely to refuse. They showered and kissed under the running water, soapy hands caressing until, aroused again, Will lifted her, balanced her against the shower wall and was inside again. 'You are unbelievable,' she said, as he strained to hold himself back. He'd always been the most considerate lover and she knew he wanted to see her orgasm again. He'd told her once, in their early days together, that he loved to see that rare look of complete abandonment on her face. She was more than pleased to oblige, giving way to the first wave of pleasure and then allowing herself to drown in wave after wave. She felt his release afterwards and wrapped legs and arms around him, holding him inside, close. For a moment, everything except the two of them was forgotten.

Giggling like children, they dried each other, finger by finger, toe by toe. Will wrapped a towel around her dripping hair. 'You should dry it before you go to bed,' he said, tucking the towel in, 'you might catch cold.'

Ellie kissed him on the cheek, took the towel from her hair and replaced it more securely. 'It'll be fine,' she said, 'I used to do this all the time.'

In bed, Will's arms wrapped around her, she snuggled into him, loving the smell of him; so different from her despite the same shower gel they'd both used.

'We should market it,' she said sleepily. 'Eau de Will.'

'What?' Will said, hanging on to wakefulness by his finger-tips before falling over into sleep before Ellie had time to explain.

She heard the change in his breathing and carefully moved herself from his embrace. She loved him, but she couldn't sleep wrapped in his arms. Moving to the other side of the bed, she stretched out. There was nothing like great sex to promise a good night's sleep. On that thought, she closed her eyes and was gone. She slept soundly, moving so little during the night that the towel was still in place when she woke. Will was already up. Ellie's hand slid over his side of the bed and found it still warm, he hadn't been gone long. She lay a minute, a smile curving her lips and then, with a sigh, she threw back the duvet and swung her feet to the floor.

In the bathroom, she unwrapped her still-damp hair. It would be a mess if she didn't do something with it. She opened a jar, dipped her fingers into the gel and smoothed it over her hair before using the hairdryer to finish drying it and tying it back in a knot with several hairpins. In the competitive world of finance, looking like she'd been caught up in a cyclone was not the impression she wanted to give. A last check in the mirror and she was satisfied; none of the excess of the night before showed on her face.

Downstairs, she met Will's smile with a slight blush and a smile of her own before saying, 'hi,' to Tia who was watching breakfast television in the living room.

The coffee machine gurgled and steamed. She reached for a cup, poured some and added milk. Lifting it to her mouth, she looked across to where Will still looked at her, a smile lingering on his lips and in his eyes. 'We're like naughty school-children,' she said quietly to him, shaking her head.

He glanced around to see that Tia was still engrossed in the television and then said softly, 'Nothing schoolgirl about you last night.'

Ellie grinned and finished her coffee. 'I'd better leave this grin behind when I leave for work,' she said, putting the cup in the dishwasher. They left together, briefcases bumping as they walked along the street, and parted in the tube-station with a final smile and a lingering look.

20

The next few weeks vanished. Ellie made what seemed like hundreds of phone calls to the company who were developing the residential complex in Brighton, but pleas to allow Tia to move into one of the completed bungalows fell on deaf ears. They were already reserved, she was told. Ellie even went so far as to take the exhausting and, as it turned out, worthless step of going to Brighton to speak to the developer in person. He was pleasant and charming and promised he'd do his best and she came away hopeful only to be told, during a follow-up call to a sales agent, that, as she'd been told several times, Tia couldn't move in until her designated bungalow was finished.

'I was told by Mr Davidson there was a chance there might be one available sooner,' she said.

The sigh on the other end of the line was audible and sounded as frustrated as Ellie was. 'I'm very sorry,' the sales agent said. 'Mr Davidson, as I'm sure you discovered, is very charming. Problem is, he doesn't like to say no to people, so he makes vague promises to do his best. It's his standard answer to all requests, Mrs Armstrong. The development is on target and there should be no reason your sister can't move in on the agreed date, but that is still two months away.'

There was nothing she could do but be gracious and hang up. 'It's just two months,' Will said when she told him. 'It'll fly by.'

Maybe it did for him but, for her, the days crawled.

She started to count down the days, ticking them off on a desk calendar at work. There were only fourteen to go when she had a phone call from the sales agent to say the completion date had been pushed back.

'Newts,' she told Will that night. 'They've found *newts* right where the final phase was to be built.' She dropped her head into her hand. 'Some blasted rare type of goddamn stupid newt,' she said, her voice muffled. She lifted her face. 'They have to wait until the ridiculous creatures have been assessed by some environmental team. And if,' she said, her voice trembling with fury, 'the blasted things are breeding, they may not allow them to be moved until the breeding season is over. So, we just have to wait for their assessment.'

It was two more weeks before she heard the good news. The newts could be moved.

'A two-week delay isn't too bad,' Will said, putting his fork down. 'I was afraid it was going to take months,' he added.

It was Sunday and they were doing what they sometimes did if they didn't feel like cooking the usual 'Sunday morning bliss' – having breakfast in a local cafe. Tia, glued to a movie at home, shook her head when she was asked if she wanted to come. Ellie lazily turned the pages of the Sunday paper, her eyes scanning for anything interesting.

'What?' she asked, looking up.

'I was just saying,' he repeated patiently, 'that a two-week delay isn't too bad. It could have been a lot worse.'

Ellie's brow furrowed. She'd told him the good news on Friday. 'Uh-huh.'

'When do you think we should tell her?'

Without looking up, Ellie said, 'There's no point in telling her until the day she's going. She won't remember and then I'll have to tell her again.' In fact, Ellie was less and less convinced that Tia's memory was that bad. Her reluctance to tell her was more to do with those calculating looks her sister continued to give her. Ellie wouldn't admit, even to herself, that she was starting to feel a little nervous around her. She turned a page, straightened the paper and only then looked across at him. 'Trust me; I know the best way to handle this, Will.'

He shrugged and then reached across the table for her hand. 'Maybe it's a good time to talk about our future then,' he said.

Ellie wanted to pull her hand away and stop a conversation that was destined to cause them both pain before it started. Instead, she left her hand in his and looked down at the table.

'We should think about surrogacy, Ellie,' he said gently. 'It would be our child, even if you didn't carry it. We'd be the child's biological parents.'

She kept her gaze on the table for a few seconds more and then lifted her face, eyes swimming with tears, and pulled her hand away. 'I'm sorry. I'm being terribly selfish because I know how much you want a child, but I cannot...' She swallowed a gulp. 'I just *cannot* face going through something so...' She sought for the right word, settling for, 'Unnatural.'

She saw his mouth open to argue the point, but he must have seen something implacable in her face. A look of sorrow crossed his before he turned back to his newspaper, giving it his undivided attention.

It would have been easy to reach out, grab his hand and say

she'd do it. But it would have been a cruel lie. She could never have gone through it; it was irrational, she knew it was, but the thought of surrogacy appalled her. She picked up the paper she'd been reading but the words blurred. Wondering if Will was having the same problem, she shot him a glance from under her eyelashes.

If he were, it wasn't obvious. She sighed and turned a page before folding the paper and putting it down.

Will did the same. 'We'd better go,' he said, his face sombre. They left the cafe, and parted at the corner of their street. 'I'll be home for dinner,' Will said, kissing her on the cheek. 'Have a nice relaxing afternoon.'

She brought her hand up to his face and patted it gently. 'I love you,' she said with unusual seriousness.

He bent to kiss her on the lips, a lingering kiss that said, more than words could, that he loved her too. But she saw the confusion in his eyes and knew he still didn't completely understand.

She forced a smile. 'Enjoy the match. Give my love to the others.'

'You can change your mind,' he said, putting his hand over hers before adding, 'And come with us.'

She lifted her chin. 'I know,' she said, 'but I won't.' She watched the confusion in his eyes turn to sadness and turned away. 'I've had an exhausting week, and I really fancy just chilling out on the sofa. Go, enjoy the match. I'll see you later.'

At home, she changed into pyjamas and her cashmere robe. Comfort dressing. Perfect for the afternoon she'd planned. A good movie, nice chocolates and a glass or two of wine.

Coming out of her bedroom, she was surprised to see Tia coming out of hers. 'I thought you were downstairs watching television,' she said.

'The movie is over,' Tia said. She turned to close her bedroom door, caught for a moment in the weak spring sunshine that flooded in from the tall windows in her room.

Ellie's eyes widened as Tia was silhouetted for a moment, her body clearly outlined by the light shining through the fine cotton shirt she wore. She swallowed when she saw the curve of her belly. No. It wasn't possible, was it? She watched as Tia smiled at her, the corners of her mouth wavering under Ellie's intense look.

She shook her head. 'Sorry,' she said, taking a step backward. As Tia passed, Ellie's eyes dropped once more to her belly. She was just being stupid. A smile of self-ridicule curved her lips briefly. Honestly, she was becoming quite paranoid.

She went into the main bathroom and stood sideways in front of the large mirror, opened her robe and smoothed her pyjama top over her stomach. But even tilting her hips forward couldn't make her flat belly curve in the same way.

She sat on the edge of the bath, her mind in a turmoil. What if she weren't imagining it? She'd thought that seeing evidence of Tia's fertility every month would distress her, but when did she last see *any*? When did she last see wrappers and empty tampon boxes? She couldn't remember. Months?

Had Tia's flirtatiousness gone a step further? 'Oh, dear Lord,' she muttered, standing and shifting her weight from foot to foot. What on earth was she going to do?

Finally, with her lower lip caught between her teeth, she went downstairs and opened the door to the kitchen.

Tia had found another movie to watch. She was sitting relaxed, her feet resting on the pouffe, looking as if she hadn't a care in the world. Maybe she hadn't? Ellie chewed harder on her lip. She had to be sure.

'I need to talk to you,' she said, waiting for Tia to turn down the volume. When she didn't, Ellie sighed. 'Can you turn that down, please?'

The silence was sudden and uncomfortable.

Ellie paced and then turned to look at her sister, narrowed eyes assessing her.

Surely, she was wrong. Of course, she was wrong! What had she been thinking? She was about to smile an apology and leave her to her television when Tia raised her arms to put her hands behind her head, a pose so studiously relaxed she wondered, much later, if it had been deliberate. It was a pose that defiantly showed off the gentle swell of her belly.

Feeling the world tip under her feet, Ellie moved to the other end of the sofa and sat heavily. She felt her sister's eyes on her but, for the moment, she stared straight ahead. Finally, she managed to pull herself together. 'Tia,' she started, searching for the correct words, not sure if there were right ones for this occasion. 'Tia, have there been men in the house while we've been out, or at work?'

There was no hesitation. Nor was there any puzzlement at the question. 'No.'

Ellie bit her lip. Was there any point in being subtle? She changed tack. 'Do you... er... know how babies are made?'

Tia thought a moment, her eyes crinkling with the effort of concentration. 'I think so,' she said finally.

Ellie squirmed slightly. 'Tell me how?'

Tia's eyes widened. 'Don't you know?' She laughed. Leaning closer, she dropped her voice and said softly, 'Men have man bits, and women have woman bits. Men put their man bits inside the woman bits and make a baby.'

Ellie had to smile. As explanations went it was basic, but accurate. Then her smile faded. 'Tia,' she said, leaning forward so that they almost touched. 'Has any strange man done this?'

No reaction. She ran a hand over her face in frustration. 'You know, put his man bit into your woman bit?' She watched as her sister processed the question, her eyes blinking more rapidly, the tightening of her lips.

Finally, just as Ellie was going to ask if she understood the question, Tia answered.

'No,' she said.

Ellie sat back with a sigh of relief. Honestly, she did get some stupid ideas. Tia was probably just eating far more than she ever did in St Germaine's. 'Fine,' she said. 'Sorry, I was checking that you knew.' She smiled and stood. 'I'm going to go and watch the television next door,' she said and, to make sure Tia wouldn't join her, she added, 'There's a documentary on that I want to watch.' As she moved away, once again, her eyes drifted to the slightly rounded belly. 'Are you sure, Tia?'

Tia laughed, stood and took a step closer to Ellie. There was a strange look on her face that Ellie couldn't identify. Shivering, she looked away.

But Tia didn't move. She took another step closer, until they were almost touching. Ellie could feel the warmth of her breath on her cheek and turned to look at her again, meeting her gaze, held by it, her stomach tightening.

She knew with blinding clarity that something was very, very wrong.

'No *strange* man did,' Tia said quietly, that curious look still on her face. 'Just Will.'

21

Ellie stood rooted to the spot for a long time after Tia left the room. She didn't even move to switch on the light, Tia's parting two words whispering on a loop in her head. *Just Will.* Over and over. She didn't notice the tears as they dropped from her chin and peppered the soft-pink cashmere, multiplying as the implications of Tia's pregnancy and Will's unfaithfulness grew.

Because Tia was more attractive, softer, less argumentative? Or because she could bear him the child he wanted so badly. The thought made her cry out. She pushed her hand into her mouth, biting down on it, feeling no pain. Only when she heard footsteps on the stairs signalling Tia's return did she move and then quickly, in a rush to be gone before she had to see her, pushing open the door to the sitting room and collapsing back against it as the footsteps passed by.

She slid to the floor and sat there in the darkness, sobbing, unable to shut off the loop of Tia's words that wound tighter and tighter until she thought her head was going to explode.

Finally, exhausted, the sobbing ceased. But the words didn't; she guessed they were imprinted on her brain and probably tattooed on her heart. She gave a final gulp and moved onto the sofa, dragging her knees up, huddling, trying to hold herself together, going over and over the *when, why* and *how could he* until her head spun and a wave of nausea swept over her.

She pressed trembling lips together when she heard the sound of the front door opening and Will's heavy footstep in the hallway.

She heard him humming, dropping his keys into the drawer and then head into the kitchen where he'd expect to find her fixing dinner like the good, loyal wife she was. Ellie imagined his face, the puzzled lines deepening between his eyes. Through the wall she heard the deep timbre of his voice as he spoke to Tia. He'd come through soon.

The door to the sitting room opened at last. She saw his face, the startled look in his eyes when he saw her sitting in the darkness. 'What's wrong?' he asked as his hand slid up the wall and flicked the light switch. In the bright light, her tear-stained face was obvious. He rushed forward and dropped to his knees beside her. 'Ellie,' he said, grabbing her hand, 'tell me.'

'You've been fucking Tia.' She said it quietly. It wasn't a question; the pregnancy left no room for doubt.

Will fell backwards in shock. 'What?' he said, getting clumsily to his feet, blinking rapidly and then sitting in the chair opposite. 'Why on earth would you say that?' he asked, reaching out for her hand, a look of confusion on his face.

She swung her feet to the floor, gasping as pins and needles gave her something else to think about for a wonderfully painful moment. She sat hunched forward and looked at him.

'For God's sake, Ellie,' Will tried again, 'why would you say that?'

Ellie's voice was calm. 'Tia is pregnant. The only man who,

as she so elegantly puts it, put his man bit inside her woman bit, was you.' She hesitated a moment, feeling her heart thumping hard against her chest. Or maybe it was just breaking in two. 'You. She was quite clear about it, Will.'

He ran a hand over his forehead. 'She told you I had *sex* with her? She's lying, Ellie. How can you even begin to believe her?' He stood and paced the room, one trembling hand pushing into his hair. 'She's lying, of course. It must be someone she let in,' he said, 'maybe someone she met in the shop, or on the way.'

Ellie frowned. She'd known him a long time, could always tell if he was stretching the truth to suit the occasion. If someone had asked, she'd have said he was incapable of lying. He didn't look like he was lying now, but... 'She said it was you, Will. Not a stranger.'

He crouched down beside her, holding her hand tightly before she had a chance to snatch it away. 'You have to believe me, Ellie. I never touched her. I swear.'

'But she's pregnant.'

'Are you sure?'

She pushed him away and stood to face him, forcing him to his feet. 'Am I sure?' She slapped a hand dramatically onto her forehead. 'Of course, because how could *I* be sure? I've never been pregnant, have I?' She closed her eyes and felt his hands move to grasp her arm, holding her still.

'That's not what I meant, Ellie,' he said. 'I meant, maybe she's lying about being pregnant?'

She pulled away and moved to the other side of the room to get some space to think clearly. 'She doesn't know,' she said and then, seeing his puzzlement, added, 'It's unmistakable to me. Her body is my body, and I can tell, clear as day. But she has no idea.'

'She eats a lot,' Will jumped in, 'maybe she's just getting fat.'

She shrugged. 'Even if I'm wrong about her being pregnant, she still said that you had sex with her. How do you explain that?'

'Why would I? I love you. Only you. And it's not like I'd mix you up, is it?'

She gave an unamused snort. 'You've done it before!'

'That's not fair, Ellie,' he said, looking hurt, 'that was when I first saw her. A simple misunderstanding. This is a bit more than that.' He ran a hand through his hair again, pulling at it in frustration. 'Why would she say something like that?'

Ellie looked at him. 'I don't know,' she said. She frowned. Tia could be lying to cover for someone else. She remembered how flirtatious she'd been with the young men in the cinema. Maybe she met someone in the shop? 'She seemed to know what she was talking about. Her description of sex is pretty basic, but she does understand, and she was quite clear that you were the only man she'd been with. "*Just Will,*" she said.' Ellie's voice quivered as she said the words.

He turned to pace the room. 'I don't underst—' He stopped, turned around and looked at her. 'Oh, dear God,' he said, his voice a shaken whisper.

'No,' Ellie cried, reaching a hand toward him. 'Please, tell me you didn't?'

He dropped into the sofa and put his face in his hands.

A wave of utter shock and disbelief swept over Ellie. 'When?' she asked, barely able to breathe out the word.

'Remember the night out I went on with the lads?' he asked, lifting a face that was grey from shock.

Ellie nodded.

'We'd had that row.' He looked up at her, his eyes entreating. 'I came home late, so drunk that I fell in the door and landed flat on my face in the hallway. I heard footsteps on the stair and looked up and you were there, like an angel, and I remember thinking how beautiful you were and how much I loved you. There was a light behind you, I could see all your curves through your nightdress. When you came down, I pulled you into my arms and... and... we made love.' He didn't have to ask, he could see in her face that he'd been wrong. Horrified, he whispered, 'It was... Tia?'

'Well, it bloody well wasn't me, Will,' Ellie spat, her voice lemon-sharp with the bitterness that coursed through her. It was as if all her nightmares had come true. Her head was reeling. This couldn't be happening. Was he telling the truth? 'When did you ever see me wearing a nightdress? I don't even own a bloody nightdress!' she said, focusing on this one stupid part of it all because the rest was just too damn painful.

'I was so drunk,' he pleaded, the look on his face showing he knew it wasn't even close to any kind of excuse.

'You were sober enough to get hard for your sister-in-law,' she said, a world of hurt and defeat in her voice.

'It was a mistake. My God, Ellie, I thought it was you,' he said, dragging his hands down his face like it would wipe away the memory.

'Did you?' she said, unable to stop herself. 'Or maybe you wanted to fuck a real woman, one who could give you what you've always wanted.' She turned away. 'And whoopee-doo, you did it first time!' Then, suddenly, she turned back. 'Or was it? How do I know you haven't made this particular,' she curled her forefingers twice as she bit out, '"*mistake*" before?'

Will rested his elbows on his knees and dropped his face into his hands again.

'Well?' Ellie said, refusing to relent.

He lifted his face. 'I love you, Ellie. I'd never do anything to jeopardise our marriage. It was a mistake, I'm so, so sorry. I don't know what else I can say?'

Ellie looked deep into the eyes of the man she loved and knew, in her heart, that he was telling the truth. He was never a good liar. All the fight suddenly left her, and she dropped to the sofa beside him. 'What are we going to do?' she said in a small, frail voice she didn't recognise as her own.

In the silence, as they both considered this question, they heard Tia call.

'She's probably wondering what has happened to dinner,' Ellie said with the ghost of a smile. 'She doesn't even know she's eating for two.'

The words hung between them for a moment. The reality of it all. What were they going to do? Ellie had no idea. Her head ached. Holding a hand up to stop him reaching for her, she fled the room.

It took another thirty minutes before she'd composed herself enough to return. Will, she saw, was still sitting where she'd left him, his head in his hands. 'We need to eat,' she said quietly, leaving him to follow her into the kitchen where she pulled a selection of food from the freezer without much thought. When it was ready, they sat around the table in their usual places, Tia tucking in with her normal appetite, Will and Ellie pushing food around their plates and stealing glances at her across the table. When Tia stood to help herself to seconds, Ellie's eye's raked over her body. There was a chance she was wrong. *God, please let me be wrong.* She looked across the table to where Will was picking at his food. Maybe she'd forgive him for the mistake, eventually, but she wasn't sure she could ever forgive him for getting Tia pregnant. She closed her eyes briefly as a fresh wave of fear swept over her.

A baby. Wasn't it what he'd always wanted?

Will wanted to talk about it again once dinner was over and Tia had gone back to watching television, but Ellie held up her hand. 'There's absolutely no point until we know for sure,' she said. 'I'll pick up a pregnancy testing kit tomorrow. We can talk tomorrow night.'

'You do believe me, don't you?'

Ellie pushed her plate away and stood without replying. She cleared the table, scraped the mass of uneaten food into a bin and loaded the dishwasher, all the while conscious of Will's eyes following her. Without looking at him, she said, 'Whether I believe you or not isn't the point, Will. It's...' She broke off, unable to finish, grabbing hold of the counter-top and letting out a quiet keening sound that held in it a sob for something lost.

'Ellie, please...'

She tried to compose herself. '*The* most intimate thing we do together, Will,' she said, her voice heavy with sorrow. 'Didn't she *feel* different, *sound* different... Something? Anything?' She wrapped her arms around her body and turned to look at him, her face pale. 'Are we so fucking alike,' she said, using the crude word deliberately, 'that fucking her was the same as fucking me?'

'I was drunk, Ellie,' he tried again. 'I thought it was you. For God's sake, she even smelled like you.'

She screwed up her face. 'What?'

'Your scent, I mean,' he said, wiping his face with his hand. 'That perfume you always wear.'

'You make me sick,' she said, before turning and leaving the room, the slam of the door echoing through the house.

She locked their bedroom door. He could sleep somewhere else. There was too much sorrow and pain coursing through her, she needed time to deal with it.

In the ensuite bathroom, she went through her usual nightly ritual automatically. The room was small, space limited. As she put her moisturiser back, her gaze landed on her perfume. It was almost empty but she knew there was another, unopened, in the larger main bathroom cabinet.

Suddenly, something Will said came back to her, making her blink.

She even smelled like you.

Her reflection in the bathroom mirror wore a look of disbelief tinged with horror. She shook her head slowly. That would just be too crazy. But she couldn't rest until she checked. Opening the bedroom door, she slipped across to the main bathroom.

She stood, her hand on the handle of the bathroom cabinet, and took a deep breath before pulling it open, letting it out on a sigh of relief when she saw her perfume exactly where she had left it. But, reaching for the box, her breath caught. She didn't usually take the cellophane wrapper off until she was going to use it. Had she done so this time? She couldn't remember. She opened the box and took out the bottle. It was impossible to know if any had been used.

And then she was suddenly very sure that some had, and a wave of nausea swept over her.

There was no point in telling Will, he'd tell her she was being silly, that the absence of cellophane meant nothing. He'd never believe that Tia had deliberately set out to seduce him. Ellie's eyes narrowed as she gripped the bottle between her hands, feeling her stomach lurch as she suddenly remembered the strange look that had crossed Tia's face when she'd said 'Just Will.'

Had it been a look of satisfaction?

22

The next day, Ellie left work early pleading illness, the bags under her eyes and drawn face telling most of the lie for her. There was a pharmacy nearby, but she didn't risk using it in case anyone from the office saw her. Instead, she took a tube to a part of London she rarely visited and found one there. It was a busy shop; she wandered up and down the aisles, hoping to find what she wanted herself, reluctant to ask for it. Wouldn't they see she was a fraud? Could they see her barrenness as keenly as she could feel it?

Her vision suddenly blurred with tears. She stopped in front of a display of nail varnish, picking up one bottle after the other until her tears dried and she could continue her search.

With the pregnancy kit bought and safely tucked into her briefcase, she headed home, the journey seeming endless. On her doorstep at last, she hesitated with her key in the lock, suddenly afraid to find out the truth. Everything was going to change, wasn't it? The thought of Will and Tia together made her stomach lurch. No, everything had *already* changed.

Tia was, as usual, watching television. She was also, bizarrely, listening to country music on the radio at the same time; Ellie was affronted by a deafening clash of sound that made her wince. 'For goodness' sake,' she shouted across the noise, turning off the radio and waving at Tia to mute the television. 'I'm surprised our neighbours don't complain.'

'They're not there during the day,' Tia said reasonably, adding, 'The noise keeps me company.'

Ellie tried to brush aside her guilt at this sudden and unexpected revelation, and the unfair suspicion that Tia had only said it to make her feel bad. The pregnancy kit was burning a hole in her briefcase, and the thought crossed her mind that Tia might not be lonely for much longer.

'I need you to come upstairs with me,' she said.

'Upstairs?' Tia remained seated. 'Why?'

'I'll explain when we get there,' Ellie said, moving into the hallway. She smiled encouragingly at her sister when she followed her out.

In the bathroom, it took several minutes of repetitive explanation before Tia understood what Ellie wanted her to do. 'You want me to wee into this?' Tia examined the small bowl in her hand, turning it this way and that as if she expected it to turn into something else.

Ellie repeated the instructions once more. 'Yes, I want you to wee into that bowl, then leave it on the shelf behind the toilet. Understand?'

Tia looked as if she were going to say more, but one look at the serious expression on Ellie's face and she nodded.

Five minutes later, she came out. 'I didn't have any,' she said, handing the empty bowl back to Ellie.

'Oh, for goodness' sake.' Ellie said, taking the bowl from her hand, putting it on the shelf in the bathroom and dragging Tia down the stairs by one arm. In the kitchen, she poured a pint glass of water. 'Drink that,' she said, pushing the glass into her hand.

Tia drank a little and went to put the glass down.

'Finish it, please,' Ellie encouraged. 'This is really important.'

'I don't like water,' Tia said, eyeing the glass with a frown.

Ellie took it from her, water sloshing over both their hands as Tia held on to it for a second too long. Emptying the water into the sink, she opened the fridge, took out a carton of juice and refilled the glass. 'Fine, drink this then.'

With a sigh, Tia took the juice and drank it all.

'Okay,' Ellie said, taking the empty glass. 'Now go back and watch television for a bit.'

Ellie made a cup of coffee and sipped it as she watched the minute hand of the clock drag through thirty long minutes, until she decided she'd waited long enough. 'Try again now please, Tia,' she said, raising her voice to be heard over the television.

Tia looked over at her, a puzzled look on her face. 'Try what?' Ellie's hands gripped the almost empty mug in frustration, trying to keep her cool. Taking a deep breath, she went over to where Tia sat, muted the television, and went through the same explanation, word for word. 'Understand?' She waited for her to nod, blinking when she saw Tia's lips curl in what could only be described as a sneer.

'Oh, I think so,' Tia said and left to head upstairs. A few minutes later, she returned. 'I've done it,' she said before sitting and unmuting the TV.

Without a word, Ellie took the pregnancy kit out and went

up to the bathroom. The smell from the bowl of straw-coloured liquid made her nose crinkle as she lifted it carefully from the shelf behind the toilet, placed it into the sink and opened the kit. The directions were easy; she opened the enclosed packet, took out a stick, dipped it into the urine and waited. One line would tell her that she'd been worried about nothing. Two lines would shatter her world. Two lines, twins, the irony wasn't lost on her.

There were two test sticks in the box, and she used both. Each told her the same story.

Tia was pregnant.

A wave of nausea made her hold her head over the sink and retch until she was so weak she had to sit on the toilet seat. She grabbed a towel and held it over her face.

Pregnant.

The word thumping in her head, she stood, turned on the hot tap and let it run for a long time over the bowl until all traces of Tia had washed away. If only everything could be so simple. Turning off the water, she picked the bowl up with the tips of two fingers and dropped it into the waste-bin. She turned on the cold tap, let it run for a few seconds and filled her cupped hands with cold water to wash out her mouth. Swirling and spitting, she rid herself of the acid taste, dried her face and hands and looked at her reflection in the mirror.

The hand she saw lifting to brush away strands of hair was trembling, she lifted her other hand to steady it, placing her palms together. She was reminded of a long-ago school friend who would put her hands together and pray every night before bed. Was that what she was doing? Praying for strength to a God she didn't really believe in?

She wanted to climb into bed, curl up under the duvet and

hide from a world that had suddenly become too difficult, too painful to bear. Instead, she went downstairs on unsteady feet and sat in the sitting room, her head spinning as she tried to see a way out of the mess. She was still sitting there when Will returned home that evening. She stood when she heard him in the hallway and opened the door. 'Come in here,' she said from the doorway. 'We need to talk.'

She stood waiting, watching while he dropped his brief-case, threw his coat over the banisters and took a deep breath. She met his gaze, watched the colour leach from his face as he saw her expression and then returned to her seat leaving him to follow. 'Sit down,' she said, nodding to the chair opposite.

He did as he was told, his eyes fixed on her face. 'She's definitely pregnant.'

His body slumped, his mouth opening and shutting while he sought words. 'Ellie,' he finally managed, his voice barely above a whisper. 'I'm so sorry. I—'

She held up a hand to stop him. 'I'm not interested in apologies, Will, I'm interested in how we deal with this. Neither of us can afford for this to come out. Tia has special needs and is living in our care, I have no idea what the implications would be, but I'm certain they wouldn't be pleasant. And if you think it wouldn't be in the papers, you're living in dreamland. It's the kind of story the gutter press loves. We'd be humiliated, disgraced. Everything we've worked so hard to build would be over.'

She waited a moment for the implications to sink in, watching as his already pale face turned a sickly shade of grey.

'I think the safest idea,' she said, twisting her hands together, 'is to go to the continent, France, maybe, or Germany. To a private clinic of some sort and have a termination there.' She watched his eyes widen. 'She could use my passport, you could pretend she was your wife. It would prevent the kind of problems I've mentioned.'

'A termination?'

Ellie nodded. 'Thank goodness it's still early. If it happened that night,' she said ignoring his expression, 'she's ten weeks pregnant. We have time to get everything organised.'

Will nodded. 'Of course. We'll do whatever you say.' He ran a hand over his face.

Ellie watched as a range of emotions passed over him. The guilt she expected, maybe even the confusion, but it was the look of regret in his eyes that made her insides churn and her head jerk back as if he'd hit her. She looked at him with wide eyes and her mouth hanging open, unable for a moment to formulate a single word. Clenching her fists, she took a deep breath. 'You want...' she said, her voice faltering despite her best efforts. She gulped and tried again. 'You *want* this baby?'

He opened his mouth to speak, shut it again and then shook his head before reaching for her hand. 'I love you, Ellie, and I would have loved more than anything to have a child with you, but that isn't possible. You're dead set against the idea of surrogacy, you said so yourself, and if we consider adoption, it's a long, difficult process with no promises. This... you know, you must know, I never meant this to happen, but—'

She snatched her hand away. 'But, what? Now that you've got my sister pregnant it's the next best thing? You're out of your mind, Will.'

'Stop putting words in my mouth, Ellie,' he shouted, standing, walking to the other side of the room and glaring at her. He ran a hand through his hair and turned away. 'I hate the thought of what I've done, of what I've done to you... to us... but it could be my only chance, *our* only chance.'

Ellie felt suddenly nauseous, the colour draining from her

face. Will rushed to her side. 'Oh, Ellie,' he said softly, putting his arm around her and drawing her into his arms. She wanted to resist, wanted to pull away and tell him to go to hell, but how could she? He was right. It was his baby. His and Tia's. The pain of her own shortcomings was so unbearable, she finally gave in to it, buried her head in his shoulder and sobbed.

23

Will held her tightly for a long time without saying a word. When the tears eased, Ellie pulled away, wiped her face with her hand and got to her feet.

'I'm going to bed,' she said, stopping with her hand on the door to add, 'Sleep on the sofa tonight, I need time to think.' She left without a glance in his direction.

He heard her heavy, slow tread on the stairs. He hated to see her in such pain... hated having been the cause of it. But, as he dropped his head back and wondered what on earth he could do to make amends, all he could think of was the baby. *His baby!*

He knew it was wrong, on so many counts, to feel in any way pleased about this. But, bad as it was, it had happened. It was an accident. An awful accident he'd spend the rest of his life paying for. But was there any point in making another dreadful mistake by getting rid of his child?

He tightened his lips in a firm line. There had to be a way around this mess that would keep everyone happy and allow them to keep the baby. There had to be, and if he had to sit there all night, he was going to find it.

He'd been sitting there for an hour and couldn't think of anything that made any sense when he heard the kitchen door open, followed by quick, light steps on the stairs as Tia went up to bed. He wondered what she'd make of it all.

The quiet of the house settled around him, helping to calm his thoughts. Perhaps Ellie was right and Tia should have a termination. Perhaps. He ran a hand through his hair trying to accept it was the best way. Ellie's idea to pretend Tia was her was crazy but there was no reason it wouldn't work. They'd explain to Tia and go abroad. A few days and it would be over.

He closed his eyes. *His baby*.

His eyes snapped open. There *was* no reason it wouldn't work. He sat forward, suddenly alert, with a bizarre, crazy idea running through his head. 'It could work,' he muttered. 'To pretend Tia was Ellie.'

He sat for another hour, going over and over a plan that was ridiculously daring and absolutely crazy. But the risks were low, weren't they? He needed to speak to Ellie.

It was almost midnight but he knew she'd still be awake. This crazy plan of his could be the answer to everything, but he needed her to agree. She had to.

He listened at their bedroom door for a second before slowly pushing it open. If she were asleep he'd have to wait until the morning. But he'd been right. In the light that came through the window from the streetlights outside, he could see she was lying with her eyes open, staring at the ceiling.

'Ellie,' he said, moving to sit on the bed beside her. 'I have an idea.'

She said nothing, closing her eyes as if to shut him and his idea out. Will reached for her hand and held it tightly. 'Actually, it was your idea,' he said, 'I just built on it. You suggested we pretend Tia was you, she could go abroad and have a termination. Nobody would question it.'

Ellie opened her eyes and turned to look at him. 'It's the only way,' she said quietly. 'Nobody would question it. They might be curious as to why we didn't have it here in the UK, but they are unlikely to ask.'

Will nodded eagerly. 'Nobody would question it,' he agreed. 'Tia would say her name was Ellie and she'd have the termination.'

He watched a look of puzzlement cross Ellie's face and squeezed her hand again. 'But what if she says her name is Ellie and she *has* the baby?'

Ellie snatched her hand away, threw the duvet back and got out of bed. Naked, she stood staring at him, eyes wide in disbelief. 'Are you out of your mind?'

'It could work,' he pleaded. 'She uses your name and has the baby. Meanwhile you pretend to be pregnant—'

'Stop!' she yelled at him, grabbing her robe from the hook on the back of the door and leaving, running barefoot down the stairs.

He followed her to the sitting room where she paced the floor, hands clenched by her side. 'You cannot seriously think I'm going to pretend to be pregnant while Tia goes ahead and has your child?' she said, brushing off his hands as he tried to hold her. 'That is the most deranged thing I have ever heard.'

'It could work,' he repeated. 'It was your idea.'

She stepped up to him and, before he could move away, she lifted her hand and slapped him hard across the face.

Both of them were stunned into silence. She took a step backward, lifting her hand to her mouth. He lifting his hand to the stinging pain on his cheek.

Ellie sat on the sofa, her anger gone, a look of deep sadness on her face. 'It was my idea for Tia to pretend to be me for a couple of days to get us out of this mess. You're talking about a charade that would need to last for months and fool so many people.' She looked at him. 'I can't believe you're seriously entertaining this idea. Have you thought of the consequences? The lies we'd have to tell?'

He sat in the chair and leaned towards her. 'For it to work, we'd have to plan for every eventuality, consider the risks. You know business deals, Ellie, how to look at all the implications, weigh up the options and devise a strategy. It's what you're good at.' He took a deep breath. 'I want this baby, it may be my only chance.'

She looked at him with her mouth open. Shutting it, she attempted a laugh that ended in a croak as she realised how serious he was. She stared at him for a moment, lost for words that would, in any way, suit the occasion before standing to pace the room again.

Finally, she returned to stand over him. 'It's impossible,' she said firmly, 'I can't do it.' She turned away, then looked back at him and shook her head. Her next words were less emphatic. 'You can't ask this of me, Will. Anyway,' she added, turning to sit on the sofa beside him, 'it wouldn't work.'

He leaned back to look at her. 'It could work,' he said. 'But, as I said, it needs planning.' When she didn't reply, a look of consternation lingering on her face, he continued, 'It's the only way. We book into a private clinic, register her as Ellie Armstrong, my wife, and for the next few months, we live the lie.'

She shook her head. 'That's the craziest thing I've ever heard, Will. I still think a termination is the best option.'

He stood abruptly and then sat again and dropped his head

into his hands. A moment later, he raised his face and looked at her. 'I'm sorry, Ellie. But I want this child. I know it's not going to be easy but this way we also avoid any potential problems. Nobody will ever need to know.' He leaned towards her and smiled grimly. 'There has to be some advantages to being a twin, Ellie. Why would anyone suspect?' He watched as she digested what he'd said, chewing her lower lip as she tried to make sense of it all. She shook her head emphatically. 'It's impossible. You're talking about deceiving our friends and co-workers for months, never mind the doctors and nurses we'd have to deal with. We'd never get away with it.' She reached a hand out to him. 'I know how much having a child means to you, I do, but this is just madness.' He nodded. 'I didn't say it was going to be easy, but I think we can do this.' He took her hand and gripped it tightly. 'If we work together, Ellie, we *can* do this.'

She frowned and looked at him. 'What about Tia? Won't she give the game away?' Then she shook her head. 'No, of course, she'd do anything for you,' she said, the words out before she thought. She watched as his cheeks reddened. 'It's the truth, you know it is.'

He shrugged and nodded. 'Okay, you're probably right. What do you suggest we do?'

Ellie shook her head. 'You ask me, I tell you, but you don't listen,' she said, her voice rising in frustration. 'I suggest we go ahead with a termination.'

He cut the air with an impatient slice of his hand. 'I want this baby,' he said again, his voice firm, a hard look in his eyes.

'And if I don't cooperate?' She lifted her chin and met his gaze. 'This is too much to ask of me. You know how badly I feel not being able to give you the child you want. And now you expect me to sit back and take part in this charade while my sister... my twin sister... gives you what I can't?' Her voice broke on the last words, her face stricken.

Guilt shot through him, not just for what he had done, but for what he was about to say. 'Don't you owe it to me, for the secret you kept from me? Deep down, you must have known you'd never be able to have a child. There were signs...'

She reeled back as if he'd hit her.

He looked away from the pain on her face. He'd make it up to her. He just needed her to do this one thing. There was silence in the room broken only by her heavy breathing and the occasional gulp that told him she was trying her best not to cry.

'Fine,' she said eventually, sounding defeated. 'I'll do it.'

He kept his tone of voice serious, despite his relief, and said, 'It's not going to be easy. We'll need Tia to play her part.' Chewing on his lip for a moment, he avoided her eyes. 'We'll get her registered with an obstetric clinic. She just needs to attend for scans and such. I can tell them she's very shy, that I have to be with her every moment. They won't suspect a thing, why would they?'

If it felt like they'd wandered onto the set of a very bad play where everyone made up their own lines, neither of them said, both sitting silently, thinking of the parts they'd have to play, wondering if they could really pull this off.

Will looked at Ellie from the corner of his eyes. She looked pale, desolate. The guilt stung but then he thought of the baby. It would be worth it. He'd find a way to make it up to her.

'And, meanwhile, you'll have to pretend to be pregnant.' It wasn't a question. A statement. He needed her to do this. For him. For them.

* * *

Ellie shut her eyes for a second. He made it sound like a walk in the park. The idea of pretending to be pregnant was horrific but, as bad as that was, the thought of watching Tia grow large with her husband's child was even worse. But Will was right, she had deceived him... not deliberately... not really, but the result was the same. She couldn't give him the child he desperately wanted. Maybe going along with this insane plan would go some way towards putting things right. She took a deep breath; he was right, she did owe it to him.

'...will have to stay indoors,' Will was saying.

'Sorry?' she said, with a shake of her head, 'I missed that. What did you say?'

'I said Tia will have to stay indoors from now on,' he repeated slowly. 'We can't risk one of the shop staff noticing or bumping into someone we know if we go out together.' He looked at her face. 'You look like a rabbit caught in the headlights,' he said with a slight smile. 'I feel more like a rabbit caught in a huge snare, the more I wriggle the more I'm trapped.' She looked at him. 'This is a crazy idea, Will. I'm really not sure we should go through with it.'

His face became set. 'We *can* do this. It's just getting all the nitty-gritty sorted,' he said.

Conceding defeat with a shake of her head, she asked, 'How are we going to get her to stay indoors, she'll never remember?'

He shrugged. 'I'll tell her it's not safe to go out any more. She listens to me.'

She blinked but said nothing. And then something else occurred to her, making her shake her head. 'What about that gynaecologist we saw, Dr Gardiner? He'll know I can't possibly be pregnant.'

She watched irritation cross his face. He'd not thought

about that. Or about the amount of lies they'd need to tell. She was already starting to lose count.

Will pursed his lips as he thought, his face clearing as an idea came to him. 'We'll register her under your maiden name, well, her own surname, actually. It will be easier anyway if anyone asks her, she'll be able to tell the truth without causing confusion. It won't be that unusual, plenty of women keep their maiden name, after all. When we register the baby's birth we can revert to Armstrong.'

He frowned. 'It might be better to go somewhere discreet, just in case. Somewhere they're used to dealing with the rich and famous and their secrets. I'll look into it and get an appointment.' He tapped his chin with his finger. 'I wonder if we need to go to our GP first. That might be awkward.'

Ellie shook her head. 'If you're going privately you'll be okay. Money cuts corners.'

Will smiled. 'Good. One worry less.'

One worry less? She looked at him with a sinking feeling in her stomach. He was so focused on this baby that he was ignoring the reality. Of course, she thought bitterly, he wasn't the one who had to pretend to be pregnant.

Weariness hit her. 'I'm heading to bed,' she said, 'we can finish this tomorrow.' She stood up. 'I'll explain the situation to Tia. It might take a few days to get through to her.'

'Just a second,' he said, stopping her. 'What about afterwards?'

Her hand on the door-knob, she took a breath. 'What about it?' she asked, playing for time, she knew exactly what he meant but she wasn't sure he was ready to cope with the answer.

'Well, Tia's going to have to stay, isn't she?'

She turned back then, holding onto the door to support her

suddenly shaky legs and stared at him coldly. Was he really that stupid? Did he think they were all going to play happy families together? A ménage à trois? She thought of the perfume bottle and felt her gut twist. 'Oh no, Will,' she said, keeping her voice calm with difficulty. 'We will bring up your child, but Tia will go to Brighton as planned. That part is non-negotiable. *Non*-negotiable,' she repeated and then, without another word, turned the door-knob and left the room.

24

Ellie slept little, her mind whirling with too many emotions. She was crazy to have agreed to this ridiculous plan. She'd tell him it was impossible. Tia would have to have a termination. It was the only sensible way.

But each time she reached this conclusion, guilt lashed her. She *had* misled him, hadn't she? She knew how desperately he wanted a family. And it would only be for a few months. She calculated quickly. Seven. Less, maybe. She would go ahead with the charade. But then anger would burn her. How cruel was he to ask this of her? How utterly selfish? She'd insist that Tia have a termination.

And round and round it went.

At six, she crawled out of bed and stood under the shower for a long time. It was tempting to ring her office, say she'd come down with something. One look in the mirror made her smile ruefully; it looked as if she had.

But if she stayed at home, she'd have to face Tia. All day. Work was infinitely preferable. Dressed, she looked in the mirror again. Make-up had helped. She'd pass.

She saw sad eyes looking back at her. 'You've made up your mind, haven't you?'

She had and, deciding there was no time like the present to start the charade, she went to tell Tia the news.

She was already awake, watching television, the volume low. 'Hi,' Ellie said, pulling a chair near to the bed. 'I need to talk to you.'

Tia said nothing, eyes wide.

Ellie cleared her throat. There was no point in being dainty or subtle about this. 'Remember when I asked you if you knew how babies were made and you told me you did?'

Tia hesitated and then nodded.

'And then you told me that only Will had been... with you,' she gulped, unable, unwilling to go into the details.

Tia smiled. 'Yes.'

Ellie looked away. She would have sworn that smile was of pleasure. 'Well,' she said, her voice hard from the effort of trying to keep her emotions in check, 'it appears that you are now going to have a baby.'

She looked back. Tia's expression had changed. Now she looked confused. 'I don't understand.'

'You know how babies are made,' Ellie tried again, waiting until Tia nodded. 'Well, when you and... Will... did that, you made a baby.' She nodded to where the duvet covered Tia's stomach. 'You've already got a little bump where the baby is.'

Immediately, Tia threw back the duvet and pulled up the T-shirt she was wearing. The bump was small but distinct. Her hand caressed it as Ellie looked on aghast before standing abruptly. She'd done enough for the moment.

She was about to go downstairs when the image of the bump came into her head. She looked down at the figure-hugging top she was wearing and groaned. If she was going to go along with this mad scheme, she had to do it right. Back in her bedroom, she flicked through the hangers in her wardrobe and finally decided on a loose, floral shirt. A slight smile of amusement curved her lips as she wondered how long it would be before tongues would start wagging? The smile vanished. They'd wag a lot harder if they knew the truth.

Downstairs, Will was already up and dressed. She reached for the pot of coffee he'd made. 'I've told her,' she said, pouring a cup. 'She seemed to understand. I'll talk to her again about it tomorrow.' She sipped her coffee. 'I'll make the appointment with the obstetrician. I doubt if we'll get an appointment for a week, at least, so we'll have a few days to get her ready.'

She ignored his grateful look. 'I'm going with you on this, Will,' she said, 'but I still think it's crazy.'

He reached a hand across and laid it gently on her arm. 'We'll get through this.' Taking his hand away, he added, 'We should start calling Tia by your name today. Give her a chance to get used to it. In a couple of days, she won't even notice and will answer to it automatically.'

Ellie looked at him, her lower lip trembling. 'So now, not only do I have a twin, but a twin called Ellie who is pregnant with my husband's child.' She watched his eyes turn hard, defensive. 'That is what you're asking me to face, Will.'

He shook his head, his eyes softening. 'For a few months, Ellie,' he pleaded. 'Please, you know how much it means to me.'

She nodded, ever so slightly. 'Okay, Ellie it is. But you explain to Tia. Don't leave that one for me.'

He nodded. 'I'll tell her it's for the baby's sake. She won't question it.'

Ellie didn't know what he said to her but, the first time she called her Ellie, Tia merely blinked rapidly and said nothing.

After about two days she answered to it with only a little hesitation.

A few days later, while she was getting dinner and Tia was setting the table, Will came into the room with the newspaper in his hand. 'Have you seen this article, Ellie?' he said without looking up.

Both women looked toward him and said no, almost simultaneously. In the ensuing, uncomfortable silence, Ellie closed her eyes, her head suddenly spinning at the absurdity of what they were trying to achieve.

Will, with an embarrassed glance in her direction, left the room quickly. From then on, she noticed, he never addressed either of them by name when the other was present.

* * *

Two days before the appointment, she was sitting in her office trying to catch up with work she'd let slide. She was worried. Over the past few days, she had gently broached the subject of babies with Tia a number of times. It was hard to know how much she took in, she smiled and nodded as if she understood everything she was told, but Ellie wasn't convinced.

Suddenly, she had a brainwave. One quick internet search later, a few clicks of her keyboard and she sat back. A DVD on childbirth would be delivered to her home address by express delivery that afternoon.

Putting it out of her head, she concentrated on the report she was trying to write, working through lunch in order to finish it, then sighing with relief when she was able to press send. She put her arms over her head and stretched, her eyes flicking to her watch. Almost four, it would have arrived by now. Tia would need to watch it several times before it would sink in.

Decision made, she stood. 'I have to leave early,' she told her secretary, ignoring the look of surprise on her face. 'I'll see you tomorrow.'

The offices were modern; glass and steel, leaving little opportunity for moving about unnoticed. It was the second time she'd left early recently, and some eyebrows raised as she walked toward the exit carrying her bag and coat. Ignoring the looks, keeping her pace slow and steady, she kept her eyes focused on the exit and left the building. It would work in her favour when she eventually broke the news about her pregnancy.

The DVD was, as promised, waiting on the doormat when she got home. She picked it up and, without waiting to take off her coat, opened the door into the kitchen. Tia was in her usual place in the living room watching a movie. Ellie wondered, not for the first time, how her sister managed to keep the house spotless, yet never seemed to leave the sofa.

There'd be no more flowers now, of course, since she wouldn't be going to the shops. She knew it was petty to be pleased.

'Hi, Tia,' she said, picking up the remote control, stopping whatever it was she had been watching and sliding the DVD into the player. Pressing the play button, she stood in front of her to get her attention. 'I've got this movie I'd really love you to watch,' she said, looking down at her sister who returned her pointed look with a docile one. 'Remember when we talked about being pregnant? It was a bit confusing, wasn't it?' She then waved toward the screen where a hugely pregnant woman had appeared, her face all smiles. 'Well, watch this and I think you might understand a bit more about what I mean.'

Dropping the remote beside Tia, she turned on her heel and left the room, knowing that watching it herself would break down the wall she was carefully building around her own feelings. Instead of watching, she went upstairs, ran a bath and tried to relax. It didn't work and, ten minutes after getting into the warm soapy water, she'd had enough. She pulled the plug and let the water run out around her.

Half an hour later, she headed back downstairs in a pair of cotton pyjamas, with a robe tied tightly around her. She stood at the kitchen door, straining to hear, her eyes rounding in surprise when she heard the distinct sound of... laughter?

She pushed the door open, convinced that Tia had switched back to one of her usual programmes. Instead, she was taken aback to see her sitting cross-legged on the floor directly in front of the television where a small baby was cooing into the camera. She was laughing at – no – *with* the baby on the screen.

Ellie stood watching her sister, her fists clenched against the crash of emotions that assaulted her. Fear and anguish coursed through her with a hundred unanswerable questions. How was she ever going to pull this off? Was she doing the right thing? Did Tia really deliberately seduce Will?

Composing herself as much as she could, she crossed the room, picked up the remote and switched the DVD off.

The screen went blank, and Tia's laugh faded with the picture. She turned and looked up at Ellie, an unusually serious expression on her face. 'That's going to happen to me, isn't it?'

Ellie watched her silently for a moment before taking a deep breath and letting it out slowly. It was what she'd wanted, wasn't it? For Tia to understand. 'Yes,' she said gently and then, seeing a tremor of fear pass over Tia's face, she sat on the floor beside her. 'You'll be okay though,' she said, resting her hand on her sister's arm. 'We'll make sure you're well looked after. When you need to go to the doctor, Will is going to take you.'

Tia's slightly worried expression cleared. 'Will is so nice,' she said.

'Indeed,' Ellie murmured, standing up and moving away. Her suspicions of Tia seemed suddenly churlish, wasn't she as much a victim of this mess as any of them? She turned around to offer more words of comfort, the words catching in her throat when she saw her sister staring at her with a look so cold she froze to the spot. They held each other gaze for a moment before Tia returned to her seat on the sofa. Shaken, Ellie stood where she was for a few minutes. No, perhaps her suspicions weren't unfounded after all. She had an awful feeling this pregnancy was going to feel very long indeed.

Will explained to Tia that she needed to stay indoors. 'It's not safe for you to walk to the shops any more,' he said. When her response was her usual serious look edged with puzzlement, he added, 'There are a lot of bad people out there.' The irony wasn't lost on him, and he stumbled slightly saying the last two words. 'Bad people,' he repeated, putting heavy emphasis on *bad*, knowing it was a word she understood well.

For days afterward, he refused to meet his own eyes when he looked in the mirror and, guilt pressed heavily on his shoulders.

Tia made no complaint about staying indoors but he wondered if she remembered the freedom she'd had just days before. He watched her closely for the first few days, but she seemed as unperturbed by the change in this as she did about the change in her name.

He felt the tension ease, just a little, his plan was going to work. Wasn't it?

25

The obstetrician Ellie chose was Sir Philip Carson, his knighthood a result of services to obstetrics. If his secretary was surprised that Tia had not already seen someone, she was too well trained to say so and booked her appointment without comment.

On the morning of the visit, Ellie chose a pair of navy trousers and a white silk shirt from her wardrobe for Tia to wear. She needed to look wealthy and refined, to fit in and go unnoticed. 'Why don't you wear these?' she said, handing them to her with a tight smile. 'The shirt is loose so it should fit, and the trousers have a bit of stretch so they should be okay.'

Tia looked at the clothes and shook her head. 'I don't like them,' she said.

'You need to look the part,' Ellie said and then, knowing it would work, added, 'after all, Will will be wearing a very smart suit.' It looked as though even this would fail but, with a sigh, Tia took the clothes and left returning, dressed, several minutes later. 'Much better,' Ellie said with a smile, pushing the cereal packet toward her. 'Have something to eat. You remember what I told you about today, don't you?'

Tia sat on a stool at the island, poured cereal into a bowl, added milk and started to eat before she replied. Swallowing, she nodded. 'I'm going with Will to see a doctor about having a baby,' she said and then, eyes down, concentrated on her breakfast. Relieved, Ellie poured some coffee and sat on the sofa to watch the news. She'd taken the day off at Will's insistence. 'You can't be with me at the obstetrician's and at work. We need to be consistent.'

He was right, of course. She told her boss the day before that she had a doctor's appointment, noticing with a flash of irritation how his eyes flickered quickly to her waist and away. It had been the plan, after all, when she'd started to wear looser blouses and dresses; she shouldn't be annoyed at its success. The hint had been well and truly dropped.

She'd pulled her hair back in a bun so tight that her head ached. Closing her eyes, she bit her lip. Her head ached, her heart ached and her eyes shone with tears she refused to allow to fall.

Tomorrow, she'd tell her boss the happy news.

26

Will was startled when he came downstairs to find Ellie sitting in Tia's usual place in the living room watching TV, Tia sitting at the kitchen island eating breakfast, wearing clothes he knew to be his wife's. It was probably the reason Ellie had tied her hair into a severe bun. She didn't take chances any more. While she ignored him, concentrating hard on whatever she was watching on the television, Tia gave him her usual sunny smile.

He sat on the stool opposite Tia and smiled back. 'You remember where we're going today?' he asked.

Tia spooned more cereal into her mouth and nodded. 'To see a doctor about the baby.'

Good; at least she remembered.

The appointment was for nine; with traffic the way it was sure to be, they needed to leave at eight. He drank coffee, watching the minute hand of the clock as it moved toward the hour. He wanted to stand and pace the floor, wanted to grab Ellie and hold her tight, tell her he loved her and that this would all be over soon. More than anything, he wanted to turn the clock back. *And not have a child?* That was the problem, wasn't it? He wanted to turn the clock back to avoid causing Ellie such pain, but he wanted the child. No wonder his head was thumping. Ellie didn't move an inch the entire time he was in the kitchen. Even when he stood and told Tia it was time to go, she sat, unmoving, unspeaking, as if the role he was about to take on was too hard for her to bear.

* * *

Ellie listened to them as they put on their coats, hearing the front door shut with a loud sigh of relief. She got up and poured more coffee, carrying it back to the armchair with a packet of biscuits. She ate hungrily, drowning out the silence in the house with the rustle of wrapping and the soft crunch of chocolate chip cookies. The television blared on; programme after programme flickering by unwatched, the images just a distraction, the noise an attempt to silence the screaming thoughts of everything that could go wrong.

The pain was intense. It should be her with Will, heading off full of excitement about the child she carried. She clasped her belly with both hands, envying Tia as she'd never envied anyone, this sister of hers having her husband's child. 'You couldn't make it up,' she muttered, reaching for the remote control in the hope of finding something to watch that would take her mind off what was happening in a private clinic only a few miles away.

It was three hours later before she heard the front door open again. She jumped at the sound, reorganising herself into a more relaxed pose before the kitchen door opened and Will entered, the sound of footfall on the stairs telling her that Tia had gone up.

'Hi,' Will said. 'Have you been there all morning?' Ellie bit her lip and nodded. 'How did it go?'

He shrugged. 'I wasn't sure what to expect. The secretary gave us some quite detailed forms to fill in.' He gave a short laugh. 'I had to pay a retainer up front.' He mentioned a figure that made Ellie's eyebrows rise.

'Bloody hell,' she exclaimed.

He shrugged. 'We're paying for his name and for the very discreet service, I guess. Sir Philip was very pleasant. When I told him that Tia was very shy and didn't really like speaking to strangers, he immediately addressed all his questions to me.'

'And the exam, she didn't object?' This was the part Ellie had found difficult to explain to Tia, unsure how to explain that another man would touch her. She was afraid Tia would go hysterical.

Will laughed. 'Not in the slightest. He said everything seemed fine. There was a bit of a problem when he asked her the date of the first day of her last period.' He shrugged, a puzzled look crossing his face. 'That's how they calculate when the baby's due, not from the...' he stopped, colour flooding his face. 'It doesn't make sense to me,' he added vaguely.

'Not from the day sex took place,' Ellie filled in the end of his sentence, annoyed that she hadn't thought of this. Truth was, she hadn't known. 'She didn't know, I suppose,' she guessed.

'She looked blankly at him. But Sir Philip appears well used to it all. He told her not to worry. He said they'd have a better idea at the next scan, but he's estimated she's about twelve weeks' pregnant.'

'And they did the ultrasound?'

He nodded. 'Yes, it was fine. And... and there's just one, in case you were worrying.'

Ellie felt herself relax, suddenly aware that this had been adding to her anxiety. 'They were certain?' she asked. 'I've heard stories—'

'Relax, I told him you were a twin—'

'You told him Tia was a twin,' she corrected him.

He closed his eyes for a second. 'Yes, alright, I told him Tia was a twin, and he was very careful. One baby, one heartbeat. One.'

Ellie nodded.

'He wants to see her again in a couple of weeks.' He shrugged when she looked surprised. 'It seems things happen quickly at this stage.' *Not when you have to sit around the house, waiting.* Ellie thought, but she said nothing.

'And then she'll have a further ultrasound at twenty weeks,' he added.

Ellie conjured up a smile. They were in this together and resenting any time he spent alone with Tia wasn't going to achieve anything. 'I know you wanted to go back to work but why not stay home. I'll order in some Indian food later, open a bottle of wine. We could watch a movie.'

* * *

Will hesitated. They needed him in the office, but she was making the effort and he knew he should stay. He opened his mouth to say he would when the door opened and Tia walked in, her eyes glued to what she held in her hand. A sharp breath escaped him when he saw the photo of the ultrasound. He should have guessed she'd forget her promise to put it away.

There was nothing he could do. He saw Ellie's eyes fall on it, comprehension dawning, her face turning pale. She turned her gaze from it to him, her eyes accusing. And then, in one elegant motion, she stood and left the room.

Will sat and looked across at Tia, who was still gazing at the picture of the baby. The baby. That's what Ellie called it and he'd been careful to follow suit. He didn't tell her how amazing it had been when Sir Philip pointed out the head and the limbs to the background of the baby's heart pounding loudly, how he'd caught his breath at the wonder of it all and squeezed Tia's hand, meeting her eyes and smiling at her wide-eyed awestruck face, knowing his probably looked the same.

Nor did he tell her that he'd held Tia's hand through it all.

And he certainly didn't tell her that Sir Philip had looked at him and asked if he wanted to know the sex of the baby and he'd nodded, mesmerised by the screen where he could see his child, unable to take his eyes away even for a moment.

'It's often difficult to tell at this stage, usually we wait until the second ultrasound, but I'm confident that it's a boy,' Sir Philip had said.

A boy! His son! His grin was so wide his face ached.

He couldn't share any of this with Ellie. He would, eventually, but not then. He didn't want to have the intense pleasure he felt at seeing his son... his *son*... ruined by having to remember the guilt, by having to see his wife's face twist in pain.

Sighing, he crossed the room to stand beside Tia. Her face was serious, a rare enough occurrence when he was around. Gently, he reached for the photograph, expecting her to let it go, surprised when she held onto it tightly. 'I'll give it back to you,' he lied. 'I just want to have a look at...' – he hesitated, feeling disloyal to Ellie, but then Tia smiled at him and handed over the photograph, so he swallowed the doubt and finished – 'our baby.'

There was no sign of Ellie's return. With a quick glance at the clock, he decided to follow his original plan and go back to work. But he couldn't leave Tia with the photograph. She was smiling at him now, a return to her normal sunny disposition. He took the chance that she'd have forgotten the promise he made and slipped the photograph into his suit pocket and with a far-from-casual wave he turned and left the room.

His briefcase was in the hall. He picked it up, took the photograph from his pocket and put it safely inside just as Tia came out.

She held her hand out, her face once again serious.

Throwing a glance up the stairs, he took the photograph out again and showed it to her. 'I have it safe,' he reassured her. 'I want to take it to work, to show my colleagues.'

Dropping her hand, she smiled. 'That's good. They'll like to see our baby.'

Will gulped. If Ellie heard her, her heart would break.

'Bye now,' he said, opening the front door. He locked it behind him and stood frozen on the doorstep, guilt souring his belly as he remembered the pain on Ellie's face.

Then, unable to resist, he reached into his briefcase again and took out the photograph. He couldn't help the flood of pleasure when he looked at it.

His son.

27

Will hadn't mentioned the antenatal classes they had been told to attend. 'Are they essential?' he'd asked Sir Philip, who looked at him quizzically before replying.

'I would classify them as being highly recommended rather than essential,' he said. 'They certainly contribute to a healthier and safer birthing experience.' He smiled at Tia. 'They show you the delivery room, go over breastfeeding if it's something you're keen on, give advice on what to pack for your stay, the delivery, breathing, and what to expect when you go home. Personally,' he said, and this time he looked at Will, 'I would advise attending.'

When Will rang, the following day, he was surprised to find the classes were busy and he was unable to get the time of his choice. The only availability was Friday evenings at seven, a time he and Ellie usually spent together, enjoying a wind-down at the end of a busy week.

Sighing loudly and audibly to make a point that was lost on the person on the other end of the phone, he said, 'If that's all that's available.'

'I'm afraid so.'

'Okay,' he said begrudgingly. 'That's Friday week?'

'And the three Fridays after that,' the voice told him.

He shut his eyes. *Oh God!* 'Fine,' he said, and then asked, 'Do we need to go to them all?'

'That's up to you, of course,' he was told. 'We do advise that you attend as many as you can.'

He certainly had to pay for them all, he noticed, taking out his wallet for his credit card. The total price up front. His eyes watered at the cost as he read out the required numbers and hung up. But paying for it faded into insignificance compared to telling Ellie that for four weeks, every Friday night, he'd be attending antenatal classes with her sister. The obstetric appointments were one thing, a clinical visit to make sure all was as it should be, but antenatal classes were different. They were for couples, for expectant parents. They were intimate.

Over the next week, Tia's belly became more pronounced. Ellie arrived home one evening with a bag of oversize T-shirts that she left on Tia's bed without explanation. When Will suggested they weren't very suitable for her clinic visits, Ellie raised an eyebrow and said nothing, not even a few days later when he arrived home carrying a bag from a well-known and expensive mother and baby shop.

Tia lifted the tissue-wrapped garment out, opening it with an ecstatic squeal of delight.

'You can wear it for your next doctor's appointment,' he told her, smiling as she held up the gauzy teal blouse.

When the day of the appointment arrived, she came down wearing it and he nodded. It had been a good choice. The colour suited her and the material settled gently around her bump. He wanted to tell her she looked nice, but he could feel Ellie's eyes boring into him.

The appointment was short; a quick examination that Tia accepted without blinking, a short conversation about her general health and that was it.

They were back home by eleven thirty. 'Nothing new,' he told Ellie who said a terse, 'Fine,' before grabbing her briefcase and coat and rushing off to work.

They could have gone together and spent the fifteen minutes it took to walk to the Highbury and Islington tube-station talking.

Perhaps, if they had, he would have gathered enough courage to tell her about the prenatal classes. Only two days away now, he'd chickened out at every opportunity that had presented itself, unwilling to increase the level of tension that had become the norm in their home. It was like negotiating a minefield. If he spoke to Tia for too long, Ellie would glare at him, but guilt made it impossible for him to criticise her; the plan had been *his* idea. Everything was his fault, so he danced around, afraid to tell her the next step.

The next morning, she mentioned she was doing fillet steak for dinner that night. He visited a wine shop on the way home from work and bought her favourite, a Pinot Noir the assistant behind the counter promised was excellent.

'Wonderful,' Ellie said, turning to him with a smile when he came through the door, the bottle in his hand. 'Open it, will you, let it breathe for a while. Dinner will be ready in about fifteen minutes.' He liked it when she cooked. It was good to sit and watch her work, humming as she switched the grill on and leaving it to heat up while she made the salad. They chatted about work in the way they used to. He told stories of work that, while not particularly amusing, were sufficiently so to raise a smile on her face and he laughed at her latest gripes about Jeff. She picked up a fork and turned the steaks in the same marinade she always used, a simple mix of olive oil and red wine. At the weekend she'd add garlic, but never during the week.

He poured a glass of the Pinot and handed it to her. She sipped appreciatively. 'Very nice,' she said, putting her glass down and turning to deal with the steaks.

The satisfying hiss as she put a steak on the hot grill made his mouth water. Tia had complained before about blood on her plate, so it was hers that went on first.

The food smelled good, the chat was pleasant and Ellie was smiling at him for the first time in days. It was like old times.

Maybe he didn't have to tell her that night. He finished his wine, poured another and held it to his lips before putting it down. He couldn't keep putting it off. What kind of a man was he?

It was better to tell her while he was sober, certainly better to tell her while *she* was sober, while there was some hope of her accepting the need for the antenatal classes without too much fuss. He closed his eyes. How did he expect her to act? He'd betrayed her, the worst kind of betrayal. He swore he'd spend the rest of his life making it up to her; he just hoped she'd let him.

'Ellie,' he said, bringing her attention to him. 'There's something I've been meaning to tell you.'

She didn't have to ask if it was good news, he knew she could read him too well for that. She put down the chopping knife, quickly picked up the fork and turned their steaks in the marinade before she sat and looked at him.

'Tell me,' she said.

Her smile, so ready a minute ago, was gone. Her serious face was ready for another blow.

'There are antenatal classes,' he said quietly. 'Four, starting this week.' When she said nothing, he clarified, 'Every Friday, at seven, for four weeks.'

The smell of burning meat filled the room. She turned, swore loudly and removed the grill pan. Tia's steak was charred around the edges. He watched her hesitate before turning it over. Draining the marinade, she took her time putting one and then the other of the remaining steaks onto the pan and put it back under the grill. Then she turned back to him and picked up her wine glass, taking a large mouthful, swallowing, and then taking another. 'And I suppose you have to go with her,' she said, flatly. 'Won't that be a lovely night's entertainment for you both.'

He ran a hand through his hair and then over his face. What could he say? They'd agreed to go ahead with the pregnancy under this huge pretence, and that meant going along with all the necessities. He didn't dare mention that the antenatal classes weren't compulsory. Sir Philip had made it quite clear it was better for the health and welfare of both mother and baby.

She stood staring at him for a few minutes before turning to look after the steaks. 'Call her down for dinner,' she said, putting Tia's steak onto a plate. He watched as she threw some salad on the plate with her fingers and hoped the steak didn't taste as dry as it looked. Dinner was eaten without a word spoken; the clink of cutlery, the sipping of wine, small sounds breaking an uncomfortable silence. Tia was the only one unaffected by the tension, but she rarely spoke unless spoken to and, although there were several glances thrown her direction, nothing was said.

Usually, Ellie and Will went into the sitting room after dinner, leaving Tia to watch the movies she liked in the living room. Tonight, Ellie pushed her plate away and stood. She took her wine glass and the almost empty wine bottle and left the room without a glance in his direction. If she didn't precisely slam the kitchen door, it was close enough. Seconds later, the door to the sitting room closed. Will listened out for the sound of the television. When it didn't come, he heaved a sigh. She'd sit in silence, in the dark, drink the remaining wine and probably cry. And there was nothing he could say to make it any better. They just had to get through the next few months and hope to come out the other side sane.

He watched as Tia stood and started to clear the table. She said nothing, scraping the food into the correct bin, rinsing the plates and putting them into the dishwasher. She did everything properly. He wondered how she'd cope with the baby and, more importantly, how she'd cope with letting him go. The image of her holding the picture of the ultrasound played on his mind. Would she give the baby up so easily? *Should* she?

The photograph from the scan wasn't mentioned again. Now and then, he took it out and looked at it. His son. He'd shown it to a few people in work, basking in the good wishes sent his way, the new father advice he was given, the jokes at his expense. And he loved every moment. The only sadness was that he couldn't share any of it with his wife.

Sometimes, when he got home before Ellie, he mentioned some of the things people at work had said to Tia. It felt good to be able to share his growing excitement with someone. Because something good had to come out of it all. A baby. His baby. He couldn't help the smile that came to his face whenever he thought about him. He wasn't even aware of it until one day Tia appeared in front of him and gently touched the creases around his mouth.

'You're happy,' she said, looking him in the eye.

He looked at her, and then let his eyes slip to her swollen

belly. She hadn't asked him a question, she was stating a fact as she saw it. And she was right, in that moment, with his thoughts on his son, he was happy.

But then he thought of the deceit, the pain, a future littered with problems so vast it made his head spin to think about it, and he thought he'd never be happy again.

28

On Friday morning, Will explained to Tia that they'd be going to a special baby class that evening. 'We'll be leaving here around six,' he said, 'so make sure you're ready.'

'Okay,' she said, immediately.

Will's smile held a hint of guilt. Ellie was right, she'd do anything he asked. But would she give him their baby and move out? Their baby. It was the first time he'd thought of the baby as *theirs* not just his. He was sure Ellie wouldn't appreciate the change in thinking. He hadn't mentioned the future beyond the birth again. It worried him. Could he really ask Tia to give up her child?

He looked across to where Ellie was sitting having breakfast. She finished early on a Friday and was usually home before him. He wanted to ask her to remind Tia and to make sure she was dressed appropriately but, seeing her steely expression, he bit his lip. He'd just have to hope Tia remembered.

He left the office a little early and was home at five forty-five. Ellie hadn't arrived. He guessed she was deliberately late so she wouldn't have to witness their departure. Hanging his coat over the banisters, he went into the kitchen and put the kettle on. He'd have time for a coffee before they left. Tia wasn't there. Hopefully she was upstairs getting dressed. He went back to the hall and called up the stairway. 'Tia, are you nearly ready?'

'Coming,' she shouted down and, relieved, he went back to make coffee.

He'd almost finished a whole mug before she appeared. He looked her over with a critical eye. She looked the part. The teal blouse he'd bought her was having its second outing. 'You look good,' he said, with a satisfied nod.

She grinned at him. 'I like going out with you.'

Since the only place they'd been together recently was the obstetrician, Will wasn't sure how to take this. 'Let's go,' he said, smiling politely.

They arrived with time to spare and sat in the waiting room as the others arrived. Four other couples, the nervous-looking ones he reckoned to be first-timers like themselves. He guessed the bored looking couple had done it before.

On the dot of seven, a woman dressed in a white tunic top and trousers came in. 'Good evening, everyone,' she said. 'My name is Julie.' She looked around the room and then down at the clipboard she held. One by one she read out names, pausing between each pair so that each couple could introduce themselves and tell the others a little about themselves.

When their turn arrived, there was a painfully long pause before Tia uttered the words, 'My name is Ellie,' and he rushed in with, 'And I'm Will and this is our first baby,' too quickly after her, feeling his cheeks redden as everyone looked at him.

Julie smiled at them all and for the next few minutes spoke about the practicalities of childbirth, handing out leaflets and notes as she spoke. Then she waved to the screen behind her. 'Most of you are first timers so this is all new to you but I'm sure Peter and Jane, who are on their second, won't mind watching the video I'm about to show you of a young couple having their first child. Everything goes exactly the way it should, so it's wonderful to watch. Afterwards, we'll have some coffee and chat about it, and you can ask any questions then. Okay?' She looked around and then switched out the light and started the video.

Will knew Tia had watched the childbirth video Ellie had bought several times so he wasn't concerned she'd be shocked by it. What he wasn't expecting was to be enthralled and fascinated himself. There was a collective gasp in the room when, finally, the child slipped out and gave its first cry. He looked at Tia who was staring at the screen with a smile on her face. *Their* child.

She must have sensed his eyes on her because she turned to look at him, her smile faltering slightly when she saw his serious face. She was so like Ellie he thought, with a deep sense of regret that it wasn't his wife sitting beside him to share these special moments. When he felt a hand slip into his, he thought for a moment that he was imagining Ellie being with him, but then he looked down and saw the hand resting in his. Tia's, of course it was Tia's. He gave it a gentle squeeze and kept hold of it until the video ended.

After a quick break for tea or coffee, there was a question-and-answer session.

'The video was pretty straightforward,' Julie said, 'but does anyone have any questions about it or anything else?'

Several hands immediately shot up and for the next several minutes Will listened to aspects of birth he'd never considered. To his surprise, he noticed Tia appeared to listen intently.

She'd put her hand back into his as soon as they'd taken their seats after coffee, he looked down at it now and shook off the twinge of disloyalty he felt at holding another woman's hand while his wife was sitting at home. He covered his sigh of frustration with a quick cough.

'Next week,' Julie said, when there were no more questions, 'you'll be given a tour of the facilities. And then the following two weeks we'll be covering breathing and relaxation exercises.' She gave a nod of dismissal and left.

Outside the clinic, Will was about to head for the tube when he looked at Tia and saw the pallor in her cheeks. 'You're tired?' he asked, unsurprised when she nodded.

'We'll get a taxi,' he said, taking her by the arm and moving to the side of the path, his eyes scanning the roads. He was in luck when one turned the corner near where he stood, its light on. He waved it down and, minutes later, they were on their way home.

He checked his mobile. There were no messages, no missed calls. The house was dark when they arrived, and Ellie still wasn't home. Will wasn't too surprised, but he was disappointed. Inside, he picked up the house phone and keyed in the four-digit code to check for messages, relieved to have one, more than relieved to hear her voice even if the message was brief.

'I'm staying with friends tonight,' she said, the strain obvious in every word. She didn't bother to tell him which friend.

Replacing the handset, he stared at it for a moment and then ran a hand through his hair. There was absolutely nothing he could do. He imagined her voice, *you've already done it*, and shook his head.

In the kitchen, he opened the fridge. He could cook something but he didn't have the heart. 'How about we get a take-away again?' he said to Tia, who'd switched on the television in the living room and was sitting, relaxed, on the sofa.

He left the money ready in the hall, ran upstairs and changed from his suit to sweatpants and a T-shirt. Barefoot, he went back down and opened the sitting room door to settle in for the evening but, finding the dark room cold and unwelcoming, he suddenly didn't feel like being on his own.

Back in the living room, Tia was giggling at some movie. He took a beer from the fridge and went over to see what she was watching. '*Ghostbusters*,' he said with a smile, recognising the scene. He'd watched it years before. It had been fun.

When the takeaway came, he brought it over and opened it on the table beside her. They helped themselves, Tia's eyes hardly leaving the television as she chuckled at the characters.

It wasn't long before Will was laughing along too. When it was over, he reached for the remote and switched the television off. It was, he knew, the only way to get her undivided attention. Tia, who usually went from movie to movie, turned to him, surprised.

He smiled at her. 'I just wanted to ask you what you thought of the class,' he said.

She looked at him for a moment. 'It was okay,' she said.

He tilted his head. 'Did you understand everything they were talking about?' He watched her face turn unusually serious, her resemblance to her sister suddenly frighteningly close, as if he was speaking to Ellie and not Tia. Sometimes, he felt like he was wading in a quagmire of complications. They were so alike, both so beautiful, the only obvious difference between them was the rounded belly of this woman who was carrying his child.

Just when he thought she wasn't going to answer, she said,

'It was about what will happen to my body before the baby comes, about how it will stretch to let the baby out, about feeding the baby and how to keep baby safe.'

Will was stunned. There had been more, of course, but she'd remembered the salient points. 'That's really good, Tia,' he said, wondering if he sounded insufferably condescending.

'Ellie,' she said.

Confused, he looked around expecting to see his wife at the door. 'What?'

'You're supposed to call me Ellie,' she reminded him.

He was taken aback. For a second, looking at her serious face, he wondered if Ellie was right, that maybe Tia was sharper than they'd been led to believe. Then she smiled, her expression becoming a little distant and unfocused, and he gave a little laugh. He was being foolish.

'Yes, of course, Ellie,' he said and then, deciding he'd had enough for one day, he stood. 'Goodnight,' he said and headed upstairs where he tossed and turned restlessly all night.

He was sitting in the kitchen when Ellie arrived back late the next morning, the newspaper spread open, drinking tea and working his way through a packet of biscuits. 'Hi,' he said, looking up from the paper. 'Did you have a good night?'

She nodded and then, as if deciding to relent, she dropped her bag, went over to him and dropped a kiss on his head. 'I stayed with Adie,' she said. 'She spent the whole evening complaining about the people who've moved into the apartment above her. According to her, they tap dance across the floor morning, noon and night.' She checked there was water in the kettle and flicked it on. 'I never heard a thing the whole time I was there,' she said, taking down a jar of coffee. 'You want some?'

He shook his head. 'She was always prone to exaggerating,' he said, remembering the tall, leggy woman from his college years. 'Yes, well, it will be a long time before I stay with her again,' she said, taking a biscuit from the packet in front of him and dunking it into her coffee.

'You didn't have to stay out, Ellie,' he said softly. 'I know it's hard for you but isolating yourself just makes it harder.'

'What is it you suggest I do, Will?' she said with more than a touch of sarcasm to hide the sadness that curled inside her. 'Go on, give me your advice. How should I handle it when my husband goes to an antenatal class with my sister, the mother of his child?'

'Maybe with a little more understanding,' he said, hoping he hadn't just lit a fuse.

But she didn't explode, she sipped her coffee, the glare fading. 'You're right, I suppose,' she said. 'After all, I did agree to carry out this charade. I can't very well complain when you're doing such a good job of it. So, are you going to tell me how it went?'

He took another biscuit. 'It was incredibly boring,' he lied, 'a bunch of women talking about stretch marks and how many centimetres' dilation was necessary for an easy birth. It made me squirm.'

Ellie laughed, her face losing some of its tension. 'What did you expect,' she said, 'a wine reception?'

'Something more interesting,' he said with a shrug, and then, because it had fascinated him and was something he could talk about truthfully, he told her how surprised he was by how much information Tia had retained of the class.

Ellie reached for the biscuits again, took one out and

nibbled the edges thoughtfully. 'I've often wondered if she isn't a lot brighter than we were led to believe,' she said. 'There are times when she appears...' She caught Will's look and shook her head. 'Don't mind me,' she said with a forced laugh. 'What's the next class about?'

'It's to show us round the facilities,' he told her. 'I think we get to see the birthing pool and a few other options.'

'You don't need to go to that, do you?' she asked. 'Can't you skip it?'

Hiding his reluctance, he shrugged. 'Yes, I suppose we could.' He saw a pleased look cross her face and was sorry he'd have to remove it. 'The following two, however, are going to be important. They cover breathing techniques during labour and other essential stuff.' He reached a hand out and caught hers. 'We'll need to be there for that.'

With a sigh, she nodded. 'I do understand,' she said, pulling her hand away, 'but that doesn't mean I have to like it.'

* * *

Will hadn't thought to tell Tia they weren't going to the class the following Friday so was surprised to arrive home and find her sitting in the living room, dressed in the teal blouse, her coat over her arm.

'I tried to tell her,' Ellie said from the kitchen, tearing open an M&S meal. 'She wouldn't listen.' Picking up another meal, she tore the wrapping off before commenting, 'I hadn't realised she was so stubborn.'

'Well, you are twins,' Will couldn't resist saying before going to speak to his sister-in-law. 'Tia,' he said, 'I'm sorry—'

'Ellie,' she said, interrupting him, 'you're supposed to call me Ellie.'

'Oh, for goodness' sake,' he said exasperated, 'All right, Ellie then, I'm sorry, I should have told you, we don't have to go tonight.'

'Why?'

He'd had a tough day at work, he was tired and wanted to relax with a drink. 'Because we don't need to go this week. Next week and the following week, they're the important ones. They show you how to breathe when you're having the baby. We'll definitely need to be there then.'

Tia nodded slowly, mollified. 'We'll definitely need to be there then,' she said, repeating his words. He smiled at her and then looked across at his wife to find her staring at the pair of them with a look in her eyes that he couldn't identify.

He joined her. 'Let's have dinner next door,' he said, 'just the two of us.'

'Okay,' she said. 'Tia will be happy, she can have hers in front of the TV.'

Relieved he'd moved past that strange moment, he kissed his wife gently on the cheek and made for the door. 'I'll just get out of my suit,' he said, 'then I'll open some wine.'

He stood in the hallway for a moment, looking down on the floor where it happened. One night's drunken stupidity. He stepped over the empty space and took the stairs slowly, his tread heavy, the pressure of the weeks ahead weighing him down.

He forced his thoughts onto his child; he had to believe it was all worth it.

29

Ellie broke the news at work, receiving the congratulations from her colleagues with a pasted-on smile. The loose clothes she'd been wearing had worked to set rumours flying, but lately she'd started wearing a prosthetic pregnancy bump she'd bought online. She couldn't help but be amazed by the endless variety of materials, sizes and shapes available.

Wearing it wasn't uncomfortable, but she hated this evidence, not only of the lie they were living, but of a condition she would never feel for real. Every morning, she strapped it on and, every evening, as soon as she was through the door, she'd take it off and drop it on the hallway floor like it was made of lead.

She never once picked it up, but every morning she would find it in in her wardrobe, waiting to be strapped back on again.

Her office building was air-conditioned, but in the cold weather it was overheated, and the silicone bump made her hot and sticky. It was easy to unclip, so sometimes she'd do that sitting at her desk, feeling the release with a sigh.

Once, she had a near-miss, her boss stopping at her door and asking her to come with him for an impromptu meeting.

She'd looked at him and nodded. 'I'll be just a minute,' she said. But he waited.

She'd wondered what he'd have done if she'd stood, her bump hitting the floor with a silicone bounce. She'd had to bite her lip to stop a chortle escaping. But she'd looked at him calmly and said, 'I just need to pop to the loo. Pregnancy does that, I'm afraid.'

And he'd rushed off with a slightly embarrassed look on his face.

Minutes later, her bump firmly in place she strode into his office.

It was the only near-miss, but there were dozens of irritations she had to deal with. The conversations about morning sickness, stretch marks, to epidural or not to epidural. That was a blasted question she didn't want to discuss. She hadn't realised how many of her colleagues had children until now but, over the course of a few months, every one of them recounted their experience in minute detail.

Bad as it was in work, it was worse at home. The T-shirts she'd bought Tia had been a mistake, the fine cotton clinging to her bump, emphasising it. Annoyingly, she didn't appear to put on weight anywhere else, and they were as identical as ever except for that one big, glaring difference, the dual insult – evidence of her husband's infidelity and her own barren state.

She tried to avoid being in the same room as her, made easier by the fact that Tia preferred sitting in the living room anyway. And, if they were in the same room, she kept her eyes averted, as much as possible, from her belly.

It didn't help seeing Will's eyes constantly drifting toward it.

'Do you have to keep looking at it?' she challenged him one evening. 'It's not going to pop open, you know!'

'Sorry,' Will said. 'It's just—'

'A great big seed-pod,' she interrupted him, 'think of it that way and maybe it won't seem so endlessly fascinating.'

* * *

Later that night, he reached for her as he had done several times since finding out about the pregnancy. Once again, she brushed his hands away. 'No,' she said, refusing to offer an apology or an excuse, hearing his heavy sigh of frustration with a flicker of satisfaction.

The next day, she ordered proper maternity tops online, voluminous garments designed to conceal rather than display. When they came, she left them on Tia's bed, expecting to see them on her the following day. To her annoyance, she arrived down in another of the T-shirts.

'I bought you some nice tops,' she said, trying to sound cheerful and encouraging, 'didn't you like them?'

Tia shrugged. 'I prefer these,' she said, pulling at the soft fabric that covered her bump. 'They're comfortable.'

'So are the others,' Ellie tried, her voice hardening, 'you should try them.' But, to her annoyance, Tia didn't.

The Friday of the next antenatal class came around too quickly. Ellie felt an uneasiness in the pit of her stomach all day. Perhaps she should have gone to stay with a friend or even checked into a hotel. But it was too late.

She could have hidden in the sitting room until they'd gone but, instead, she decided to make a point and took the seat Tia normally sat in, switching on the television, channel-surfing until she found some light romance movie to watch. Pressing pause, she went to fetch a glass of wine. She was pouring it when Tia came down, dressed in the same teal blouse.

Will arrived home moments later. She saw him glance at the glass and raised it in a toast. His getting drunk had been the cause of this mess, getting drunk might help her get through it. They left almost immediately, Will checking his watch anxiously. She held her glass tightly as she listened to the murmurs in the hallway and the front door opening and closing. When she had stupidly agreed to this charade, she'd known it was crazy but she hadn't expected it to be a nightmare from which she never woke. Seeing Tia, day after bloody day, blooming in her pregnancy was killing her.

She could hardly bring herself to look at her any more, and avoided speaking to her if she could help it. It wasn't fair, she knew, Tia hadn't asked to be part of the charade, hadn't been given a choice. But then, really, neither had she.

And now it was too late. The game had begun, and they all had to play their parts.

She sipped her wine and wondered what they were doing just then. Was it as boring as Will had implied? Was he holding her hand and pretending to be a devoted husband? Her mouth twisted in pain and the tears she'd been holding back since they'd left slowly began to fall.

30

Will wasn't holding Tia's hand. When they'd arrived at the clinic they were asked to sit on mats on the floor. He'd helped Tia sit, her bump, while not as big as some of the others, making the act of lowering to the floor awkward. And then he did what the other men were doing and sat on the mat behind her, his legs extending both sides of her, her bottom nestling against his groin. Ellie would never know, but he felt a sense of betrayal with this intimacy.

Her hair smelled of coconut, and from her skin came the fresh smell of lemon. Completely different to Ellie, he thought frowning and wondering how he'd ever got confused. He felt her body relax back against him, heard her sigh as she did, felt the disloyalty and sense of betrayal course through him even as he adjusted his position to support her better.

The woman leading the class, a nurse whose name was Merry, made the class fun. Thirty minutes in, she told them they were doing wonderfully. 'I suggest we take a break,' she said. 'Some of you may want to use the facilities and when you return, we'll have a chat about what you've learned so far and I'll answer any questions you may have.'

There were smiles and head nods of agreement. Will clambered to his feet and reached a hand down to assist Tia to hers. She stood, brushed herself down, and then looked at him, her brow furrowed. 'I need to wee,' she said, moving uncomfortably from one foot to the other.

Her un-hushed voice carried to the couple who were sat next to them. The woman laughed. 'Me too,' she said, struggling to stand, her bump more cumbersome than Tia's neat mound. 'Let's go together,' she said with a smile.

There was nothing Will could do except hope Tia didn't say anything awkward. The other woman, her name already forgotten, seemed to be the chatty type, perhaps she wouldn't have the opportunity to get a word in edgeways.

He stood with the other men making small talk, his eyes constantly darting to the doorway, desperate for Tia to return. He laughed meekly at one of the other dad-to-be's jokes, even though he hadn't heard the punchline. Where was she, he wondered, looking down at his watch and then back up at the door.

Relief flooded through him when the sound of laughter announced the return of the five women who'd left en masse for the bathroom, including Tia. She was smiling; a real smile this time, not the faraway grin she often wore.

'Everything okay?' he asked as she joined him.

She nodded and moved closer to him. Looking around the room, he saw that the other couples had connected in some way, hands held, an arm around a shoulder or waist. It seemed churlish not to do the same. He slipped an awkward arm around her shoulder and immediately she relaxed into him as if it was the most natural thing in the world.

He tensed as dismay washed over him; she didn't know it was all pretence, that it would soon be over and she would leave, and he would stay with his wife with their baby. He felt suddenly claustrophobic. Sweat pinged on his brow and trickled between his shoulder blades. He looked toward the door, his mouth dry. It seemed a long way away. His heart was thumping so loud he was surprised nobody heard. Eyes flicking to the door again, he knew he had to get outside before he made a fool of himself.

Luckily for him, Merry returned just then and asked them to take their seats. He saw Tia to her seat and excused himself with a nod toward the door through which she'd gone earlier.

The door led to a short corridor. To his relief, he saw the exit door on his right and pushed it open, almost falling out into the street. He staggered a few feet and then stopped and leaned forward, his hands on his knees trying to catch his breath. He took a deep breath of the cold night air, letting it out slowly, trying to regain some semblance of control. For a moment in there, he felt as if the world was slipping out from under him. It was ten minutes before he could return.

He avoided Tia's eyes when he did go back in, taking his seat as quietly as he could. The rest of the session was spent in an almost endless run of questions and answers. Checking his watch, Will was appalled to see it was eight fifteen.

'Any more questions?' Merry asked, seemingly uncaring that she was running over.

Will gritted his teeth when a woman raised her hand and asked a question that required a rather detailed answer.

'Anything else?'

Will stood, taking Tia by the hand. 'I'm terribly sorry,' he said as the group looked at them. 'I'm so sorry,' he repeated, 'it's getting late, and Ellie is exhausted. I think we had better head off.' Merry nodded sympathetically. 'Of course.' She looked around the small group. 'Let's finish here. Thank you, everybody, and see you all next week.'

The others didn't appear to be in a hurry to leave, starting to chat amongst themselves as soon as the nurse had turned her back to start clearing things away. If Ellie had been beside him, if things had been different, he'd have stayed and talked through the normal fears and excitement of any first timers. But he couldn't. His fears were more terrifying, more horrifying. These honest, normal people would be shocked if they knew the truth.

He needed to get home to his wife. In the mess that was his life, he had to cling to what was important. Ellie. With an arm around Tia to hustle her forward, he made a dash for the door.

Opening a taxi door for Tia, he helped her in and ran around to the other side. He gave the driver the address before sitting back with a sigh. It would have been more honest if he'd told Merry it was he who was exhausted. He was bone-weary, and sometimes, although he was loathe to admit it even to himself, he was afraid of what they were doing.

A chuckle from Tia brought him from his thoughts. 'What's so amusing?'

'I like being Ellie,' she said, smiling at him.

He looked at her in shock. 'You're not Ellie,' he said, 'you're Tia. We're just pretending, for the baby.'

The mulish set to her mouth reminded him so much of Ellie it startled him. He knew when his wife got that stubborn look there was no point in arguing with her. There didn't seem much point here either. After all, they wanted her to be Ellie, for the moment. He didn't know if she would understand the importance. Didn't know if she'd understand the truth could destroy their lives. She liked being Ellie, at least. Looking at it that way, he could deal with it for a few more months.

He turned and looked out at the dark London streets, his eyes bleak.

31

As the days passed, cloaked in their web of deceit, Will felt some relief that nothing untoward happened before the next and final class.

On Friday afternoon, he looked around his office. He would lose all of this if they were found out. His colleagues would be horrified, no, disgusted.

What the hell had he been thinking? This charade, this mind-boggling deception, was never going to work. He found himself waiting, every day, for something to go wrong, knowing that just one wrong step would send everything falling down around them.

He sat back in his chair and rested his hands on the desk in front of him. Just this morning, one of his colleagues asked how Ellie was doing, and it took him a few seconds of looking blank before he remembered he meant Tia, and not his wife. Because although Tia was blooming, pregnancy suiting her very well, Ellie had started to look gaunt and pale.

His colleague had looked at him strangely as he over compensated and told him how well his pregnant wife was and how wonderfully she was doing. 'First-time father excitement,' he had finished, hoping this would explain everything.

He rubbed a weary hand over his face and stood. It was time to leave to collect Tia.

She was waiting for him when he got home, wearing her teal shirt once again. Tia obviously liked the blouse he'd bought better than the new clothes Ellie had given her. It suited her, she looked – the only word that suited – radiant.

She smiled when she saw him, a hand resting on her bump, drawing his eyes to it before they flicked to where Ellie was standing, a glass of wine in her hand. There was a hard look on her face and he flinched. He should have been more careful.

'We're going out again,' Tia said, bringing his eyes back to her. 'Yes,' he said to her, checking his watch. 'In fact, we'd better be leaving.' He turned to say goodbye to Ellie. 'We'll have dinner when we get back?' He waited patiently, refusing to leave until she nodded.

When she did, he gave a quick smile and left.

The final class was a rehash of all they'd heard in the others and Will was bored by the end and grateful it ended slightly early. He hadn't realised he was quieter than usual until Tia reached out a hand and laid it on his arm. 'You okay?'

Surprised, he smiled at her and put his own hand briefly over hers. 'Yes, I'm fine. Just a bit tired. It's been a busy week. I'm glad these classes are over.'

'I'll miss them,' Tia said. 'I liked being out with you.'

He gave an uncertain laugh. 'Well, we have the next ultrasound appointment in a couple of weeks to look forward to.'

* * *

The days fell into an uneasy routine. Every evening, he picked up the prosthetic bump that Ellie dropped on the hall floor and brought it to their room, placing it in her wardrobe so she couldn't miss it and every morning he watched his fake pregnant wife studiously avoid his pregnant sister-in-law before rushing out the door to work.

The pain in Ellie's eyes most days made him squirm; so, he found himself looking to Tia's promise-filled bump for solace when Ellie was out of the room or otherwise occupied and wouldn't notice. So many pitfalls to avoid, they danced around each other trying not to trip up. Tia was the only person who seemed unfazed by it all.

Pregnancy suited her. She looked well, glowing in fact.

Taking a sly look at her bump when Ellie was making dinner one night, he looked up to catch Tia watching him, a strange expression on her face. He remembered what Ellie had said, more than once, about Tia staring at her. Was this what she meant? Because there was something odd about her expression. Not that it was serious, which in itself was unusual, but it was hard and – what had Ellie called it? – calculating.

And then it was gone, and Will shook his head. He was getting as bad as Ellie, seeing things that weren't there. 'You feeling okay?' he asked Tia, quietly.

Her pleasant smile in reply was as it always was. Shaking his head at his silly fantasy, he left her to join Ellie who was pottering about in the kitchen.

'How about we go out for dinner tomorrow night?' he said, putting his hands around her waist, pulling her back into his arms. He felt her go rigid before she turned and glared at him. 'Go for a meal wearing my fake bump in case we meet anyone we know? I don't think so.' She pulled away from him and left the room, the slam of the door telling him he'd got it wrong yet again.

He shook his head, feeling like a swarm of wasps was buzzing about over his head.

* * *

The day of the ultrasound arrived. It was at midday, so once again Ellie had to take a day off work to sit at home. She stayed curled up in bed with a book and was still there that evening when they returned home.

'It went okay,' he said, sitting on the bed beside her. 'And that's it with appointments now, as long as everything goes according to plan.' He waited a moment, seeing her eyes reading his face. She knew immediately he had more to share. 'It's a boy,' he said, as if he'd just been told the news that day.

He saw her eyes go bleak, felt his own eyes water. A son. But not *their* son.

Reaching for her, he pulled her into his arms and held her tightly. 'It's all going to be okay,' he whispered into her hair. 'We love each other, that's enough to get us through this.'

He felt her tremble and then heard her whisper, her breath warm on his cheek. 'You're getting just what you've always wanted.'

She was right. But the expression *Be careful what you ask for* slipped into his head and sent a shiver down his spine.

32

Ellie was a fake, a fraud and the pain of it all, the lies and secrets, the whole charade, was taking its toll. At work, she began to notice the sideways glances, the concerned stares, the conversations that stopped when she entered a room.

'Are you sure you're not overdoing things,' the CEO, Alex, asked one afternoon, popping into her office unexpectedly. 'You can take maternity leave sooner if you wish.'

Tough at work, it was even tougher at home. Take early maternity leave? Stay at home and watch Tia blooming? Try not to see Will glancing at her bump when he thought his wife wasn't looking? She couldn't face it. 'I'm fine,' she said.

She told Will what Alex had said that evening over dinner and saw his eyes darken with concern.

'You do look pale,' he said. 'I didn't think—'

'What?' she interrupted him. 'You didn't think it would be so hard to play make-believe for weeks, months on end? That the constant lies wouldn't take their toll?'

Tia chose that moment to stand. She looked at them both

for a few seconds before she took her plate, put it in the dishwasher and went to sit on the sofa. All without a word spoken.

The blare of the TV shattered the uneasy silence, bringing Ellie's attention back to Will. She ran a hand over her face, feeling weary. 'Do you know,' she said sadly, 'I had thought that because Tia has hardly put on any weight apart from her bump that we still looked identical. Then, this morning, I saw my reflection and realised we didn't any more. I look like her frailer, *older* sister.'

'You're being ridiculous,' Will said. When she shook her head, he reached for her hand. 'You're just tired. I know how hard this is for you.' Ellie looked at him. He didn't. He had no idea of the intense feeling of worthlessness that came over her in waves as she watched Tia blooming in her pregnancy, swelling with *his* son, looking so damn pleased with herself.

* * *

She began to count down the weeks to the due date in February. Christmas was a nightmare, all of them trapped in the suddenly too-small house, trying to avoid one another. She insisted, more than once, that Will took Tia out in the car for a drive.

'For God's sake,' she said, 'she's been shut in here for weeks on end, at least you and I get out. Take her to a park where you won't meet anyone we know.'

There were numerous invitations to festive parties, both for Christmas and the New Year. She insisted they turn down every single one. 'I can't,' she said firmly. 'I just can't go to our friends' homes wearing that *thing* and pretend to be happily pregnant. Lie. To our friends.' She shook her head. 'I won't do it.'

'I'll tell them you aren't feeling up to socialising,' he said, 'they'll understand.'

She snorted. 'I'm sure they wouldn't,' she said, and left him to it.

The days after Christmas dragged, the weather wet and bitterly cold. Ellie bundled herself up and headed to work.

'You need to be careful,' one of her colleagues said, eyeing her court shoes with wary eyes. 'It's icy on some of the paths. Should you be wearing heels?'

Ellie bit her tongue on the *mind your own business* she wanted to say. She'd learned that people saw her pregnant state as the right to give unwanted advice and smiled instead. 'I'm fine,' she said.

'Every blasted person I meet has a comment to make,' she said to Will that evening. She frowned. 'You know, maybe I will take maternity leave earlier than I'd planned.'

The next day she went to see the CEO. 'I was thinking I might take maternity leave soon,' she said.

Alex Gilmartin nodded so emphatically it brought an amused smile to Ellie's face. 'Yes, of course,' he said, 'we are quite concerned about you, you know? Finish today, go home and rest up. Keep us updated with the news.'

Ellie blinked. She'd been about to say she'd go in two or three weeks but then she shrugged. Why not immediately? She'd get away from the constant, unwelcome scrutiny.

'Thank you,' she said. 'That's very kind of you. If you're sure?'

Ten minutes later, she was heading to the tube-station, a spring in her step despite the cold. She hadn't realised until that moment how exhausting it was to live the lie every day. And if the pain of facing the truth at home was the alternative, so be it.

She tried to avoid Tia by staying in her bedroom reading until late morning and then watching television or using her laptop in the sitting room during the afternoon. Only when she needed coffee or something to eat did she go to the kitchen, and then it would be in and out as quickly as possible with a quick flick of her eyes to check where Tia was.

It was in the evenings that things became difficult. She wanted to suggest that she and Will have their meals in the sitting room, leaving Tia to have hers watching TV, but she couldn't bring herself to say something so divisive, so down-right mean.

But then things came to a head. She was making dinner when Will came home one evening. He stopped to give her a kiss before his attention was claimed by a news item on the television.

She put the tray into the oven and set the temperature. Suddenly, she was conscious of the hairs on her neck standing on end and turned abruptly, biting her lip to stop the groan of distress escaping at the sight of Will with his hand resting on Tia's bump, a look of rapture on his face.

And then her eyes locked on her sister's as Tia stared at her over Will's shoulder, an intense look of satisfaction on her face. Ellie took a deep breath and walked to join them. 'Is the baby kicking,' she asked, pushing Will's hand out of the way, laying her own, fingers splayed, over the tense dome. She felt it then, a definite kick and was unable to stop a look of wonder creeping into her eyes. Looking at Tia's face, suddenly wanting to say something enthusiastic and encouraging, her mouth shut with a snap when she met her sister's cold, hard eyes.

From that night on, Ellie ate her dinner in the sitting room. Will wasn't happy, arguing it was better to eat together, but since Tia showed a distinct preference to eat in front of the TV, she ignored him and set his dinner on a tray to bring through.

* * *

Over breakfast, one morning in late January, Will mentioned redecorating one of the spare bedrooms as a nursery. 'We could paper the walls and buy a cot, plus we need to get a pram or whatever they call them these days and all the other paraphernalia that a baby needs.'

Ellie looked at him with one eyebrow raised. 'Do you want to go shopping with your pregnant sister-in-law while I hide at home, or shop with me and my pregnancy prosthesis while the mother of your baby stays at home?' She ignored the flash of pain that crossed his face. 'Either way is impossible,' she said. 'Just leave it to me.'

What she didn't tell him, what she couldn't tell him because it hurt too much, was that she'd already planned the nursery. A year before. She'd spent hours poring over various sites on the internet, a smile curving her lips as she chose item after item for their child. *Their* child. The memory brought quick tears to her eyes. She'd planned it all as a surprise for Will. A surprise. Imagining them decorating the room together. Making plans as they painted, papered, laughed and dreamed. But that was before she got the news that she'd never be able to bear a child.

She sat in the sitting room with her laptop and, with a few clicks on her keyboard, brought all the saved items up. The beautiful handmade cot. The brightly coloured furniture to store all the baby stuff. The delightful wallpaper. A comfortable chair where she could sit to breastfeed. Her gulp was loud. Where *Tia* could sit to breastfeed.

Her fingers hovered over the keys for a moment before clicking to purchase all.

She paid extra to have it delivered the next day so when the doorbell rang late morning she knew why. 'Can you come and help me,' she said to Tia who was sitting reading a magazine. Seeing the reluctant look on her face, she added, persuasively, 'It's something nice, honest.'

The delivery men obligingly brought the heavier of the boxes up to the room they'd designated as the nursery. Leaving Tia to start opening them, Ellie went downstairs to fetch the stepladder they kept in the garden shed.

When she returned with it, she was surprised to see Tia had most of the boxes open and was in the middle of removing the wrapping from the chest of drawers, her eyes wide with pleasure.

'You like it?'

Tia, opening and closing drawers that had animal figures for handles, turned and grinned. 'For the baby?'

Ellie bit her lip. For *the* baby. Not *her* baby, never her baby. She swallowed the pain that seemed to have lodged in her throat and forced her lips to curve in a smile. 'And this too,' she said, holding up a roll of wallpaper. 'If you help me, we could get this done before Will gets home and surprise him.'

Tia nodded and then frowned. 'Do you know how?'

Ellie had never wallpapered in her life but how difficult could it be? The paper was self-adhesive and, according to the internet, easy to apply. 'Of course,' she said, unrolling the first roll.

Luckily, she'd ordered a spare roll because *easy* wasn't a word she'd have used to describe the process. It took almost three hours, and a lot of swearing, to get the small room papered but when it was done the two women stood back and grinned.

'I like those,' Tia said, pointing to the fat cartoon rabbits along the bottom.

Ellie had chosen well. Above the rabbits, large cuddly bees buzzed around big white daisies and, higher still, fluffy yellow birds flew in and out of cotton wool clouds. It was delightful and completely charming.

'I like it all,' Ellie said, her smile fading. She'd loved the paper the first time she saw it, a lifetime ago. She sighed loudly, drawing Tia's eyes to her. Ignoring her gaze, she said, 'You'd better go and rest now, I'll manage the rest.'

It took her another couple of hours to get the furniture unpacked, all the baby clothes, creams, lotions and potions put into the drawers and the room organised. The cot was as beautiful as she expected. Standing over it, she stared and then blinked to stop the tears forming, wrapping her arms tightly around her waist. *Swaddled.* The word leapt into her head. She looked down at the cot and imagined the baby lying there. Will's baby.

She was still there when Will came home. She heard his footsteps going into the kitchen, the low murmur of voices as he spoke to Tia and then the sound of his feet on the stairs.

'Ellie?' he called.

'In here,' she said, her voice thick with tears. She heard his gasp when he came in and saw what she'd done, felt his arms around her, resting back against him for a moment before she gave way to the tears she'd been holding. She turned in his arms and cried for the mother she'd never be, and for the baby that wasn't hers.

33

One day before Tia's due date, Will and Ellie were reading the papers in the sitting room when the door opened and Tia stood in the doorway. 'I've got a pain,' she said, rubbing her belly, her face slick with sweat.

Both of them jumped up. Will rushed to Tia's side, putting an arm around her waist and leading her to the couch. 'Sit down,' he urged.

Ellie hovered. 'How often are the pains coming?'

'It hurts,' Tia said, gritting her teeth, a groan escaping, a low plaintive wail that went on and on.

Will looked up at Ellie helplessly.

'We need to know how often they're coming and when they started,' she said. 'If they're not too close, you'll be okay, I think, to drive her in.'

Tia's wails increased in volume and then stopped abruptly.

Both Will and Ellie leaned toward her, surprised. 'Tia?' Will said gently.

'I'm wet,' she said.

Ellie looked at the growing stain on the front of her pyjamas with startled eyes. 'Bloody hell,' she said, 'her waters have broken.'

Tia looked at her blankly.

Ellie asked her again, 'How often are the pains coming, Tia?'

'It doesn't matter now, Ellie, she's in labour,' Will said, his voice tight with anxiety. 'Ring an ambulance.'

They arrived almost thirty minutes later. Minutes where Ellie paced the floor as Will mopped Tia's brow. When they heard the sound of sirens in the distance, he looked at Ellie. 'You'd better go upstairs and out of the way.'

She stopped pacing. 'What?' she said, frowning.

'They can't see you,' he said, reaching a hand towards her to pull her close for a moment before, with sad eyes, he pushed her away. 'We can't risk it, Ellie. I'll go with her and ring you as soon as I have any news.'

Ellie said nothing. She wanted to wish Tia good luck, wanted to wish her well, but she couldn't. Instead, she nodded to Will and left the room, climbing the stairs with leaden feet to stand on the landing until the ambulance pulled up outside. Afraid they might glance upward and see her, she moved further back and finally, with a shake of her head, went into their bedroom.

Sitting on the bed, one hand gripped the other as she listened to the sounds that filtered up from below. She strained to hear what they said, wanting to know, to be a part of what-ever was happening but all she could hear were the deep calm voices of the two ambulance men and Tia's high-pitched cry followed each time by Will's anxious voice. But she couldn't make out what they said.

It didn't matter. None of the words were for her.

She lay on her bed, ignoring the tears that trickled sideways into her hair and imagined what was happening. The fuss over the pregnant Tia, the professional concern in the ambulance crew's eyes, the anxious look in Will's as he took everything in.

She laid her hand over her eyes, shutting out the light, listening as the voices became louder as they moved from the sitting room. She could hear the trundle of wheels on the wooden floor of the hallway and imagined Tia's swollen body lying on a gurney. She wondered if Will was holding her hand, staying in character. She knew how scared Tia would be, so she bit her lip and hoped he was. There was more noise, rattling and louder voices as they negotiated the steps from the front door and then the bang as the front door was shut. Triple-glazed windows meant she heard almost nothing from outside. She could have gone to the window and peered around the edges of the curtains like some sad peeping Tom, but she didn't, she lay and waited until she heard the muffled but distinct sound of an engine.

Finally, it was quiet. But only for a moment before Ellie's tears broke, loud and heart-rending to fill the house with sound once again. She curled on her side as she sobbed until the tears ran out and she was exhausted. It wouldn't be silent in this house again for a long time. Everything would change as the baby filled the house with cries, gurgles and laughter. She uncurled, lay back and stared at the ceiling. Will would have the baby he wanted.

She threw her arm over her eyes and, in the darkness, admitted what she'd been afraid to until now. *She* would have the baby she wanted, Will's baby. She couldn't have children of her own, wasn't this the next best thing? After all, Tia's DNA was as near to hers as was possible.

It was almost *their* child.

Tia would move to Brighton. They would bring the baby up as theirs. Nobody would ever know.

34

Ellie finally went to bed around midnight, only to toss and turn fitfully until morning. The phone didn't ring once and when she still hadn't heard anything by nine, she began to worry.

A mug of coffee in hand, she switched on the radio to listen to the news and try to drown out the voices in her head. There were no reports of major disasters, no earth-shattering events that could have prevented their arrival at the hospital. She sipped her drink. There could only be one reason she hadn't heard from them. Complications.

The mug crashed to the table with a bang, coffee shooting up to splash her jumper. What if Tia died? It happened. Their mother had died in childbirth, after all. A feeling of intense sorrow hit her. If Tia died, how would she feel? Bereft. The word came without hesitation. She'd always resented being a twin, but it was who she was. The thought made her shiver. If Tia died, she wasn't sure who she'd be.

She frowned. And the ramifications of her death? They'd be a nightmare. What would they do? They'd have to admit the truth and open the floodgates. It would be a catastrophe.

Her frown deepened. What if something were wrong with the baby? She held her hand over her mouth as the horror of that thought struck her. Their baby. Right at that moment, it didn't seem to matter whose baby it was. As long as the child was well. 'Please,' she muttered, feeling tears gather once more.

Letting them fall, she reached for a cloth, mopped the spilt coffee and dabbed at the stain on her jumper before throwing it into the sink. Tears were still falling when, at last, the phone rang. Wiping her eyes with the back of her hands, she let it ring three times before picking it up, steeling herself to hear bad news. 'Hello?'

'Ellie, it's me,' Will said.

He sounded exhausted. 'Is everything okay? I thought I'd have heard from you ages ago.'

'There were complications,' he said.

Ellie, despite preparing herself for the worst, gasped.

'It's okay,' he rushed out. 'They're both all right.' His voice was gentler when he continued. 'The baby is fine, and Tia will be when she's recovered. She was bleeding and they couldn't stop it. They had no choice but to do an emergency hysterectomy. But she'll be fine.'

Ellie couldn't find the words. Luckily, Will took her silence as shock and hurried to reassure her. 'The doctors say she'll be okay in a few days, Ellie, don't worry. They were able to do it non-invasively so there'll be no scars to heal. She'll be on her feet in no time.'

'That's good,' was all Ellie could manage, relieved when Will said he had to go. She put the phone down with a trembling hand. Her worries had been unfounded, they were both okay and she was pleased, of course, but she started laughing out of shock and at the utterly insane irony of it all, the laughter turning to tears and then back to laughter, the hysteria lasting for several minutes and leaving her weak.

Tia had had a hysterectomy – now they were more alike than ever.

Will arrived home three hours later. Ellie stood when she heard the door open and watched as he came through. He was pale, his eyes red and puffy, but he couldn't hide the smile that curved his lips. She ran to him, holding him tightly, burying her head in his shoulder, wanting reassurance. For what, she wasn't sure. 'How is she?' she asked, moving away but keeping her hands on his upper arms. Now that Tia was safe, now that she was sure she was okay, she needed the next part of their plan to fall into place.

He smiled. 'She's doing fine, don't worry. They say she can come home soon.'

'And the baby?' She couldn't hide the excitement in her voice. 'He is beautiful,' he said, grinning. His smile dimmed. 'The nurse asked her if she wanted to breastfeed. Tia said she did.' Ellie's eyes widened. Her grip on his arms tightened.

'It's okay,' he said, 'It didn't happen. Tia tried but the baby screamed blue murder and eventually the nurse took him away. They said she could try again later but I think the experience frightened her and she shook her head when they suggested it again. She's bottle-feeding him.'

Ellie couldn't hide her relief, but Will didn't seem to notice. 'She was managing the bottle-feed without any problems when I left. She's a bit weak after the operation, of course,' he said carefully. 'It's going to take her a while to get her strength back.'

'Of course.' Stepping back into his arms, she held him tight, feeling his arms snake around her with relief.

The worst was over.

35

Three days later, Tia and the baby came home. Will managed to get parking right outside the house, the car pulling up just as Ellie peered out the sitting room window to see if there was any sign of them. She watched as he jumped out of the car and rushed around to open the passenger seat, saw him bend to help Tia out, keeping an arm around her as she moved toward the gate. He left her holding onto it for support while he went back for the baby. He returned with the carrycot, holding it as if he'd been doing it for years. At the gate, he stopped beside Tia and, with a shared smile, both of them peered into the cot. Ellie, hidden behind the curtain, felt pain engulf her, unable to stop a cry of despair at being excluded from this emotional homecoming that should have been hers. It would never be hers. 'Never,' she muttered, gulping, her eyes fixed on her husband, her sister and their child.

They hadn't moved. Tia was saying something, she thought she could hear Will's gentle laugh in response. She wanted to look away, to move away, but she was rooted to the spot by jealousy, bitterness and a terrifying sense of fear. She reached out to grip the curtain, her knuckles white. They looked so damn good together. She took a deep breath and released it, letting go of the drapes and smoothing the creased curtain before stepping away, straightening her shoulders and taking another couple of deep breaths. She'd get through this. The firm belief that things would return to normal once Tia was gone was her mantra, the only thing that enabled her to get up in the morning. She refused to listen to the little voice that whispered, '*Things would never be the same again.*'

The click of the front door opening was loud in the uneasy silence of the house. As she stood, composing herself, Ellie heard the hallway filling with laughter and cooing and Will's deep voice. Such excitement. She'd never felt so lonely in her life.

She waited a moment, her hand resting on the door-knob before pulling it open with an inane grin on her face. 'Hello,' she said, moving forward to give her sister a hug, pulling back to look at her, noting the paleness of her face, the circles under her eyes. 'You must be exhausted.'

'She is,' Will said, 'we both are. A cup of tea would go down well.'

Ellie blinked. *We both are.* For a moment, she felt disorientated, confused, as if the world had changed and nobody had told her. She brushed the thought away. 'Yes, of course,' she managed. 'Let me see the baby first and I'll go and put the kettle on.'

'Of course,' he smiled, turning the carrycot in her direction. 'Isn't he just gorgeous,' he said, reaching down to touch one fat, round cheek.

The baby chose that moment to open his mouth and wail. For such a tiny scrap, the noise level in the hall was incredible.

Both parents smiled at the demonstration of their son's vocal strength. 'What a pair of lungs he has.' Will beamed.

Ellie looked down at the crying baby and thought she'd never seen anything so beautiful in her life. Then she saw Will's proud face and Tia's satisfied expression and felt a lump in her throat.

'He's just gorgeous,' she managed, before stepping back and adding, 'I'll go make that tea.'

Tia followed her into the kitchen, taking her seat on the sofa in the living room as if she'd never been away, her hand reaching automatically for the remote control. Moments later, the room was filled with noise as the TV blared and Will came through from the hallway, the wailing baby now in his arms. Hands trembling as she filled the kettle, Ellie tried to shut it all out.

She made tea, filling three mugs, adding sugar to Will's and extra milk to Tia's. The wailing had stopped and, with a sigh, Ellie picked up a mug and brought it across to Tia. 'Here you—' She stopped abruptly, her mouth dropping open, the mug tilting slightly so that hot tea slopped over the edge, burning her hand. And still she couldn't move, couldn't take her eyes from the sight of Tia with the baby in the crook of her arms, a bottle tilted to a mouth that guzzled as if he couldn't ever get enough.

'He was hungry,' Tia said, shifting herself slightly on the sofa. 'Yes,' Ellie said, unable to think of another word, unable to take her eyes away from the picture of maternal bliss. Finally, with a shake of her head, she put the tea down on a table within reach and turned away.

She took her tea to the sitting room hoping to find Will sitting there, needing some time with him, some reassurance in the face of all this change. The room was empty. She could go to look for him but, with a sigh, chose instead to sit, sip her tea and wait for him to come and find her.

He did come eventually, opening the door quietly, smiling when he saw her. He had the tea she'd made him in one hand, a piece of cake in the other, crumbs dropping to the floor.

She smiled at his untidiness. Not everything had changed.

He took it as a good sign and sat down beside her. Putting his tea down, he took her free hand in his. 'You okay?' he asked, looking at her with concern.

'Fine,' she said, squeezing his hand, feeling him squeeze back. For a moment it was like old times. Just for a moment. Then she heard it.

'Will, are you there?'

Instantly, he released his grip on her hand. 'I'll go see what she wants and be right back,' he said. But he wasn't. Ellie sat until the light began to fade before getting up. Dinner needed to be organised. She'd forgotten to take anything suitable from the freezer. It would be takeaway again. Running her hands though her hair, she felt a reluctance to go next door where she'd probably find Will sitting with Tia and the baby. She felt like an intruder in her own home, in her own marriage, in her own life. Could she survive this for much longer? She wasn't sure.

She braced herself and opened the kitchen door. Tia still sat reclined on the sofa while Will paced up and down, the baby lying across his shoulder, his big hand gently rubbing its back.

He saw her. 'Sorry,' he said, keeping his voice low, 'Poor little fella's got wind.'

Unable to stop herself, she lifted her hand and laid it on the baby's warm, downy head before meeting Will's eyes. 'He's so beautiful,' she said softly.

They stood a moment, the three of them, and Ellie felt a moment's peace before the mood was broken by Tia calling from the sofa. 'I'll take him now,' she said, and Will immediately took the baby to her and laid him in her arms.

Ellie bit her lip and moved back to the kitchen. 'I'm getting a takeaway for dinner,' she said, pulling open the drawer and taking out the well-used sheaf of menus. 'Anybody got a preference?' She shoved the drawer closed with her hip, the sound loud enough to startle the baby who immediately started to wail.

'Oh, for goodness' sake, Ellie,' Will snapped, 'look what you've done.'

Look what you've *done, mate*, she thought and then shook her head. 'I'll order Italian,' she said over the baby's cries, 'the usual unless anyone has any other preference.' She didn't wait for a reply and, taking the menu with her, she left the kitchen to make the call in the relative quiet of the hallway.

By the time it arrived, calm had been restored, and the baby was asleep in his cot. Ellie dished the food up onto warmed plates and brought them to the table. Opening a bottle of wine, she poured a large glass for herself and a smaller one for Will. She picked up her fork, pulled her face into a smile and looked at him as he took his seat. 'What are we going to call him?' she said, twirling spaghetti around her fork with practised ease. 'We can't keep calling him *the baby*, can we?'

Tia looked up from her carbonara. 'We don't call him *the baby*,' she said, 'we call him Bill.'

Pasta fell from the loaded fork that was just inches from Ellie's mouth. 'Bill?' She looked from one to the other, noticing the slight blush on Will's face and felt a rising tide of emotion cross her own. 'Ah.'

'We thought we'd stick to tradition. You know, calling the first son after his father,' said Will.

She closed her eyes for a second. Was he even aware what he'd just said? 'First son?' she said, raising her eyebrows.

Will put his knife and fork down. 'You know what I meant, Ellie.' He pushed his barely touched food away and stood, holding onto the back of his chair, looking down at her. 'It was just an expression,' he said, his voice gentler, 'you know, like from the Bible; the first-born son.'

She put the reloaded fork into her mouth and pulled it away clean, then stabbed it back into the plate of pasta and focused on twirling the spaghetti around the tines. She felt him move away, watching from the corner of her eye as he went to the cot and looked down at his child. Bill. She hated the name.

Lifting her fork again, Ellie caught and held Tia's gaze across the table. Her lips were pressed together, eyes hard. She looked annoyed, even a little angry. Putting her fork down, Ellie closed her eyes for a second before looking back at her sister, a question on her lips that died when she saw Tia wearing her usual expression. Nothing more.

She shook her head. The stress was getting to her. She toyed with the pasta for a few seconds and then pushed the plate away. Without a word, she picked up her glass and left the room.

In the sitting room, she didn't turn on the lights, the dark silence suiting her mood. She finished the wine, sat back and hoped Will would come to find her. She wasn't sure what she'd do if he didn't.

She was only waiting a few minutes before the door opened and he came in. 'You managed to drag yourself away, did you?' she said, her words sharp and cold to disguise the hurt in her eyes Instead of taking the chair opposite as she had expected, he sat beside her, put an arm around her shoulders and pulled her to him. She resisted briefly before relaxing against him with a tired sigh. 'What have we done?'

Perhaps he was happy to hear the *we* rather than *you*, because he said nothing for a moment. And then, she felt his lips brush her hair. 'I know this is hard, Ellie,' he said. 'It'll just be for another few months, honestly.'

I want it to be just you and me, the way it was. That's what she wanted to say. But what was the point? Things were never going to be as they were.

'A couple of months,' she conceded, 'no more than that.'

36

A couple of months. Will smiled in relief. By then, it would be easier. Tia would have completely recovered, and Ellie would have formed a bond with Bill. He'd seen how her eyes softened when she looked at him. It was only a matter of time.

He'd explain to Tia and she could move to the bungalow in Brighton; he'd tell her it was important that the baby stayed with him. She'd understand. And everything would return to a version of normal. He shut his eyes briefly. If he said it often enough, he might start to believe it was all going to be that easy.

'How about another glass of wine?' he said.

'Yes, please,' Ellie answered, pulling away from his embrace to allow him to get up.

He took her glass and went back to the kitchen. Tia was still sitting with her elbows on the table, chin resting in her cupped hands. She looked pale. 'You okay,' he asked, feeling guilty that he hadn't helped her back to the sofa. 'Let me give you a hand,' he said, putting an arm around her. 'You'll be more comfortable on the sofa, where you can put your feet up.'

She stopped at the cot where Bill was awake, lying quietly. 'He's so sweet, isn't he?'

Will smiled at her. 'Sweet,' he agreed. He felt her hand slip into his and, for a moment, he held it before guilt shot through him and he pulled away.

Tia didn't seem to notice, her attention now on her child. She bent and picked him up, supporting the head just like she'd been shown and holding him close to her as she shuffled the last couple of steps.

Will made sure everything she wanted was at hand before leaving her. 'You sure you're all right?'

'I'm a little tired,' she said, looking up from the baby.

He frowned. Maybe she should be in bed? 'Do you want me to help you up to bed?' he asked.

Tia shook her head. 'Not yet.'

A last look at Bill, nestling comfortably in her arms, and he turned away. If he wasn't careful, Ellie would arrive looking for the wine he'd promised her several minutes ago. He breathed a sigh of frustration. He wanted to be with her, he wanted to be with his child. There was no easy answer.

He took a bottle of wine from the fridge. 'Give a yell if you need anything,' he said to Tia before he left. At the door, he looked back; unusually she hadn't turned on the television, instead she was cooing softly down at the baby.

He gulped, opened the door and stepped into the hallway, staying there for a few minutes overwhelmed with regret. It should be Ellie cooing over their baby. This should be a happy time. Turning to the door he'd just shut, he reached for the knob to open it. He'd take his son from Tia and go to Ellie. The spurt of determination faded as quickly as it had come, and he released the knob and turned again to lean against the door.

Caught between the Devil and the deep blue sea, he thought, his eyes on the door to the sitting room.

When he went in, the bottle of wine in one hand, he saw the accusation in Ellie's eyes.

He'd forgotten her glass.

37

At first, Tia kept Bill in her bedroom, Will carrying the cot upstairs at night and down again in the morning, but after two nights of broken sleep Ellie was exhausted. 'How can something so small make so much noise,' she said, rubbing a hand over her face. 'Do you think maybe he could sleep downstairs?' she asked Will.

He nodded. 'It might be easier. Tia is finding the stairs a bit of a struggle anyway. I can bring a bed down for her.'

Tia, when she was asked, shrugged. 'That's okay, I can sleep on the sofa.'

Ellie shook her head. 'Bring the bed down, Will. She needs a proper night's sleep or she'll be too exhausted to take care of him.' She looked at her sister. 'You need some rest too, Tia.'

'We could put it in the sitting room,' Will suggested.

Ellie shook her head. She needed that room. 'It makes more sense to put it in the living room. Then Tia has easy access to the kitchen to heat bottles and stuff.'

While Will tackled the more difficult task of dismantling and moving the bed, Ellie reorganised the dining/living room to make space. She pushed the dining room table against the wall. That done, she moved the sofa and television down to free up the far end of the living room for the bed. It would fit neatly under the window.

Once the bed was in, Ellie narrowed her eyes, and directed Will to help her move a large bookshelf to screen off the bed.

'It will give it a bit of privacy,' she said, as they hauled the heavy piece of furniture across.

She viewed the final result with satisfaction. 'That's not bad, is it?' Tia came and sat on the corner of the bed. 'It's fine,' she said and then pointed to the foot of the bed. 'Bill's cot will fit there.' Ellie gauged the space. She was absolutely right; it would, just about.

'Where am I going to sit to watch the television?' Tia asked, her attention moving from the make-shift bedroom.

'Well, it's not finished yet.' Ellie said and then, with Will's help, she proceeded to push the furniture into place. It took a while to untangle the mess of electrical cables at the back of the television to allow them to move it down the room. A final push of the sofa, and it was done. 'There,' Ellie said finally, 'how's that?' Tia sat on the sofa and picked up the remote control. Only when the television screen lit up with one of the mindless programmes she liked to watch did she look up and say, 'This is good.'

The new arrangements suited very well. With the baby sleeping downstairs, Ellie and Will slept well and Tia didn't have to negotiate the stairs while she recuperated. She was, Ellie had to admit, very good with the baby. So good that it took her a few days to realise that any time she wanted to hold the baby, Tia would prevent her with some comment about Bill being cross, tired or hungry. Two days later, Ellie came into the kitchen to find Will holding the baby. 'He's so gorgeous,' she said to him with a smile, 'let me hold him?'

'I'm just going to feed him,' Tia said, coming into the room and immediately reaching for the baby. 'Maybe later?'

But later never did come.

* * *

Ellie had no intention of taking her full maternity leave and went back to work two weeks later. If eyebrows were raised, nobody commented, and she slotted back into her position as if she'd never been away. She showed photos of Bill on her phone to her colleagues when they asked, a genuine smile of pleasure on her face when they oohed and aahed and said how gorgeous he was. In that moment, Bill was hers and she relished it.

'That's the end of you working late,' one of them said with a smile that faded when Ellie snatched her phone out of his hand. 'I'll be putting just as much into my work as I ever did,' she said, determined to nip that attitude in the bud; she'd worked damn hard to get where she was. 'And if that means working late, then I'll be working late.' She was tempted to say that she had a very capable live-in nanny, but she didn't feel she owed him an explanation. Instead, she fixed him with a cold stare until he gave a weak smile and left.

Her female colleagues made no comments about her hours. She guessed those who had children didn't have to ask, they knew how difficult it was to juggle home and work commitments. She found them friendlier now than they'd ever been, as if by having a child she'd joined some exclusive club. To her surprise, she found she enjoyed it.

In the evenings, over dinner, Tia surprised them both by filling them in on how Bill had been during the day. If Ellie was surprised at how chatty her normally quiet sister had become, she had no illusions; the conversation was solely for Will's benefit. But she listened to the stories and borrowed the anecdotes to share in the office the next day, watching her colleagues smile, laugh or nod in understanding. 'He's so gorgeous,' one of the women said as Ellie showed her the most recent photo. 'He seems such a happy baby too, your nanny is obviously very good. You're very lucky.'

Ellie kept her smile in place with difficulty and took her phone back. 'Yes,' she said, 'I am.'

* * *

If, in the office, she was the lucky mother with the adorable baby and the wonderful childcare, at home the reality was different.

Tia continued to block every attempt Ellie made to care for the baby. Will didn't appear to notice and when she mentioned it, he put his arm around her, gave her a hug and told her she was being too sensitive. 'Give her time,' he said.

Ellie wanted to remind him about their plan. That time was a factor. She was also worried about how close Tia was to the baby. How would she feel when she was asked to leave without him? Ellie opened her mouth to say something, but the door opened and as Tia walked in with Bill in her arms, she felt Will's arms drop away. She stood and watched as he held his son's tiny hand and chatted to Tia, and she felt totally excluded. Will was always home before her now. She guessed he was making excuses to leave his office early and, now, whatever time she got in, he'd be holding Bill, with Tia hovering around, giving advice or sharing stories of what they'd done that day. She joined in, asking questions, genuinely interested in the baby but always feeling at the edge of the conversation with Tia addressing all comments to Will. Even when she answered Ellie's questions, it was to Will she spoke.

It made Ellie feel isolated. Invisible.

Just when she thought she couldn't take it any longer, she had a phone call from Brighton. After delay upon delay, the bungalow was finally ready. She almost cried with relief.

'I'd like to have it fully furnished so my relative can move in as soon as possible, can you handle that?' She was assured that could be done. For a fee, of course. 'Whatever it takes,' Ellie muttered when she hung up.

She'd promised Will that Tia could stay two months to recover from her operation. With the bungalow now ready, she began to count down the days. She also became more assertive when it came to spending time with Bill. Sneaking in to pick him up for a cuddle when Tia popped out of the room.

'I'll take him,' Tia said, returning to find Bill in Ellie's arms. 'I need to feed him.'

But Ellie had been watching. 'No,' she said firmly, holding him closer, 'he's not due a feed for another hour.'

She took a deep breath when she saw the look of annoyance on Tia's face. 'He's perfectly safe, you know,' she said gently, 'and I can feed him too. Give you a rest.'

Tia shook her head. 'I like to feed him.'

'Fine,' Ellie said, 'you do the next feed, and I'll do the one after. It's time you had a proper nap.'

A few hours later, she lifted her head when the door opened and Will walked into the room. She saw his eyes widen and slide between her, the bottle gripped tightly in her hand as Bill guzzled, and Tia who was sitting staring at them. She could see the doubt on his face and in his eyes before his face cleared. 'I don't usually see you feeding Bill, Ellie,' he said, coming over and dropping a kiss on her head before caressing his son's cheek.

'I've not been allowed up to now,' she said, looking up and holding his gaze, 'but it's time, I think.'

She saw by the look in his eyes that he knew what she meant.

It was time to start planning for Tia's departure.

'The first thing we need to do is to find an experienced nanny,' she said to Will the next morning as he finished getting ready for work, knotting the silk tie she'd bought him for his last birthday. 'We'll need to advertise. I think live-in for the first year or two, don't you?' She watched his hands freeze for a moment before he finished and turned to her. 'A nanny won't sleep in the living room,' he said. 'Bill will have to come back upstairs.'

Ellie frowned. She hadn't thought of that. 'He can stay downstairs, can't he? Don't they start to sleep through the night after a couple of months?'

Will had no idea, but he shook his head. 'I don't think they do until they're a few months old but, anyway, it will vary from child to child, I'm sure. Maybe we should let Tia stay for a few more months.'

Ellie chewed her lower lip. She couldn't afford to have sleepless nights; her job was stressful enough without adding that to it. Then she brightened. 'I know what we could do,' she said, 'we could make the sitting room into a bedroom.'

'And all of us sit on top of one another in the evening and at weekends. Absolutely not,' Will said. He could see by the look on her face that she agreed. 'We have two choices. We put up with sleepless nights until Bill starts to sleep through, or we let Tia stay with us until he does.'

Feeling cornered, Ellie turned away. 'Let's think about it for a while,' she said. When he'd gone, she took out her phone and did an internet search for information. She wanted to find out that all babies slept through the night from two months; unfortunately, that wasn't what she discovered. 'Nine months!' She pressed a few more keys and swore loudly. 'Twelve months?'

She sat on the bed reading the information before slamming the phone down on the bed beside her. Maybe they'd be one of the lucky few whose baby slept through from three months. She could cope for another month; after all, it wasn't as though she had much choice.

And it probably would have gone on like this, the decision being put off month after month, if she hadn't felt unwell a few weeks later. Reluctantly, she left work early and arrived home to find Will and Tia sitting on the rug in the sitting room, Bill on the floor between them chuckling as one and then the other tickled him.

Engrossed with the child, they hadn't heard her come in. She stood in the half-open doorway watching them. Watching Will. When had he last looked at her like that? Heartache twisted and squeezed her until she felt weak and dizzy. Grabbing onto the edge of the door she fell forward as the door swung open under her weight, falling to her knees, adding more pain to the gut-wrenching ache in her heart.

Will and Tia turned at the same moment. Will rushed to her side while Tia picked up the baby and held him close as if he was in danger.

'Ellie, are you okay?' Will asked, kneeling beside her and peering into her face, his creased with concern. 'What happened? How on earth did you fall?'

The laugh Ellie tried had a hint of hysteria around the edges. She tried again. Better. 'Just me being clumsy,' she said, accepting his helping hand and struggling to her feet. Her knee hurt, the wooden floor was unforgiving. 'I'm going to have a bruise there,' she added, pulling her hand from his and bending to rub her knee. She straightened and looked over his shoulder to where Tia still stood with the baby in her arms. As she watched, Tia placed a kiss on the child's head, and then held her lips to his ear and whispered words only he could hear.

Telling him secrets? Or telling him lies? Ellie felt her lips tremble.

'You're home early,' Will said, and sat down in the sofa to stare up at her. 'That's not like you.'

'I wasn't feeling very well. I think I've caught a bug,' she said, rubbing a hand across her forehead. 'I've a bit of a temperature.'

Will looked suddenly alarmed, his eyes darting from Ellie to his son. 'Mind Bill doesn't catch whatever it is,' he said.

A dart of annoyance swept through her. It went straight to her spinal cord and strengthened it. 'Thanks for your concern for me, Will,' she said, lifting her chin.

'Infection is more of a risk for him,' he said, pursing his lips.

'The great childcare expert,' she replied. She picked up her bag from the floor and turned to leave, adding with even heavier sarcasm, 'I'd better take myself off before I contaminate the room.'

In their bedroom, she stripped off her suit and put on a pair of cotton pyjamas. The image of the three of them on the floor came back. It would haunt her for a long time. In the bathroom, she opened the cabinet. She felt awful and her head ached. She rummaged among the bottles and packets. There was definitely paracetamol in the kitchen cupboard, but she wasn't going back down. 'Aha,' she said, finding a packet tucked at the back. They might have been there for years, but at this point she didn't care.

Popping two from the foil, she swallowed them, turned the tap on, and took a drink of water to wash them down.

She climbed onto the bed, lay back against the pillows, and, for several minutes, didn't move and barely blinked. Then, with a loud sigh, she closed her eyes. That look of love on his face. Was it just for Bill? Or was he falling in love with the mother of his child? He hadn't mentioned why he was home early. How often was he coming home and playing happy families?

They'd been rock-solid before Tia came along, before the baby came along. They could be again. She wanted Will, she wanted his son. Something had to be done.

An hour later, despite the ideas that were spinning around her head, the pain had gone. She still felt a little queasy, but there was no time to delay. She made a quick phone call to her office, explaining she was feeling much worse and wouldn't be in for a few days. The plan she'd come up with wouldn't take longer than that. A couple more phone calls and it was taking shape. She tossed her phone onto the bed beside her and lay back feeling the headache returning with a grunt of annoyance. She needed to be better in the morning. There was no putting it off any longer. Despite feeling poorly, she felt energised by action and when Will came up a couple of hours later to see if she wanted anything, he was surprised to find her almost cheerful. 'I'm sorry,' he said, responding to her uplifted hand, taking it and sitting beside her on the bed. 'I've become a bit obsessed with Bill, I know.'

'A bit,' she said, smiling to show him she was joking.

He laughed. 'Okay, a lot. It's just that I've wanted this for so long. You do understand, don't you?'

Instead of replying, she patted the bed covers. Will kicked

off his shoes and swung his legs onto the bed to snuggle up beside her. 'How are you feeling?' he asked, rubbing his hands up her leg and lingering on the inside of her thigh.

Ellie pushed his hand away. 'I'm feeling terrible,' she said, 'my head is thumping, and I feel sick.'

He rolled away and sat up. 'We haven't made love since we found out about the pregnancy. You're never going to forgive me, are you?'

She reached out and laid a hand on his back. 'I have forgiven you, Will. It's the forgetting I'm having a problem with.' She moved her hand gently up and down his back. 'Tomorrow,' she said. 'I promise.'

He leaned back and kissed her, his lips lingering. 'Tomorrow,' he said and stood up.

Ellie declined his offers of food or drink. 'I'll be fine,' she said, 'I've taken some pills.'

'I'll come back and check on you in a while,' he said. 'Try to close your eyes, get some rest.'

Ellie closed her eyes but when the bedroom door shut they flicked open. Her plan had to work, she thought. Her marriage depended on it.

38

Luckily, whatever bug she'd had was gone by the next morning and, as soon as Will left for work, she jumped up and got dressed. One of the previous day's phone calls had been to an agency. If they were as good as their word, the doorbell should be ringing in about fifteen minutes. When it rang dead on time, she decided it was a good omen.

The conservatively dressed, middle-aged woman who stood on the doorstep was the picture of reliability and competence. Just what she hoped for. 'Come in,' she said, with a relieved smile, 'I'm Ellie Armstrong.'

'Sally Watson,' the woman said, looking around the hallway appreciatively. 'This is nice.'

'Thank you.' Ellie opened the door into the sitting room. 'Please, take a seat in here for the moment. I've just a couple of things to do and then I'll bring you in and introduce you to the baby.'

She waited until the woman sat before closing the door and then stood listening at the kitchen door, trying to hear what Tia was doing. There was no sound from inside, so she went in. To her surprise, for a change, Tia wasn't lounging in front of the television, feeding the baby or holding him in her arms. The thought crossed her mind that she was much more tactile with him when Will was around.

Now, perched on a stool at the island, she was reading a newspaper and looking bored.

'Goodness,' Ellie said, moving into the room. 'I've never seen you reading the newspaper before. Are there no magazines?'

Tia looked up slowly and smiled. 'I'm just looking at the pictures,' she said, folding the paper and putting it behind her on the shelf.

Ellie frowned and then shook her head. What did it matter what she read? Pasting on a smile, she said, 'I've got a treat for you.'

Tia's face showed no interest.

'A treat,' Ellie said again, 'you know, a surprise.' This got a slight reaction but not what Ellie expected.

'Really?' Tia said.

Her tone told Ellie, as if she'd put it into words, she didn't believe her. 'Yes, really,' she said, trying to instil a measure of enthusiasm into her voice. 'I'm going to take you shopping for some new clothes.' This time there was a slight smile on Tia's face, so Ellie went a step further. 'I thought we could buy some nice things for the baby, too.'

The smile died. 'His name is Bill,' Tia said, her voice sharp, 'he's not *the baby*.'

Ellie blinked in surprise at the note of irritation in her sister's voice. She held her hands up. 'Sorry,' she said, 'yes, of course, you're right. We'll go and buy some nice things for Bill.'

'When he wakes up,' Tia said, looking over at the sleeping child in his cot.

'No need,' Ellie said, with false brightness she hoped Tia wouldn't notice, 'that's the rest of the surprise. I've hired a nanny to look after him while we're gone. You can't shop with a baby.' She smiled sympathetically. 'It wouldn't be fair on him, would it?'

A slight frown appeared between Tia's eyes and her lips tightened.

Ellie, who'd expected her sister to be easily persuaded to go shopping, was flummoxed. What could she say to make her go? 'If we're going to have Bill christened, we'll need to get him something nice to wear. Will said maybe a cute little sailor suit of some sort?'

Tia's face brightened. 'Will said that?'

Ellie bit her lip. If anything convinced her she was doing the right thing, this did; her sister's crush on Will was getting worse. But, if using his name succeeded in convincing her, she'd use it. She'd use whatever she needed to. 'Yes,' she lied, 'he's very excited about it.'

At last Tia nodded. 'Okay,' she said. But her face was still wary. Before she could change her mind, Ellie sent her upstairs to get a coat. 'You'd better say goodbye to Bill first, Tia. While you're getting ready, I'll bring the nanny through to explain about his feeds.' When she saw her hesitate, a frown appearing between her eyes, Ellie smiled sweetly. 'Unless you'd prefer to give her all the important instructions?' She laid heavy emphasis on *important,* watching as Tia's eyes flickered. 'About the feeds, the steriliser, the emergency phone numbers etc.'

As she guessed she would, Tia baulked at having to explain the details, especially to a stranger. 'You'd be better explaining,' she said, and moved to say goodbye to her child, cooing over the sleeping baby as Ellie watched with a twinge of guilt that she quickly brushed away. She could come and visit, or they could bring Bill down to see her. She'd be far better off in Brighton.

She clenched her fists. Far better. They'd all be far better. When, finally, Tia went to get a coat and bag, she brought Sally in and introduced her to the baby, pointing out the supplies and where the emergency phone numbers were. 'I should be back by around four, Sally,' she said, 'help yourself to whatever food you want.' She took a card from her bag and handed it to her. 'If, for any reason, you've concerns you can get me on this number. Okay?'

Sally took the card and put it into her trouser pocket. 'There should be no problems, Mrs Armstrong,' Sally said with a smile.

'Go and have a nice break. I've been doing this job a long time. There's nothing I can't handle.'

In the hallway, Ellie grabbed her coat and looked up the stairway. 'Tia,' she called, keeping her voice cheerful, 'come on, let's get shopping.' The footsteps on the stairs as Tia made her way down were slow and reluctant, but Ellie kept up a one-sided conversation about baby clothes as they walked the short distance to where the car was parked. When she pulled out into the traffic, she relaxed a little. They were off.

'There's a good shopping centre a few miles out of the city,' she said. 'We can park there and go straight to the shops.'

Tia stared out the window. 'You're sure that woman knows what to do?' she said eventually.

'Absolutely. She is one of the best. That's what the agency said. In high demand; we were lucky to get her. I only wanted the best.' That seemed to reassure Tia. Her face lost its pinched look and she looked a little more relaxed. Ellie kept up a stream of inconsequential chatter for the whole journey, surprising herself with the amount of stuff she knew about babies and baby clothes. Finally, after more than an hour, they arrived at the shopping centre. 'Here we are,' Ellie said, indicating and pulling into the queue of traffic that snaked into the underground car park. She had to drive around for a few minutes before finding a place to park, pulling in with a sigh of relief.

After an hour's shopping, she was carrying several bags filled with underwear, nightwear, jeans, jumpers and shoes. If Tia was surprised at the number of things she bought, she didn't comment, following her without a word.

'Okay,' Ellie said finally, 'that's us sorted. Now we'd better start looking for baby outfits.'

They walked around a couple of shops that were dedicated to baby clothes. Sailor suits, unfortunately, seemed to be out of fashion. Ellie watched as Tia's face dropped when the assistant in the second shop told them they hadn't stocked them for a long time.

'But I want one for Bill,' Tia said, her voice shrill. Ellie kicked herself for choosing something so specific.

She reached for a blue outfit. 'What about this?' she said. 'He'd look cute in this.' But even adding, 'I think Will would like it,' didn't work this time and she could see tears beginning to gather in the corners of Tia's eyes.

Looking around her in desperation, Ellie spotted a blue and white striped outfit in the corner of the shop. 'What about this,' she said, rushing over and grabbing it. 'This could almost be a sailor suit.'

Tia took it from her and rubbed the soft fabric gently between her thumb and forefinger, a smile slowly appearing on her face. 'Yes, this is nice,' she said.

Ellie raised her eyes to heaven and muttered, 'Thank you, God.' The assistant bagged the item, she handed over her credit card to pay for it and, within minutes, they were heading back to the car. She threw all their purchases into the boot and slammed it shut. Starting the engine, she smiled across at her sister. 'That was a good morning's shopping,' she said. 'Now you can sit back and relax.'

There was another hour's drive before they reached Brighton.

39

To Ellie's relief, ten minutes into the drive, Tia fell asleep.

Taking a deep breath, she let it out slowly and felt her shoulders relax. The agency had said Sally could stay with them until they managed to find a suitable, permanent, live-in nanny. Ellie hoped it wouldn't take long; Sally, with all her years of experience, was astronomically expensive.

Switching the radio on to a classical radio station, she went over what she'd say to Will. He'd be annoyed, maybe even furious, but faced with a fait accompli there wasn't much he could do, was there? Sally would take good care of the baby and things could return to normal. She frowned. Well, perhaps as near to normal as was possible.

She was more worried about Will's reaction than she was willing to admit. What could he do? Drive down and bring Tia back? If there was a small part of her that worried he might do just that, she ignored it. She had to, because she just didn't know how their marriage would survive if he chose Tia over her. He loved her, she loved him, that had to be enough.

They were fifteen minutes' drive from Brighton when Tia

woke up. She looked around, then looked at the dashboard clock, her face registering some confusion.

'Are we nearly home?' she asked, stretching and looking across to Ellie.

'Nearly.' The residential home, just outside Brighton, was approached down a series of twisty country roads. She indicated and turned off the main road, ignoring Tia who was twisting in her seat to look out the rear-view window.

'This doesn't look like it's nearly home,' she said, a note of rising panic in her voice. 'It looks like the roads around St Germaine's.' Ellie had never considered the comparison and refused to do so now. It wasn't the same. Here Tia would have a certain amount of independence, maybe even a job. And it was a new build, there'd be no damp, no peeling wallpaper and she imagined there wouldn't be the pervasive smell of cabbage. It would be a little bungalow of her own. A better life than she had before. She shook her head, she didn't have to convince herself – she knew it was the best thing for all of them. It was Tia she had to convince, and it was time to tell her the truth. 'No, it's near Brighton, Tia. It's another surprise. We've bought you a place of your own,' she said, throwing her a swift look. 'Your own home. You can buy nice things for it. Move furniture around if you want to, have friends around.'

When there was no word from her, she continued. 'Married people need to have their home just for themselves, Tia. That's Will and me, you understand. You can still come and visit, of course, and we'll come and visit you, but you won't live with us any more. We'll look after Bill too so you can enjoy yourself and not have to worry about him.' As there was still no response from her, Ellie gave her a quick glance, but Tia had her head turned away. 'It will be better for him to stay with us, and I know you want what's best for him.'

The narrow, winding road needed her concentration, so it was a few minutes before she chanced a look in her sister's direction but when she did what she saw shocked her.

Tia was staring at her, looking furious, eyes narrow and hard, her mouth, usually curved in a smile, downturned and pursed. 'You think you're going to keep Bill?'

'He'll be better off with two parents to look after him and Will is a great father. We're going to keep the nanny until we find someone more permanent to look after him.'

'I can look after him,' Tia said, her voice growing harsh. 'I love him. He's mine.'

'It's just not working with us all together.' Ellie tried to keep her voice calm. 'Will and I want to get back to the way things used to be.'

There was a moment's silence. 'The way things used to be. Before me?'

'Yes,' Ellie said and threw her a grateful smile. Maybe she did understand.

'And before Bill?'

Ellie's grip on the steering wheel tightened. 'Bill is different,' she said, her eyes flicking to the satnav. Ten more minutes.

'Because Bill is Will's baby, and he loves him?'

Ellie nodded, almost reluctantly. Where was she going with this?

'Me and Will, we both love him.' Tia twisted in her seat to look across at Ellie. 'Maybe you should be the one to move out.'

Startled, Ellie looked at her. 'Will is my husband,' she said, but even to her own ears the argument didn't hold much weight.

A husband who'd fathered a child with her sister. Her identical twin sister, her mirror image.

'But Bill is not your child, Ellie,' Tia said.

Ellie blinked. She didn't think she'd ever heard Tia say her name before. It was a shocking realisation, almost as shocking as the realisation that she had seriously underestimated her sister. But she wasn't giving up.

'You don't understand, Tia,' she said, hearing the pleading note in her voice. A raucous laugh made her turn her head, her eyes wide.

'I understand,' Tia said. 'What *you* don't understand is that I am never going to give up my baby. Take me home.'

Ellie shook her head. 'I can't do that, I'm afraid.'

Both sisters glared at one another for a moment. Then, without warning, Tia reached for the steering wheel with both hands. 'Turn around, I want to go home,' she said, pulling on it hard.

'Don't be stupid, let go.' Ellie tried to push her away, to prise her fingers off the wheel as she desperately tried to keep control of the car.

'Take me home!' Tia shouted, and continued to struggle.

With a last, desperate attempt to push her away, Ellie turned toward her and hit out with a clenched fist, feeling it connect hard with her neck. Tia, stunned by the blow, held onto the wheel for another moment before, suddenly, collapsing back in her seat. Horrified at what she'd done, Ellie was taken by surprise and was unprepared for the wheel to suddenly become free. Frantically, she tried to compensate but it was too late. The car veered to the right, crossing the other lane. Going way too fast. Her foot, on the brake, went to the floor. There was a screeching sound of rubber, but it was all too late and the car swerved into the ditch at the side of the road.

It should have been a soft landing, the ditch wide and lined with nettles, ivy and a mass of weeds, but a tree, brought down by storms months before, lay across it, hard and unyielding.

The car hit it at speed, somersaulted over it and tumbled down the slope behind to the sound of cracking branches and groaning, shrieking metal.

It slammed to a halt on its side against a tree and there was silence.

* * *

Ellie's eyes fluttered and then opened. She'd no idea how long she'd been unconscious. Pressed tightly against the door, she blinked and tried to clear her vision to look around, but there was something in her eyes. She raised her hand carefully to wipe them and blinking rapidly finished the job. She could see, and what she saw terrified her.

Her fingers were covered in blood and there were jagged pieces of glass embedded in her left arm, blood trickling from the multiple lacerations. To her right, it was dark and it took her a few seconds to understand why. The car had landed on its side, smashing the side window. That's where the glass had come from. But the blood was trickling, not pumping she realised. She wasn't going to bleed to death.

With the car on its side, Tia should be above her. 'Tia,' she called but her voice came out a weak whisper. She tried to turn her head to look up, the movement causing her to groan in pain. Taking a shallow breath, she attempted instead to move her position in the seat but the effort made her black out for a time. When she came to, she tried again. The pain was intense. She wasn't sure what she'd broken but she guessed her right arm and, since breathing was painful, probably some ribs. Moving slowly, crying out in pain, she used the seat belt to pull herself around, inch by agonising inch, until finally she managed to see her sister.

Tia's body was slumped in the seat above her, the seat belt preventing her from falling down. She took the deepest breath she could manage and called, 'Tia.' But her voice cracked barely above a whisper. She tried again. 'Tia, are you okay? Can you move?' There was no answer, no movement. Ellie caught the smell of petrol in the air and felt panic rising. She'd seen enough movies, she knew what could happen. They needed to get out of the car.

She was about to call her sister again when she noticed a slight movement of her hand. 'Tia? Tia, we need to get out of the car. Can you hear me?'

It was a few seconds before she heard a reply, the first an inaudible mumble, the second a slightly louder, 'Yes.'

Ellie closed her eyes briefly. *Thank God*. It wasn't going to be easy to get out. If Tia undid her seat belt and fell on top of her, they'd both be stuck.

'Okay,' she said, 'we need to get out of the car. You're going to need to push the door open first. Can you do that?' There was silence and no movement. Ellie felt tears sting her eyes. She took another deep breath, ignoring the sharp pain, and called out, louder. 'Tia, I need you to open the door and push it back so that it stays open.'

Once again, there was no answer but then, just as Ellie was about to call again, she heard a grunt and the sound of the door handle being tried.

'It's stuck,' Tia said.

Ellie felt her eyelids droop again. She had to stay conscious. If they were going to make it out alive, it was up to her. She took another wheezing breath and, as calmly as possible, said, 'You have to try again, Tia. We must get out. Will would want you to try, and Bill needs you.' If that didn't work, she didn't know what would. There was no way she'd be able to climb over her.

Twisting again, feeling a grating in her side as splintered ribs shifted, she put as much force into her voice as possible. 'Tia, push the door open.'

To her relief, it seemed to work. She watched her twist and push at the door. It opened but the angle was difficult, and it fell back. 'Harder,' Ellie encouraged, 'push the door back, hard as you can.'

Finally, Tia pushed and the door swung back. This time it stayed open.

'Well done. Now, this is going to be tough, but you can do it. Wedge your feet onto something, hold on tight to the edge of the door with one hand and gently undo your seat belt with the other. You have to be very careful, or you'll fall down here on top of me, okay?'

She braced herself when she heard the seat belt being released, relaxing a little when Tia didn't fall down immediately.

But it could happen yet. She needed to pull herself up and get out.

'My arm hurts,' Tia said.

Ellie wanted to close her eyes, to get away from the excruciating pain that seemed to be in every part of her. But if she did, they were lost. 'Bring your legs up, Tia,' she said. 'That's right. Use them to push yourself up.'

Tia hesitated, then did as she was told, reaching for the opening with one hand, her feet using the seat as leverage. She was almost up, when she slipped.

One foot hit Ellie hard on her left side; there was a loud crack in her ribs followed by an intense pain that made her scream before everything faded to black.

When she woke once more, disorientated and confused, pain hit her again and made her cry out. It took a few seconds before she remembered what had happened. She bit her lip against the pain and looked up to the passenger seat. Tia was gone.

Her hand felt for the seat belt. She struggled to open it, her hands slippery with blood. Stopping, she took a breath, wiped her hand on her shirt and tried again. This time, she managed it, feeling the belt open and slipping it from over her shoulder. Without its support, she slumped heavily against the door, crying out again.

It took several minutes before she could twist around and make the attempt to climb out. The distance to the opening seemed enormous. Gulping, she brought her legs up and reached for the passenger seat to pull herself up. Was Tia okay? She called her name, but her voice didn't carry beyond the confines of the car. With broken ribs on both sides, and one arm almost unusable, every movement was painful and the going slow. There was no sound apart from her own grunts and whimpers. She'd no breath to spare to call out again for Tia.

Finally, she managed to get a foot on the edge of the passenger seat and push herself up through the opening, crying out as she knocked against the side, feeling bones shift and scrape before collapsing onto the side of the car.

She lay for a moment while another wave of pain gripped her, biting her lip and taking shallow breaths through her nose. It was the strong smell of petrol that made her move again.

Ignoring the pain, she raised her head to look for Tia and saw her lying a few feet from the car. She wasn't moving. 'Tia,' she cried out. There was no response.

Gritting her teeth, she pushed herself up, swung around and let her legs dangle over the side of the car. It probably wasn't more than four feet, but that was a long way to drop with broken bones. Rolling onto her belly, she used her good arm to push herself down, holding on for as long as possible before making that final drop. She tried to stay on her feet but they wouldn't hold her, and she slipped, falling backward to the ground, her shoulder hitting a rock as she landed. She rolled away with a groan and lay face down, the clean smell of pine needles replacing the stink of petrol. She could have stayed there, her head cushioned on the layer of pine, could have closed her eyes and just let go. It would be good to be away from the pain. Her eyes flickered and closed for a moment before sanity kicked in. She had to move away from the car.

Unable to stand, she crawled, one painful inch at a time through the layer of leaf mould, banging knees and elbows off hidden rocks. Woodlice and ants scattered out of her way as she dragged herself to where Tia lay, unmoving.

The last year vanished. This was her twin. She was supposed to be looking out for her. Her father would be disappointed in her again. Will would be disappointed. She'd failed everyone.

'Tia,' she rasped. Reaching her sister, she put a hand on her leg and shook it. There was no sign of life. With a cry of despair, she crawled further until she was eye-level with her face. All she could see was blood. She reached out bloody, muddy fingers and touched her gently. 'Tia, please, wake up.' She couldn't see whether she was breathing or not. Moving closer, she gave her cold cheek a gentle kiss. 'Tia,' she begged, 'you have to be okay. Think of Will, think of Bill. I'm sorry I tried to make you leave, you can stay with us. Of course, you can stay with us. Tia?'

There was no sign that Tia heard, no movement. Ellie, tears streaming down her face, lay beside her and, finally, gave into the pain that rushed in, wave after wave.

40

Will was in the middle of a Skype meeting with colleagues in Edinburgh when his office door opened suddenly. He looked up from the screen with a frown. His secretary, Maisie, knew not to interrupt. Opening his mouth to ask what was going on, he shut it when he saw her unnaturally pale face and felt blood drain from his own when he saw the two uniformed police officers behind her.

'I'll have to get back to you,' he told his colleagues, shutting the programme down without further explanation and standing to face whatever it was that was coming. 'Ellie,' he whispered, watching as Maisie stepped back to allow the police to enter the office. She shot him a sympathetic look before closing the door.

He saw the look in their eyes and sat heavily. 'Ellie,' he said louder, an edge of despair in his voice.

PC Norman, grey eyes in a grimly serious face, stepped forward and introduced herself and her colleague, PC Woods, before taking a step closer. 'There's been an accident, Mr Armstrong. Mrs Armstrong has been injured. She's in hospital.'

Will felt a wave of relief sweep over him. Ellie was alive. 'There was another woman in the car,' the officer said. 'We believe her name was Tia Bradshaw. Do you know this woman?' Will nodded.

'She's my sister-in-law, my wife's sister. Her twin, actually.' He looked at them, frowning, his face pale. 'They were in the car together?'

PC Norman nodded. 'A few miles from Brighton.'

Will, looking a little grey, blinked. 'Brighton? I don't understand.' He ran a hand over his face. 'Is she okay?'

'I'm sorry to have to tell you,' PC Norman began, starting with the same words she always used in these situations, 'that Ms Bradshaw sustained a severe head injury and didn't survive the crash.'

'Tia's dead?' Will's face paled. He gulped, stood up and then immediately sat back down again, his eyes wide. 'Bill? Oh God, my son, Bill? Is he all right?'

PC Wood quickly held up his hand. 'Your son wasn't in the car, Mr Armstrong. He's with the nanny.' Noting his blank face, he added. 'Sally Watson.'

Will shook his head. 'I've never heard of her, there must be some mistake.'

PC Wood looked to his partner, a slight shrug of his shoulder telling her he was out of his depth here.

Narrowing her eyes, she took out her notebook. 'Your car registration, Mr Armstrong, what is it?'

Will reeled it off. 'It's Ellie's car,' he said, 'not mine. We only had the one car, there didn't seem to be much point having two in London, we use the tube for work and a taxi if we're going out...' He stopped abruptly. He was babbling.

'That's the registration of the car involved in the crash, Mr Armstrong. Your wife regained consciousness for a brief time and identified herself. There is no doubt we have the right person. We called to your house first and met Ms Watson, she gave us your details. Perhaps your wife organised a temporary nanny at the last minute?'

Perhaps. It still sounded a bit odd but there were more important things to worry about. 'What hospital is she in?'

'The RHB,' PC Woods told him and then gave a shake of his head. 'Sorry, the Royal Hospital, Brighton.'

Will nodded and stood. 'I have to get there.' He looked at them and then gave a rueful smile. 'I don't know what to do.'

The police officers took this in their stride. 'Leave it to us,' PC Norman said. 'We'll organise a car to take you there and contact the nanny to ensure your son is cared for. She said she worked for an agency so there should be no problem.'

Will nodded, relieved to be able to leave everything in their hands. His head was muddled. Ellie injured, Tia dead. None of it made sense.

He remained in the same daze during the drive to the hospital, the driver taking one look at his face and keeping his mouth shut throughout the journey. Parking outside the main entrance of the hospital, the police driver turned to look at his passenger. If he'd been pale when he picked him up, he looked paler now. 'You going to manage?'

'I'll be fine, thank you,' Will said and pushed open the door and got out.

It was dark, and the lights of the hospital were glaring. He blinked away a tear and took the first step slowly, then the second, concentrating on each one, afraid that if he didn't, he'd stop and not be able to move again. The doors opened automatically, and he moved inside the huge reception area, his eyes darting around for something familiar. But there was nothing.

He didn't know how long he stood there, people milling about ignoring him, everyone focused on their own problems, nor did he know how much longer he would have stood if he hadn't felt a hand on his arm.

He turned to see the driver. 'I couldn't leave you,' the man said. 'Come on, let's see where you need to go.'

Will allowed himself to be led toward the reception desk where there was a short queue.

'Wait here,' the driver said and, courtesy of his uniform, dealt with the short queue by skipping it, taking only a few minutes to find out where Ellie Armstrong was.

Returning to Will's side, he told him, 'She's in the intensive care unit.'

Will felt his legs weaken.

'Come on, mate,' the man said kindly, 'I'll take you up.'

In a daze, Will followed, getting a measure of reassurance from the firm hand on his arm. At the door to the ICU, a sign advised them to ring the bell and wait. The driver pressed the bell and stood silently at his side.

'I have to go now,' the driver said, when a nurse finally appeared. 'Will you be okay, Mr Armstrong?'

Will, feeling a moment's panic, wanted to beg him to stay. He took a steadying breath. 'Yes,' he said, gratefully, 'and thank you, you've been extraordinarily kind.'

The driver nodded and turned to the nurse, 'Look after him, will you? He's pretty shook up.'

The nurse glanced at Will and then looked back at the driver and gave a quick, sympathetic smile. 'They always are,' she said. 'Don't worry, we'll take care of him.'

Will watched the driver go and then felt the nurse's hand on his arm.

'Follow me, Mr Armstrong,' she said, leading him a short way down the corridor and stopping outside a door.

Will, who was beginning to feel as if he were caught in a dream sequence where he was led from place to place by a succession of people, felt a moment's panic when she opened the door.

Panic, and a deep sense of dread as the horrific truth started to sink in. Ellie was injured. Tia was dead.

41

The reality behind the door, however, was a large waiting room where grouped seating and large, obviously artificial, plants didn't take away the feeling that it was a place of sadness and despair. Will let the breath he'd been holding out in a hiss that was loud enough to draw a startled look from the nurse who still held his arm.

Taking her hand away, she indicated a chair. 'Take a seat, Mr Armstrong,' she told him, her voice gentle. 'I'll go and get one of the nurses who is looking after your wife to come and speak to you, okay?'

It wasn't a question, Will guessed, as she left, disappearing back through the same door. He turned and sat, ignoring the grim, grey faces that occupied some of the other chairs.

It was ten minutes before the door opened and a scrub-suited woman came in, a frown on her face, a clipboard in her hand. 'Mr Armstrong?' she asked, looking around.

Will hesitated and put up his hand. It seemed the easiest thing to do.

'There's a room where we can chat,' the woman said, indicating a door to one side.

Will didn't want to chat, he wanted to see Ellie. But he stood and followed the woman's back as he was told. For a gut-wrenching second, he thought of Tia. She'd have done the same, followed without question. She always did.

The room he was taken to was small and functional. One large table stood in the centre, surrounded by several uncomfortable-looking chairs. It wasn't a place to stay for long. It was a place to hear bad news. Will sat, his face in his hands. 'She's dead, isn't she?'

The nurse sat beside him and put an arm around his shoulder briefly. 'No, she isn't, I promise you. She's badly hurt but she's doing okay.' She took her arm away and sat back. 'My name is Casey Jarvis, I'm the lead nurse looking after your wife.'

Will took a deep breath and looked at her. 'How badly hurt is she?'

'She has multiple lacerations from the glass, a couple of which needed sutures. The seat belt probably saved her life but it also broke her clavicle and some ribs, one of these perforated a lung and another nicked her heart.'

'Nicked?' Will asked, his eyes wide as he tried to absorb everything. 'How seriously?'

The nurse smiled reassuringly. 'The cardiology team have already been, they don't seem too concerned but we'll be monitoring it, of course. The most serious of her obvious injuries was the perforated lung, the thoracic team have inserted a chest drain which will remain in situ for a few days. There's also a simple fracture of her left arm and a badly sprained right ankle, neither of which are causing any serious problem.'

Will frowned. He latched onto one word that puzzled him. 'You said *obvious* injuries, what do you mean?'

She put down the clipboard. 'Your wife regained consciousness briefly at the crash site while the paramedic was with her but has been unconscious since. She's breathing independently, a good indicator that there's nothing too seriously wrong, but she was badly shaken. Until she wakes up, we don't know if there's some damage.'

'You mean brain damage?' Will said, appalled.

The nurse's face gave nothing away. 'We don't know,' she admitted. 'If she doesn't regain consciousness by tomorrow, they'll do an MRI scan. It may just be her body's way of dealing with the shock.' She looked down at her clipboard briefly. When she looked up again, her eyes were softer. 'I had a call from the police a short while ago, they informed me that the woman who was killed in the crash was your wife's sister. Her twin. It may be that, on some level, she is aware of her death.'

Of course. The link was there, even if Ellie so often wished it weren't. He nodded. 'It's possible.'

The nurse smiled at him as if he'd given the right reply. He wanted to scream at her but instead he smiled back dutifully before asking, 'Can I see her?'

She nodded and stood. 'Don't be frightened by all the tubes and monitors,' she said, moving to open the door, 'we're keeping a close eye on her.'

Going through the heavy doors into the intensive care unit was like entering a different world. Nothing could have prepared him for the array of equipment or for the number of people who hovered around every bed, their faces creased in concern, hands everywhere, adjusting, checking, scribbling notes on clipboards. And everything was done to a symphony of beeps.

He followed the nurse to the end of a bed where she stopped and hung the clipboard she carried. 'Here we are,' she said.

Here we are? Will looked at the person in the bed, and his mouth fell open. This couldn't be his wife, couldn't possibly be his Ellie.

Approaching the head of the bed, he tried to see his wife through the bruises, the multiple cuts and the many tubes that snaked around her. He wanted to hold her hand but didn't dare disturb the drip line in one, and there was a plaster cast on the other. He wanted to pull her into his arms and hold her tight, but he couldn't. All he could do was stand and stare.

'There's a chair,' said the nurse, pointing to one as if he wouldn't recognise it, 'you can pull it up and sit beside her. We'll tell you if you're in the way.'

'Thank you,' he managed, with a brief smile in her direction which she took as her cue to leave. He perched uncomfortably on the edge of the chair trying to think of the right thing to do, left alone with his battered wife and her attendant technology.

'Oh God, Ellie,' he said, reaching for the only part of her that wasn't either broken and bruised or attached to something, his fingers stroking her elbow, reassured somewhat by the feel of warm flesh. 'You have to pull through, you can't leave me.'

Alone with his thoughts and the steady beep-beep of the monitors, it didn't take him long to figure out why they'd been on the road to Brighton, and why there was a strange woman looking after his child. He knew his wife too well to be in any doubt. She'd organised the nanny and somehow persuaded Tia to go for a drive, a long drive, all the way to that damn bungalow.

'Did you really think you could just leave her there,' he

muttered, 'that Tia would stay there without Bill.' He leaned closer, his eyes filling with tears. 'I could have told you it was a waste of time, Ellie. But you didn't ask me, did you?' His fingers moved back over her elbow, the contact small but reassuring. 'And now look at the mess we're in.'

He stayed sitting beside her, leaving reluctantly when the nursing staff insisted and then he paced the reception until given the signal to return. By early morning, his skin was an unhealthy ashen colour and when he'd nodded off for the third time, he knew he had to find somewhere to sleep. The nurse on duty took his mobile number and promised, more than once, to ring him if there was any change.

'Of course,' she said, 'now go and get some sleep. You must look after yourself, she's going to need you.'

There was nowhere for him in the hospital, the only family beds available reserved for the parents of children, so he was directed to a nearby hotel where he was able to check in immediately.

Opening the bedroom door, he moved to the bed, lay down fully clothed and was asleep within seconds.

He slept deeply until noise in the corridor woke him and then he lay unmoving for a moment in the hope that it had all been a horrifically bad dream. But, of course, it wasn't. Tia *was* dead. Ellie unconscious. He checked his watch, midday. He needed to ring home and find out how Bill was and, more importantly, who on earth was caring for him.

Sally Watson answered the phone on the second ring and immediately put his mind to rest. 'These are unusual circumstances, Mr Armstrong. I'm happy to remain looking after your son until everything has been sorted. I'm aware you've not met me but if you'd like to ring the agency, I'm certain they'll put your mind at ease. I'm very experienced.'

'No, no,' he hurried to reassure her, 'I'm sure my wife employed the best. I'll keep you informed and let you know what's happening as soon as I know.' He hung up with a sigh of relief. She seemed competent. He hoped she was. A couple of days, he'd told her. It was a polite lie; he'd no idea how long they'd be there. He called the office and told the same lie. Deaf to their sympathy, he finished the call as soon as possible.

He slipped his jacket on and headed back to the hospital. The heavy door into ICU didn't open at a push and he stood back puzzled until he noticed a key pad on the wall to his right. A politely phrased sign beside it advising visitors to ring the bell ONCE and wait.

The nurse who came out to him asked his name and vanished.

She returned in a minute, an apologetic look on her face.

'Mrs Armstrong's condition is unchanged,' she told him. 'Unfortunately, you can't come in just now, the staff are doing personal care. It will be another ten or fifteen minutes before they finish.' Seeing his bloodshot eyes and ashen skin, she pointed down the corridor. 'Why don't you get something to eat, the canteen is nearby.'

He thanked her and did as she suggested, following the corridor back to a large, busy restaurant. He bought a few things, sudden hunger spurring him on, and took his laden tray to a window table where he sat with a sigh. The lasagne he'd chosen looked appetising and he picked up the knife and fork, dropping them quickly when a wave of nausea swept over him. Pushing the tray away, he rested his head in his hands and took deep breaths, letting them out slowly. He sat back and used a paper serviette to wipe the perspiration from his brow before reaching for the tea with a trembling hand and taking a sip. A few sips later, he felt a little calmer and pulled the tray back.

The lasagne now looked cold and unappealing, the muffin he'd bought not looking much better. He was debating going back for something else when two men appeared at his side.

'Mr Armstrong,' one said. 'May we join you?'

Will looked up at them. Not doctors, he guessed. 'Sure,' he said.

The men sat, the older of the two reaching into his pocket for a card that he slid across the table as he introduced himself and his partner. 'You have our sincere condolences on the death of your sister-in-law, Mr Armstrong,' he said.

'Thank you,' Will said, wondering how often he'd have to hear those words before the reality sank in. *Tia was dead.* Feeling tears prickle, he dropped his eyes and picked up the card, trying to concentrate on the words written on it. *Detective Inspector Walker, Brighton Constabulary.* 'You're investigating the crash?' he asked, breaking the silence.

'In a sense,' the detective inspector answered. 'We're investigating Tia Bradshaw's death.'

Will bit his lip. *Tia is dead.* 'It's hard to believe she's gone.' He drew a shuddering breath and let it out before meeting the inspector's rather pale blue eyes. 'What can I do for you?'

'We need someone to identify Tia's body, Mr Armstrong. I know it's difficult with your wife being in ICU, but it does need to be done so that the investigation can progress.'

'Of course,' Will said. 'I understand.' It was a lie, he didn't understand anything. But he didn't know what else he was supposed to do except follow instructions.

He was about to ask when they wanted him to do the identification when they stood and waited for him to follow. Now, he guessed, getting up and falling into step between the two men, dwarfed by their six-foot-plus height, feeling both intimidated and anxious. They didn't speak to him as they made their way along long hospital corridors, down three flights of stairs to the basement level, and in through a door marked *Mortuary*.

'If you would just wait here for a minute,' Walker said, opening the door and vanishing inside.

Tia is dead. Will wanted to scream, but he didn't. He bit his lip, feeling his eyes water, praying he wouldn't cry and then, realising tears were already rolling down his cheeks, he gave in to them.

Walker returned a few minutes later. He saw the tears and frowned. 'You sure you're all right to do this?' he asked in genuine sympathy.

Will dried his face on the back of his sleeve and nodded. Without another word, he followed the detective down a small corridor to a window where, on the far side, he could see a small, coldly clinical room and a table holding a sheet-covered body.

Tia's body.

He recognised the tiny part of himself that still hoped it was all a big mistake. That they'd pull the sheet back and he'd look at Walker in confusion and say he didn't recognise the woman. He wanted that bad TV script, the one where Tia would run in saying it was all a mistake, a dream, a nightmare, any bloody thing, just not this awful truth.

An attendant in scrubs entered the room and stood respectfully by the body. Will ran the tip of his tongue over dry lips and clasped his hands together, forcing his eyes to stay focused on the sheeted figure.

With a nod from Walker, the attendant grasped the corners of the sheet and, with a deliberateness that caused Will to clench his fists and his teeth, slid the sheet down to her shoulders.

Will's gasp was automatic and loud, drawing Walker's attention. His first thought was that they *had* made a mistake, a terrible one. It wasn't Tia on the table, it was Ellie, her hair pulled back from her face, desperate to distinguish herself from her twin. His second thought was that Ellie would be furious that he'd mixed them up again. Because of course it *was* Tia, her hair tucked under a white disposable mop-cap. Of course, it was Tia.

'Is that Tia Bradshaw?' Walker asked after a minute. Will nodded.

'She and your wife were twins? Were they alike?'

'Yes, identical twins,' Will gulped. 'But you could tell them apart if you knew them.' *Unless you were drunk.* He caught a strange look from the detective and wondered if he'd said the words aloud.

Will nodded, took a final look at Tia and turned away. 'Do I need to sign something?'

'Yes, please, if you would,' the detective said politely and led him into a small office.

'What happens now?' Will asked, placing the pen he'd used back on the table.

'There'll be a post mortem and a coroner's inquest. The crash investigator has already given his findings. There appeared to be no obvious reason why the car went off the road, you know. Your wife's phone was checked, she wasn't using it at the time. The likelihood is a rabbit or deer jumped out and startled her. It's more common than you think.' He shook his head. 'They were unfortunate, if it hadn't been for that felled tree they probably would have stopped in the ditch with only minor injuries, but that tumble down the valley was a bad one.'

Will closed his eyes, imagining the horror. He didn't want to know the details, but he needed to. 'Were they thrown from the car?' Walker shook his head. 'No, it looks like they managed to get out after the car came to a halt. They were found close together, several feet from the car. It's amazing, actually, that they both got out, especially your sister-in-law with such extensive head injuries.' *Amazing.* Will, picturing the scene, gulped and then nodded.

'I'd better get back to my wife. Is there anything else?'

The detective shook his head. 'No, that's it, thanks.' He indicated the exit door. 'I have more work to do here, will you be able to find your way back?'

Will had no idea. 'Yes. Of course,' he said. How hard could it be?

Walker offered him a hand. 'Thank you for your assistance, Mr Armstrong,' he said, shaking his hand firmly. 'I'm sorry for your loss and I hope your wife pulls through. You've a tough road ahead.'

'Thank you,' Will said, glad the detective had no idea just how tough that road was going to be.

42

Will negotiated the corridors and found his way back to the ICU where he found Ellie still unconscious. He sat beside her, staring, trying to see any sign of change. But there was none. Her face was still fixed and rigid, her breathing peaceful. Strangely, the staff had brushed her hair so that it was loose, framing her face, dark waves on the white pillowcase. *Tia is dead.* His heart twisted as he realised Ellie could wear it loose all the time now, there was no reason to tie it back. He'd never be able to make that mistake again. Suddenly, his wandering attention was brought back to Ellie's face. Were her eyelids flickering? He looked around for one of the nurses, but they were all busy. They'd told him to ring her call bell if he saw any changes but he wasn't sure if this counted. He leaned forward to watch her face closely, but there was nothing more. He was about to sit back when it happened again and this time, he was convinced she was trying to open her eyes. Looking around, he saw Nurse Jarvis hanging a clipboard on the next bed and waved to attract her attention.

'I think she's waking up,' he said, when she joined him.

She peered closer and, reaching out, lifted one eyelid, then the other. 'You might be right,' she said, checking the equipment and the intravenous line. 'Just keep talking to her.'

He was beginning to think he'd imagined it when Ellie's eyes suddenly opened. She stared at the ceiling for a moment and then turned her head to look at him. 'Will,' she murmured. One word, but it was enough.

'Ellie,' he said, moving closer, 'thank God.' This time he did ring the call bell. Nurse Jarvis had gone off shift, so it was another nurse who attended.

'Well, well,' said the nurse, smiling, her eyes quickly assessing the monitor display. 'You've decided to wake up, have you? How are you feeling?'

Ellie tore her eyes from Will's face and looked at the nurse. Blinking rapidly, she looked to Will. 'What happened? I don't remember.'

He caught the nurse's eyes. How much was he to tell her at this stage?

The nurse transferred her smile to him. 'Don't worry your wife with details, Mr Armstrong, and don't you worry about what happened for now, Mrs Armstrong, just concentrate on getting better.'

Ellie's eyes flicked from one to the other. Then, without a word, she closed her eyes.

Will's eyes met the nurse's gratefully. 'It's hard to know...'

'Don't worry about it for the moment,' she said. 'She'll probably drift in and out for a while. Time enough for her to know what happened. I'll let the consultants know she's regained consciousness.'

A few minutes later, Ellie opened her eyes again and Will watched as her brow creased, making the small dressing that was there concertina up. 'It's a bit different to that hospital in

Italy, isn't it?' she murmured, bringing her eyes to him, managing a small smile.

The holiday where she'd had food poisoning so badly she needed to be hospitalised, had been three years ago. If she remembered that, her head injury couldn't be so bad. He breathed a sigh of relief. 'A bit different,' he agreed, smiling gently. With the smile still on her lips, she closed her eyes again. 'I just need to make a few phone calls,' Will said later, softly, unsure if she were asleep or not. When she gave no indication of hearing, he stood and stepped outside the unit to ring Sally and check on Bill, followed by a quick update to his office and then the call he'd been putting off. Ellie had insisted he put Adam's number as an emergency contact in his phone years before. He remembered laughing at the idea. 'What on earth is the point? He can't do a lot from Barbados.' But she'd insisted and he'd put it in to keep her happy. He found it and pressed ring.

He wasn't sure what time it was in Barbados, but the sleepy voice that answered made him think it was the middle of the night.

'Adam?'

'No, it's Tyler, hang on.'

He heard a lot of muttering before hearing the familiar voice of Adam Dawson. 'This better be very good, or very serious,' he said.

'Serious, I'm afraid. It's Will, Will Armstrong.'

'Will? It's the middle of the night. What's wrong?'

There was no easy way to deliver the news, so he went straight to the facts. 'There's been an accident, Adam, it's Tia, she...' He gulped, the words he'd said so often in his head difficult to say aloud. 'I'm sorry, Adam,' he managed, 'it's just so hard. Tia... she's dead.'

The silence that followed lasted for so long he thought they'd been disconnected. 'Adam? Are you still there?'

'Yes, yes, I'm sorry, it's...' There was silence on the line for a few seconds and then his voice came again, a distinct quaver in the words. 'What happened?'

'She was in the car with Ellie, and they crashed. Ellie was injured but I think she's going to be fine.'

'Thank God,' Adam said, cutting in.

'She's still in ICU,' Will carried on, 'but she's come around and she recognised me so that's a good sign. Luckily, Bill wasn't with them. He's being looked after by a nanny.'

'Bill?' Adam asked, puzzled.

Will held his hand over the mouthpiece and said, 'Shit.' In a sudden fit of panic, he muttered, 'Hello? Hello?' through his fingers and cut the connection. He didn't redial, nor did he answer the phone when it rang back. He needed time to think.

He knew Ellie emailed Adam now and then. He'd assumed she'd kept him up to date with things. It seems she'd left out one important detail. How on earth was he going to explain Bill?

He paced the corridor for a few minutes before redialling. This time the phone was answered immediately. 'Sorry, Adam,' he said, trying to sound apologetic, 'bad signal. I've moved to a better area.'

'That's okay,' Adam said, 'you were telling me about Bill?'

'Our son,' Will said. 'Ellie never told you?' He held his breath as he waited for his reply. If Ellie had mentioned being unable to have children, he'd have to think on his feet.

When the reply came it was both puzzled and disappointed. 'No, she never told me. We haven't spoken in a while, you know, and her last email was a few months ago. She's always so busy.'

'I think she might have tried to contact you, but you were away,' Will tried to explain. It was a shot in the dark, but it had some hope of success; Adam and Tyler were frequent travellers.

'We have been away a lot in the last year,' Adam said, the hint of puzzlement fading. 'I'm so happy for you both, I know you were keen to have children.

'Keep me up to date on Ellie's recovery, Will, won't you? Such a shock, this. Hard to take it all in.' There was a moment of static on the line when Will thought he'd lost the connection before Adam spoke again. 'Let me know when you'll be able to have Tia's funeral. I'll have a look at flights.'

Promising to keep him informed, Will hung up, thankful for once they had no other relatives to inform. He headed back to sit with Ellie, who lay with her eyes closed. She didn't open them when he pressed a gentle kiss to her cheek, so he sat to wait.

It puzzled him that she'd not told Adam about Bill. He'd have found out sometime, wouldn't he? Perhaps she was worried he'd come over to visit before they were ready, before Tia was relocated to Brighton. If he had, he'd have known immediately that Tia was the mother.

There was no risk of that now.

The thought surprised, frightened and appalled him. Was he seriously looking at Tia's death as a way out of the mess he'd landed them all in? He dropped his head into his hands and groaned quietly. What level had he stooped to?

'Will?'

Ellie's frail voice dragged him from his thoughts. He ran a hand over his face and put a smile on his lips. 'Hello,' he said, squeezing her elbow. He was about to say more when a commotion at the nurses' station caught his attention.

Within minutes, a group of medics was at the foot of Ellie's bed. The unit manager, whose name Will had never heard, introduced the consultant. 'This is Professor Grosschalk, the consultant neurologist.'

Grosschalk picked up the clipboard and scanned the information before putting it back and looking at Ellie. 'It's good to see you awake, Mrs Armstrong,' he said. 'You've had a rough time of it, but all the results look good. Your recovery should be smooth.' He gave her a smile and switched his attention to Will. 'Perhaps I could have a few words, Mr Armstrong?'

Without waiting for an answer, Professor Grosschalk headed back to the nurses' station. Will stooped to plant a kiss on Ellie's forehead and said, 'I'll be back in a minute.' He waited until she gave some recognition of what he'd said before joining the consultant.

Grosschalk held out his hand as Will reached him. 'Mr Armstrong,' he said, 'I thought it was important to have a word with you away from your wife.'

Will shook his hand, surprised at the strength in the slim, well-manicured hand. 'Is there a problem?' he said. 'Ellie is awake. Isn't everything going to be all right?' He suddenly realised he was still holding the man's hand and gave a shaky smile. 'Sorry,' he muttered, dropping it and rubbing his eyes to keep himself focused. An alarm from a monitor sent staff rushing to one of the other patients and, for a moment, there was organised chaos. Professor Grosschalk took Will by the arm, drew him to the corner of the station and indicated a couple of stools. 'We may as well sit here out of the way,' he said with a slight smile. He waited until Will sat before continuing, his face serious. 'Head injuries are difficult things to deal with, Mr Armstrong. It isn't always easy to identify residual damage. Until your wife's physical injuries have healed, we won't know the outcome for sure.'

'Are you saying she could have brain damage?' Will asked, appalled.

'It's a possibility that we should keep in mind.'

'But she's awake. She knew me, said my name,' he said again. 'She even remembered things from ages ago. That's a good sign, isn't it?'

The professor nodded. 'Yes, of course, and they're a good indication that she may make a full recovery but, sometimes, following a head injury there can be slight personality changes that people are unprepared for.'

'Personality changes?' Will wiped his face with a trembling hand.

Grosschalk shrugged. 'Sometimes very minor; a person who was very ebullient may become quiet, and vice versa. It can be more troubling if a person who was very mild-mannered becomes aggressive. Often, these changes are short-term, but they can be persistent, and it may happen that the patient needs to adjust to this lifestyle change.'

Will's frown eased. 'Is this just a worst-case scenario?'

Professor Grosschalk stood and held out his hand again. 'I find it is best to be prepared for all scenarios, Mr Armstrong. It is my hope that your wife makes a full and complete recovery. I will certainly do my utmost to ensure she does.'

Will sat where he was for a few minutes, watching the hustle and bustle of the unit before standing and making his way back to her bedside.

'How're you feeling?'

'Okay,' she said with an attempt at a smile. It wasn't much, but it reassured him. He sat with her until late evening and then, with a kiss, he left her and returned to his hotel.

He ordered room service and sat eating a mediocre meal, watching a movie he'd seen before. It filled the silence but didn't stop him thinking. He'd have to tell Ellie about Tia eventually and he wasn't sure how she'd take it. Her feelings towards her sister were ambivalent; she was her sister, but she was also her twin. And she hated being a twin. Would she be devastated or relieved at Tia's death? Would she feel guilty? Whatever the reason for the crash, there was no dispute as to who was driving.

And he? He was still appalled at the thought that had crossed his mind earlier. That he was sad, went without saying. But he couldn't deny a modicum of relief that it was unlikely now that the whole mess would ever come to light. Nor could he deny a certain sense of satisfaction that things could go back to the way they used to be between he and Ellie, but now with the wonderful addition of a son.

He put the half-eaten meal outside the door and switched off the television. The bedroom was on the fifth floor of the hotel and not overlooked so he'd left the curtains open and lay on his bed staring out at the new moon. He vaguely remembered reading something about seeing a new moon through glass. Wasn't it supposed to be unlucky?

* * *

The next morning, he headed back to the hospital and was greeted at the unit door by the news that Ellie had been moved to a different ward in the early hours of the morning. 'There was a fire in a local hotel,' a nurse explained. 'We'd some very badly burnt and injured people admitted so we needed to free up some beds. The consultants agreed Mrs Armstrong was doing so well she could be moved out.'

It was excellent news, and he felt some of the tension of the last few days ease.

Ward II, where she'd been sent, was a large, sprawling ward comprised of several four-bedded units. The nurses' station was manned by an efficient-looking clerk who found where Ellie was with a few key taps and directed him to room five.

She was lying in the bed by the window, morning light streaming in to emphasize her pallor. Standing in the doorway, looking across at her, he could see the chest drain was gone, so were most of the monitors. Just one stood beeping softly, its ECG trace reassuringly constant. She was sitting up slightly, her breathing slow and even.

He felt his eyes well up. She was going to be all right. He took a chair and positioned it beside her, sitting near enough to touch her when she woke. She was almost free of tubes; one still snaked up from her left arm to a bag of clear fluid that dripped slowly. The bed table beside her held a cup and an empty plate. She was eating and drinking; he'd have cheered if it wouldn't have startled the other patients.

When, at last, her eyes opened, squinting slightly in the sun from the window, Will took her hand.

'Feeling better?' he asked.

'Much,' she said, her lips curving in a smile. She looked at him and her smile faded. 'Tell me what happened?'

He couldn't put it off any longer. 'There was a crash, Ellie.' There was a spasm in the hand he held, he gripped it tighter. 'Do you remember?'

'I remember being in the car, and then trees.' Her face creased in anguish. 'Tia? She's dead, isn't she? I feel it.'

He stood and gathered her as close as possible. 'I'm sorry, Ellie,' he said softly into her ear, 'you're right, she didn't make it.' Afraid he was hurting her, he settled her back gently against the pillows and kissed her softly on the mouth. Her breath was stale, her lips dry. 'I am so sorry,' he said. 'She didn't suffer. It was a massive brain injury... She hadn't a chance.'

Ellie lay dry-eyed, her face set. 'I knew, Will. As soon as I woke, I had the strangest feeling, and I just knew she was gone.' She gulped. 'And it was my fault,' she said.

'No,' he hurried to reassure her, 'the investigators think an animal may have run in front of the car. You'd have braked instinctively, Ellie. You know you would. It was just bad luck, there was a huge tree trunk at the side of the road, the car hit it and flipped over. If you'd been a few feet further up the road you'd have gone into the ditch and escaped with bumps and bruises.'

'If we hadn't been there in the first place!'

There was no point in getting into that conversation. She was right, of course. What the hell had she been thinking? But if they were going to play the blame game, he only had to look in the mirror to know where to start, didn't he?

'Everything will be okay,' he said, wishing he could think of something original, something more reassuring to say. 'That woman you hired, Sally, she's agreed to stay and look after Bill for as long as we need her.'

'That's good,' Ellie said. 'Tia would like that.'

Before he could say more, a white-coated doctor came into the unit, clipboard in hand. He smiled at the other three patients but moved directly to Ellie's bed.

'I'm Dr Clare,' he said, smiling. 'Dr Pai's registrar.'

Will had no idea who Dr Pai was but he inclined his head a little.

Dr Clare obviously took it as permission to continue because he spent the next five minutes going over Ellie's various injuries. 'You'll need to organise an orthopaedic appointment with your local hospital,' he said. 'It was a simple fracture, I can't see there being any problem. They'll take off the plaster when the time comes. The ankle sprain isn't severe, keep the strapping on for support and keep it elevated when you can.' He dropped the clipboard to his side. 'The nursing staff will get you walking this afternoon, Mrs Armstrong, and I don't see why you can't go home tomorrow.'

Will looked at him with his mouth open. 'Tomorrow?' he said. 'She only left ICU this morning.' He pointed at the monitor and drip. 'She's still connected to those things.'

The doctor picked up the clipboard again. 'The monitor can be taken down and, since she is drinking adequately, the drip can be discontinued.' He looked from one to the other, his eyes unsympathetic. Finally, he fixed his eyes on Will. 'There's no reason to keep her in longer. Recuperation is best done in the comfort of her own home with her own things around her, you know. I've spoken to the consultant neurologist, the thoracic consultant and the cardiology team. They're all in agreement and happy for her to be discharged.'

Will felt cornered. 'How will we get home?' he asked. 'The police drove me here.' His face tightened when he read the message on the doctor's face. *That wasn't his concern.*

'Have a chat with the nursing staff,' he said, 'they'll be able to point you in the right direction.' And with that, he left with a final quick smile that never quite made it to his eyes.

'Don't worry,' he said to Ellie, reaching for the hand he'd dropped at the doctor's approach. 'He is right, anyway, you'll be better off at home.'

43

The hospital organised an ambulance to take them home. The nearest Will could pin them down to a time was late morning, so he arrived at ten and sat chatting to Ellie or flicking through magazines when she closed her eyes until finally, at eleven forty-five, the ambulance crew arrived.

There was a bit of friendly chat before they helped Ellie slide onto the gurney, Will fussing around getting in the way, giving advice nobody listened to.

It wasn't until they were moving out of the ward, Will holding Ellie's hand, that he remembered the last time he'd walked beside a gurney. Tia, in labour, a look of fear and excitement on her face, her hand gripping his with a strength he hadn't realised she possessed. The memory made him feel weak with guilt and remorse; both made all the worse for the knowledge that it would be so much easier now.

* * *

It was late afternoon before they pulled up outside their house. Will bustled up to the front door while the ramp was lowered and the gurney wheeled out, the crew negotiating the steps to the front door without a problem.

'Where do you want to go, love?' one of them asked, looking around the hallway.

'You can sit in the sitting room,' Will answered for her, pushing open the door. 'And put your feet up on the sofa.'

Minutes later, Ellie was settled on the sofa and Will waved goodbye to the crew before closing the door and taking a breath. For a moment, he felt the silence overpowering, almost threatening. He wasn't sure why. It was better now, wasn't it? He closed his eyes to the memory of Tia reaching for the photo of the baby scan. He regretted now not having given it to her. Regrets. Too many, he thought shaking off the uncomfortable feeling and going back to Ellie.

She was lying with her eyes closed. He was about to leave when they opened. 'You must be exhausted,' he said with a smile.

She nodded. 'A bit,' she admitted.

They both turned as they heard a door open and, moments later, the cheerful face of the nanny appeared in the doorway. 'I'm Sally,' she said, holding her hand out to Will, who shook it.

'You've been a lifesaver,' he said, giving her a smile of gratitude.

Sally nodded as if such praise was her due. 'I've put the kettle on,' she said, 'I'll have tea ready in a minute.'

She was true to her word and, just over a minute later, she appeared with a tray.

Will eyed the biscuits and suddenly realised he was starving. 'I'm going to order a takeaway. I could eat a horse.' He turned to Ellie. 'What about you? Sally?'

Ellie nodded at the tray. 'I'm fine with this. My appetite hasn't returned yet.'

'No, I'm fine, thanks,' Sally said. She stood for a moment and when neither asked, volunteered, 'Bill is awake. Would you like me to bring him in?'

Guilt swept over Will's face. In his excitement at having Ellie home, he'd forgotten about the child. He looked at Ellie and saw her smile. 'I'll come and get him,' he said, standing and following Sally from the room.

Bill was in his cot, his hands waving in front of his face. Will bent over and picked him up, holding him close, breathing in that baby smell he loved. Was he imagining it or had he grown in the few days?

'He looks well,' he said, turning to the woman who stood watching them. 'I'm so grateful for you filling in as you did.'

She shrugged. 'I get very well paid, and I like what I do.'

'You wouldn't be interested in staying full time, I suppose?'

'No,' she said without the slightest hesitation, and with no apology. 'Agency work suits me better. I'll stay until you've found someone, though, but only because I appreciate you've been through a tough time. It's not something I normally do. The agency will send someone else tomorrow for a few hours to give me a break, but I'll be back tomorrow night.'

Will knew when to give up. 'We do really appreciate that,' he said. Looking across the room, he saw Tia's bed neatly dressed. 'Are you sleeping down here?'

'I thought it was best and it's certainly more convenient,' she said.

It was perfect. Will wondered if the permanent nanny would be so accommodating.

Back in the sitting room, he sat on the edge of the sofa, Bill in his arms. 'Here he is,' he said, tilting the child so Ellie could see him. 'He looks well. Sally is a marvel.'

He watched as Ellie reached out and caressed the baby's cheek with a trembling finger and felt a rush of love for her, for them both. He placed Bill gently in her arms and reached around to embrace them. It was all going to be okay. Wasn't it?

Bill chose that moment to remind them he was due a feed by wailing. With a grin, Will picked him up. 'I'll take him back to Sally,' he said.

Handing the crying child over, he ordered a takeaway, returned to the sitting room and took the other chair. *Tia's chair*, he thought with a chill as he sat into it.

Ellie, he noticed, was very quiet. Probably exhausted. 'You should go up to bed,' he suggested, leaning forward.

'No, I'm fine,' she said.

He dragged the chair closer to the sofa, noticing her eyes had filled with tears, one slowly tracing a path down her cheek and making little detours around the scabs. 'Ellie, are you all right? Are you in pain?'

She shook her head. 'I was horrible to Tia, Will. And now I can never make it up to her.'

'Shush,' he said, reaching forward and pulling her gently into his arms. 'You weren't horrible to her. You brought her here, remember? Gave her a home.'

'You don't understand,' she snuffled into his shoulder. 'Brighton. I was taking her to the bungalow. I was going to leave her there.'

Will tightened his grip on her. 'I guessed that was it, Ellie. It wasn't difficult, there was no other reason for the two of you to be together in Brighton.' He took a deep breath. It was hard to criticise her now, but he had to say something. 'You should have talked to me, Ellie. I could have told you she was never going to go.'

'You said she'd go in a few months,' she said, raising her head to look at him.

He moved away from her and shrugged. 'I said what you wanted to hear, Ellie.' He rubbed his face with his hands. 'I suppose I was trying to convince myself too, but when I saw her with Bill, I just knew it wasn't going to work the way we'd planned.' He stood up and paced the room before turning to her. 'We were crazy to think it would ever work.'

The doorbell announced the delivery of the takeaway. Feeling he was escaping from a conversation that could only end in the realisation that she didn't have to worry about Tia now, he went to answer the door.

The takeaway food was probably good, but he'd lost his appetite and, after nibbling on a little, he pushed it away and turned to Ellie, surprised to find her looking at him with a serious expression on her face. He reached for her hand. 'If I hadn't got drunk that night,' he said, 'I'd never have made that stupid mistake, we wouldn't be in this situation and Tia...' – his gulp was audible – '...would still be alive. I'm going to have to live with that guilt, Ellie, but you don't have to. The crash was an accident, out of your hands.'

Ellie looked at him, her hand lying passively in his. 'What about Bill? He's the result of that stupid mistake. Would you wish he was never born?'

Mixed emotions ran through him, and he took his hand away. 'Of course not,' he said. He dropped his face into his hands and sat for a while. 'We have much to forgive each other for, don't we?' he said, his voice muffled.

The sound of a baby's cry broke the silence. He lifted his face and looked at her. 'Can we get through this, Ellie?'

She looked at him. 'I love you. So yes, I think we'll get through it.' It was as much as he could hope for. She loved him, he loved them both. That was a lot of love going around, there was enough to spare for his son. He looked at her. Their son.

* * *

At midnight, Will slept heavily. Ellie woke and looked at him before turning and slipping out of bed. Barefoot, barely limping, she made her way downstairs, her good hand holding tightly to the handrail. She listened for a few minutes at the kitchen door. Even through the heavy door she could hear Sally's snore, and slowly, quietly, she turned the door-knob and pushed it open.

Sally had left the blinds open. It was a clear night with enough light coming from the sliver of moon to guide her to the cot where Bill lay sleeping. She stood and looked down at him, her face set.

He was all that stood between her and the life they'd had.

44

Will put down the phone and turned to Ellie who sat at the other end of the sofa, her eyes still fixed on the television even though he had muted the sound when the phone rang. It was two weeks since the crash. Her recuperation, after a quick start, had slowed. She tired easily, her appetite was poor, and he frequently found her sitting, gazing into space. 'Ellie?'

She dragged her eyes slowly from the screen and looked at him. 'Bad news?'

He reached for her hand and held it tightly. 'That was one of the police officers who were investigating Tia's death. He rang to tell us that the coroner has ruled it was accidental.'

Ellie frowned. 'Accidental? Was there ever any doubt?'

It was Will's turn to frown. 'No, of course not. It's just red tape. The important thing is that it means we can organise Tia's funeral.'

Her frown vanished and she smiled sadly. 'We can pick out a nice casket.'

'Yes, we can.' He pulled her close. 'I've already had a word with Whitechapel Crematorium. I'll give them a ring and fix a date.'

'Crematorium?'

'That's okay, isn't it?' He kissed the top of her head. 'If you would prefer a burial, I can look into it?'

'No, no,' she hurried to assure him, pulling back to look up at him, 'that's fine. I'm sure Tia would be happy with that. After all,' she smiled, 'it's what I would choose. And she is my twin.'

He laughed uncertainly. It was the first time in a long time that she'd referred to Tia as her twin. Maybe no longer having her made it easier.

Checking the time, he nodded. 'It's late morning in Barbados. I'll see if I can get through to Adam.' He moved away to pick up his phone and after a quick search for Adam's number, hit dial. 'Do you want to speak to him?' he asked, turning to look at her.

She shook her head. 'I'm too tired.' Will smiled understandingly.

The phone rang a number of times before it was picked up. 'Adam, hi, it's Will. I've just heard from the police; Tia's body will be released for burial. I've spoken to the funeral directors and agreed a tentative date of the fifth, I just wanted to check with you before confirming.'

'Sounds fine, Will,' Adam replied. 'That gives me time to arrange things this end.' There was a brief pause before he continued. 'How's Ellie doing?'

'She's doing fine. It's going to take a while to make a full recovery, but the doctors were happy with her progress at the hospital so it's just a matter of time. By the fifth I'm sure she'll be back to herself.'

'Can I speak to her?'

'She's resting at the moment. Would you like me to get her to ring you later?'

'No, that's fine, Will. Send her my love and tell her I look forward to seeing her in a couple of weeks.'

'You're welcome to stay here with us?' Will added, hoping the answer was no. But he didn't need to worry.

'No, thanks, Will. I'll book us into a hotel. Perhaps you and Ellie will join us for dinner one night. We're going to stay for a few days; Tyler wants to have some suits made.'

Arrangements made, Will hung up, sat back and ran a hand through his hair. It would be a relief when things returned to normal. *If they returned to normal.* He looked at Ellie who was once again watching the muted television. He reached for the remote and turned the sound back on.

He'd taken yet another day off to be with her. The company were being understanding, but he could see it starting to fray at the edges.

'Of course,' Alistair Metcalf the CEO said when he'd dropped into his office the day before. 'You must do what you think fit. After all, it's only been two weeks since the accident.'

Maybe Will imagined it, but he thought there was a touch of sarcasm in the *only two weeks*.

From the living room he heard the sound of Bill crying. It lasted a moment before stopping. The wonderful Sally had been replaced by an equally wonderful Mary, a woman as plain and old fashioned as her name suggested. She came for an interview, took a look at the sleeping arrangements and nodded. 'This'll do for the moment,' she said agreeably. 'I'm assuming there is a bedroom I can use eventually?'

He brought her to see the small spare bedroom and she looked around with narrowed eyes as if judging what would fit where. 'I'll use this as a sitting room while I sleep downstairs,' she said. 'I like my bit of privacy.'

'Of course,' Will said.

'I'll need a television and an armchair,' she said.

'Absolutely,' he agreed, 'I'll get that organised.' If these were her only conditions, they were easily met. 'My wife was in a car accident,' he told her, 'she'll be here during the day recuperating until she's ready to go back to work.'

'Sally told me all about it,' Mary said.

Will was relieved he didn't have to go into explanations but was also taken aback that Sally had gossiped. He was about to shake off concerns with an *after all we've no secrets* attitude when he remembered it wasn't true and sighed.

Mary Parks moved in immediately and, within a couple of days, it was as if she'd always been there. Bill took to her immediately, his crying miraculously stopping when she picked him up.

At first, every time he needed to be fed during the day, she asked Ellie if she wanted to feed him and she declined. After a couple of days, she stopped asking. They quickly settled into a routine, Mary and Bill in the kitchen or living room, Ellie on the sofa in the sitting room. Except to get coffee or something to eat, Ellie didn't bother her. If Mary were surprised at this lack of concern, she said nothing, merely shaking her head and giving Bill extra cuddles.

It wasn't long before she was running the house. 'You should be getting out of the house, Mrs Armstrong,' she started saying to Ellie after a few days of letting her recover slowly. 'You won't get better lying on the couch, day after day. Why don't you take Bill out in his pushchair? It would do you both the power of good.' But each time Ellie would shake her head. 'Maybe tomorrow, Mary.'

Two weeks after her arrival, Mary approached Will while he was reading the morning paper with a coffee before going to work. 'I'm worried about Mrs Armstrong,' she said. 'She does nothing except watch television. It's not good for her. And she shows no interest in her baby at all.'

She didn't say *it's not natural,* but it hung in the air.

Will gave her a sharp look. 'She's had a difficult time. That's why we need you to look after Bill,' he said. 'Leave Mrs Armstrong to me.' Mary pressed her lips firmly together, nodded and turned away.

A wave of guilt washed over him. The woman was just trying to be kind. If he were honest, he was worried about Ellie too. He'd expected her to have recovered by now. She wasn't taking painkillers any more. The cuts on her face had healed, the bruises fading to a sickly yellow. She was walking without a limp. The plaster cast on her left hand did impact a little on what she could do, but she could use her fingers, so she wasn't totally incapacitated. She was always so energetic and active before the accident. Maybe she was depressed? Leaving his empty cup on the counter, he folded the newspaper and headed back to their bedroom. 'Hi,' he said, seeing her eyes open when he walked in.

He sat on the side of the bed, reached out and brushed the hair from her face. 'Sleepyhead,' he teased with a smile. 'I'll be heading to work in about twenty minutes, but I'm in no hurry this morning so I thought you might like to go to your office and say hello. Make your presence felt? Let them know you're alive and kicking,' he said, resorting to clichés in the face of her blank look. 'You don't want Jeff Harper getting any clever ideas, do you?'

The blank look was replaced by confusion. 'Jeff Harper?'

Will laughed uncertainly. 'Jeff? The man you always suspected was after your job?'

Ellie's puzzled look cleared, and she laughed. 'Of course. Funny, it took a car crash for me to stop worrying about him.'

'Well, something good came out of it then,' he said, bending down to kiss her cheek. 'I'll wait for you to get dressed, if you want.'

She shook her head. 'It's too soon,' she said, reaching a hand up to touch his cheek. 'Maybe next week.'

* * *

That afternoon, Ellie told Mary she was going out for a walk.

Mary's round face creased in a smile. 'Some fresh air will do you the world of good. Do you want to take Bill? The pushchair is easy to manoeuvre, you'll have no problem – even with the cast.'

Ellie shook her head. 'I think I'd like some time just for myself today.'

It was a beautiful day. She stepped out of the front door and took a deep breath. Unsurprisingly, she felt a little shaky. After a few steps she wanted to go home but she persevered and made it as far as the local shop. She walked around inside with no intention of buying anything and was about to leave when a cheery voice called out, 'Hello! We haven't seen you here in ages.'

She turned to face the caller, a young assistant who was packing fruit onto a shelf without any attempt at display. Her smile turned to a grimace when she saw the plaster on her arm. 'Oh dear, what have you done to your arm?'

'I broke it,' Ellie said, realising in that split second the woman thought she was Tia. Should she tell her, or smile and leave?

'Poor you,' the assistant said, and returned to her unpacking. Ellie shrugged, turned and left. She wouldn't come this way again. The journey home was slower, every step a struggle. She was shocked at how weak she'd become in such a short space of time. Tomorrow, she'd do better.

'I'll have to build up gradually,' she told a delighted Will when he arrived home. 'But tomorrow, I'll walk the other direction.' She told him about the assistant.

'Of course, they thought you were Tia,' he said reasonably. 'She was always going in there. Why didn't you just tell her who you were?'

Ellie stared at him. 'Tia's twin? I don't want to be a dead woman's twin, Will.'

Surprised at her vehemence, Will held up both hands in surrender. 'Sorry, sorry,' he said. 'I didn't think, I'm sorry. Of course, you don't.'

She let her head flop back on the sofa. 'No, I'm sorry, Will. I suppose I haven't really come to terms with the fact she's dead yet.'

He sat beside her and rested a hand on her knee. 'We'll get through this, Ellie. You, me and little Bill.'

She looked at his hand and rested hers on top. 'Don't you ever wish it was like it was before? When it was just you and me? No baby, no nanny?'

Turning his hand, he grasped hers. 'Sometimes, I suppose,' he admitted. He was looking down at their joined hands and didn't see the look that passed over her face. 'But,' he added, looking up, his other hand reaching to brush her cheek, 'with Bill, I think we'll be stronger. Even the secrets that have made him, have brought us closer. Don't you feel that?'

She met his eyes, hers softening as she saw in his what she wanted. Unconditional love. Perhaps there was enough to go around after all. Perhaps she'd done enough. 'Secrets,' she said softly, rolling the word around in her mouth. 'I suppose it means you can never leave me, doesn't it?'

Will was slightly taken aback and laughed uncertainly. 'If I wanted to leave you, would you tell on me?'

'Maybe,' she said with a serious face. Then she squeezed his hand and gave him her biggest smile, watching as his face immediately relaxed. 'But you'll never want to leave me, will you?'

45

Adam and Tyler flew into Heathrow two days before the funeral. Will toyed with the idea of hiring a car to pick them up but, in the end, decided a taxi would be easier. He told Ellie the time the taxi was due, so he was surprised when, fifteen minutes beforehand, she was still in her pyjamas.

'You better hurry,' he said, checking his watch.

'Why?'

He blinked in surprise. 'Have you forgotten? We're going to meet Adam and Tyler.'

She looked at him with a blank look, then shook her head and smiled. 'Oh gosh, I forgot,' she said. 'I'll go and change. I can be ready in ten minutes.'

It was almost twenty minutes before she came down the stairs dressed in a fitted, low-cut navy dress, her hair tied back in the nape of her neck. She'd replaced the hospital-supplied sling with a silk scarf. It was her only accessory.

A cream coat hung over one arm, she reached the bottom step and handed it to Will who draped it over her shoulders.

'You look amazing,' he said, kissing the back of her neck. 'We'd better hurry, the taxi is waiting.'

Ellie nodded and moved to the door, looking back in surprise when Will didn't follow. 'Okay?' she asked.

'I'll just go and say goodbye to Mary and give Bill a kiss goodnight.'

She didn't follow him, waiting almost impatiently at the door until he returned minutes later.

'Why can't you make a little effort, Ellie?' he said, opening the door for her.

It was the first time he'd criticised her since the crash and she looked at him in surprise. She looked down at her dress. 'You said I looked amazing.'

He looked puzzled for a moment and then frowned. 'You know damn well I wasn't taking about how you look,' he said.

In the taxi, he turned to her again. Her attitude was really beginning to grate on him. 'Mary is wonderful,' he said, 'but she's a nanny. She could up and leave at any time. Bill needs a mother. I want us to be a family, but you're not making any effort with him. He's a lovely child; Tia and I used to enjoy playing with him, making him giggle.'

Hearing the regret in his voice, her face suddenly turned hard. 'You miss her?'

He sat back in the seat and said nothing for a while. 'Don't you?' he asked eventually. 'Even a little?'

Ellie nodded. 'Of course, I do. How could I not?'

'I miss how she was with Bill,' Will said. 'She really loved him. That's why I think our plan to separate them was never going to work. She'd have found a way to come back to him.'

'To *you*,' Ellie said. She looked at him, her eyes cold, hard. 'She was only good with the baby when you were around. It was all for your benefit. When you weren't there, she didn't pay him as much attention.'

He blinked. 'I don't believe you.'

She shrugged dismissively. 'I knew you wouldn't believe me so I never said anything. Anyway, it doesn't matter. She might have found a way to come back from Brighton, but not from where she's gone now.'

If he was stunned at her words, he was horrified at coldness of her voice. He'd never heard it before, not even in the worst of their rows. He remembered, years before, meeting her colleague Jeff at a work party. He'd described Ellie as a ruthless, cold negotiator. He'd not been able to reconcile the description with the woman he loved. Now, for the first time, he could.

The taxi pulled up at the airport and they moved through the crowds to Arrivals without further discussion, both their faces set and grim. The flight was delayed, and they stood looking resolutely ahead, neither knowing what to say to break the uncomfortable, frosty silence between them.

It was a long forty-five minutes before they saw the tanned face of Adam Dawson and his partner coming through, both men pushing laden trolleys.

'How long are they staying for?' Will muttered, looking across at her to see if this raised a smile. It didn't. He sighed and waved at the approaching men, pasting a smile in place, hoping she was doing the same, afraid to look in case she wasn't.

The two men, exhausted from the long flight and the free champagne, greeted them with bear hugs and smiles. 'So good to see you both,' Adam said before pulling away from Ellie to stare into her face. 'How're you holding up, my dear?' he said with genuine concern, before looking toward Will with a slight frown.

Will gave a quick shake of his head and Adam said no more

as they moved en masse towards the exit to join the long queue for a taxi.

'Are you going to replace your car?' Adam asked, when they'd settled inside one, ten minutes later.

Will shook his head. 'We hardly used it, it doesn't make sense to buy another. In London, it's more convenient to use the Tube or get a taxi. We could always hire a car if we needed one.'

'Makes sense,' Tyler said, yawning widely. 'Sorry,' he smiled apologetically. 'I need my bed.'

The taxi dropped them off at the elegant Mavern Hotel on Grosvenor Street, before taking Will and Ellie home, silence returning as soon as the two travellers had departed.

Once inside, Ellie went upstairs without so much as a good-night. Will, his eyes bleak, stood a moment; should he go and speak to her? While he was trying to decide, he heard the sound of the bath filling. He smiled grimly. Decision made.

Restless, he went into the kitchen to find Mary preparing a bottle for Bill. She turned with a smile that dimmed slightly when she saw he was alone.

'Ellie's not feeling well,' he lied and then, as if trying to convince himself, he added, 'Tia's funeral is going to be hard on her.'

Mary finished what she was doing and leaned back against the counter. 'I was going to make some coffee, would you like a cup?' Will nodded gratefully. He'd take kindness and sympathy wherever he could get it these days. He sat at the table and rested his chin in his cupped hands until she put a mug in front of him and then cupped it instead, feeling the heat and enjoying the coffee-laced fumes.

Mary stood sipping hers.

'Sit down, for goodness' sake,' he said gruffly, but kindly.

Her grunt was wary, but she pulled up a chair and sat. While he stared into his coffee, she ventured a question. 'There are no photographs of Tia, were they very alike?'

He looked up, surprised. 'She only came to live with us a short time ago,' he said. As explanations went, it wasn't good, but he saw her nod. 'And to answer your question, yes, they were very alike to look at, but different in temperament. Tia was a gentler soul, not very bright, but very loving. She was good with Bill too, used to make him laugh.'

'He's a happy baby,' she said. 'It's a shame Mrs Armstrong spends so little time with him.'

Since, as far as Will was aware, Ellie had spent almost no time with Bill since she returned from hospital, he guessed Mary was being kind.

'It's been difficult for her. I'm sure, once the funeral is over, things will go back to normal.' He said it with a conviction he didn't feel.

He slept on the sofa, waiting until he heard the living room quieten before switching out the light and stretching out. He could have gone upstairs and grabbed a blanket and pillow but in a spirit of martyrdom he lay uncomfortable all night, sleeping fitfully. At two, he was wide awake. What was it Ellie had said? *Tia might have found a way to come back from Brighton, but not from where she's gone now.* It had been a terrible thing to say, almost as if she were truly glad Tia were dead.

He tried to get back to sleep but the words spun round and round. He remembered Ellie's face when she'd said it. How hard she'd looked. His eyes snapped open. What was it that detective had said? He racked his sleepy brain to remember something that had seemed of little importance at the time, but now... What was it?

When the answer came to him, he sat bolt upright, letting

out a groan of despair. The detective inspector had mentioned something about how amazing it was that Tia had managed to climb from the car with such an extensive head injury.

But maybe she hadn't.

Maybe Tia hadn't been badly injured in the crash at all.

What was he thinking? The blood drained from his face. It was sleep deprivation making his brain imagine stupid things. He flopped back on the sofa and closed his eyes.

Don't you ever wish it was like it was before? When it was just you and me? No baby, no nanny? When had Ellie said that? Days before? He'd thought nothing of it. In the light of his fears, the words took on a new meaning. His eyes snapped open again. If Ellie were presented with the opportunity to get rid of Tia for good, would she have taken it?

Wasn't that why she was on the road to Brighton in the first place?

Maybe she was presented with an opportunity too good to pass up. The detective said both women had made it out of the car and were lying close together. Tia might have been unconscious. One blow from a rock would have sufficed to cave in her skull.

He gulped. Was he seriously entertaining this idea? Did he seriously think Ellie capable of murder?

When it was just you and me?

If he was right, was Bill next?

46

Late the next morning, feeling weary, he was relieved to see Ellie come into the kitchen with a smile on her face.

'Good morning, everyone,' she said, pouring herself a cup of coffee. 'My goodness, I can't believe I slept so late. Did Bill have a good night, Mary?'

Mary stopped taking baby clothes from a basket and looked at her in surprise. 'Yes, Mrs Armstrong,' she said. 'He slept until two, had a bottle, then slept until six.'

'That's good.' Ellie put her coffee down. She moved to the cot where Bill lay cooing and stood for a moment looking at him; then, to Will's amazement, she stooped down, picked him up and cuddled him for several minutes before putting him back.

Will met Mary's eyes. Maybe things were going to be all right. In the bright light of the day, his night-time fears seemed preposterous. Ellie was smiling, she looked brighter. Perhaps she'd taken his criticism on board and now things would start returning to normal.

They'd arranged to meet Adam and Tyler for lunch at one. 'We'd better leave soon,' Will said, glancing at the clock.

Ellie nodded and finished her coffee. 'I'll get my coat.' Before leaving she bent and gave Bill a kiss on the forehead and then turned to Mary with a friendly smile. 'I can't thank you enough for looking after him so well.'

'Well, well,' Mary said when Ellie left. 'She's like a different woman.'

'No, she's like her old self,' Will said, reaching down to caress his son's head. 'It's just taken her a long time to recover from that terrible crash. Everything will be better now, you'll see.'

Looking down at his son, he hoped he was right.

They took the tube, getting out at Bond Street and walking through Grosvenor Square Garden. Even on a cold, grey day, the park, though small, was beautiful. With its statue of President Roosevelt, the Eagle Squadron Memorial and the memorial to those who died on September 11, he and Ellie had always joked that it was like having a little bit of the United States in the heart of Mayfair. He held her hand tightly as they walked through the park and along Grosvenor Street. Usually, Ellie would comment on how much she loved the Georgian buildings but, today, she walked silently, lost in thought.

'You feeling all right?' he asked. It was only a ten-minute walk but maybe it was too much.

'Yes,' she said, with a quick smile. 'I feel fine.'

They arrived just before the prearranged time to find the two men waiting in The Mavern's elegant foyer reading newspapers.

'Good morning,' Adam said, folding the paper and dropping it on the table. He gave Ellie a hug, reached out a hand to Will. 'You look tired,' he said. 'Bad night?'

Will waved a hand dismissively. 'It's been a difficult time for all of us.'

Adam and Tyler nodded in sympathy. 'I thought, unless you have another preference, we'd have lunch here,' Adam said.

Will looked at Ellie who smiled. 'Sounds good to me,' she said. 'I've always liked this hotel.'

Tyler dropped his newspaper on the table and stood. 'I'll go and make a reservation,' he said. 'And get some drinks. What will you have?'

They all looked at Ellie, who suddenly looked flustered. 'I don't—' She stopped.

'Have a gin and tonic,' Will said, slipping an arm around her. 'You always like one before dinner.'

She smiled at him gratefully. 'Yes, that would be lovely.'

The foyer was too noisy for comfortable conversation. 'There's a lounge further back,' Adam said and led the way to a large room where comfortable chairs were grouped informally around low tables. 'Better?' he asked.

Nodding, Ellie and Will sat. Tyler returned followed by a liveried waiter carrying a tray of drinks.

'Well, I think this calls for a toast,' Adam said, lifting his glass. 'To Tia.'

'To Tia,' they all chimed.

An uneasy silence followed the toast as they all sought for something unexceptional to talk about. It was Tyler who came up with the old reliable. The weather. 'It's hard to get used to this cold again,' he said with an exaggerated shiver.

As a conversation opener it was banal, but they jumped on it, comparing the advantages and disadvantages of constant sunshine. 'You must come and visit us, see for yourselves,' Adam said.

Will laughed. 'You're hardly ever there.' He looked at Ellie.

'We could do with some sunshine though. Would you like to go? I can look at flights.'

Tyler chirped in. 'Do come, we go home in a week and then we've nothing planned for ages. It would be lovely to have visitors.' They were still discussing this when it was time for lunch and, by the time they'd finished that, a tentative date had been set.

Adam pushed his plate away and sat back. 'I hope we get to meet Bill while we're here,' he said. 'I still can't believe you didn't tell me about him.'

'I'm afraid that's my fault,' Will said. He picked up Ellie's hand and kissed it before looking back at Adam, an apologetic expression on his face. 'I'm so sorry, *I* was supposed to tell you.' Dropping her hand, he held his up, palms out. 'When Bill was born, Ellie asked me to ring you to let you know the good news but, with all that was going on, unforgivably, I forgot.'

'It must have been a huge adjustment,' Tyler commented.

'Huge! He was a fretful baby and cried all hours so Ellie was exhausted,' Will said, the lies coming far more easily than he'd expected. 'Tia was great with him though, and she looked after him when Ellie went back to work.'

'And now? You have an au pair?'

'A nanny,' said Will with a smile. 'A mature, serious woman called Mary.' He reached into his inside pocket and took out some photographs. 'There you are,' he said, handing them over. 'That's Bill when he was just a few weeks old.'

'He's a handsome boy,' Adam said without much enthusiasm. 'They all look the same at that age, don't they?'

'Adam's not into babies, really,' Tyler said apologetically. His face creased in concentration as he looked at the small, squashed scrap of humanity in the photograph and clearly tried to think of something complimentary to say. 'He's lovely,' he said in the end, handing the photos back.

'You'll get to see him tomorrow,' Ellie said.

Will nodded. 'Yes, of course. We can call in to see him after the service, if you like, or maybe it would be better after lunch. I've booked a Japanese restaurant, by the way. They do the most wonderful sushi.'

Adam and Tyler may have shown a lack of interest in the baby but the mention of sushi had both men's faces wreathed in smiles and, over coffee, they discussed a recent visit to Japan. Tyler managed to find an endless supply of photographs on his phone to show them.

Finally, Will called a halt. 'I think we'll head off,' he said. 'It's Ellie's first time out since the accident, she shouldn't overdo it.'

'Yes, yes, of course,' Adam agreed, jumping to his feet and rushing around to envelop Ellie in a hug. 'Until tomorrow, my dear,' he said.

Will quickly gave the details for the following morning, handing them a card with the crematorium's address. 'It's arranged for eleven thirty,' he said, and then, with an arm around Ellie's shoulder, they left the hotel.

He caught her hand as they walked along the street. 'You were very quiet,' he said. 'You feeling okay?'

She nodded absently. 'Just tired and a bit emotional.'

Of course. Guilt shot through him. Wasn't it all bound to take its toll? And she'd had quite a lot to drink too; Adam and Tyler were gracious hosts but a bit heavy-handed when they poured wine. How many bottles had they got through? Three or four?

He saw a vacant taxi approach and quickly hailed it. 'Let's get you home,' he said.

Once there, he encouraged her to go to bed for a couple of hours. 'You'll feel better afterwards,' he said, helping her out of her coat and giving her a gentle push toward the stairs. He watched her go, her bottom swaying in the soft fabric of the dress. There was a time the sight would have turned him on, he'd have followed her up and tried his luck. A lot of things had changed. The house was quiet. Hanging her coat over the newel post, he went to the kitchen door and held his ear to it, listening for sounds. Nothing. He knew Mary sometimes went for a nap while Bill was having one, having walked in on her once when she was asleep. She'd woken in great embarrassment and he'd had to spend considerable time reassuring her that it was perfectly all right to have forty winks when she could. He didn't want to repeat the experience. Maybe that's all Ellie meant by her remark. That it was easier when it was just the two of them and they could do what they wanted in their own home. Of course, he decided, that was what she'd meant.

With a feeling of relief, he retreated to the sitting room and flopped onto the sofa. He felt a headache brewing, too much alcohol in the middle of the day, too little sleep. Kicking off his shoes, he swung his legs up, rested his head on a cushion and closed his eyes.

He didn't think he'd fall asleep but he did, just for a moment, waking in a cold sweat when he dreamed he saw Ellie standing over Tia's unconscious body, a rock in her hand and a terrifying look on her face.

He didn't sleep again, switching on the television with the sound muted and watching reruns of an old comedy show. But it was the footage in his head that was on an endless loop and, for a moment, he wondered if he were losing his mind.

47

The day of Tia's funeral arrived with blue skies and a bitterly cold breeze.

He'd slept on the sofa again, bringing a pillow and duvet down without explanation. He half expected Ellie to question him but she said nothing, accepting his decision when he told her without as much as a flicker of an eyelid.

In the morning, he'd showered and dressed in the main bathroom. It took him several minutes to find the black tie he'd bought for his uncle's funeral several years before. He tied it and straightened the knot. Carrying his dark-grey suit jacket, he headed downstairs stopping at their bedroom door to listen for movement, reluctant to go inside. The hum of the electric shower satisfied him that she was getting ready and he carried on down. He was eating a slice of toast when the door opened and she came in, swallowing with a gulp when he saw her. She looked stunning. The black sheath dress she wore accentuated every curve and showed off her ivory skin. Normally, she wore more make-up, but today she'd settled for mascara and muted lipstick.

She'd left her hair loose, simply pinning it back at the sides with jewelled clasps he'd never seen before.

'I don't think I've ever seen you look more beautiful,' he said, standing up and planting a soft kiss on her cheek.

She tilted her head, a curious expression on her face. 'Not even on our wedding day?'

'Not even then,' he smiled.

'Thank you,' she said, and her eyes shimmered with tears. 'That means more than you could ever imagine. Especially today.' She handed him a scarf. 'Would you fix this for me, please. It's not black, but it's the closest I have.'

Will took it and folded it along the diagonal before tucking it around her cast and tying it at the nape of her neck. 'It will be good to have this off,' he said, tapping it lightly. 'Two more days and you'll be free of it.'

She smiled absent-mindedly and walked over to Bill's cot. 'Hello, gorgeous,' she said, putting her hand on his stomach and rocking him gently. He gurgled up at her. 'He slept well, did he?' she asked Mary, who stood waiting for the kettle to boil.

'Seems to have fallen into a regular pattern now, Mrs Armstrong.'

'Good.' She rocked the baby gently again and smiled when he gurgled. With a final caress she left him and moved to the kitchen to get coffee. She poured a mug and looked at Will. 'More?'

He shook his head. 'I've had some, thanks. You should have something to eat. A slice of toast or some cereal?'

She shook her head. 'Just coffee will be fine.' She took her mug and sat at the table.

'It's very cold out, Mrs Armstrong,' Mary volunteered. 'I was putting some rubbish out a while ago, that breeze is bitter.'

Will frowned. The black dress was stunning but it was also sleeveless. 'Maybe wear a cardigan,' he suggested. 'Remember, you're still recuperating.'

To his surprise, she stood and left the room, returning a few minutes later with a black cardigan. She slipped one arm in and pulled the other side over her shoulder.

Touched, Will reached to help her, tucking the empty sleeve neatly into the cardigan's pocket. 'Better?'

'Yes,' she said with a laugh. 'I have to admit, I was a little chilly.' He checked the time. 'The taxi will be here any moment. Where's your coat?'

'On the banisters.'

He fetched it and helped her with it just as the doorbell announced the arrival of the taxi. Putting on his coat, he said, 'We won't be very late, Mary. As usual, any problems, give me a ring.'

'I hope it goes as well as these things can,' she said.

Ellie smiled, took a last look at Bill and headed out into the hallway, Will following close behind.

He looked at her from the corner of his eye as they travelled through the usual mayhem that was London traffic. She seemed calm, peaceful even, and a changed woman from a few days before. Perhaps she'd taken what he'd said to heart and decided to make more of an effort with Bill? If so, it hadn't put his mind at ease; he felt more confused than ever.

They picked Adam and Tyler up at their hotel and arrived at Whitechapel Crematorium with five minutes to spare. They stood, a small, almost pathetic group of mourners to wait their turn.

The hearse arrived from the undertakers, the casket he and Ellie had chosen from their online catalogue gleaming in the sun as it drew up outside.

'Would you like to carry the coffin in?' the undertaker asked, his voice pitched low to suit the solemnity of the proceedings.

Adam made the decision. 'Yes,' he said firmly, 'it's the last thing we can do for her.'

When they were given the signal, they took a corner each, the undertaker taking the fourth, and, hoisting the coffin to their shoulders, they carried it inside.

Ellie walked behind with the celebrant, her head down.

The crematorium was stark and austere, relieved only by the dramatically colourful floral arrangements Will had organised. They sat together in the front pew and listened as the celebrant read the agreed readings. She'd asked if they wanted to give a eulogy, showing no surprise when they'd said no.

Will regretted the decision, one that had been made by Ellie in the tone of voice that said she didn't want to discuss it. He'd have liked to have said a few words, to have said they'd miss her. He'd have liked to have said he'd take care of her child, but they were words he could never say. Even now, at her funeral, secrets had to be kept.

He glanced at Ellie. What had she said? That their secrets meant he could never leave her? A chill ran through him and he felt his eyes fill. Looking at the sad coffin, he wished they were tears for Tia, but he was honest enough to admit they were for himself.

Thankfully, it was a short service, no sooner started than over. To the strains of 'We'll Meet Again' the curtain slowly moved across, and Tia was gone. Will's eyes dried as he stared, unblinking. She was gone. His face hardened. And if there was any evidence that Ellie had a hand in her death, that was gone too.

He could live with it, he didn't really have a choice. But for Bill's sake, he had to know one way or the other.

48

A taxi took them to the Japanese restaurant, Tyler and Adam making small talk while Will and Ellie sat lost in their thoughts. There were no other customers at the early hour they arrived, the quiet venue adding to the sombre mood of the small party.

Only when the food arrived did they start to speak about Tia. There were few anecdotes they could share to lighten the mood, certainly no funny stories of things she did or happy memories of times they'd had together.

Adam did his best, speaking of times he'd gone to see her at St Germaine's. 'I never bothered ringing ahead to tell them I was coming,' he said, 'after all, she was always going to be there. The staff would go and fetch her, and she'd come into that awful visitors' room and greet me with, "*Hi, Adam,*" as if she'd just seen me the day before. Sometimes,' he smiled ruefully, 'there would be months or more between visits but her greeting never changed. We'd sit in that grim room over a pot of tea and cheap biscuits and I'd ask her how she was. She always laughed and said the same thing, "*I'm okay.*" She didn't volunteer much apart from that, but she'd ask me about where I'd been and sit and listen to me talk. When we finished the tea, she'd get up, put the cups and saucers back onto the tray, say, "*Goodbye, Adam,*" and leave.'

He laughed. 'The first time I went to visit her, I sat there waiting for her to come back. She never did.'

'I only went once,' Tyler admitted with a defensive shrug. 'I felt depressed for days afterwards. God, it was so grim.'

'She was happy there,' Adam said, scowling at him. 'I made sure of that. There are fewer and fewer places available to provide assisted living.'

Tyler patted his arm. 'I wasn't criticising,' he said, 'I know you did your best. But I'm glad she spent her last months living with Ellie and Will. I'm sure she was much happier.'

Will pasted a smile in place. There was no point in telling them it wasn't working out, that Ellie was unhappy with her twin living with her, that the day Tia died, she was heading for an assisted living bungalow in Brighton. No point at all.

The stories he could have told about her, the episode with the obstetrician, the antenatal classes, the moment they realised she was in labour, the smile on her face when she held Bill, the times they spent playing with the child – he couldn't share any of them. Instead, swallowing the sadness and the bitter guilt, he told them the very mildly amusing story of the first time Tia had fillet steak. 'She was afraid to eat it because she didn't know what it was,' he said with a chuckle.

After that, they made light conversation and ended the lunch as soon as they could. Adam, pleading tiredness, promised to call around to see Bill in the next few days rather than going back to their house that afternoon. They all knew he was lying. He'd done his duty in memory of his old friend, but his heart had never been in it. Now that Tia was gone, and

Ellie the mother of a small child, the relationship between them would continue to fade with the passing years.

Outside the restaurant, they hailed separate taxis, Ellie and Will heading home, Adam and Tyler heading elsewhere. 'You'll let us know if you decide to come and visit,' Adam said, shaking Will's hand, 'remember there's always a bed for you.'

Will didn't bother reminding him that they'd already made a tentative date. He'd known it was never going to happen. 'Perhaps we'll meet up for lunch before you go back,' he said.

'Absolutely,' Adam said, opening the taxi door, 'we'll be in touch.' Ellie sat silently until they reached home. Inside the house, she turned to Will. 'I'm going to lie down for a while. I'm so tired.'

'Shall I bring you up a cup of tea?'

She shook her head, turned and went up the stairs.

The kitchen door opened, and Mary stood with a sympathetic smile on her face. 'The kettle's on to make some tea,' she said, offering the age-old panacea.

He smiled gratefully. 'A cup of tea would be just right, thank you. I have a few phone calls to make, could you bring it into the sitting room for me?'

His laptop was where he'd left it. He pulled it out from under the sofa, switched it on and waited for it to power up. His mind drifted to Adam; he'd bet they didn't hear from him again. It made it easier, with the secrets they had, to have as few people as possible close to them.

With a sigh of regret, he focused on his laptop and, within minutes of starting his search, had the information he wanted. And, more importantly, the phone numbers of the people to contact.

Mary arrived, carrying a tray she deposited on the table in front of him. She'd taken extra pains with it. One plate held sandwiches, neatly cut into triangles, another a selection of biscuits. She'd used a china teapot they rarely bothered using and china cups and saucers instead of mugs.

'How kind,' he said, genuinely touched.

A slight blush of pleasure crossed the woman's face. 'Is Mrs Armstrong holding up?' she asked.

He tilted his head side to side. 'She's gone for a lie down. It's been tough for her.'

'Of course,' Mary said, nodding her understanding. 'If there's anything I can do, please let me know.'

When she'd gone, he poured tea. He didn't want anything to eat; he seemed to have no appetite these days. But, unwilling to offend Mary, he forced himself to eat a couple of sandwiches as he wrote out the phone numbers he needed.

'Hello,' he said, when the first call was answered. 'I'd like to speak to Detective Inspector Walker, please. He was involved in the investigation of a crash my wife was involved in, and I have a few questions I'd like to ask him.' If he'd expected to be put through to him he was quickly disappointed; Walker didn't work in the divisional headquarters of the Brighton constabulary.

'I can give you the number of the station where he works,' he was told. Armed with the new number, he hung up and redialled. This time it was right place but wrong day. Detective Inspector Walker, he was told, was not on duty.

'Is he back tomorrow?' he asked. Getting an affirmative, he hung up.

Tapping the phone against his chin, he considered whether it would be better to go there. Face-to-face conversations were often easier. Once there, he could visit the Brighton coroner's office. He wanted to see the coroner's report into Tia's death.

Decision made, he looked up the addresses of Walker's

station and the coroner's office. They weren't too far apart. Making a note of the directions on the piece of paper, he closed the laptop, folded the paper and tucked it into his pocket.

He'd taken the rest of the week off work. On Friday, he needed to take Ellie to the orthopaedic clinic to have the cast removed.

But tomorrow he was free to do some investigating.

49

He went to see if Ellie was awake. The door was partially open and, listening carefully, he could hear her gentle breathing. Back in the sitting room, he sank into the sofa, reached for the remote and switched on the television. There was a movie on, one he'd not seen before. He relaxed, let his mind go blank and watched it.

The movie was almost over before the door opened and Ellie appeared, wearing a carelessly tied robe, her hair messy. 'Hello,' she said, coming in and sitting beside him. She pulled her legs up, curling them under her. 'I didn't think I'd sleep,' she said, smiling at him.

He reached for her and pulled her close, her head settling onto his shoulder where it belonged. 'You needed it,' he murmured into her hair, feeling closer to her than he had for a long time. *Before Tia.*

The thought had come unbidden but, once there, it wouldn't go away. Especially as he realised he'd never asked Mary how Bill was, nor had he gone to see him. His eyes closed in the face of the wave of guilt that washed over him. Had Ellie been right? His contentment – was it because, for just a moment, he'd forgotten about him, about Mary? It was just as it used to be. Just the two of them.

Guilt had him push Ellie away. 'Sorry,' he said. 'I just remembered something.' He stood. 'I'll be back in a minute. Do you want anything?'

She stretched and yawned. 'I'm feeling a little peckish. The sushi was lovely, but it wasn't very filling.'

He smiled. Just what he'd thought. 'How about I order a takeaway?' he said. 'Maybe Italian?'

'Perfect,' she said and reached for the remote control.

Leaving her to it, Will went next door to do what he should have done hours before. He smiled at Mary, who was stirring something in a pot, and went to peer into Bill's cot. He was awake, his little hands reaching toward a mobile Mary had attached to the cot.

Bending, Will gently brushed his forehead. 'Hello, Son,' he said, and watched as the child gurgled happily and waved small chubby hands. 'He's looking well, Mary,' he said.

She turned to look at him without stopping her circular stirring motion. 'He's a happy child,' she said. 'They're easy at this age. As long as they're well-fed and kept warm, and given a bit of love and affection, they usually do well.'

He smiled. 'You make it sound easy.'

'Babies aren't complicated. That comes a lot later.'

He gave the child another glance before taking a menu from the drawer. 'I'm going to order a takeaway, Mary. Would you like anything?'

'No, thanks,' she said, stirring faster, 'I've something almost ready.'

He left her to it, ringing the Italian from the hallway.

'It'll be here in about fifteen minutes,' he said to Ellie a few minutes later, setting the plates and glasses he'd gathered on the table, a cold bottle of Chardonnay wedged under his arm. Handing Ellie a wine glass, he twisted the lid and poured her a glass.

'A toast,' she said, raising her glass. 'To Tia.'

Surprised, he lifted his glass and echoed her words. 'To Tia.' They touched glasses, the ping on contact loud in the quiet room. Before the sound had faded Ellie had reached for the remote control and turned the volume up.

She'd spread out on the sofa and didn't move her legs to allow him sit. He stood for a moment, confused at her sudden change of mood, before stepping back and sitting in the single chair.

She was watching a chick flick, an unusual choice for her, and was obviously enjoying it, laughing and smiling at regular intervals. It was good for her, he decided, smiling at her infectious laughter. It was the most relaxed he'd seen her in a long time.

He'd expected her to be sad, maudlin even, expected he'd be needed to console and support, instead, he felt redundant. Shouldn't he be pleased with how well she was coping? Why did he feel it was just a tad strange to be so apparently happy? He didn't want to relate her relaxed mood to the words that still echoed in his head. *When it was just you and me.*

The sound of the doorbell interrupted his thoughts. He stood, giving Ellie a glance as he left the room. Her attention never wavered from the screen. Who knew chick flicks were so addictive? When he returned, moments later, she didn't stir. Laying out the containers, he took off the lids, arranged spoons in each and sat back on his heels. 'Will you put that on hold,' he asked her, slightly irritated.

Her eyes flicked over him and then over the food on the table. With obvious reluctance, she nodded, and, even more grudgingly, she aimed the remote at the television and put the movie on hold. Unfortunately, it stopped just as the heroine of the tale had opened her mouth to scream, her wide-jawed face frozen in time.

'Not exactly the most pleasant of sights,' Will said, reaching for a plate.

Ignoring him, she helped herself, sat back with her plate and started to eat.

'I need to go into work tomorrow,' he said, the lie coming easily. 'There's a meeting I can't miss. I'm sorry, I had hoped to be here for you.'

His rehearsed words seemed silly in the face of her obvious lack of grief.

'That's fine,' she said, spearing a piece of chicken with her fork. She put it in her mouth and chewed, waiting until she'd swallowed before adding, 'I'll be fine. The weather is supposed to be good, I might take Bill out for a walk.'

The piece of beef Will was swallowing caught in his throat causing him to cough convulsively. There was no water; he reached for his wine glass and swallowed the contents. 'Sorry,' he said, wiping a serviette over his red, perspiring face. 'Do you think that's wise? You've only been out a few times yourself. The baby buggy is more awkward than it looks, especially with your cast.' She shrugged. 'I'll be fine. After all,' she smiled across at him, 'I can use it a bit like a walking frame to support me, can't I?'

What could he say? Are you planning to murder my son to get your wish? It sounded crazy even to him. Maybe that's what it was. He was going crazy. Suddenly, he was no longer hungry. Putting his plate down, he refilled his glass and sat back in his chair.

As if this was a signal she could resume her movie, Ellie curled up with her plate and pressed play on the remote. The room filled suddenly with the sound of a woman's scream.

50

Like most lies, the one he told grew legs. He had to leave at the same time he normally left for work and, although he'd have preferred to wear jeans and a casual jacket, he was forced to wear his usual work uniform of suit and tie, and to take his blasted briefcase.

He caught the eight o'clock train to Brighton from Victoria station and, eighty minutes later, he was standing outside the police station, staring at the formidable door with a feeling of panic.

Why was he here? To find out, without the shadow of a doubt, that Ellie couldn't possibly have killed Tia? Because then his fears about Bill's safety would also be unfounded?

And if there was still doubt or, worse, if his fears were proven, what then? Could he live with Ellie knowing she was a murderer? He ran a hand over his face. It appeared he didn't have any choice. They were, as she so clearly pointed out, tied together by their secrets.

He sighed and turned away. He needed more coffee before

he could face what he had to do. Looking down the street, he saw a familiar sign and headed toward it.

With a large cappuccino in front of him, he considered what he'd come to find out. He had to tread carefully with his questions; the man was a detective, he didn't want to give him cause for suspicion. He sipped his coffee and faced the truth. If his fears were proven, it wouldn't change how he felt about Ellie. He loved her, had done from the first day they met. Whatever she did, he'd still love her.

He wasn't sure what that said about him.

The cafe was busy with friendly staff and a pleasant atmosphere, but the coffee wasn't good. He pushed it away and stood. He loved her, but he also loved his son, and he needed to know if he was at risk. Back outside the police station, he didn't hesitate, taking the steps to the door two at a time and pushing it open without allowing time to think or change his mind. The desk clerk looked him up and down, taking in his smart suit, his neatly tied tie. 'Can I help you?'

'I'd like to speak to Detective Inspector Walker, please.'

The clerk looked at him without speaking, as if waiting for more information before he could proceed.

'Detective Inspector Walker investigated a crash my wife was involved in. I wanted to ask him a few questions about it. At least,' he babbled on, 'I was hoping he'd be able to answer some questions.' He stopped, feeling embarrassed.

'Take a seat,' he was told, the calm, indifferent clerk waving to a waiting room.

The room was small and stank of a combination of odours, which, he decided, it would be wiser not to try to identify. The chairs, bolted to the floor, had seen better days. Will tried to find one where he wasn't at risk of contamination, choosing one separated by an empty chair from his nearest neighbour, quickly realising why it was empty when wafts of foetid air drifted from the man, causing his nose to twitch. He hugged his briefcase, and hoped he wouldn't have to wait too long.

His hopes, unfortunately, were doomed and it was over an hour before his name was called. He jumped up immediately. 'Here,' he said, hoping it didn't sound as public school boyish to everyone else's ears as it did to his.

He needn't have worried, nobody paid him the slightest attention.

The clerk who had called him waited for him at the doorway and then walked briskly ahead of him, forcing Will to increase his pace. Finally, they stopped at a doorway that the clerk opened without knocking before standing back to let him in.

Expecting to be led into a busy office, Will was surprised and annoyed to find himself in an empty room.

'The inspector will be with you soon,' the clerk said, closing the door and leaving him alone before he had a chance to ask what *soon* meant in the Brighton police vocabulary.

He sat on one of the two chairs in the room, putting his briefcase on the scuffed, worn table in preference to the floor and settled down to wait. In his experience, *soon* usually meant five or ten minutes but it was another twenty before the door opened and a harassed-looking inspector appeared in the doorway.

Will barely recognised him as the man he'd met in the hospital. His skin was pale and dull, dark circles under his eyes hinting at excess of some sort. Standing, he reached out a hand. 'Thank you so much for agreeing to see me,' he said with a smile.

If he expected an apology for being kept waiting, he was disappointed. Walker took his hand briefly, took the chair opposite, and sat looking at him with a distinct lack of interest. 'You wanted to see me?' he said.

Will tried the smile again, feeling it fade in the face of the man's lack of response. He'd practised what he was going to say. It had sounded perfectly reasonable to his reflection in the bathroom mirror. He pasted on the same unconcerned look he'd tried then. 'I'm so sorry to take up your valuable time,' he started, hoping the man didn't think he was being sarcastic. 'We buried my sister-in-law yesterday and Ellie, my wife, is slowly coming to terms with her loss.' He brushed away the image of Ellie laughing at that stupid movie. 'She's finding some aspects of it difficult. If we had more information, I think it would be easier for her to move on.'

Walker ran his hand through lank hair. 'I'm sorry,' he said, 'and I don't mean to be rude. But I've no idea who you are.'

Will blinked in surprise. Of all the reactions he'd expected, this wasn't one of them and he was lost for words. Then he remembered. Of course. He was so used to thinking of Tia in relation to Ellie, he'd forgotten she'd an identity of her own. 'Tia Bradshaw,' he said, waiting for the penny to drop.

It did, Walker's puzzled face clearing a little. 'Ah yes, I remember now. You came to ID her. I'm sorry, your name didn't register.' He ran a hand over his face, rubbed his eyes and added, 'I've been up all night on a case. So how can I help you?' he asked.

Will slipped back into his practised lines. 'My wife drove the car, so is understandably feeling guilty.' He waited for a nod of understanding. It didn't come, the detective's face still registering puzzlement. 'I know it's splitting hairs, really,' he gave a little laugh, 'but if I could tell her that Tia's head injury didn't actually happen in the crash, that it happened afterward when she fell... or something... it might help.'

Walker's frown deepened. 'Splitting hairs indeed,' he said, his eyes narrowing. 'Whatever way you look at it, Tia Bradshaw died as a result of that crash.'

'But not *in* the crash,' Will said, pushing the matter.

The detective shrugged. 'If it makes any difference, no, not in the crash as such. Our theory, and one the coroner agreed with, was that she was relatively uninjured in the actual crash and acquired the head injury as she was getting out of the car. It is quite a drop from the side of an upturned vehicle to the ground, she probably jumped, missed her footing and fell, hitting her head as she did so. The terrain is rocky and we found blood on a number of rocks.'

'Tia's blood,' Will said sadly.

Walker pursed his lips. 'Blood from both women to be exact. Your wife bled extensively from cuts she sustained. She was lucky.'

'Yes,' Will said, 'she was.'

Walker stood abruptly. 'If that's all, I really need to get going.'

'Just one last thing,' Will said, holding a hand up to stop him, 'I'd really like to visit the crash site. Could you tell me how to get there?'

'Are you sure that's wise?' the detective said, looking down with a puzzled look on his face.

Will had prepared for this. 'I promised Ellie,' he said, dropping his eyes to the table. 'It's in the way of a pilgrimage, I suppose you could say.'

Detective Inspector Walker continued to look at him for a moment and then, as if he couldn't find any reason not to, he gave him the directions. With a brief nod, he left the room.

Opening his briefcase, Will took out a notebook and scribbled them down. He sat for a moment thinking over the conversation. It could have happened just the way he said. Tia could have fallen onto a rock and then crawled away from the car. Head injuries were like that, he'd heard many stories of people getting a bang on the head, being able to talk and walk and then collapsing a short while later. It could have happened that way.

Picking up his briefcase, he left. Next stop, the coroner's office. It was, to his surprise, more straightforward.

He told the receptionist at the front desk what he wanted. She pointed him toward the correct department where a helpful administrator asked for proof of identification. Looking at his driving licence, she smiled and handed it back. 'Do you want the full report, including photographs?' she asked him.

'Yes please,' he said.

Leaving him to stand and wait, she headed off and returned a few minutes later. 'That'll be ten pounds, please,' she said, handing him a thick A4 envelope.

He handed over the money and took it from her, putting it into his briefcase without looking at it and, smiling his thanks to the woman, left.

Out in the street, he couldn't see anywhere to have coffee, but this was Brighton, he wouldn't have to go far. In fact, he just had to turn the corner to see a large sign proclaiming a cafe to be the *Best coffee shop in Brighton*.

It might be the best, but he was glad to see it wasn't the busiest. He asked for a flat white and, glancing at the menu board, chose a sandwich to go with it, nodding to a table in the corner when he was asked where he'd be sitting.

He took out the envelope and put his briefcase on another chair. There was nothing written on the outside of it, but he stared at it until his coffee and sandwich arrived. Then he reached for the envelope and opened it.

The report was comprehensive and detailed. He flicked through it all and then started at the beginning, reading line after line, looking for something, anything to prove that Ellie couldn't have been responsible.

The paramedic, the first professional at the scene, reported finding Tia face down. The theory was that she'd fallen as she dropped down from the side of the car and cracked her head on a rock, managing to crawl away from the car before collapsing. Will put the report down and picked up his coffee. So far, it was much as the detective had said. Taking a deep breath, he took out the photographs he'd been avoiding. Most were of the scene of the crash, the skid marks on the road, the tree trunk they'd hit before somersaulting down the slope, the car on its side.

Markers indicated where the women had lain. He was surprised at how closely together they were. And there were photographs of blood on various surfaces including the rock that they theorised Tia had fallen on. There was a report on her head injury, a diagram showing exactly where the injury had occurred and an X-ray showing the concave indent in her skull. He looked at it, frowning. She had come down heavily on that rock.

Or the rock had come down heavily on her.

He read the rest of the report. There was no indication there was any doubt. But then, they didn't know Ellie had a motive, did they? They never asked.

Did his suspicion hold more weight than their theories?

Maybe he should just forget about it all, accept that he'd never be sure, and move on. Words echoed in his head, *just you and me.* Reaching into his pocket, he took out his mobile and hit the speed dial button for home. 'Mary,' he said when the phone was picked up. 'Is Mrs Armstrong awake yet?'

'No, not yet, Mr Armstrong,' she said, 'do you want me to bring the phone to her?'

'No, that's fine, Mary. I just wondered how she was this morning. She mentioned yesterday about taking Bill out in his buggy. I wasn't sure it was a good idea. She's not very strong as yet.'

'It's not a good idea anyway, Mr Armstrong. Bill has a bit of a cough this morning. I'm keeping a close eye on him.'

Feeling relieved that Ellie couldn't take him out, he immediately felt guilty for being pleased his son wasn't well. 'Good,' he said, 'I'll check in with you again later.' He hung up and put his phone away. He thought about getting more coffee, looking toward the server to see if a raised hand would do the trick. But the small coffee shop was busy and she was tied up with other customers. Forgetting about it, he put the coroner's report into his briefcase, left the cafe and headed back to where he'd seen a taxi rank earlier. He was in luck, a taxi stood waiting. Climbing into the back seat, he thought to himself the day was going fairly well, even if he hadn't managed to prove anything. He gave the driver directions and sat back.

'Where?' the taxi driver asked, turning around to look at him, his eyes taking in the smart coat and briefcase.

Will leaned forward and repeated the directions. 'Twelve hundred metres from the junction of the A27 and B2123.' He frowned when he saw the puzzled face of the driver. Surely the directions were clear. 'Is there a problem?'

'Do you have a postcode for where you want to go?'

He'd tempted fate by thinking his day was going without a hitch. 'No postcode,' he said. 'There isn't a building, I just want to go to that stretch of road.'

The taxi driver stared suspiciously. His eyes lingered on the briefcase. 'This isn't something dodgy, is it?'

Will closed his eyes briefly and let his breath out in an exasperated huff. 'No, it's not,' he said emphatically. He shouldn't need to explain why, but it was that or find another taxi. 'It's in the way of a pilgrimage,' he said finally, using the same line he'd used on the detective. 'My sister-in-law was killed in a crash on that part of the road. I promised my wife I'd visit.'

Not convinced, the taxi driver nodded at the briefcase. 'Gonna lay flowers, are you?'

Cursing the lie that necessitated his bringing the briefcase, Will nodded. 'Something like that. Now, either you're going to take me, or I get out and find someone who will.'

With a final speculative glance, the driver shrugged, turned on the engine and pulled into traffic. Will tried to relax but he couldn't. The man's suspicious looks had increased his own doubts. What was he hoping to find there?

Thirty minutes later, the taxi turned onto a tree-lined road. He sat up straight, his eyes peering down the road ahead. Was this where it happened? Moments later, the taxi pulled to the side of the road and stopped. 'Here we are, twelve hundred metres, give or take a few centimetres.'

Will ignored his sarcasm and looked around. The detective had mentioned a fallen tree. It shouldn't be too hard to locate. 'I'll be twenty minutes or so,' he said to the driver.

'Meter is running, mate, take as long as you like.'

He thought about leaving his briefcase in the cab but, catching the driver's eye in the rear-view mirror, changed his mind.

Getting out, he looked up and down the road. Which way? He walked back down the road, hoping he'd chosen correctly. If he didn't see the fallen tree in a few hundred metres, he'd turn and go the other direction.

He was in luck. Minutes later, he saw it. It had to be the one.

There was damage to the upper curve of the trunk which he imagined had been caused by the car. How unlucky they had been. It was the only fallen tree around. He agreed with the consensus that had they come off the road a few metres away, they'd have been slowed by dense undergrowth and might have escaped with just minor injuries.

He circled the fallen tree and headed downward. There had been a lot of rain in recent days, and the undergrowth was lush and slippery. It wasn't the place for leather-soled shoes. Before long, he'd slipped to the ground. Swearing loudly, he hauled himself to his feet with the help of a sapling and eyed the grass stains on his coat with disgust. They weren't going to be easy to explain away. Standing a moment, he looked around. Straight down from the tree, the detective had said. Only by using his imagination could he see evidence of the car's tumble down the slope, imagining the broken branches here and there as proof of its passing. Truth was, in the six weeks since the accident, the undergrowth had covered any evidence there was.

He should have given up, gone back to the taxi and headed home to his wife and child. But he didn't, clinging tightly to his briefcase, he slipped and slid onward, until he came to the clearing where the car had finished its journey.

The car, of course, had gone, but it was easier to imagine the scene here. The police hadn't bothered to remove all evidence of their presence; some of the tape they'd used to cordon off the area from curious dog walkers still hung limply from the trees.

The undergrowth, well trampled by all involved, hadn't, as yet, recovered, so it was easy to identify the area where Tia and his wife had lain close together.

A pilgrimage, he'd told the taxi driver. He wished it were that simple. Opening up his briefcase, he took out the coroner's report, removed the photograph of the crash scene and, with it, figured out where the car had landed. As the inspector had said, the terrain was rocky. It could have happened just as they said.

Moving back to where the bodies had lain, he looked around. More rocks. He kicked one with his foot and it rolled a few inches. Bending, he picked it up, weighed it in his hand and then dropped it. It could have happened that way too. But if there had been evidence, it was long gone.

He'd been fooling himself; he was never going to know the truth. A last look around, and he turned to head back up the slope.

It was time to go home.

He slipped again on the climb back to the road, coming down heavily on his knee, feeling the wet mud seep through. Back in the taxi he looked at it and swore under his breath.

'What was that?' the taxi driver said.

'Nothing,' Will said, irritated. 'Just take me to the train station.'

He arrived at the station, paid the driver without bothering to tip, and walked off hearing sarcastic comments fading behind him as he marched briskly into the station. He swore viciously when he realised he'd just missed a train and would have an hour to wait before the next.

In the gents, he tried his best to rub the mud from his knee, but it was wet and his endeavours simply spread it over a larger area. He'd have been better to wait until it was dry and then he could have brushed it off. Too bloody late now.

The stain on his coat was less visible; he ignored it, took a final look at his knee and, with a groan, left. He was going to sit and have a coffee while he waited but changed his mind. Something stronger was in order. Leaving the station, he headed to a nearby pub and ordered a whiskey. 'Make it a double,' he said.

There was a fire lit. He sat beside it and sipped his drink. Before he'd finished it, he took out his phone and dialled home. 'Just checking on how Bill is?' he said when Mary answered. 'He's much the same,' she said. 'He's been a bit fretful because he's not so well, poor boy, but Mrs Armstrong has been soothing him. He seems happier now.'

Will couldn't think of anything to say apart from, 'Oh, that's good.' Ellie was looking after Bill. That was good, wasn't it? He finished the whiskey and ordered another double. By the end of the second, he didn't know what he thought any more. Maybe he was just thinking too much. Maybe, he was so consumed with guilt for that night with Tia that his brain was addled. After all, wasn't it then that everything had started to go wrong?

Tempted to order another drink, he glanced at his watch. The train would be leaving in ten minutes. If he wanted to catch it he needed to leave now. He staggered slightly when he stood. Hard spirits weren't really his thing, and two doubles was a lot of alcohol on a fairly empty stomach.

The train was a few minutes late, giving him time to order a large takeaway coffee to sober himself up. He sipped it as he waited, taking the remainder on board and finding a window seat where he drank it as the train chugged towards London, and continuing to sip it long after it had gone cold.

It was the heartburn rather than the caffeine which sobered him up before he arrived in Victoria. He walked around until he found a pharmacy. Armed with antacids which he sucked on the Tube, popping one after the other until the pain subsided, he headed home.

51

Ellie was holding Bill in her arms when Will arrived home. He was conscious of the mud on his trousers, the stain on his coat and a lingering reek of whiskey that the faint smell of mint from the antacids didn't disguise.

If Ellie noticed, she said nothing, but Mary gave him a strange look before offering him a mug of coffee. He took it, colour appearing in cheeks already red from the alcohol and drank it staring across the room at the unusual sight of his wife comforting the fretful child. They looked good together, and this was what he'd wanted; so why did the sight make him anxious?

'Don't overdo it, Ellie,' he said, moving to her side. 'You should give him back to Mary, have a rest.'

She shook her head. 'I'm fine, Will.' It wasn't until he mentioned that he was hungry an hour later that she stood up and handed the sleeping child to Mary, who immediately put him into his cot.

'Hungry?' Ellie said, looking around the kitchen for inspiration. She turned to him with a bright smile. 'Let's get a takeaway.' He tried to look enthusiastic. It was all he seemed to eat these days. She'd never been a great cook, but she could unpack an M&S dinner and make it look as if she were. The only thing she really enjoyed cooking was steak. Maybe he'd get some tomorrow on the way home.

Adam rang while they were waiting in the sitting room for the takeaway to arrive. Will spoke to him briefly and handed the phone to Ellie, leaving her talking to him while he got the plates and cutlery ready. He took the last bottle of wine from the fridge. The cupboards were definitely getting bare.

Ellie had put the phone down by the time he got back. 'Are they coming to visit?' he asked her, handing her a glass of wine. She shook her head. 'I mentioned Bill wasn't well. They don't want to risk coming in contact with an infection when they've a long flight ahead of them in a couple of days.'

Will shrugged. 'I got the impression they weren't really interested in seeing him anyway,' he said.

She sipped her wine. 'I'll send them a photograph; at his age it's just as good.'

For a moment, he thought she was joking and waited for her to smile. When she didn't, he gave an uncomfortable laugh. 'Hardly the same as meeting him, is it?'

The look she gave him was critical. 'Hardly,' she said and turned back to the television.

Will didn't bother asking her to mute the television while they ate. He filled his plate and sat back into the chair that was quickly becoming *his* seat in the sitting room as Ellie's preference to spread out on the sofa continued. Normality, he sighed, didn't appear to be heading back his way.

* * *

The next morning, Bill seemed worse. Mary frowned when he came into the kitchen. 'I've been up most of the night with him. His cough seems a lot worse.'

'Do you think he needs to see a doctor?' Will asked, peering into the cot. Bill's round, chubby face looked much the same as usual, but what did he know?

Mary shook her head. 'He doesn't have a temperature, so it's probably just a cold. If you think I should take him, of course, I will.'

'Perhaps it would be as well to wait another day or two,' he said, taking his cue from her. 'As you say, he doesn't have a temperature so there's no point in exposing him to all the bugs that a GP surgery will have.'

She smiled. 'My sentiments exactly,' she said, apparently relieved. 'I'll make sure he has lots of fluids and keep him warm and comfortable. He'll be fine.' She hesitated and then added, 'Mrs Armstrong was great with him yesterday. It seems like she's feeling much better and her maternal instinct is returning.'

He pulled his lips up in a smile, hoping it didn't look as forced as it felt. 'Good,' he said and then, because he couldn't think of anything else to say, he nodded and repeated, 'Good.'

He didn't bother with coffee and headed off to work.

During the day while at his desk, Ellie's change of heart continued to bother him. Was he being too hard on her? 'After all,' he muttered, 'Mary seems to be happy with her.'

His secretary appeared in the doorway. 'Were you calling me?' He looked at her puzzled for a moment and then shook his head. 'Mary, not Maisie,' he said as if that explained everything.

Maisie blinked uncertainly. 'You didn't want me?'

He shook his head, waved her away and reached for the

packet of antacids he'd been chewing with increasing regularity. Popping a couple into his mouth, he resumed his thoughts. Perhaps there was nothing sinister about Ellie's increased interest in Bill. The idea that she was trying to pull the wool over his eyes was ridiculous. 'Ridiculous,' he muttered, unaware he'd said it aloud until he saw the wary eyes of his secretary look his way.

He got up and shut his office door.

* * *

He rang late morning to be told that Bill seemed to be improving and Ellie was still in bed. Mid-afternoon, the improvement had continued. 'Mrs Armstrong has him now,' Mary said. 'She's said she'll look after him while I go and have a lie down.'

'Is that wise?' he said hurriedly. 'She's not very strong.'

There were a few seconds of silence before Mary's voice came again, a little cooler. 'I'm only going to lie down for an hour, Mr Armstrong. She can call me if there's a problem.'

'Yes, of course, of course,' he said, running a hand through his hair. 'Sorry, Mary, it's just that I worry when I'm not there.'

'There's absolutely no need,' she said, but her voice was still cool.

He hung up and sat staring at the phone for several minutes before picking it up and dialling home again. It rang several times before switching to answer machine, his own voice inviting him to leave a message. Hanging up, he dialled again, this time it was engaged. He waited a moment and dialled again. Still engaged. *Just the two of us.* 'Oh God,' he muttered, running a hand over his face. 'She wouldn't, would she?' He tried once more, got the engaged tone again and stood. Should he ring the police? And say what?

That he thought his wife was planning to kill their child... well, not exactly their child, officer, his child with his dead sister-in-law who he suspected his wife of killing.

He laughed, heard the edge of hysteria and stopped, his eyes growing hard. It was time for action.

Slipping on his jacket, he grabbed his coat and told Maisie he felt so unwell that he had to go home. It wasn't precisely a lie; he felt sick to his stomach. Ignoring her raised eyebrows, he rushed from the office.

The underground was fifteen minutes' walk away. Running, he made it in ten, rushing into the station, stepping onto the elevator and pushing past people who stood on the wrong side blocking people like him who were in a hurry. On the platform, he stood too close to the edge and had to step backward when the tube stopped and the door opened to a mass of people getting off. Pushing forward again, he got on, staying near the door while it travelled the four stops to Highbury and Islington.

He couldn't make the Tube go any faster, but he couldn't stand still, stepping from one foot to the other, drawing apprehensive looks.

At his stop, he was out of the door before it had finished opening. He took the elevator, mercifully almost empty this time, racing upward two steps at a time, tripping when he got to the top, righting himself before running on, shouting at people to get out of his way.

He was breathless by the time he reached his house, armpits damp, a trickle of sweat down his back, heart thumping. Leaning on the front gate, he took a shuddering breath. Whatever he was going to find inside, he needed to be calm before he could face it. The key shook in his hand as he tried to insert it into the lock, the sound of metal on metal grating. Finally, he got it in, the key turned, and he pushed the door open.

The house was quiet, but then it usually was. What was he expecting? Screams?

Taking a deep breath, he let it out slowly and walked to the kitchen door. He rested his ear against it but there was nothing to be heard. His hand, sweaty from the race to get home and from the fear that swept over him in waves, slipped on the door-knob. He wiped it against the arm of his coat and tried again. This time it turned, and he pushed the door open.

He was so pumped with fear that he gasped when he saw Ellie standing by the kitchen island, drinking coffee, one hand lazily turning the pages of the newspaper. The gasp brought her face up and she stared at him in surprise. 'I wasn't expecting you home so early,' she said, giving him a friendly smile. The smile faded when she took in his dishevelled look. 'Are you feeling all right? You haven't caught Bill's bug, have you?'

He moved over to the cot. It was empty. 'Where is he?'

A frown creased her brow. 'What's the matter with you?' she asked, moving across to him and laying a hand on his forehead. 'You're all sweaty,' she said, drawing her hand away, 'for goodness' sake don't go near him if you're coming down with something. The poor mite is just getting over his cold.'

Feeling suddenly weak, he pulled a chair from the table and sat. 'I don't feel well,' he admitted. 'You're right, I'd better stay away from him.' He looked around the room. What had she done with him?

'Good idea,' she said kindly. She tousled his hair as she passed by. Will watched as she headed to Mary's bed and bent over it. 'He's still out for the count,' she said, coming back to stand beside him.

His world kept tilting at crazy angles. 'Why is he sleeping over there?'

She laughed. 'I was pointing to birds on the bird-feeder when the phone rang, so I plopped him on the bed. When I got back, he'd fallen asleep, and I didn't want to disturb him. He's been sound asleep since.'

'You took the phone off the hook,' he said, understanding hitting him.

'It's only ever cold calls during the day. Mary said you'd rung so I didn't think you'd call again. When Bill wakes up, I'll put it back on.' She looked at him in confusion for a moment. 'I did right, didn't I?'

'Yes, of course you did,' he hurried to reassure her. His paranoia wasn't her fault. 'I think I might go lie down for a while, until I feel better.' He stood, then looked at the bed. 'I'll just go and look at him first,' he said.

'He's perfectly safe, Will,' she said, with a worried look on her face. 'He's right in the middle; even if he woke and squirmed, he wouldn't fall off.'

She seemed genuinely concerned about him. Will reached out his hand and caressed her cheek. 'I'm sure he's fine,' he said gently. 'I just want to have a look at our son.'

Her hand came up to hold his and she smiled. 'Go have a look, but don't get too close in case you're coming down with something, he doesn't need more germs.'

It was just as she'd said. The baby was lying on his back, his arms stretched above his head, fat fingers curled into fists, his face turned slightly to one side, lips moving now and then as if he were, in his dreams, sucking on a bottle. He was the most beautiful thing Will had ever seen.

He felt Ellie behind him. 'I love you both so much,' he said quietly. 'Both of you make my life complete.' He turned. 'You, me and Bill,' he said, 'we're going to be the happiest of families.' He looked straight into her eyes and said again, 'You *both* make my life complete.'

She moved into his arms and put her hands around his neck. 'I love you too,' she said. 'I know these last few weeks have been hard, but I'm feeling so much better. And I can feel the bond growing between me and Bill.' She smiled. 'Just the way you hoped it would.'

They looked down at the sleeping child.

'I was thinking,' she continued, turning back to him. 'I might not go back to work at all. After the crash, and losing Tia, the job seems to have lost its allure somehow. I think I'd like to be a stay-at-home mum. Not yet,' she added quickly, 'but when I'm completely better, maybe in a few more weeks. We could do without a nanny, have the place to ourselves. Just the three of us.' Will pulled her close. He loved her with every breath in his body. *Just the three of us.* With those words in his head, he stood with his wife in his arms and thought he'd been wrong, stupid, paranoid. Everything was just fine. Just the way he'd hoped it would be.

52

The following days sped by and, before they realised it, it was eight weeks since the accident. Ellie was better. Her cast had come off and physiotherapy had restored full function to her wrist. All the cuts had healed without scarring and the bruises had faded and gone.

There were some residual problems from the concussion. Will noticed she was slower to pick up things than she had been and she was less assertive about what she wanted or didn't want. Mostly, he missed the fire and passion in their relationship. They used to have heated rows, followed by the most incredible make-up sex. It made him smile to remember.

But now, he'd see her with Bill and think the change was for the better. He couldn't imagine the old Ellie sitting down and reading stories from a children's book or just holding him for hours, singing childish nursery rhymes.

'How soon do you think we could manage without Mary,' he asked her one Sunday afternoon. They'd taken Bill to a local park and were sitting watching children in the playground.

She looked at him. 'She is so kind, so lovely, but it would be nice to have the place to ourselves. Sometimes, when I come down in my robe, I can almost feel her disapproval.'

He laughed. 'She's old school, she probably expects you to be up and dressed at cockcrow the way she is.' He felt the sun on his face with pleasure and then peered down at Bill to make sure he was out of it, tilting the parasol slightly to shelter his skin from a sneaky sunbeam.

'We have to give her a month's notice,' he said, reaching for her hand. 'We could do it this evening and then by July, we'll have the place to ourselves.'

'Just the three of us,' Ellie said, squeezing his hand.

Will breathed deeply, catching the scent of roses that drifted in from a local garden. The sky was blue, the sun shining and all was definitely right with his world. He rested an arm on the bench behind him, letting his eyes drift over the scene in front. In a few years, Bill would be playing in the playground. It would be good if he had a brother or sister to play with. Looking at Ellie, he wondered if it was worth broaching the subject of surrogacy again. There had been a lot of changes since her absolute refusal to think about it.

After all, she'd gone from *just the two of us* to *just the three of us*. Could he persuade her to go with *just the four of us*? It was worth thinking about. But perhaps, he grinned, one change at a time. They gave Mary the news that evening. She didn't seem surprised. 'I knew this was coming,' she said with a smile. 'Actually, this is my last job. I've been planning on retiring for a while, so it's come at a good time. I don't know if you want me to work a month's notice, I'd be happy to leave earlier if it suited.'

They agreed she would leave in two weeks. Will opened a bottle of wine, persuaded Mary to have a glass and they drank to her retirement and to their future without her. 'We'll probably be begging you to come back within a couple of days,' he said with a laugh, finishing his glass and pouring another.

'No,' Ellie said, her face serious, 'we won't, I can manage. I'm not an idiot, you know?'

Silence followed her remark. Will looked at her, horrified, his head woolly from the wine too quickly drunk on an empty stomach. 'Of course, you're not,' he said, trying not to slur his words, wondering if it would be bad form to ask Mary to make some coffee.

She didn't need to be asked. There was silence as she filled three mugs with coffee and brought them back to the table. Seeing Will's shocked face, she took it upon herself to smooth troubled waters. 'He didn't mean anything by it, love,' she said, resting a hand on Ellie's arm. 'It was just a silly joke. You'll cope perfectly well without me.'

'Of course, you will, I was teasing you,' Will said, 'you're wonderful with Bill.'

'I am, aren't I?' Ellie said, her eyes wet. 'I'm just going upstairs for a bit. I'll be back.'

They watched her go, Will running a hand through his hair. How thoughtless he was. He gave Mary a rueful grin. 'I put my feet in it there, didn't I?'

She smiled and patted his hand. 'She seems strong but she's still recovering from the accident and her sister's death, Mr Armstrong,' she said. 'I don't know if you know it, but she spends a lot of time in her sister's room.'

'Really?' Will said, more than a little surprised. He'd never told Mary about the tension between the two sisters so she wouldn't have known there was little love lost between them. 'Tia didn't bring an awful lot with her from St Germaine's,' he explained, 'most of the clothes she had were bought when she moved in here. I suppose we should pack it up, turn it back into a guest bedroom. To be honest, I hadn't really given it a lot of thought.'

'I think it gives Mrs Armstrong some comfort, being close to her sister's things,' Mary said, 'so be careful. She might rely on it for a bit longer.'

Will nodded. What she said made sense. After all, despite the tension between the two, they were still sisters.

Mary hesitated before saying, 'You haven't thought about taking her back to the doctor... You know, about her head injury?'

Will looked at her in surprise. 'It wasn't a head injury, as such,' he said. 'She had concussion. She came out of it very quickly, within hours, actually.' He cocked a head to one side. 'What made you ask?'

She looked down at her hands clasping the coffee mug. 'Don't forget, I didn't know her before her accident, so I don't know if she's changed much. It's just that you mentioned she had a very high-powered finance role...' She looked at him apologetically. 'You'd never guess from the way she is.'

'I don't understand,' Will said, feeling a sudden chill.

'Well, for instance, I asked her to help me when I was making lunch the other day. Just to weigh out four ounces of butter. The scales were on the counter, all she had to do was cut some butter and put it on it, but she just looked at it blankly and turned away. And there was the other week when I asked her to sign my attendance sheet, you know, the one you do for me?' She waited until Will nodded before continuing, 'Well, she started and then grabbed the piece of paper and tore it up... angrily like... before telling me to get you to do it.' She sighed. 'I feel bad telling tales, but there have been a few other things; her absent-mindedness for one. She says she's going to do something and then forgets completely. I just wondered if you'd noticed and whether perhaps you should speak to the doctor again?'

Will frowned. Hadn't he thought the same thing? Mary was looking apprehensive, as if she'd broached a subject she shouldn't have. He nodded. 'They said there might be some residual problems,' he admitted. 'I keep thinking if I'm patient and give it time, she'll recover completely.'

'It's been more than eight weeks,' she said. 'It might be worth checking in with them. Make sure everything is as it should be.' He put his mug down and pushed it away. 'Tell me honestly,' he said, 'do you think she'll manage to look after Bill without you?' Mary smiled reassuringly. 'Goodness, yes. I didn't mean to worry you about that. To be honest, she's been doing most of the work looking after Bill recently. She makes up his feeds quicker than I do, now. I did have to show her several times, but now she's a whizz.'

'That's good to know. But you're right, I'll give the consultant who looked after her a ring and have a chat.' He smiled. 'At least it will put my mind at ease.'

He slept little that night, worrying about what Mary had said. She hadn't known Ellie before the crash, but he had and he couldn't deny she'd changed. Maybe there was something the doctors in the hospital had missed. If so, her condition might get worse.

* * *

At work the next day, he contacted Professor Grosschalk's secretary and asked if he could make an appointment to see him, biting his lip with frustration when he was told it would be the following week. Having, at last, decided to do something, he wanted to do it today.

It wasn't to be. Despite emphasising the urgency of the situation, the secretary wasn't budging with dates and, in the face of his persistence, said, 'I would advise if you are very concerned about your wife, Mr Armstrong, that you should take her to your local hospital.' Knowing when he was beat, he took the appointment for the following week and hung up. It was probably just as well. Between now and then, he'd observe Ellie, take notes and then would have a clearer picture to present. He sat back in his chair and flicked through emails he'd not bothered to read, frowning when he read one.

His office door was open. 'Maisie,' he called out, seeing his secretary's head immediately lift.

She came in and stood looking at him, her hands clasped in front, thumbs tapping.

Will had known her for years, he'd never seen her looking so uncomfortable. 'I was just reading an email about a meeting last week,' he said, nodding to the computer screen. 'I don't remember being informed about any meeting.'

Maisie licked her lips and dropped her eyes to the floor. 'What's going on?' he asked, suddenly realising how many strange looks he'd been getting recently. He supposed he'd taken quite a bit of time off in the last couple of months. 'I wasn't invited, was I?' he asked gently.

'Mr Metcalf said not to bother you, that you had enough on your plate,' she said. 'I'm sure it doesn't mean anything.'

Will nodded. 'I'm sure,' he said, 'thanks, Maisie. Close the door after you, will you?'

'You sure you're okay?' she asked, her brow furrowing.

'Yes,' he smiled, 'of course.' When she'd gone, he dropped his face into his hands. Shit. When the CEO leaves you out of management meetings it most certainly did mean something. He wondered what else he'd been left out of. What was it

Maisie had asked, '*You sure you're okay?*' He seemed to be hearing that a lot recently.

He could check through all the emails to see what he'd missed, he could even ask Maisie, but he didn't do either. Instead, he sat staring into space until it was time to leave.

* * *

He started preparing for his appointment with Professor Grosschalk that evening. They'd got into the habit of having dinner in front of the television in the sitting room, leaving the living room to Mary. Tonight, when Ellie brought dinner in, he reached for the remote and switched off the television. He caught her surprised glance and smiled to himself.

'We never get a chance to talk any more,' he said. 'I thought we could chat over dinner. The way we used to.'

'Just the two of us,' she smiled, handing him his plate. 'Exactly.'

He waited until she sat before asking, 'What do you think of the election campaign so far?'

To his surprise, she shook her head. 'Remember,' she said firmly, 'we said we'd never discuss politics over dinner again after you got so animated you broke that lovely china vase a friend gave me.'

He laughed. 'Gosh, I'd forgotten about that,' he said. 'It was one you particularly liked too.'

'You bought me another,' she said with a smile, reaching for her wine glass, 'but you promised, no more politics at dinner.'

He lifted his fork and waved surrender. 'No more politics,' he agreed. Remembering the vase reminded him of the friend. 'Are you still in contact with her... Miranda, was it?'

'Amanda,' she corrected him. 'I haven't seen her for a long time. She moved to Cardiff when she got married.'

'Perhaps you should contact her, go for a visit. You were very close.'

'Perhaps,' she said without much enthusiasm.

They chatted until the conversation flagged. With a sigh, Will reached for the remote and switched the television on. From the corner of his eye, he could see her relax. Nothing wrong with that, he was doing the same himself.

By the day of his appointment with Professor Grosschalk, he had nothing written on the A4 pad he'd put aside for his notes. There was nothing definite to say. She hadn't forgotten anything recently or said anything inappropriate. She was quiet, less assertive than she used to be and there was a certain indefinable something about her that was missing.

'How are you feeling these days,' he'd asked her two days before he was due to go for the appointment. 'It's a couple of months since the crash, do you think you're back to yourself?'

She'd looked at him, surprised but slightly wary. 'Don't I appear back to myself?'

He'd heard the slightly sarcastic note in her words and knew he needed to tread warily. 'You seem a little quiet at times,' he'd said with a shrug. 'Maybe you need a vitamin or something?'

'Quiet?' She'd looked at him for a long time.

Long enough for colour to rush to his face. 'Just a little,' he'd tempered.

She'd picked Bill up and jiggled him on her hip before picking up the bottle she'd heated for him and settling into the sofa. 'Quiet,' she'd said again, slipping the teat into the child's mouth. When he was sucking away happily, she'd looked back at him. 'You don't think I have reason to be quiet?' she'd asked.

The colour still high on his cheeks, he nodded slowly. 'Yes, of course you do,' he'd said and, after a few minutes, left the room.

If he'd given any consideration to bringing her along to the appointment with the professor, he certainly wasn't going to do so now. If she was changed since the accident, she either didn't want to face it, or was in denial. He'd go on his own, see what the man had to say. He went by train again, settling into his seat and trying to relax as he watched first London, and then rolling fields, pass by. The train, chugging gently, lulled him to sleep before they were halfway. He woke when it pulled into Brighton, brushed off the initial disorientation from waking in a strange place and stepped off the train onto a crowded platform.

A taxi took him to the private hospital where Professor Grosschalk had his consulting rooms. He arrived twenty minutes early, checked in with his secretary, and sat drinking excellent coffee while the minutes ticked by. He checked his watch when it reached the appointed time, and the secretary made no move to call him. Waiting five minutes for politeness, he approached her. 'My appointment was for 2 p.m.,' he said, nodding to the clock behind her head.

'That's correct, Mr Armstrong,' she said. 'Unfortunately, he is often delayed. You're his first appointment, as soon as he arrives, I'll direct you in.'

And with that he had to be satisfied.

It was two thirty before the professor arrived. He came in without the appearance of rushing, taking his time to greet his secretary and listen to the messages she had for him. Will, he ignored, walking past the waiting area and opening his office door. It was another five minutes before he heard the words he'd been waiting thirty-five minutes for. 'Mr Armstrong, you can go in now.'

Professor Grosschalk sat behind his desk, a pair of narrow glasses perched on his nose. He looked over them at Will. 'Mr Armstrong,' he said pleasantly, 'please take a seat. My apologies for keeping you waiting. Now,' he said, sitting back, forearms resting on the arms of his chair, the slim manicured hands that Will remembered noticing in the hospital, dangling. He wondered how hard he had to work at appearing so relaxed.

Now that he was here, Will wasn't sure what to say. He'd hoped to have facts; what he had were vague suspicions and the opinion of a woman who'd only known his wife a few weeks.

'You looked after my wife when she was in hospital after her crash,' he said slowly. 'We had a few words about her at the time.'

Grosschalk nodded but said nothing.

Will wanted to take out a handkerchief and wipe his brow but was afraid of what it might show so he ignored the beads of sweat he could feel ping on his forehead. 'You said, at the time, that it was impossible to say if she'd sustained any long-term damage from her concussion.'

'Yes, I remember.' The professor moved to pick up a file. 'She recovered very quickly, I gather,' he said. 'I sent her notes to your GP but no further information was requested from me.'

Will nodded. 'She has been fine,' he admitted. 'It's just that...' He stopped, realising suddenly that he couldn't tell this man everything. He was aware of the physical damage Ellie had sustained, and would guess at some of the mental damage that would have affected anyone involved in an accident. But he couldn't tell him about the baby, about what he'd put her through beforehand.

'It's just that...?' The professor encouraged him, his eyes flicking conspicuously to his watch.

'She's different,' he went on, 'quieter, more docile.'

The professor opened the file and took out a report. 'Really,' he said, putting it down, 'her concussion was relatively minor. She was breathing on her own. Her observations were stable the whole time. An EEG was done – it was normal. Before we discharged her from ICU she had a brain scan, and it showed no damage.'

Will hadn't known about the EEG or brain scan; the doctor who'd come to see them had never mentioned them.

The professor closed the file. 'Your wife had a bad car crash, Mr Armstrong. But her physical injuries weren't serious. However,' he added with a sympathetic glance, 'sometimes the mental damage takes a lot longer to heal. You've heard, I take it, of post-traumatic stress?'

Of course, Will had. His face cleared. 'You think it could be that?'

Grosschalk shrugged. 'It's more common than people like to think. And, of course, there is the issue that she was driving the car in which her sister died. Her twin sister, wasn't it? That has to have had an impact.' He opened a drawer in his desk and took out a card. 'This is the number of the British Psychological Society,' he said, handing it to him. 'They will be able to direct you to someone who is an expert in PTSD.' He waited a second and then stood, holding one of his slim hands out to Will. 'I hope it all works out for you, Mr Armstrong.'

Armed with the card, Will took the obvious dismissal lightly.

He felt better than he'd felt in weeks.

It wasn't until he was on the train home that reality hit him. Could Ellie go to a psychologist and not bring up all the lies, the secrets? And if she had to hold back on them, what would be the point in going? He stared at his reflection in the train window. He'd speak to her, at least give her the choice.

He waited until after dinner to bring it up, reaching for the remote to switch off the television, ignoring her look of irritation. 'I've something to tell you,' he said, looking across at her. 'I was a little worried about you, so I went to see that consultant neurologist who looked after you in Brighton. Professor Grosschalk, remember him?' When she didn't nod, just kept staring at him, he went on, 'I was concerned you were still suffering from effects of the crash. He doesn't think there's any physical problem but he did suggest you might be suffering from post-traumatic stress.'

He waited for a reaction, any reaction.

Her voice, when she did finally speak, was cold, 'You went to see him about me? Without asking me?'

'I was worried about you,' he said.

'A couple of days ago, you accused me of being quiet. Now I have this... this whatever it is.'

'Post-traumatic stress,' he said, keeping his voice level. 'It's very common.' He hesitated before continuing. 'Professor Grosschalk just suggested you *might* be suffering from it.'

When she said nothing, he ran a hand through his hair in frustration and moved to sit beside her, pushing her legs out of the way. 'I thought I was doing the best for you, Ellie,' he said. 'You have to admit, you haven't been the same since the accident. You're giving up the job you loved without a blink. You've not been out with your friends, in fact you rarely leave the house.'

He reached for her hand but she pulled away, her face set and hard. 'I read up about it when I got home,' he went on, trying to get through to her. 'One of the ways PTSD can manifest itself is in the person withdrawing and becoming isolated, giving up things they used to enjoy. It's called emotional numbing, Ellie. You don't want to think about the crash so you're dealing with it by trying not to feel anything about anybody. Even me,' he added.

She blinked. 'What do you mean, even you?'

He shook his head. 'You have to admit, Ellie, our sex life has taken a bit of a nosedive. It used to be fun and passionate, but nowadays...' He stopped abruptly as she turned away from him. He knew he'd hurt her, but he needed her to face reality. 'You need to get help,' he said. 'Grosschalk gave me a number for the British Psychological Society, but you can go to your GP first. There's medication that helps as well, antidepressants.' He waited for her to say something. When she did, it wasn't what he expected her to say.

'You're a fool,' she said, turning back to look at him, her upper lip pulled up in a sneer. 'There's absolutely nothing wrong with me. You, on the other hand, I'm not so sure about. Since you fucked Tia, you've been sucking antacids like they're smarties. And just how many days have you taken off work, using me as an excuse but really because you couldn't get out of bed, eh?'

She got to her feet and stood, arms crossed, looking down on him. 'I'm not the one who is constantly stressed and whose clothes are hanging off them because they've lost so much weight. Just how much weight have you lost, Will? A stone, two? It isn't me who needs help, it's you.'

He stood shakily and faced her, his mouth opening and closing as he desperately sought words to defend himself.

But she wasn't finished. 'You screwed my sister and you can't get over it, can you?' She jabbed her finger at him, stopping before she came in contact. 'You talk about *emotional numbing,* Will, just when was the last time *you* picked up your son?'

He felt his knees grow weak and collapsed heavily back onto the sofa and looked up at her stunned, feeling a shiver running down his spine. *My God, was she right?* When *was* the last time he'd picked Bill up? Blinking rapidly, he realised he couldn't remember. He ran a hand over his face and rubbed his eyes. It would explain the strange looks he'd been getting from his colleagues at work and the numerous times people had asked if he were okay.

She was right about it all. He *had* lost over a stone in weight and he'd been aware, somewhere in the back of his mind, that he wasn't staying home for her benefit. He faced the truth now. Sleepless nights had left him so tired he didn't want to get out of bed in the morning. And, when he did, when he dragged himself into work, he couldn't focus. No wonder he was left out of meetings. And hadn't his workload become a lot lighter just recently?

He cupped his face in his hands and rubbed it before looking at her.

It all made sense now. There was nothing wrong with her. He was just looking for someone to blame, for a way out. Because guilt was eating him up, the awful, gut-rotting secret that he had slept with his sister-in-law and was glad, yes, he could admit it, he was glad she was dead because now, it would never come out.

All his suspicions about Ellie were a smoke screen to hide what he really believed: he was to blame for Tia's death.

'Oh God, Ellie,' he said, his voice thick, 'I'm so sorry. I don't know what I'm doing.'

53

Watching him for a moment, she sat beside him and held her arms out, an invitation in her eyes. His face cleared, just a little, and he moved closer and buried his head in her chest.

She held him for a long time, until his sobbing stopped and she felt him relax, then she lifted his head and looked at him, her brown eyes serious. 'I love you with all my heart,' she said, 'we'll get through this. Tomorrow, I'll make an appointment for you to see the GP. You need to get some help, Will.'

Waiting until he nodded in agreement, she went on, 'You'll get better and then it will be back to the way it used to be.'

A few minutes later, she sat back. 'I think I'll head to bed,' she said, 'I'm shattered.'

'I'm going to stay up a while.' He smiled up at her, his eyes full of gratitude, and then he said, 'I love you, Ellie.'

Blowing him a kiss from the doorway, she closed the door. She should go and say goodnight to Mary and Bill, but she'd had enough for one day. She hadn't lied; she was absolutely shattered.

Still, there'd be no more talk of her being *quiet*, or of visits to psychologists or doctors. Not for her anyway. She smothered a laugh, holding her hand quickly over her mouth, and then headed upstairs.

He wouldn't come upstairs for a while, she guessed, it was safe to go into Tia's room.

She'd not visited as much recently but for the first few weeks after the crash she'd spent some time there every day. It helped keep her life in order.

It was tidy, she'd kept it that way. 'Like a shrine,' Mary had said the only time she'd gone in. She'd asked her to leave it alone and, as far as she knew, the woman had done so. She'd be gone in a few days; it would be better without her. Safer.

Will never visited. He'd thought it was maudlin to keep her room as it was, suggested they should clear it out, but she'd dropped a hint in Mary's ear that it was important to her and that seemed to have worked. There'd been no more talk of it.

Sitting on the bed, she looked around. It was a pretty room, decorated nicely for the poor simple woman from St Germaine's. She should have been happy here, shouldn't have wanted anything else. Certainly, shouldn't have wanted Will. But she had, from the first day she'd met him when he'd mixed them up and thought she was Ellie.

That was when the idea first came to her. That she could live as Ellie, *be* Ellie.

With a smile, she took a folder from the shelf and opened it. All the letters, neat and tidy in their own poly-pocket, every letter from the very first. There was a whole shelf of them. Twelve folders. She turned page after page, all the intimate details of her sister's life, all the secrets, things she guessed even Will didn't know. She supposed Ellie believed she had burnt them, she'd never asked. Her lip curled. How little insight she had to ask her to do such a thing! Did she really think her simple sister had access to matches? She had tried to destroy them, however, every week going to the office and asking permission to use the shredder, every week chickening out. Did she know, even then, that they'd be useful someday?

Closing the folder, she put it back on the shelf with the others. She knew she wasn't clever, but she had an excellent memory for stories and knew the ones in these letters like the back of her hand. When she'd woken in the hospital after the crash, she'd seen Will there beside her and her mind had raced through them all. *It's a bit different to that hospital in Italy.* It was a perfect reference, convincing him, if he'd ever had a doubt, that it was his wife lying there and not her twin.

He would never know. And she'd make him happy. She went a little wrong for a time but his criticism that she wasn't making an effort had been enough to make her understand she wasn't playing it quite right. But now, she was doing better. Soon, Mary would be gone, and it would be just the three of them.

She bit her lip. She still wasn't sure about Bill. The life in the letters, the one Ellie and Will had lived, that was the one she'd wanted. But he seemed to really love the child so maybe it would be okay.

Maybe she'd learn to play happy families.

First, though, she'd help Will to get over this guilt trip he was on. Poor man, to go through life thinking he'd seduced his simple sister-in-law. What a shame she could never tell him the truth.

Secrets and lies. Guilt and regrets.

She had listened to Ellie's whinging apology after the crash. *I'm sorry I tried to make you leave, you can stay with us. Of course, you can stay with us.* And in her pain, the truth came to her. It would always be this way. Ellie would always be the one to decide Tia's future.

But although Tia might be simple, she wasn't stupid. The opportunity had arisen, and she'd taken it.

She had no regrets, felt no guilt. Why should she?

It was her turn to have it all.

* * *

MORE FROM VALERIE KEOGH

The next pulse-pounding psychological thriller from Valerie Keogh is available to order now here:

https://mybook.to/NewKeoghBackAd

ACKNOWLEDGEMENTS

There are so many people to whom I owe a debt of thanks that I could write a whole extra chapter. So, I'll keep it short.

To my readers, for reading, reviewing and taking the time to send emails and messages – without you, none of the writing would be worthwhile.

To the wonderful Boldwood team especially my editor, Emily Ruston.

To my wonderfully supportive and encouraging friends who offered help, support and time. Too many to name here – you all know who you are.

Finally, I couldn't have done any of it without my family.

I love to hear from readers – you can find me here:

Facebook: https://www.facebook.com/valeriekeoghnovels
Twitter: https://twitter.com/ValerieKeogh1
Instagram: https://www.instagram.com/valeriekeogh2
BookBub: https://www.bookbub.com/authors/valerie-keogh
Author Central: https://www.amazon.co.uk/Valerie-Keogh/e/B00LK0NMB8

ABOUT THE AUTHOR

Valerie Keogh is the internationally bestselling author of several psychological thrillers and crime series. She originally comes from Dublin but now lives in Wiltshire and worked as a nurse for many years.

Download your exclusive bonus content from Valerie Keogh here:

Follow Valerie on social media here:

facebook.com/valeriekeoghnovels

x.com/ValerieKeogh1

instagram.com/valeriekeogh2

bookbub.com/authors/valerie-keogh

ALSO BY VALERIE KEOGH

THE *Murder* LIST

**THE MURDER LIST IS A NEWSLETTER
DEDICATED TO SPINE-CHILLING
FICTION AND GRIPPING
PAGE-TURNERS!**

**SIGN UP TO MAKE SURE YOU'RE ON
OUR HIT LIST FOR EXCLUSIVE DEALS,
AUTHOR CONTENT, AND
COMPETITIONS.**

**SIGN UP TO OUR
NEWSLETTER**

BIT.LY/THEMURDERLISTNEWS

Boldwood

Boldwood Books is an award-winning fiction publishing company seeking out the best stories from around the world.

Find out more at www.boldwoodbooks.com

Join our reader community for brilliant books, competitions and offers!

Follow us
@BoldwoodBooks
@TheBoldBookClub

Sign up to our weekly
deals newsletter

https://bit.ly/BoldwoodBNewsletter

Printed in Dunstable, United Kingdom

75118678R00202